# The Devil in the Dark

## (The Dark Solar System Series)

C.K. Prothro

For my family; immediate and extended, living and dead. Thanks for the strength, wisdom, and support.

Also for those of the Lincoln Program (1977 through 1981). You were my brothers and sisters of my youth. This is for you, and thanks for both the memories and the nightmares!

# Location Map of Surface of Titan

Portion of Cassini Composite Map -2006
Courtesy of NASA's Cassini Mission

# CHAPTER ONE

Out of the cold, a sharp, wailing siren announced itself to the four corners of the world. The siren was followed almost immediately by a panicked male human voice that shouted, "Attention! Attention! We are under attack! Get to the nearest shelter!" The message repeated, but there was a commotion in the background that sounded like fighting punctuated by muffled shouts and weapons fire. Before the brief announcement could repeat itself for a third time, it was interrupted by an agony-filled scream, and an earsplitting screech, like sharp, heavy fingernails on an ancient slate chalkboard.

Lieutenant Demitri Sloan was instantly jolted awake by the shriek of the public address system that echoed around him. He immediately recognized the dormitory of the mining camp in which he had been assigned. Scanning the room, Sloan realized he was alone. The two dozen other bunks in the huge room were empty.

"Okay, this is fucking different," spat Sloan in an emotionally raw voice that spoke of an unhappy surprise.

Jumping out of his bunk, Sloan quickly donned his outerwear, a collection of dirty and worn garments, pants, shirt, and jacket, standard corporate mining industry issue. Spurred by the distant sounds of weapons fire, and the screams and cries for help, Sloan yanked on his boots and dashed out of the workcrew dormitory into the icy street.

As the report of weapons fire and screams of pain and fear echoed through the complex of low buildings, a thick fog moved

1

slowly along the empty, dust-covered lane that was outside of the rusty dormitory structure. Old forklifts, used equipment, broken crates and garbage lined the narrow street. The light wind created swirls and eddies in the drifting fog. It looked to Sloan as if the hanging clouds of mist were slowly breathing, pulsing in time with the blaring and echoing sirens. There was more weapons fire and shrieks of human suffering that shattered the gloom of what looked like dawn or dusk, Sloan did not know which.

Surprisingly, there was no one else on the cold, stony street, given the time of day. Only the fog, growing and flowing like an amoeba, spreading among the garbage and artifacts of human toil and wastage. Somewhere in the distance, something exploded, throwing a black mushroom cloud high into the depressingly dull sky.

With the sounds of yet more weapons fire and shrieks of pain, Sloan raced off toward the sounds of combat. The strands of cold fog slithered out of the way of the running lieutenant. In a few turns, Sloan was halted by a rain of debris from a nearby explosion.

As the echo of nearby blasts faded, Sloan heard screams of men and women booming out of a building with a sign that read: **Dining Hall # 3.** The heavy metal door leading into the cafeteria had been torn off of its motorized sliding track as if an explosion had bent the door and knocked it off its rails.

As the last screams of the cacophony of horror and pain died away with a hollow echo, Lieutenant Demitri Sloan entered the darkened building. The second he stepped into the structure, Sloan encountered four dead men, or at least he thought it had been four men. They were ripped apart, and their innards had been sprayed around the shattered room like some sick version of a child's finger painting. Heads, feet, booted and unbooted, along with spinal columns and other internal human organs were all over the common area of the dining hall.

"*Scheisse!*" hissed Sloan, choking down panic. During previous missions, he had seen gore and violence that rivaled anything recorded or hinted at by all the ancient war records. Stunned, the lieutenant stumbled backward out of the nightmare, into the street amidst the sounds of a raging battle, both near and far. He knew what this was and he was not ready for it.

Swirling fog moved and flowed down the narrow passage of the street, much thicker and denser than when Sloan had entered the dining hall. The clouds of mist contracted, strengthened, and expanded again around Sloan as if they were alive and about to devour him. Glancing down into the fog, Sloan could see for the briefest of moments several enormous bloody, clawed footprints leading into the building from the street.

Horrified, Sloan ran. He raced back to the dormitory from which he had come. The situation he was confronted with was not what he had expected or envisioned. ———

More explosions bloomed around him, near enough to shower him with gravelly bits of building and street. One explosion hurled dozens of flaming objects in his direction. Sloan watched the arc of the smoke trail of one of the fiery objects as it narrowly missed him. It was the smoldering remains of a gutted human torso. Sloan kept on running, the remains of destroyed buildings and other debris continuing to come down on him from all sides.

Barely reaching his dormitory, Sloan was thrown through the entranceway by a concussive blast. He laid there on the cold, hard floor for what seemed like an hour, but was only a few seconds. His ears were ringing, and his vision blurry, as he climbed back to his feet. "*Ich bin nicht bereit für diese noch,*" he screamed as he continued towards his bunk. The building trembled from the numerous explosions outside, pieces of street debris and other buildings flew through the shattered windows and landed at his feet.

Reaching his bunk with its duroplastic footlocker, he began to search frantically for the weapon he had hidden there. He tossed aside clothing and other personal items as he dug through the footlocker looking for the weapon. That is when he noticed it. The sounds of the carnage outside had ceased. There was nothing but silence, punctuated every few seconds by a single, blood-curdling shriek of a dying person.

Pausing for an instant, Sloan knew it was coming, and this was it. He continued to search for the weapon. He had taken it from the mining museum during the robbery. Now he could not find it, and he cursed under his breath.

He needed it because he was dead without it.

He needed something, anything to defend himself. Sloan could feel it coming, like the onset of the flu, or worse yet, it was like a pending painful blow to his testicles; he felt it before it got to him. It was death. Then he heard it. A sound that signaled the

3

approach of a violent end, filled with pain and blood.

It was definitely coming for him, now, at that very moment.

Just as he was about to give up the search, he found the stolen weapon. Sloan took the dull black metal composite weapon into his hands, an ancient Glock-Whelan L-seventy-seven automatic slug-thrower. A weapon not too far removed from bows and arrows, spears and slingshots, but it was all he had.

The fog invaded the dorm, rolling masses of white and thick cumulus clouds. It surged forward like a living thing needing nourishment. It flooded over Sloan, enveloping the entire dormitory area in which he stood. He readied himself. He knew the end was near, and at some level welcomed it.

The fog moved aside for an instant and Sloan saw the frost that now covered the floor. *This would have been much easier if the damn fog was not here,* thought the lieutenant, readying the primitive weapon in his hands. The mist was precipitating ice and moisture around the base of the furniture in the room.

With a snarling hiss, something tried to emerge from the fog, but the mist instantly swallowed it again, blocking Sloan's view.

For a moment, the frightened lieutenant's nerves broke, and he cowered backward. Sloan's eyes locked on the thing hidden in the fog. From nowhere, a shadow appeared, and Sloan raised the weapon in his hand, ready to fire at the form in the shadows, all the while retreating. Finally, his back struck a seemingly immovable object. Turning quickly, Sloan looked up and saw it.

With a sudden electric-like shock and a deafening screech, Sloan's fog-shrouded world swirled into a nauseating blur of colors that exploded into a blinding white light. The man's false reality was instantly ripped away and the *true* reality re-asserted itself into his consciousness. Reeling from the suddenness of the event, he fought back the urge to vomit.

"Are you fucking kidding me!" bellowed Lieutenant Alain LaRocque. "If one of the Majors, or the Colonel or, the Divinities forbid, the General himself caught you playing VR-games while on duty, and an illegal one too, they'd have your---"

"Come on! I was just about to confront them," blurted Sloan in defense of himself, as he removed the VR-game headset with its neuro-connector. "I have been working toward this level for weeks."

Lieutenant LaRocque shook his head, "But that is an illegal version of the game." He stepped around his seated comrade to eye the small dataclip set in the VR-game headset. "You could get a year, Earth-time, in a Re-Ed facility for that."

Both men were aware that any VR-game that had been modified to depict *real* violence for entertainment purposes was against the law, everywhere in the solar system. "It's only illegal if I get caught," added Sloan.

"But you're on duty!" barked LaRocque.

"Its New Year's Eve back home, everyone here is at the party, and I am the only one in this Divinity forsaken place left on duty!" He tossed the headset on the console before him.

LaRocque motioned toward the gaming device with a coffee mug in his hand. "Yeah, but that's still trying to get the Colonel's boot up your ass."

With the arrival of their new commander, everyone on the station was now required to wear the standard-issued blue and gray UESA pseudo-uniform with its Joint Deep-Space Planetary and Titan-Base Lincoln/Saturn mission logo patches. Only the OSC personnel wore a rank insignia, the other FA or UESA scientists wore color-coded epaulets indicating the branch of science or medicine they belonged too. Both Sloan and LaRocque wore Lieutenant insignia on their uniforms. For the last couple of months, even though a hard-ass on some topics, the general had allowed the station's personnel to let the UESA dress-code slip just a little. Even the civilian Frontier Authority scientists, who were exempt from the UESA dress code, wore the uniform, some in an unkempt manner.

"Lync can do just as good a job as I can."

LaRocque furrowed his thin blond eyebrows for an instant, then he added, "Your job is to supervise Lync and make decisions Lync can't."

"Yeah, right," the sarcasm was so thick in Sloan's voice it was almost visible. "Anything like that happens, and I'm calling the Colonel." He surveyed his friend a second, concern flashing across his young face for the briefest of moments. "You aren't going to go all *delator* on me, are you?"

"What you do on your off time is your business, but seriously, this?" LaRocque frowned and indicated the VR-game headset, "I got to show our new commander that I'm on top of things?" He let Sloan hang for just a few seconds before he broke a smile and added, "Okay, cause you are going to let me play when you are done, right?"

"Of course," Sloan grinned with relief. For a moment, he was not sure about his friend. "It's the latest installment of the Rogue Colony Series."

"Darkness Falls?"

"Bet your ass," Sloan picked up his VR headset from the console and surveyed his friend, "Had a dealer on Mars ship it to me, a couple of months back, on the last supply run."

Sloan and LaRocque had been friends and coworkers for the past seven years. They had both volunteered for the Titan-system project and had trained together at both Mars and on Jupiter's moon Callisto. The two men had made the two-month voyage out to Saturn in cryosleep along with the other forty-eight members of their original team. Their group had joined the other five thousand plus scientists, engineers, and support staff who were already at Saturn studying it and its family of satellites and rings.

During the near decade he had known LaRocque, Sloan had grown to think of the man like the older brother he never had. He admired LaRocque's knowledge of AI-systems and his ability to write high-level AI-scripts, which were the governing architecture for all AI-firmware systems. Sloan also admired the man's ability to engage the women on the base. His dirty blond hair, piercing blue eyes, soft complexion, and deep voice always seemed to attract the attention of women. That is before eighty-five percent of the base was evacuated.

Like Sloan, LaRocque's thick Venusianized, neo-central European accent made people think he was a native Earth-born. They would be wrong. Both men were true native sons of the hot, sticky, claustrophobic, mining colonies of Venus. Both could trace their family ancestries back over three hundred years to the first Unified Germo-Franc Republic settlers of Venus.

LaRocque held up a ceramic mug with the Titan-Base Lincoln Mission logo boldly displayed on its bright surface, "Thought you'd like a cup of coffee." Staring back at Sloan, LaRocque was still amazed that even after nearly three years on Titan, his friend still managed to maintain his boyish appearance. The younger man, with his sun-starved central European features, neatly cut straight brown hair, and brown eyes still looked like someone's sixteen-year-old kid brother. Subordinate personnel, who did not know him, were hard-pressed to believe he was an officer in the United Earth-Space Administration's Outer Systems Command. LaRocque often felt like Sloan's older brother, keeping him from making dumb mistakes, like playing illegal VR-games on duty.

For his part, Lieutenant Demitri Sloan was an expert in micro-and nano-electronics. LaRocque and others had commented on more than one occasion, that if it had wires, gears, and a power-supply, Sloan could get it to work. Both men felt like they made an excellent team.

Sloan took the white mug from his friend with a nod of gratitude. The coffee smelled like real coffee with a hint of chocolate and nutmeg. It looked like real coffee, black and smooth, and Sloan knew it tasted like real coffee. However, he also knew that there was no trace of *real* coffee bean to be found in the cup. It was truly amazing what the autochef could do with artificial flavoring, coloring, and raw inorganic caffeine. "Thanks, Alain, but you didn't come up here to bring me coffee." Sloan fought to hold back a grin, "Nor did you come up here to check on me."

LaRocque flashed a polite smile, and patted Sloan on the shoulder, "We were all at the party, and our new General not so subtly asked if we had re-established contact with T-One or TBK?"

Sloan's eager expression vanished. "Nothing, not a peep from either of them," he sipped at his coffee, as he sat up and became all business. "Datastream is still flowing to the secure servers, but outside of that, nothing. Both the T-One crew and Titan-Base Ksa have been as quiet as a morgue."

LaRocque, knowing he did not have to ask, still did anyway. "We still transmitting hails?"

"Every five minutes, all working channels, Lync is monitoring." Sloan shook his head, "So far, nothing."

LaRocque sighed. "Just so you know Tounames and Yoshida are back. They got the MSS back up on the Enceladus-Seven, two days early. You should start to see that data feed in a few hours."

Anger flashed across Sloan's face, "*Scheisse*, Ariel forgot to log them in. I didn't even know they were back," his Venusianized accent making an appearance. He did not want to sound too hard on Lieutenant Ariel Pulgar since LaRocque and Pulgar had developed an unofficial, unprofessional relationship that was known to everyone.

LaRocque nodded his head. "Yeah, she remembered at the party. She sent you a message over the interlink, but you never replied."

Sloan glanced at his sleek, forearm bar PDI (Personal Data Interface). Indeed, the small liquid crystal device wrapped around his lower forearm showed a message from Lieutenant Pulgar was waiting, unanswered. He tapped an icon, and the message disappeared. "I take it no one ordered them to swing by the T-One drill site and have a look-see?"

"Nope," LaRocque shrugged. "T-One airspace is still off-limits."

"For Divinity's sake, there is nobody left out here but the twenty-six of us, and them." Sloan gestured with the coffee mug towards a far bank of slowly changing lights and graphs.

"From what Major Singleton mentioned at the party, the OSC has ordered us to give'em another ten days. Then if no contact has been established, we can send a team over to investigate."

"Any new theories about what is going on?" inquired Sloan.

LaRocque scoffed, "Same old, same old. Nobody knows anything, but everybody's got an idea. There are a few like Yoshida, who thinks it's a significant rare element mineral find. Then there is McGilmer and Costello who still thinks it's an outbreak of some new Titan-native disease. Capt'n Aamodt thinks they are experimenting with some new type of geo-ion power."

Sloan shot a hard eye at his comrade, "*ficken nicht!*"

"Yeah," both men were old enough to remember the failed experiment on Io when the OSC tried to develop a geothermally powered ion fusion plant.

Sloan slowly twisted his face. "If it is, I hope that it has a better ending."

"That medtec," LaRocque continued on, making a sudden cupping motion with his hands to his chest. "You know the cute one of *Newey's Newbies*. The one with the huge---"

"Lebowitz is her name," added Sloan, "Trauma-Specialist Medtec First Class Yara Lebowitz." Even though Sloan agreed, he still disliked the way his friend described the station's newest members, who had arrived with their latest commander, Lieutenant General Ronald Newey.

LaRocque indicated he did not care. "Whatever. Mama mammalian massives thinks it's all a giant training exercise."

"Has Major Nianta changed his mind or is he still thinking T-One found themselves some extrasolar spacecraft." Sloan's face was struggling with a smirk and losing.

"Well, that's what he said he heard," was all LaRocque could reply before Sloan started chuckling. LaRocque put his hands up defensively, "Hey, you know what I think."

"Yeah, it's far more likely they found another extrasolar meteorite," chuckled Sloan into his steaming mug, "than some Divinity forsaken extrasolar spacecraft from who knows where."

"I hope it is an extrasolar meteorite. I got a bet going with Ariel," LaRocque gestured, "and before you ask what the wager is, don't ask."

Both men snickered knowingly.

"Whatever it is," continued LaRocque, "our new General and that bitch of a Colonel of his, are keeping it tight." LaRocque knew, as did Sloan, no one on the base much cared for the new commander and executive officer of Titan-Base Lincoln. After the other bases on Titan and the other satellites of the Saturnian system were evacuated, a number of key personnel on Titan-Base Lincoln and Titan-Base Ksa were replaced or demoted. That fact was not sitting well with any of Titan's long-timers, LaRocque and Sloan among them.

Sloan sipped his coffee again. "Well, what every the *fick* they are doing over there, it must have gotten real sensitive. Like I said, they are not talking, but the data stream is still very active." Sloan cocked his head and stared hard at LaRocque. "You try to see what's in the data?"

A grin washed across LaRocque's face. He was the senior AI-administrator on the base and had authority and password clearance to the base's AI-network. "Of course," he chuckled, "but I can't get access to the secured servers they installed. I don't even think our gallant General has clearance for those."

"You looked at the data stream itself?"

"Of course I did," scoffed LaRocque. "It's encrypted. A high-level quantum cipher with a three-dimensional finite-based Boolean key," Sloan snickered triggering the same response from

LaRocque. "I could crack it, assuming Lync would help me, and I had about thirty-two thousand years to work on it."

Both men burst into laughter.

There was an audible beep followed immediately by the voice of Lync. "TiStar-Three is reporting an atmospheric thermal anomaly. It appears to be located directly over the T-One installation at Menrva." Lync's voice was calm and smooth, with the slightest hint of a North American Midwestern accent. Three seconds later Lync added with a hint of concern, "Seismic anomaly detected, same location."

Before Sloan or LaRocque could comment, Lync began reading out a list of remote Titan surface monitoring stations that had suddenly gone offline. Confused, and with fear beginning to mount in both Sloan and LaRocque, they listened to Lync add to the growing list of distance stations that had abruptly stopped communicating with the base.

"Lync, please run diagnostics on main communications array," commanded LaRocque.

Without breaking stride, Lync responded, "Main communication network and all sub-systems reporting back normal." The reciting of the list continued, then Lync added, "Gentlemen this isn't a systems' glitch or a test. This is a real event."

Minutes flew past as Sloan, focused on the console before him, began to mentally analyze the data. LaRocque falling into a seat next to Sloan also started accessing instruments and data sets. "Lync what is your analysis? What are we looking at?"

"A circular expanding, high magnitude seismic wave with a trailing thermal shockwave," Lync's voice was calm, yet had an edge to it. "We have just lost all data-feeds and telemetry from Titan-Base Ksa. Based on dropout rates of the nearest RTSMs, the approaching edge of the wave has an ETA of ten minutes, twenty-one seconds. I am initiating station-wide emergency protocols, and am locking down all critical systems."

Two separate alarms sounded at once, and Lync's voice was suddenly booming through the hidden wall speakers, announcing a station-wide emergency. At the same time, Lync continued to list RTSMs that were going offline.

Instantly General Newey's face appeared on Sloan's forearm PDI, demanding information. As Sloan informed the general as to the situation, he could hear Lync's voice also speaking to the general. He could tell by the motion of the man's image on his PDI that he was running. The last thing the general said before his image vanished was that he was on his way up to the com-center.

Both Lieutenants Sloan and LaRocque were becoming concerned as the two tapped glowing and flashing icons on the array of holo-touchscreens floating over the consoles before them.

"Arrival of initial seismic wave-front in fifteen seconds, Surface wave component in nineteen seconds . . . eighteen . . . seventeen . . ." announced Lync, counting down.

Staring at the holographic readout of the approaching seismic signal, Sloan swallowed and whispered, "Hold on to something, this is going to be---" Sloan's words were drowned out as a mild shuddering began to rapidly grow throughout the com-center. The shuddering was accompanied by a deep-throated rumbling that reminded Sloan of a large growling dog.

Four seconds later the com-center convulsed violently. It was followed by a series of muffled explosions that rumbled through the station from deep within its bowels. The sound and vibrations carried and echoed through the very walls and floor like the tortured screams of some medieval prisoner. The entire installation flexed and contorted as an array of consoles erupted into curtains of hot sparks. Another set of earsplitting klaxons joined the ones that had already been shrieking for attention.

Sloan and LaRocque scrambled away from the volcanically erupting equipment as the room's primary lighting failed. Instantly, a huge blob of hellish flames spilled out of a wall panel and rolled towards the opposite corners of the com-center with the hiss of bubbling carbo-plastic. Half of the holo-screens in the com-center winked out, and the others quickly became a twitching, unreadable techno-colored specter. The vibration lasted for what seemed like minutes to Sloan and LaRocque but was only a few seconds. Several more extremely violent jolts struck the installation, before the shaking quickly faded away, leaving screaming alarms and burning circuitry.

"Atmospheric shockwave estimated time of arrival twenty-seven minutes, plus or minus two minutes." blurted Lync.

Lync, Titan-Base Lincoln's Main Artificial Intelligence detected the sudden increase in temperature in the com-center and identified the source as a fire. In its annoyingly calm voice, Lync announced the presence of a fire in the com-center. Knowing that people were in the room, it ensured that the com-center doors were closed, but not locked, and the ventilation system was rerouted to prevent the spread of smoke beyond the room. It also disengaged the fire suppression system and informed everyone of the same. While it was handling the fire in the com-center, Lync was also simultaneously dealing with tens of thousands of other problems, large and small that had unexpectedly appeared throughout the vast station. However, this did little to slow its performance in dealing with the several hundred million other daily tasks it had to oversee.

LaRocque, suddenly on the other side of the room, opened a cabinet in the wall near the door and removed two mini fire extinguishers. Arcs of electricity exploded from neighboring panels and consoles. Tossing one of the emergency extinguishers to Sloan, the two men attacked the burning instrument consoles. A moment later, a second, weaker quake, hit the station and subsided with a low, catlike moan. Lync's voice instantly when quiet.

Seconds stretched into long minutes, as the two men, coughing, and hacking, assaulted the flames spouting from several of the semi-circular consoles. Great clouds of smoke crowded through the room's air vents, only to be replaced by more smoke. Numerous liquid-crystal holo-screen projectors melted into steaming masses of useless carbo-plastic composite, and the fire continued.

On the verge of becoming overwhelmed, the two officers were considering abandoning the room when the door to the com-center sounded above the cries of the fire extinguishers. A small group of people, armed with emergency equipment, rushed into the com-center, only to skid to a halt, bewildered at the state of disarray before them. The leader of the group, a graying and mature, but obviously fit gentleman, slowed to a stop. The man took stock of the situation in the room then hurriedly moved to Sloan's side. "Lieutenant! Are you two okay?"

"Yes sir!" screamed Sloan.

"What the hell happened?" coughed Lieutenant General Richard Newey, his voice booming over the wail of the sirens, the mutterings of Lync, and the roar of the extinguishers.

"I don't know sir!" shouted Sloan, glancing back at the

general and noticing the other two new arrivals, Colonel Rozsa and Major Singleton. "I'm working on it!"

General Newey, the dying firelight shining off his tungsten-gray eyes, turned and swept the room. His com-center was a smoking ruin. His officers, occupied with the disaster at hand, coughed and wheezed, and fanned dark clouds away from their stressed young faces, as they got the situation under control. It had been a long time since Newey last saw a mess like this. "Karen! Give Sloan a hand!" coughed Newey, pushing gray beard into his teeth as he covered his mouth.

Colonel Karen Rozsa glanced over at the struggling lieutenant, "I'm on it sir!" she patted Major Steven Singleton on the back as she abandoned him to battle a small, but white-hot fire at a melting console.

"Lync! Get this damn smoke out of here and kill those fucking alarms!" barked Newey, suppressing a cough, "Emergency lighting!" Nothing happened, "Lync! Emergency lights!"

Still, nothing happened.

A whispered, distorted voice suddenly made itself heard above the confusion of the com-center, "I have lost all control over primary and emergency lighting systems in the com-center." responded Lync.

"Fuck," rasped Newey, moving to the manual light switch on the wall. Hitting the switch, several of the room's emergency lighting panels winked on; however, a small number did not. Looking up, the general could see a thick cloud of gray and black smoke clinging to the ceiling. "Go manual on the air systems! Quick!"

"In the works," replied LaRocque, noticing the grimace on the general's face. He tossed the half-empty extinguisher to the floor and hopped into a wet chair at a damaged console. As his fingers danced over a surviving holo-screen, he paused with a frown, then continued. In rapid succession, all but one of the alarms failed. "Sir, Captain Arroyo is going to have to do it manually from engineering," he announced after checking the console.

Lieutenant General Richard Newey had been enjoying the New Years' Eve party with the others when Lync sounded the alarm. At first, he had hoped it was a Titanquake, and then he feared it was an explosion. Now, he just prayed they were not dying. Confused, he tried to make out what Lync was saying over the room speaker, but the secondary fire alarms were still screaming full blast. Consciously he moved to Colonel Rozsa, with Lieutenant LaRocque quickly joining the two senior officers.

"Someone needs to tell me what we are looking at here!" the general barked to no one in particular. He was hoping it was not an unpredicted meteorite impact and praying it was not a thermonuclear detonation of some kind.

"Sir, I think you need to look at this." Colonel Rozsa suggested, accessing a flickering holo-screen above a smoking console. "This is a live feed from TiStar-Three." Rozsa's voice often reminded Newey of a bad lounge singer.

Moving to Rozsa and Lieutenant Sloan, Newey took in the jittery image on the holo-screen. An expanding and fading dark ring was sweeping across the fuzzy orange atmosphere of Titan. Behind the rolling front of thick, dark clouds the atmosphere of the large moon boiled and seethe, and began to change color. It slowed and steadily darkened, moving from orange to pink to red to blood-red. "What in the name of…" the general's voice faded as he, Colonel Rozsa and Sloan stared at the ghostly image.

"It's a thermal shockwave." Rozsa tapped and re-tapped icons on the hovering holo-screen with no seeming effect. "Lync can you help me improve this image and get me some telemetry on this?"

"I do not think so," began Lync's disembodied voice. "Too many of the com-center systems have been compromised for me to improve your command and control options from your current location. All of the Marbs have been assigned priority-one tasks. I can re-task one for the com-center?"

"No!" barked Newey, understanding that Marbs stood for Maintenance and Repair-Bots. "Keep them working on the station. This can wait." Noticing the VR-game headset on the floor, the general stooped down and retrieved the unit.

Colonel Rozsa and Lieutenant Sloan traded a glance then both looked to the general, but neither said anything.

A grid system suddenly appeared over the holo-image of Titan, and Newey pointed at it. "It appears like the epicenter was located at T-One."

Sloan refocused on his job. "Sir, Lync also reported that TiStar-Three detected the atmospheric event originated over the T-

One Drill Site." He knew what that location was. So did General Newey and Colonel Rozsa.

No one articulated anything for almost a full minute, then tossing the VR-game on the control, Newey said, "Okay, let's see if TBK wants to talk to us now. Try to get them on the comms. I'll inform the OSC what's going on."

"General, I am showing that the main communications system is reporting several primary failures. All primary and secondary communications disk are reporting a misalignment error," Lync's voice now had a bad reverberation to it. "Ninety percent of the failures are external to the station. All Marbs are tasked with priority-one damage; shall I re-assign one to handle communications?"

"No." Newey was scowling at Sloan but addressing Rozsa. "Have Pulgar gear-up and get communications back online. Have Fung give her a hand."

"I recommend we have both Fung and Wong assist Pulgar," suggested Colonel Rozsa. "Environmental conditions outside are off the charts; I rather have someone out there with her who has real surface experience."

Newey nodded, "Good call."

Colonel Rozsa activated her forearm PDI and began issuing the necessary commands.

General Newey liked Colonel Karen Rozsa from the first moment he had met the younger woman. She was a quick, painfully thorough, a no-nonsense officer, who never smiled much. Rozsa was lean with a physique that was a cross between a fashion model and a long distance runner. Her pale complexion with traces of sun-damage freckles and wrinkles spoke of a deep Central Asian-North African ancestry. Her shoulder-length brown hair was wavy and unkempt, and in places, it was obviously tangled into knots. She had a nose that Newey suspected had been broken on more than one occasion, without proper medical treatment being available. In addition, her clear brown eyes hinted to Newey that more was going on in her head then she was letting on.

Pointing toward the holo-screen image, Major Singleton injected, "Sir, I recommend that we prepare an emergency relief team to head over to TBK. T-One is only about twelve hundred kilometers west-northwest of TBK. They're certain to have more severe damage than us," a look of deep concern flashing across his bronze face.

Newey gave Singleton a sharp look. "Priorities Major. Let's check all of our fingers and toes before we go offering a helping hand." Newey did not know the SatSETs team commander very well. However, like all the other personnel on Titan-Base Lincoln, the Satellite Surface Exploration Teams commander's personnel file indicated that he was one of the most experienced and knowledgeable persons when it came to the conditions on the surface of any of Saturn's natural satellites.

The major's black skin pegged him as being of African ancestry, but his narrow face and stout body frame suggested central European bloodlines that went back a thousand years or more. His short, well-kept Afro hinted at order and perfection. His eyes were a sort of chocolate brown that radiated strength and confidence.

The general turned to Rozsa, "Colonel I want all department heads in my office in one hour with a status update." With that the general turned and exited the com-center, leaving Singleton and the others staring in his wake as the door closed behind him.

"Lync, are internal communications still down?" shouted Rozsa, still staring at the com-center doorway.

"Partially," replied the AI. "Some key relays are offline."

"Lync, do what you can to contact all department heads and have them report to me ASAP." ordered Rozsa, giving up on her PDI attached to her forearm. "I'm going to roundup Pulgar, Fung and Wong and get them on the long distance communications, then I'm going to find Tounames and Yoshida and get them up here." She headed for the door. Speaking back over her shoulder, she added, "We'll talk about the VR-game later Lieutenant."

"Yes ma'am," replied Sloan, frowning and exchanging a look with LaRocque, as his friend phased out the last alarm.

The com-center door opened again as a scared young woman rushed in, out of breath, sweating, carrying a workslate in her hand. She started to speak but paused. She was shocked and bewildered at the unexpected scene that greeted her.

Rozsa abruptly took the workslate from the woman, startling her. "Zuverink, internal communications are down, I need you to get to engineering. Tell Yoshida or Tounames to get up here on-the-double." She noticed the moment of confusion in the young woman's pale gray eyes, then the sudden blink back to reality.

"Sir, engineering is a mess," announced Private-Specialist Sasha Zuverink, her young face hinting at a Lunarized Lithuanian accent. "They are all down on the engineering sub-level. Suamir is trapped by a fallen pipe, and there is water flooding into the area. Capt'n Arroyo knows the comms are down and sent me up here to report."

Without any hesitation, Rozsa replied, "Get back to engineering and help as best as you can. Tell Arroyo to pull a Marb of another assignment if he has to, but get Private-Specialist Zapollo free ASAP."

Without a word, the young woman half saluted and turned on her heels as the door moved aside again, and stepped back into the corridor.

Rozsa looked over the data on the workslate, frowned deeply, and tossed the workslate to LaRocque. "I am going to do a manual check of the main structural supports." She abruptly turned and left the com-center without another word.

LaRocque slowly scrolled down the data on the workslate. He noticed amongst the list of system outages was a note that the command and control sub-systems for Lync and the Marbs were damaged. He swore under his breath several times, as he read. After a minute, he turned to Sloan and coughed, "Happy Fucking New Year's."

# CHAPTER TWO

Private-Specialist Sasha Zuverink bolted out of the elevator onto the main engineering level. A local alarm was sounding, and red emergency warning lights were flashing. She had just left the engineering level fifteen minutes ago, and nothing had changed. Quickly surveying her surroundings, she immediately took in what the huge computerized graphic displays that lined the walls next to the elevator were telling her.

Titan-Base Lincoln was in trouble.

The integrated array of scrolling display screens and flashing indicators of the gigantic digital flowchart was lit up with multicolored lights and dancing readouts. At the moment, the majority of the lights and texts embedded in the various parts of the flowchart were flashing either red or yellow. Moreover, to Zuverink's dismay, there were even a few solid reds interspersed among the glowing colors.

"Captain Arroyo, Sir!" Looking around, Zuverink saw no one as she moved deeper into the elongated L-shaped engineering section. Only the constantly changing indicators responded to her call, in the language of blinking lights and electronic beeps. "Where are you?"

"At main terminal-A," a heavy, masculine voice, laced with stress, echoed from around the corner of the room.

The woman trotted passed a very busy Marb. Eyeing the color-coded, multi-armed Maintenance and Repair Robot, its multi-tool arms a blur of motion as it worked on an open electrical panel.

18

Zuverink knew that the machine and its kin were the arms and legs of the station's main AI.

The young private-specialist moved around the corner, and past several doors numbered in sequence and marked: **MAIN ENGINEERING STORAGE UNIT**. Zuverink was aware, as was everyone on the station, that there were several large and small storage compartments situated at various locations within the huge installation. They knew that on Titan the nearest assistance was, at best, an hour or two away. They also knew that at worse, the nearest assistance could be four months and two billion kilometers distant. Besides, Titan-Base Lincoln was designed and built to be the core of a new human settlement, one of many on Titan, and one of hundreds across the Saturnian system.

As Zuverink passed one doorway, it immediately attracted her attention. On all of Titan-Base Lincoln, it was the only red door, and she was surprised to see it open. In the entire six and a half months she had been on Titan, she had never seen that particular door open. The mysterious crimson entryway, with its warning pictograms and small illuminated key and scanner pads mounted on the wall next to it, was labeled in large, embossed black letters:

### DANGER!
### MAIN FUSION POWER PLANT
### EMERGENCY CONTROL CENTER.
### AUTHORIZED PERSONNEL ONLY.

Continuing past the red doorway, Zuverink spied her target at the far end of the room. There, seated at a sprawling control console with numerous holo-screens was Captain Vincent Arroyo. The captain was pivoting his black syntha-leather chair from one console to the next. The chief engineer was obviously dealing with multiple emergencies as best as humanly possible. To Zuverink he looked as if he were playing the ancient kid's game they use to call *whack-a-mole*.

Captain Vincent Arroyo was a mountain of a man. He was two meters plus tall, and two hundred and thirteen kilograms of muscle. From his dark curly hair, brown eyes, and faint *Japotinian* accent, it was obvious that he was a native of Earth. On days better than this one, he was proud to tell people he was born in the Aqua-farming town of Villa Angela, on the shores of the Argentinian-South Atlantic seaway. Arroyo carried his Japanese and Argentinian ancestry as a badge of honor, and that he had bettered himself with degrees in mechanical engineering and macro-scale construction management from the best Schools in the South American Commonwealth.____

The captain's huge face exhibited an expression Zuverink had never seen before. He was intense, with a focus that scared her. The hard-monitors and holo-screens in front of him indicated that the local engineering AIs were hard at work with countless tasks, and Captain Arroyo was trying to monitor all of them.

"Captain, Colonel Rozsa has been informed about the situation. She ordered me to help you as much as I can." Arroyo did not even acknowledge the young private-specialist, which left Zuverink perplexed for a moment. "How are we---"

"I haven't heard about Suamir. I am assuming he is still trapped. Chuck and Mitsu are probably still trying to free him, but the sub-level is still flooding."

"You can't stop it?"

"We have at least four different pressure seal ruptures," began Arroyo, not looking at Zuverink. "Debris and one crushed floor drain are stopping the water from discharging to the reclamation plant, which isn't functioning anyway."

Suddenly Zuverink realized that the voice of Lync was not streaming over the room speakers as elsewhere on the station. "The Colonel said to get a Marb to help with Suamir. What can I do?"

"Get down to the sub-level and help Chuck and Mitsu."

"What about the Marbs?" questioned Zuverink.

Not taking his eyes off the multitude of holo-screens, Arroyo barked, "I got no communications with the Marbs or Lync. Lync must have assigned all the Marbs priority orders before the comms went down. They are not responding to verbal commands from me." Just then, the captain turned to face Zuverink. His brown, bloodshot eyes screamed of panic. Arroyo's expression was a mask of fear highlighted in shades of sorrow. "Tell them as soon as I get the relays for the pumps back up, I can start the emergency systems for the waste-water reclamation system," his voice was hoarse and gravelly. "If the drains are clear, I might be able to dump the effluent out on to the surface."

"Untreated, that is a violation of the Environmental protection protocols," scoffed the private-specialist.

Arroyo suddenly looked menacing. "If you guys don't free him, Suamir drowns in our wastewater. It's that, or I dump our wastewater onto the surface."

"They are liable to stick you into a re-ed facility for the rest of your---"

"Move!" boomed Captain Arroyo, angry.

Zuverink swallowed, "Yes, sir." As she turned to head for the elevator that led to the sub-engineering level, a blast of static exploded over the room speakers. It sounded like a woman's voice calling for Medtec Brauer to check something, someplace. Zuverink thought the voice might have been Doctor Tan, but it was too garbled to be sure. Shouting back over her shoulder, the private-specialist blurted, "The com-center is in total disarray, most of the systems looked like they're down!"

"Dogshit!" The captain ran his hands through his dark curls and down the back of his thick neck, as he appeared to sit back and take stock of his actively changing holo-displays. "Careful Zuverink, it's bad down there too."

The young private-specialist was already through the door marked: **SUB-ENGINEERING LEVEL.**

•　　　•　　　•

Sub-engineering was an enormous dark and dank, two tiered space that underlain almost the entire TBL complex. The upper tier was a discontinuous series of porches and catwalks lined with numerous manual valves of various colors and sizes, digital graphical flowcharts and AI-interface terminals. The lower tier was a vast network of color-coded pipes and tanks and congested with machinery of all shapes and sizes. Normally the air in the seemingly endless enclosure was hot and smelled of grease and solvents, like some vast, grotesque mid-twentieth century automotive garage. Even the engineering staff preferred not to spend too much time in the place. It was the least attractive level on the station, and to most of the station's personnel, it was a medieval place, straight out of the dark mind of Dante. On a normal day, four or five Marbs would be performing maintenance and running equipment checks. However, this was not a typical day.

Private-Specialist Sasha Zuverink stepped out of the elevator expecting precisely what she saw. The dim sodium lights that normally illuminated the machine-laden basement had been replaced by the glare of several high-intensity emergency lights. The roar of an uncontrolled torrent and the waling of a siren replaced the normal sound of dripping water, and the opening and closing of computerized valves. A waist-high raging pool replaced the usual small puddles of oily water, leaked from some overworked piece of machinery.

The hollow booming of metal against metal and the hissing and whistling of steam was barely audible over the sounds of the angry water and the earsplitting alarm. Hot clouds of steam and gas moved around the sub-engineering level in the glare of the emergency lights, casting eerie shadows on the numerous machines. Condensation and seeping liquids ran down the walls, moving small blobs of dark greasy matter. Any nineteenth-century steamship boiler-room worker would have felt right at home in these conditions. However, at the moment, Private-Specialist Sasha Zuverink felt anything, but at home.

Quickly sliding down the ladder, Zuverink landed with a splash in the filthy, near chest high gray-brown water. It was then that she noticed the odor. Raw sewage, laced with the faint aroma of solvents and oils. "Mitsu! Chuck!" she yelled, trying to get her voice above the ambient noise.

"Over here!" came a shouted reply, "Hurry!"

Moving with hopping and skipping motions through the water, Zuverink headed for the sound of Tech-Sergeant Mitsu Yoshida's voice. "Where are you?"

"By number three air softener!" The reply was just audible above the chaotic noise of the sub-engineering level.

Tech-Sergeant Mitsu Yoshida was submerged up to his chest near a large gray metal pipe decorated in several colors. The sergeant was cradling Private-Specialist Suamir Zapollo's head in his hands. "Help me!"

Private-Specialist Zapollo had his arms wrapped around the metal beam in a bearhug, trying to pull himself out of the water. His face was barely above the height of the swirling water. His body was completely submerged, the large metal bean spanning the length of his body. The red blood that issued from the deep laceration on his face was just a shade darker than his hair. His green eyes were wide and filled with tears, fear, and panic.

"He's still pinned, and we can't free him!" bellowed Yoshida, his uniform top soaked through and covered in greasy dark stains.

Taking in the scene, Zuverink asked, "Where's the Sergeant?"

"Looking for something to get this off him."

"The station's a mess! Capt'n Arroyo can't get the Marbs off task because the comms are down. He is trying to get the pumps back online for the waste-water reclamation system!" Zuverink tripped over something submerged and almost fell. "If the drains are clear, he might be able to dump the effluent out on to the surface."

"I don't want to die!" begged Zapollo spitting smelly water as it washed into his mouth the moment he spoke.

Yoshida ignored Zuverink. "You'll be okay." He tried to comfort the younger man. "We'll have this thing off you in a minute, just hold tight."

"What can I do?" questioned Zuverink, fear rising in her voice as she moved in close to the two men.

"Take his head," directed the tech-sergeant. "Keep his face above the water, I'll try to get him free again." Yoshida had tried before to free the younger man, but he was pinned between the fallen beam and a piece of machinery.

"Emergency respirators?" queried Zuverink, hopeful.

Shaking his head in the negative, "Chuck's looking!" With a gulp of air, Yoshida dropped below the rapidly rising waves.

Zuverink just barely got a hold of Zapollo's head before Yoshida disappeared. "I got you." She comforted the man.

"What's going on?" he asked, obviously trying to distract himself.

Feeling the man's body move, Zuverink answered, "I don't know. The com-center is a mess; the Colonel is there, didn't see the General."

"Some party huh?" spat Zapollo as water washed into his mouth again.

Zuverink forced a grin. "Yeah, can't wait to text home about this one."

After a minute Yoshida popped out of the dark water like a cork, spitting and coughing. "Still no good, he's in there tight."

He moved around to the other side of Zuverink and Zapollo, filthy water funneling down his face in a thin ribbon. He activated his wrist PDI. "Chuck! Where the fuck are you? We're running out of time!"

"The interlink system is still down!" screamed Zuverink, her voice heavy with the notes of a Lithuanian ancestry marred by centuries of Lunar colony living.

The station's structure made an unexpected complaint, as a deep shuddering traveled through the entire sub-engineering level, like the rumbling of some obsolete freight train. The shock raised numerous tiny waves in the already crazy floodwaters, as the emergency lights lining the walls and ceiling outlined the passing wave.

As the shutter faded, there was a loud metallic bang from above the tech-sergeant, followed by a burst of warm foul air. Yoshida gagged as his reddened, whiskey brown eyes bulged at the sight of another large piece of structural support crashing down into the flooding sub-engineering level.

A wet bronze figure, covered in grease rushed around from behind a cluster of massive machines and hurried towards his coworkers and friends. "No joy! Half the fucking control circuits are shorted!" shouted Tech-Sergeant Charles Tounames.

"Cutting torch?" questioned Yoshida.

Shaking his head as he approached, Tounames replied, "The toolshed in this section is overturned, and there is no way I can move that bastard! There's a high-pressure steam line rupture in the next section, couldn't get to that toolshed either!"

"Fuck!" blurted Yoshida, slapping the water angrily.

"Worse, most of the drains are clogged with debris, and the pumps are offline. I knocked the pressure covers off half a dozen of the methane bypasses." Tounames saw the change in expression on Yoshida's face. "I know, but it was the only thing I could think of. The water pressure should be enough to keep a negative flow, and ice should form over the intakes."

Just above the sound of moving water and the scream of the local siren, was the sound of Private-Specialist Zapollo. He was starting to choke.

"Help me try and move what's under him!" bellowed Yoshida as he dived below the surface of the still rising water. Tounames followed his friend.

Still holding Zapollo's head, Zuverink could feel one of the men push her aside below the waterline. "They'll have you free in a second. Don't worry."

Spitting up gray water and gasping for air, Zapollo replied, "My back's got to be broken, I can't feel or move my legs."

Zuverink smiled, "NJ will have you fixed up in no time." She was now forcing the man's head and face as high as she could against the fallen bean, but the water was now above his chin.

"Tell'em to cut my legs . . . off if they have too," the water was rushing into Zapollo's mouth with each word, and he was spitting it out into Zuverink's worried face. "Not want . . . to die . . . like . . . this."

Zuverink tried to put her face close to the trapped man's, but the bean prevented her from getting her mouth close to his to give him air.

Just as Tounames and Yoshida re-surfaced, the water covered Zapollo's mouth and began washing up his nostrils. The young man instantly started to panic, thrashing wildly.

"Fuck! Fuck! Fuck!" screamed Yoshida as he and Tounames both grabbed the fallen beam and began to strain to move it.

It did not budge.

Zuverink let the young man's head go and moved to help the two tech-sergeants, but still, the beam did not move. They threw their bodies against the fallen piece of metal, but nothing happened.

Zapollo's crazed face became entirely submerged as he continued to thrash around, trying desperately to grab onto something, anything. He was beyond panic now, deep into the natural instinct to survive. The sound of the bubbles and froth he generated was lost to the sounds of the rushing water and groans of his colleagues, still trying to free him.

Suddenly Zuverink grabbed one of Zapollo's groping hands and squeezed it tight. He squeezed back, and Zuverink felt the bones in her hand give under the pressure. She groaned from the pain but cried for her friend. Her tears were lost in the grimy water that ran down her face.

Tounames and Yoshida both abandoned the useless attempt at moving the beam and grabbed onto Zapollo's and Zuverink's hands. The three stood there silently with a look of anger and sorrow as their coworker and friend slowly drowned.

After a minute, Private-Specialist Suamir Zapollo stopped moving and his grip on Zuverink's hand when slack. Zapollo's face was still turned upwards. His eyes were still open and dilated. His mouth was open, and small bubbles streamed out into the fast moving water around his face.

For a long moment, none of the three moved or said a word. They just stared at Zapollo and each other, as if in a minute or two something would change. Nothing did, except the water got higher and Zuverink's sobbing got more emotional.

Tounames finally grabbed Zuverink. "Get a hold of yourself! We know, but now is not the time for it!"

"He's dead!" The woman had never seen a dead body before outside of a vid or holo-image.

"Yes, but we have jobs to do!" Unfortunately, Tounames and Yoshida had both seen dead bodies before, in the real world.

"But---" sobbed the younger woman.

Something exploded in a shower of sparks, and the three felt an electrical jolt move through their bodies from the water.

"He's right," muttered Yoshida, cutting off Zuverink, "let's get the fuck out of here first."

Zuverink forced herself back under control, and after a second, she and her two coworkers hurriedly moved off, towards the exit.

*It's days like this that make me wish I had listened to my father,* Yoshida thought to himself as he waded away from the body of the young man he had tried to save.

Tech-Sergeant Mitsu Yoshida had been born and raised on Earth, in one of the Marshland preserves on the Yemen-Arabian coast. His father had tried to make him into an Environmental Health Specialist like himself, and his father and grandfather before him. For the last two hundred years, the Yoshida family had worked to improve the ecological health of that region of the earth. However, the rebellious young Mitsu Yoshida had changed his direction in his first year of college and ended up with degrees in macro-electromechanical engineering and solid-state electrohydraulics. He also ended up a long way from the Yemen-Arabian coast.

"Chuck! Did you try bypasses twenty through thirty?" Yoshida's short black hair had a hint of golden-brown, which stood out against the thick black valve grease that now covered most of his head and upper body.

"Of course I did!" Tech-Sergeant Charles Tounames' pale brown eyes darted around the flooded level surveying the damage. "Almost nothing is working down here!" Wading his way through the rampaging waves of noisy water, he turned to Zuverink. "What the fuck is going on?"

"I am in as much of the dark as you," Zuverink began, her young face a mass of sorrow. "Interlink is down, the Capt'n ordered me to report engineering status to the com-center! The Colonel ordered me back here!"

"We should have gotten Arroyo; maybe the four of us could have gotten Suamir free!" Tech-Sergeant Charles Tounames was a strongly built bronze man, who could trace his ancestry back a thousand generations to the Choctaw and Seminole *"aboriginal"* North Americans on his father's side. His mother had nearly unbroken bloodlines to the Kikuyu of Kenya, and the Nyamwezi and Sukuma tribes of Tanzania, all part of the United Nation States of Africa.

Like Yoshida and Arroyo, Tounames had been born and raised on Earth and had found himself a long way from home. Tounames had grown up in the large, industrial city of Allendale Carolina, part of the North American Commonwealth. Nevertheless, like his friend and coworker, Tounames had gone against his family's tradition and stayed out of his family's cybernetics business. Still, he had earned university degrees in both macro-electromechanical engineering and nano-electronics.

"I don't think four Marbs could have moved that beam! We needed a cutting torch!" yelled Yoshida. Just as they reached the foot of one of the access ladders, another wave of electricity flowed through them accompanied by distant bangs of exploding machinery.

As Zuverink and the two engineers began to pull their wet, slimy bodies out of the water and up the ladder, there was a loud screech above the wail of the warning alarms and sounds of rushing water. What was still working of the sub-engineering's public address system sprung to life.

"Attention everyone! Attention!" Lieutenant Sloan's static laded voice was barely understandable. He spoke slowly as if he were reading from a script, "Internal communications are spotty, but report all injuries to medical immediately. Senior staff; please begin compiling your status reports. Colonel Rozsa wants a preliminary report in thirty minutes. There will be a senior staff meeting in General Newey's office in ninety minutes. We don't appear to be in any immediate danger. I'll keep you all up-to-date as to our current situation." In the background of Sloan's announcement was the semi-human voice of Lync, droning out its systems report.

"Zuverink! Mitsu and I will start a manual inspection and run the checklists. Can you please report to Capt'n Arroyo? Tell him about Zapollo. See if he can cut the power to transformers thirteen and fourteen in this section, so we don't get electrocuted."

The young woman said nothing. She just stared at Tounames looking wet, lost and frightened.

"Also, tell him we need some help down here to get Suamir out of there," mumbled Tounames, fighting back his emotions.

Sloan's announcement continued, "A lot of key operational systems are off-line including the interlink system and long-distance communications. Heat, power, and water supply to several sections are off-line. The Marbs are in emergency repair mode until Lync can re-establish communications with them. The station's environment and structural integrity are, as best as we can tell, still within normal parameters. That's all for now, Lync will be making announcements as usual." Sloan's voice clicked off, and Lync's voice rose from the background with a polite thank you to Lieutenant Sloan.

"They definitely need a status update," blurted Yoshida, starting up the ladder again. "Let's get to it."

Just as Tounames reached the top of the ladder, the station quivered again, and a distant moan sounded as a structural support, somewhere, took a sudden unexpected load. "Dogshit, we are not in any danger." Tounames tapped out a series of commands on the flickering wall holo-screen, and Lync's voice became inaudible.

Joining Tounames and Zuverink at the upper porch, Yoshida added, "We are definitely in dogshit!"

"Yeah, the party is over all right," added Yoshida.

The station shuddered again.

# CHAPTER THREE

General Newey sat in his office, hunched over his oversized gray desk. He was thoroughly absorbed in the details scrolling across his holo-screen, comparing and cross-referencing them with the information on the digital workslate in his hand. If he focused his senses, he could still smell burnt wires and hot carbo-plastic from the numerous electrical fires that had flared up around the station during the event and had now been extinguished. He knew he needed a shower, as he glanced up and looked around at the brightly lit office, but he also knew a shower would have to wait until the water reclamation system was functioning again.

He slumped back into his soft syntha-leather seat and took in the hollow décor of his office, which was more of a status symbol than it was practical. Most of his office space was unused, but rank had its privileges, even a billion kilometers from Earth. Several exotic, bio-engineered potted plants lined the perimeter of the room, giving it that much-needed *lived-in* feeling. Colored globes and ovoids of several different sizes were interspersed among the plants, each spherical shape detailing the geography of a different Saturnian satellite. On each of the larger globes, the positions and status of the numerous installations and autonomous science experiments were highlighted in tiny, color-coded texts. The other facilities were all evacuated now, empty of the nearly five thousand personnel and staff, along with all their personal effects and perishable materials. The only other humans for at least six hundred and fifty million kilometers were located a mere two thousand kilometers away, at Titan-Base Ksa, and thirty-two hundred kilometers away at the T-One Drill Site.

Suddenly Lync's soft voice reminded the general of the time, and that his meeting was scheduled to start in five minutes. Newey stood and stared at the Intelligent-conference table that took up the center of the room and its eight black syntha-leather chairs. He was not looking forward to this meeting. He had lost a man, and the preliminary reports on the condition of the station had not been good. The upside was of course that they would not have to evacuate the station and end, what he knew was his final assignment before retirement.

*Retirement,* thought Newey, as he slowly moved to the conference table, *becoming part of the past, but not really making history. This mission, however, would most likely get him into the history texts for sure.* His eyes played over the pale blue-gray smart-walls and the numerous embedded two-dimensional digital Image-blocks, which were displayed around the room. As he took a seat at the head of the conference table, his eyes played over the slowly changing picture. The Image-blocks randomly rotated through a series of family and friends, famous spacecraft from the past, interplanetary vistas, and landscapes from distant worlds.

As Newey watched in silent thought, the pictures of the early Chinese scramjet space-plane slowly replaced images of the first American and Russian space capsules. His long deceased parents appeared; his father an artist from Indiana, and his mother a UESA officer from Utah. From the scenery, it was easy to tell they were someplace in the southwest of the North American Commonwealth. The pictures of Newey's parents were swiftly replaced by the image of the first Euro-Indian and Chinese commercial Earth-orbiting space stations of the late 21st century. The graceful image of the *Tiangong-Ross Two* suspended before the full moon steered Newey's emotions. He knew all the images in the queue of the Image-block, and had studied each of them in detail since childhood. There was the first permanent lunar outpost, Lunar-One. There were images of the earth and moon together in space, the large cities of Antarctica, Africa and Europe, along with several of the domed lunar communities like Orientale, Shatnerville, and New Jamaica, lighting up the darkened hemispheres of the two bodies.

The general mused to himself. *In the thousand years since Yuri Gagarin, we have inflated the bubble of civilization beyond the moons of Jupiter, but at what cost? Even with artificial intelligence, psytronics, and cybernetics, hundreds of people died each year in work-related accidents. Was this an accident, like some industrial workplace mishap or was it more? The work of space exploration and colonization was inherently dangerous. But only humans could do the work of colonization. Only humans could put a human handprint in the dust of an asteroid, and only a human could put a human footprint in the sulfur snows of Io. Humanity had marched across the solar system in an unrelenting quest for resources and knowledge, only to find that someone else had been there first. That someone or something had made plans for the worlds of the solar system, long before humanity had even evolved.*

In the midst of the general's reflections, there were images of the future. Eight full disk images, one for every planet in the solar system, from Mercury out to Neptune were suddenly displayed in the Image-blocks. A moment later, a parade of images depicting the principal Trans-Neptunian Dwarf planets and their Moons began. He thought of Thanatos that small world of rock and ice, slightly larger than Earth discovered back in the late twenty-first century. Unlike the other major Trans-Neptunian objects like Eris, Quaoar, Makemake, Sedna, and Salacia, that were formed in the cold and the dark of the outer solar system, Thanatos had been formed elsewhere and expelled by its parent star, only to be captured by the sun in the distant past. These worlds, Newey knew, and the thousands of other smaller main Kuiper objects exiled out there beyond the light and warmth of the Sun held mysteries and treasures beyond wonder.

Without warning the door beeped for attention, bringing the general back to the here and now. Leaning forward with a barely audible grunt, Newey keyed an icon on the Intelligent-conference table's holo-screen and grumbled, "Enter."

The pneumatic door slid aside with a low hum, as Colonel Rozsa entered with a frown. She was focused on her PDI, tapping icons and reviewing the unhappy results. As she moved to the conference table, she swore under her breath. "Okay, most of the surviving RTSMs are reporting heavy ionization in the upper thermosphere, up around eight hundred kilometers over most of Titan."

"Any contact with TBK?" Newey's voice was hard. The situation at Titan-Base Ksa worried the general.

"No sir," Colonel Rozsa returned the general's stare, "but Lync thinks we are receiving an emergency disaster beacon."

Newey bobbed an acknowledgment. "What's the status of Private Zapollo's body?"

Colonel Rozsa seemed to settle. "Lync has re-established control over the Marbs; I ordered it to temporarily pull two Marbs off of station repairs to retrieve Zapollo's body. They will take him to Doctor Tan. Lync will notify me when it's done."

General Newey adjusted himself in his seat. "Do you think this has something to do with operation Quadriga?" He knew the answer but wanted confirmation from his executive officer.

"It almost certainly did. From the preliminary data, the epicenter of this event was directly over the T-One Drill Site."

"An opinion Colonel?" began Newey eyeing the younger woman. "Do you think I should bring the rest of them in on this?" He did not like secrets but understood why there was a need for them, especially when it came to the T-One site and operation Quadriga.

Before she spoke, it was clear Rozsa's mind was working the problem. She too did not like secrets, and like General Newey, she knew how to keep them when needed. "No, sir. Not unless Commissioner Marshall or someone above him gives the okay."

"We've already lost one man, what if this is just the start of this mess going sideways on us?" Newey was now testing his young second-in-command, "what is more important, the success of this mission or our lives?"

"It's your command, sir, you make the call. If it were up to me, knowing what could be at stake, I'd do it on a need to know basis." Rozsa's workslate beeped, getting her attention.

Newey indicated he liked her answer, "Good move, Colonel."

Rozsa smiled and entered several commands into the tabletop, and a holo-screen materialized and hovered above the table. It began to scroll color-coded data on Titan and the rest of the Saturnian system. "I am just amazed that we are even receiving anything with the amount of ionization in the atmosphere."

"I transmitted a report to the OSC," Newey began, "If the transmission got out, I would expect a reply in two or three hours. Will we be able to receive it with the ionization?"

"The high-band transmitter should be able to clear the

ionization, but Pulgar would be the one to confirm that."

General Newey just nodded. He would like to have some guidance from the Outer Systems Command before he started taking action. The general began nervously fiddling with a small white ashtray on the table. He desperately wanted a cigar and a bourbon to help him through this meeting, as he rubbed his sore eyes. "Did we lose---" Newey's question was stopped by the hum of the office door.

Lieutenant LaRocque was inside the room before the door had fully opened, and he looked upset. A slim, dark-haired woman was right on his heels, looking equally displeased. LaRocque and the woman, both clutching their workslates as if they were going to use them as weapons, advanced on the seated general.

"Sir, communications systems ready to report," began Lieutenant Ariel Pulgar, with a disgusted expression on her soft face. "Is it true about Suamir?"

Newey stared at Lieutenant Pulgar for a long moment and for just an instant, she reminded him of her grandfather. She was the oldest grandchild of Commandant General Ilyich Pulgar, the first human on the fourth largest moon of Uranus, Ariel, for which the young, bright-eyed lieutenant was named. "Yes," blurted the general. Newey had known her grandfather well. He had been an instructor and mentor of his at the UESA training academy on Mars and had gotten him assigned to the Jupiter phase of the Uranus Three Project.

For her part, Pulgar was petite, attractive, very bright, and sociable. However, she, like several others of the pre-evacuation Saturn System mission was only on Titan for career advancement. He had kept them on because they knew the station and the environment, and they were the best people available for this assignment.

"AI-systems have been inspected, and I am ready to report," announced LaRocque.

Pulgar, her soft brown eyes scanning Newey's face was filled with sorrow. "Sir, did he really drown in sub-engineering?"

"Not now." LaRocque paused at the growing reaction on Pulgar's face.

Pulgar eyed LaRocque, confused. Then she added, "I guess we'll get to it."

"I didn't know him as long as you did, but he was still one of mind." Newey shifted his gaze from LaRocque to Pulgar. He heard, saw, and understood Pulgar, but his mind was focused on all of the twenty-four survivors of Titan-Base Lincoln. To make things even more muddled, General Newey, like everyone on the station, was aware of Pulgar and LaRocque's non-professional relationship. They were not the only non-professional relationships on Titan. It was hard to keep a group of isolated people from developing emotional and sexual relationships. Even though such relationships were frowned upon, all branches of the UESA took a blind eye to them, as long as they did not interfere with people's performance and efficiency.

Before he took command of Titan-Base Lincoln, Newey had read everyone's personnel file. He knew, before he set foot on Titan, who was romantically or otherwise involved with whom on the base. However, the relationship between two of his junior officers was not uppermost in the general's mind at the moment. Newey closed his tired eyes and once again massaged them.

For a third time, the office door opened. Major Singleton and Captain Arroyo entered side by side, with Arroyo a half dozen centimeters taller than Singleton. It appeared as if the two officers had just ended a heated conversation. Following wordlessly behind them was a thin, middle-aged woman, with faded reddish-blond hair highlighted with streaks of gray. She had the air of a classic schoolteacher or librarian from the eighteen hundreds of North America. The woman was sporting a slight frown that did not fit her face. It was like an ugly color on a nice vehicle.

"Okay, let's get this underway," instructed Newey, as all of them quietly took seats around the table. The redheaded woman took the seat next to Newey and acknowledged him with a nod, as he slid the ashtray down the table, past the six others gathered with him. "First off, so we all are on the same screen with this," the general spoke to the disembodied AI. "Lync give us a summary report on the condition of the station." He already knew all of the bad news.

"There are eleven hundred and seven pipelines, and conduit ruptures in sections A through E, levels one through five, including the engineering and sub-engineering levels." A holo-screen appeared in front of each person seated at the conference table, and the screens began to scroll color-coded data on the damage. "Sixty-two electrical and material fires were detected." A multicolored, rotating three-D schematic of Titan-Base Lincoln appeared over the middle of the table. The location of every fire was indicated by a flashing icon, "The auto-fire suppression system extinguished them. There is structural damage in sections A through E, with the worst being in the north end of section E. The Marbs are all engaged with repairs, addressing these issues in priority order."

"Lync, how many Marbs do we have functional?" inquired Major Singleton.

"We had one Marb down for repairs at the time of the event. Eleven Marbs were destroyed or damaged and are currently offline. We lost two Marbs in the course of making repairs to the station systems. That leaves thirty-six operational Marbs; all but two Marbs are currently engaged in station repairs." The rotating schematic of Titan-Base Lincoln switched from showing the locations of the fires to showing the positions of the functioning Marbs. Each Marb's location had a textbox showing what the Marb was doing, the approximate time remaining before it completed its current task and the Marb's general systems' health. "Marb TBL-Nine and TBL-twenty-one are currently in the process of recovering Private-Specialist Zapollo's remains. They will take him to Medical. They will be re-assigned to repairs as soon as their current assignment is completed."

Everyone's face grimaced, and the general added, "We'll arrange a memorial service as soon as we get this situation under control."

No one said anything and Newey ordered the station's primary AI to continue with its report. The holo-diagram of the installation changed again as Lync continued, "There was a breach of the atmosphere in the east section of C, level two. Power flow to the east section and the chem and bio labs were also disrupted, but the Marbs have reestablished the circuits. Emergency power kicked in, so Professor Costello didn't lose any of her live specimens."

Major Singleton apparently did not like the sound of that and knew the other shoe was about to drop. "This gets better?"

Lync ignored the major's comment. "All the drinking water is heavily polluted, and we have only one functioning water purifier. A large portion of the waste and water reclamation systems will have to be replaced." The image of the station in the center of the Intelligent-conference table continued to highlight different issues concerning Titan-Base Lincoln. "The good news in this is that with the station's current population of twenty-five, there should be ample drinking water."

"As long as we don't all take twenty-minute long showers at once," added Captain Arroyo, grinning.

"Will the single unit hold out until we get the other units back online?" Rozsa looked worried.

"Yes," answered Lync, "however we'll have to store any chlorinated waste until the other units are back online."

"Great," muttered the middle-aged woman, who had been sitting silently up to this point.

"Flooding in sub-engineering has damaged or destroyed forty-two percent of the primary environmental control systems. Each and every nano-processor clip will have to be replaced in the main processor servers for waste treatment, water recycling, and oxygen processing. The good news is we have in stores or can manufacture the replacement parts." The AI paused.

"The bad news?" General Newey already knew the answer, so did Colonel Rozsa. Major Singleton and Captain Arroyo had been discussing that particular information on the way to the general's office. Singleton thought the captain's estimate of the repair time was grossly inflated until he tapped out some numbers on his PDI and saw the results for himself.

"The bad news," added Lync from the room speakers, "is that even with the Marbs working around the clock, it will still take approximately two thousand, one hundred and twenty-one work-hours to get primary environmental controls back on-line."

Arroyo glanced over at Singleton and could tell that the major was having flashbacks of the conversation in the corridor. "We can reduce that time estimate if we assign personnel to work crews to assist the Marbs."

Newey and Rozsa both swore under their breath. "Lync continue," commanded Newey.

"The pressure seals in the lower east section of C blew, but the emergency pressure doors sealed it off. There are no leaks. In addition, half of the emergency sensors on the pressure door subsystems are out. We can tell if we are losing or gaining pressure, we just cannot tell if a particular door is sealed or not."

"Great. Thank you, Lync." Nodding, Newey added, "Make

sure we manually check all the outer and secondary pressure doors."

Arroyo rocked his head sadly, "You know, this station was not designed to survive any kind of real shaking." The chief engineer looked toward Colonel Rozsa, who had been listening closely. "We have some critical structural damage, but if the ice under this station starts to move, we could be fucked. The pilings only go down fifty meters into the ice, and most of the piping flex-couplings only have---"

"I don't think we need to worry. The most recent geologic survey of Sotra Patera says---"

"The fucking geologists are not here," Arroyo fired back at the general.

"Lync, we didn't get a report on the graviton generators?" inquired Rozsa quickly and skillfully, redirecting everyone's attention.

"There were a couple of power spikes and a big EM surge, but the systems AI compensated, and there was no damage. I believe Captain Arroyo checked the Harlem bed personally and there are no cracks or fractures."

Arroyo's eyes traveled from the colonel to the general and back several times, but both let his earlier outburst slide. "Yeah, we're good."

Everyone in the room knew that HARLEM stood for *Higg's field Artificial Radiation and Lepton Energy Manipulator*, and for the unique crystalline composite constructed of the ultra-stable molecular isotopes of hassium, actinium, roentgenium, lead, europium, and mercury. The thick, flawless slab of carefully manufactured material, when energized, amplified the local gravity field, making it strong enough for people to move normally. Without the field, living and working in Titan's normal one-seventh gravity would become nightmarish really quickly.

Newey took a deep breath and released it slowly. He was relieved at that bit of good news, but he still wanted a cigar, badly. "Alright, now I know this is a moot point, but do we have to worry about aftershocks, atmospheric radiation, or adverse climatic effects?"

Both Rozsa and the middle-aged woman, who had been pleasantly listening to the exchange, shook their heads in agreement. "No," Rozsa's voice was confident, "but we will suffer aftershocks. The upper atmosphere is heavily ionized. Broadband communications are still down with most of the RTSMs and the satellite network," she turned to Pulgar.

"We still have most of the high gain and some of the narrow-band communications," the lieutenant added. "Lync and I don't foresee a major data loss." Lieutenant Pulgar's eyes shifted to the general. "Communications with the Inner Solar System is still on high-band."

"I'm just happy the sky isn't going to fall on us," Rozsa grinned, as she looked to the general for agreement.

The general looked relieved, "Anything else?"

Pulgar straightened up as everyone looked at her. "Yes, outside of several damaged RTSMs transmitting bad data, we are only receiving the emergency transmission from TBK. Atmospheric ionization is cutting into normal traffic."

Quickly LaRocque added, "Lync has algorithms to correct for that."

Newey stared at Lieutenant LaRocque. He knew just how lucky they were to have the man on Titan. The lieutenant had grown up being exposed to cutting-edge AI-technologies at his father's cybernetics design job, in the Venusian Tunnel-city of Avranches-Ducey, a half kilometer under Beta Regio. According to his official records, LaRocque had learned to write AI-scripts in BAIL (Basic Artificial Intelligence Language) at the age of eight, had mastered CLAISTS (Command Level Artificial Intelligence Synthetic Thought Scripting), and SAILA (Standard Artificial Intelligence Language Algorithms), by the age of fifteen, and was designing holographic memory engrams at sixteen. Newey also knew that his mother, who taught applied math, had realized her son's talents early and had gotten him into all the best schools on Venus. LaRocque's mother also felt betrayed when her son decided to apply his trade in the service of the UESA instead of in the private sector. As far as anyone knew, the two have not spoken since.

"Any response to your RFI?" Rozsa knew the answer but needed to hear it.

"Not a word," injected Pulgar, confirming that they had not received a reply to their Request for Information. "There has been no change in the signal strength, frequency, or content. Just the same signal repeating every sixty seconds. They either can't reply or won't reply. I think it's automated."

Newey indicated his understanding. "If the signal can escape Saturn's background noise, do you think they can pick up the transmission back in the inner system?"

Pulgar tapped out several commands on her holo-screen and was rewarded with the data she needed. "With the current positions of the inner planets and the measured signal strength to drop-off ratios of the transmission, I'd think one or two of the relay stations in the MAB will detect it. Maybe some of the big dishes on Mercury too."

Newey and the others knew that 'MAB' referred to the Main Asteroid Belt.

"Even with the atmospheric ionization?" question LaRocque, slightly surprised.

Pulgar nodded her answer to LaRocque's question, "Yes. It is a forced pulse signal, being broadcast on a narrow-band frequency. Kinda like the old SecureSat data-link system."

Expressionless, Newey contemplated Pulgar and LaRocque's information for a moment then turned his attention to the middle-aged woman, who had been quietly listening to the discussion. "What's your info, Lori?"

Professor Lori Eastman leaned back in her chair. She was fortyish and firm with strawberry blond hair that tended more toward blond and gray than the red. Her face was oblong but soft like a baby's behind with wrinkles. She was a planetary scientist specializing in atmospheric mechanics. Eastman had been the third Commander of Titan-Base Lincoln, since its construction over two decades ago. That was until the Outer Systems Command inexplicably evacuated most of the personnel for the Saturnian system, removed her from command and replaced her with General Newey. Now she was just the head of the scientific team. "Well, the first indications are that a meteorite or comet has impacted Titan. The data transmitted by some of the RTSM's before they went offline, seem to indicate a massive shockwave was generated by an extremely powerful explosion. It was centered at twenty point one-eight degrees north by eighty-seven point one-four degrees west, practically dead center of Menrva." She paused for a second, then added, "Directly where the T-One Drill Site is located."

"Could something at T-One have exploded?" asked Rozsa.

"I don't think so. There does not appear to be a radiation signature, and anything this big would have to be thermonuclear in nature unless it involved hypervelocity kinetics."

"How powerful?" inquired the general as he studied the professor's face. She was fairly attractive, with her eyes a shade of hazel that reminded one of something you had forgotten, and wanted to find. However, he had never seen her do anything in the way of make-up or hair styling to draw anyone's attention. Newey knew she was a widow, and that it had something to do with the loss of the McNett Research facility on Mars a number of years ago. He also knew she could be cold, uncaring, and even abrasive at times, but he also knew that she had his attention, professionally and personally.

"Best estimates put it at about one point oh-four-six times ten to the tenth gigajoules."

The room went dead quiet as everyone traded stunned looks with their neighbor.

After a moment, Eastman continued. "Luckily, somehow ninety percent of the blast energy was directed upwards. Otherwise, we wouldn't be sitting here. A blast of that size should have had a destructive radius of about forty-eight hundred kilometers. Even with the curvature of Titan, the atmospheric shockwave should have flattened this place like a tortilla. However, the Stoneley wave registered only eight point three on the Freseman-Potenza scale. We can probably expect aftershocks for some time."

Newey appeared to want to speak, but Eastman continued on, "There was a thermal wave that passed through the atmosphere. It initiated a wave of high-energy chemical reactions, both in the lower troposphere and in the main tholin haze layer in the stratosphere. The resulting chemical reactions liberated small quantities of oxygen that was rapidly consumed in an ignition-pressure wave. The wave was measured and tracked by TiStars-Two and-Three as it moved across Titan at approximately seven hundred kilometers an hour before the elevated CCR dropped below the exothermic ignition point again."

"Any danger to us?" the general beat Colonel Rozsa to the question by a millisecond.

"No. Its decay rate was too high, but if Titan had twenty to twenty-five percent more free oxygen or the reaction had liberated more oxygen and hydrogen from the water-ice and methane in the environment, we could have had a thermal flashover, and we would all be in worse shape." Eastman glanced around the table, gauging the reactions of the assembled group. "As it stands, a load of thermal energy got dumped into the atmosphere. We can probably expect a three to three-and-a-half-degree rise in the global atmospheric temperature. The normal climatic and atmospheric patterns will probably be disrupted for months to come. I'm having Lync put together a revised Martino-Quinn climate model. It should be ready in about an hour." Eastman paused a few seconds, watching the faces around her.

General Newey leaned into the conference table, "Besides the distress signal, do we have anything on the condition of TBK?"

Eastman looked to Colonel Rozsa, who tapped out a few commands on her holo-screen. The three-D schematic of Titan-Base Lincoln vanished, only to be replaced by an enhanced image of Titan-Base Ksa. The projection was such that it appeared to be facing everyone at the table. "The place has looked better," Rozsa indicated the gloomy, color image. "There is extensive structural damage. We are detecting minimal electromagnetic emissions, but due to the thermal instability in the atmosphere, we can't tell what the conditions are like within the structure."

Lieutenant Pulgar seemed to grow pale for a moment, as she understood, "You mean everyone at TBK could be dead?"

The colonel just stared back at Pulgar for a second. "Given the TiStar data, plus their proximity to the event, they were only about twelve hundred kilometers away; I think we should be prepared to declare TBK, end-of-mission."

There was silence in the room for over a minute, as the small group let that reality sink in.

"What the fuck happened at T-One?" exclaimed Singleton shaking his head.

General Newey too shook his head and stared hard at Professor Eastman. "Is there any information that can tell us what this event was or what caused it?"

"Well, TiStar Two," began Eastman, "is showing a new crater complex inside Menrva." She tapped several commands into the holo-screen in front of her. The image of Titan-Base Ksa vanished. It was immediately replaced by a multispectral composite image of the Menrva crater and its new feature.

The image, rendered in dozens of shades of blue, red,

green, and magenta, was centered on an ordinary looking flat-bottomed, ringed impact crater. According to the digital scale on the bottom of the image, the crater was a little more than thirteen kilometers in diameter. Its bright rays and fractures clearly visible in the methane ice of the hydrocarbon lake that was Menrva crater. The image indicated that the feature was of recent origin.

The new crater was set among several smaller irregular ovoid shapes. Based on the image's color code, the new crater held small, newly formed ponds and small lakes of liquid hydrocarbons and slushy methane. At the top of the image was a series of sharp linear features with smooth ridges and deep sinuous and angular channels that snaked their way between the small craters.

"Based on this," added Eastman, coldly. "The entire T-One drilling installation is gone."

"Did you redirect the platforms to take a closer look at the site?" Newey continued to study the image.

Eastman called up and scanned the translucent texts and images of Professor Yee's preliminary report, as it slowly scrolled across the holo-screen in front of her. "Yes. However, there is no unusual electromagnetic activity or radiation. All of the other images including those from both the nano-band near-infrared and micro-ultraviolet mapping spectrometers show nothing," she paused, tapped out more commands on her holo-screen. "That event wiped the entire site almost clean."

"Almost?" Newey took stock of his staff, "What do you mean, *almost?*"

Eastman read the transparent text on her holo-screen. "There is a curious, sheer-walled caldera-like depression in the center of the new structure." She put the image on everyone's holo-screen.

"It looks like a hole," commented Singleton.

"Yes, but there is little evidence of secondary cryomagmas. There are only traces of liquid hydrocarbons and ammonia compounds that would be associated with any neo-cryovulcanism. Outside of that, it looks like the site of some type of violent outgassing." Eastman refocused her attention on another holo-screen before her, as she slowly switched from one image to another, each a different collection of colors. "Fred and Lync are working on precise numbers."

Newey cocked his head. "What is the problem? It was

big."

"Well, the energies indicate an outgassing of material in the range of four hundred trillion metric tons. However, the recorded data would indicate between six hundred and eleven hundred trillion metric tons." Eastman surveyed the astonished faces at the table. "Like I said, Fred's looking at the data now, and Lync's checking his calculations." She paused, frowning hard as she deactivated the data stream before shutting down her holo-screens. She leaned back in her chair and surveyed the faces at the table. "Could the OSC have been testing some new technology out at T-One? Could that be the reason they evacuated the system because they knew it could be dangerous?"

General Newey forced himself not to look at Colonel Rozsa as he answered, "Honestly, I don't know." It was clear from several of the reactions at the table, no one believed the general.

"Are you sure," Professor Eastman was trying to give the general a way out. "Some type of experimental, heavy element hyper-ion powered engine, like the one Major Nianta tested? Or maybe a prototype antimatter power plant." She leaned forward again, her long fingers dancing over the holo-screen in front of her. "Built it under the ice at a remote place, just in case something like this happened?"

Shaking his head in disbelief, the general adjusted himself. "I have no clue. They told me not much more than they told you. Are you sure there's no sign of radioactivity?"

Eastman met Newey's stare, leaned into him, and added, "Yes I'm sure. You want to check the data yourself?"

He held up his hands defensively, "I'm not questioning your---"

"There are no indications of fission or fusion byproducts, the TiStars did not detect any abnormal gamma ray or R-emissions from anywhere in the Saturn system." Eastman sat back in her chair but continued to stare at Newey. "If it was some new tech, it is truly revolutionary. Even an antimatter blast produces a gamma-ray signature. There is nothing."

"Now, I know this is a long shot, but it could be a piece of extrasolar matter. Something coming faster than our scanners could track it. A super-hypervelocity impact could explain a lot of what we are seeing at Menrva." Pulgar ventured.

"Talk about being unlucky," Arroyo snickered. There were

several subdued chuckles from around the table, but there were also a few others who had even wilder ideas.

"An interstellar rock?" cautiously acknowledged Rozsa, knowing that only four interstellar objects had ever been found, and documented to be older than the age of the solar system. An old conversation flashed through LaRocque's head. Not counting Thanatos, he knew that three very large interstellar fragments had been found, and dated using their Rhenium-Osmium and Thorium-Lead isotopic ratios. When he was a child, he had actually seen the smallest of the three on display at the Viking-One Museum on Mars. A geology student on a field trip had discovered it nearly two hundred years ago. He remembered that the other two captured interstellar objects were circling the sun in stable, long period orbits.

Rozsa called up some data on her holo-screen. "There are absolutely no indications of objects with trajectory and velocity that would bear out an interstellar object." She punched in another series of commands, and a diagram of the Saturnian system appeared on everyone's holo-screen.

There was practically a half minute of glances, half nods, and questioning stares before Eastman added, "So, I guess we have to go take a look at the site."

The general sighed, "You are all forgetting TBK. I know there is little hope of survivors, but we are receiving a distress signal. We need to investigate and render any assistance we can before we start investigating this event. Besides, they may have some insight into what caused this." He shifted his weary gaze around the quiet table for a few seconds, then refocused on Eastman. There was a fear growing in the pit of his stomach. "Alright! Let's get some hard facts before we fuck ourselves. Colonel, I want you to lead the team to TBK. Take all the emergency and relief gear you can carry and check for survivors. On your discretion, you can proceed to the site of the event."

Looking up from her holo-screen, Rozsa added, "No problem sir, but I would like Major Singleton as copilot and Tech-Sergeant Al-Yuzwaki instead of Lieutenant Fung."

"Why Jamal? Isn't Lieutenant Fung---"

"I think we may need someone with more surface expertise, and Al-Yuzwaki worked over at TBK for a few months."

"You will need someone from medical?" suggested

General Newey, but the sudden look on Rozsa's face told him something different. "Yeah, I know, but let's err on the side of caution."

"Yes sir," Rozsa was frowning and surveying the others at the table. "I don't think we are going to need anyone from medical, but I'll take Doc Tan along."

Newey indicated his understanding of the colonel's comments. "Yeah, but take that trauma-specialist with you, instead." He looked to Major Singleton for any objections, but Singleton signaled his being okay with the assignment.

The colonel continued, "I know there is a dogshit-load of repairs to be done, but I'd like Arroyo, Pulgar, LaRocque, and Professor Eastman on this with me." Rozsa surveyed the faces gathered at the table, "They are next on the surface duty roster anyway. We were scheduled to recalibrate the high-contrast SDI and the graviton flux recorders on Epimetheus, Atlas, and Pan next week."

Arroyo and the others looked at each other in silence. No one disagreed.

"Take Yee, he's the geophysicist. Lori will stay here and help me figure out this mess. Major Nianta and Lieutenant Sloan will monitor you from the com-center," Newey's tone suddenly turned matter-of-fact. "Colonel, please no doctoral dissertations. Just find out what the hell happened out there. I want hard facts when I explain this dogshit to the OSC."

Rozsa nodded, understanding the look in Newey's eyes, "Right."

Newey continued to stare at the colonel. She met his glance straight on. "So, for the record, your team will consist of Major Singleton as command pilot, Captain Arroyo, and Technical Sergeant Al-Yuzwaki as engineering support, Lieutenants LaRocque and Pulgar as I.T. support, Trauma-Specialist Lebowitz as medical support, Professor Yee as science support, and yourself as mission commander and co-pilot."

Again, Colonel Rozsa denoted her understanding with a dip of her head.

The general looked around the table at the knowing yet somber faces, "Any more questions?"

Nothing, no one spoke or voiced their thoughts. Everyone had questions, but none could be answered yet.

"Any comments?"

The seven in the office surveyed each other's faces, trying to read expressions, looking for hidden doubts, or protected feelings. None could see past the calm expressions with the possible exception of Newey. He was a poker player, and very good at reading people. There was a round of approving nods. LaRocque gave Pulgar a smile and a wink, as Arroyo gave a thumbs-up sign. Eastman continued to frown and stare coldly at the general.

"Anything else we should go over?" Before anyone could answer, Newey added, "Regarding station systems or procedures?"

"Are you going to notify Zapollo's next of kin personally," questioned Eastman, "or should I?"

Newey noted the expression on Pulgar's face as he addressed Eastman. "Let me speak with the OSC before we do anything."

No one commented.

"Anything else?" The response from several at the table was a unified *"No,"* with several others shaking their heads in agreement. "Okay let's move to a level-two alert, and continue with repairs." Newey stood, which signaled the meeting was over, "Let's get to it."

The other six stood, and as Newey moved back towards his desk, Rozsa led the others out of the door as a group.

## CHAPTER FOUR

The uppermost of the four-tiered massive city that was the Titan-Base Lincoln installation housed the hangar-launch bay. The rectangular bay was an enormous enclosure, measured and marked off in meters with the aid of bright lines and numbered rows. Soft neon lights arranged along the ceiling imparted to the hard, alloyed walls a pleasant aquamarine hue that made the area feel even larger than its true size. However, the three white and silver skiff dirigible exploration craft and the three metallic blue hopper spacecraft brought true scale and dimension back to the hangar bay. They were like six pieces of large furniture in a small room; they ate up space.

The skiffs were glorified airships, straight out of the twentieth century European and North American aviation history. The aerostats were standard issued lighter-than-atmosphere aircraft that had been modified to function in Titan's extremely cold environment. They were propelled through the minus one hundred and eighty degree Celsius, nitrogen-rich atmosphere by twin, high-efficiency turboprop engines. Similar craft could be found sailing through the skies of Venus, Earth, and Mars.

The hoppers, however unlike the skiffs, could leave the atmosphere of Titan. The hoppers were construction transport craft, designed for work in and around the moons of the Jovian system. Their structural design and outward appearance were similar to that of the now long extinct insect the grasshopper, hence the name. The craft's two front windows stared forward like two small eyes. Its landing gear posed like a set of powerful legs about to spring off.

Unexpectedly the pneumatic hum of the airlock hatch cycling broke the quiet of the hangar bay. The noise announced the arrival of a small group of people, all dressed in bulky gray e-suits, talking busily among themselves. The group made their way to one of the parked skiffs, their bulbous environmental suit helmets in their gloved hands. Each member of the small team carried a large travel-pack loaded with specialized instruments and personal gear. The eight looked more like a team of asteroid mining inspectors going out on a ten-hour work shift than trained scientific explorers on a rescue and fact-finding mission.

"Major, please confirm the onboard AI's preflight," ordered Rozsa as she led the seven toward the skiff. She and the others on her team looked over the airship as they approached it. Each member taking in the silver and black image of a winged human, holding a sphere studded with four large stars, each surrounded by dozens of smaller stars. The figure was the logo for the UESA (United Earth Space Administration), FA (Frontier Authority), and OSC (Outer Systems Command) joint deep solar systems mission. Below the image of the winged human, Rozsa read the familiar words:

**United Earth-Space Administration**
**Saturn Expedition: Titan**
**Lincoln Base: Skiff-1.**

The words were embossed and printed across the side of the small craft in bold, highly reflective silvery letters.

Reaching the small entry ladder to the skiff, Rozsa helped her fellows into the craft, quickly eyeing their e-suits for obvious problems. She knew there would be none, but old habits die hard. First Major Singleton, then Lieutenants LaRocque and Pulgar climbed aboard, immediately followed by Tech-Sergeant Jamal Al-Yuzwaki, Trauma-Specialist Yara Lebowitz, and Captain Arroyo. As they moved up the short ladder, Rozsa almost confused the tech-sergeant's husky frame with that of the equally massive Captain Arroyo, for the two men were close in size, and their e-suits made their overall appearance very similar. Only Al-Yuzwaki's dirty blond hair and softer face distinguished him from the captain.

From the top of the ladder, Arroyo reached back to help the geophysicist, Professor Fredrick Yee on to the craft. Professor Yee paused a second. He scanned the captain for any hints of mockery with questioning brown eyes. Seeing no undue concern, he took the younger man's hand and let himself be hoisted aboard the craft. ▬

Inside the main compartment of the skiff, Pulgar and Arroyo stowed their helmets and travel-packs with the others and took seats side-by-side, facing Al-Yuzwaki, Lebowitz, and Yee across the box-like compartment way. Pulgar watched Lebowitz strap herself into her seat. The young, dark skin trauma-specialist was very busty with dark hair, brown eyes, and facial features that screamed middle-eastern ancestry, unlike Tech-Sergeant Al-Yuzwaki.

Pulgar was glad that Technical Sergeant Jamal Al-Yuzwaki was going out with them on this assignment. Al-Yuzwaki was well experienced in the skiff's operational procedures, not unlike the exploration team commander, Major Singleton. In addition, Jamal Al-Yuzwaki was a genius with all sorts of field generators. The man could literally tear apart and rebuild the enormous Boson field initiator whose resonance pulse interacted with the HARLEM bed and gave-off the station's artificial, Earth-normal gravity. He had managed to impress a number of key people, General Newey and Professor Yee among them, with his skills as an engineer and his knowledge of non-linear, probabilistic, fluidic-quantum mechanics.

Tech-Sergeant Al-Yuzwaki, his eyes a dark turquoise followed Rozsa as she moved passed him, and headed up the three-meter-high ladder to the ship's cockpit. He was glad for this trip out on to the surface, for it was delaying his assignment to a repair team. As he looked across the aisle at Pulgar and Arroyo, he caught Pulgar eyeing him. He flashed a quick grin at her, as she and Arroyo both began to strap themselves into their seats. His grin faded slowly as he studied Arroyo, wondering how the captain managed to get himself assigned to this trip when there was so much work to be done on the station.

The tech-sergeant's concentration was momentarily broken by the sudden gagging cough of the dark-haired professor next to him. The tall, thin-faced professor of Afro-Asian descent looked a little ill as he strapped himself into his seat. Al-Yuzwaki hoped that Yee had remembered his anti-nausea patch this time out. Last time, while they were on the surface of Dione, Al-Yuzwaki barely got the professor back to the hopper before he threw-up in his e-suit.

Grinning to himself, Al-Yuzwaki thought how silly it was to have a person with chronic motion sickness on any mission outside of a stable gravity environment. However, he also knew that even with the population of Saturn down to just the crews of Titan-Base Ksa, the Titan-One Drill Site, and themselves, there were still numerous research projects in and around the Saturnian system that needed human hands in order to continue working. He also knew that Professor Yee was an accident waiting to happen.

Lieutenant Pulgar watched with a silent smirk as LaRocque finished stowing his helmet and travel-pack in an overhead compartment. Spying her, LaRocque gave the woman a suggestive wink and a smile as he exited through a hatch at the rear of the compartment, headed for the craft's auxiliary AI-systems terminal.

Pulgar suddenly noticed Professor Yee's color was slightly off, and there were several beads of perspiration welling up on his forehead. "You okay Professor?" she inquired as Yee wiped his brow with a gloved hand.

Looking up with a smile, Yee replied in a voice that hinted at a strong Afrikaan influence, "Yeah. I find it just a little warm." At that moment, the powerful hum of the engines started up, and the atmosphere in the compartment noticeably changed, to the appreciation of the sweating professor.

Out of the corner of his eye, Yee saw the blond haired Al-Yuzwaki look away from his direction and begin working on his restraining straps. It was obvious to the professor that the tech-sergeant was wondering if he was going to throw-up again or cause some other problem. He was glad the new Trauma-Specialist Yara Lebowitz was going along on this trip.

Feeling a little self-conscious, Fredrick Yee was painfully aware that he had been a weakly child. Growing up in De Aar, the twenty-ninth largest city in the UNSA, he had suffered from Praghian's disease as a child, which came from eating tainted kangaroo meat. The disease had kept his skeleton thin and his muscles weak for most of his adolescent and teenage years. He had struggled at home and in school to be accepted by both his family and his peers. Not unusually smart or gifted, he had to prove himself constantly.

As soon as he was old enough, he left Earth, headed for Mars and MPIT (the Mars Planetary Institute of Technology). Graduating with advanced degrees in non-terrestrial geomechanics and applied planetary geophysics, he had joined the UESA's Frontier Authority straight out of college. In spite of his childhood health problems, Professor Fredrick Yee had become one of the most published and respected theoreticians in the field of non-terrestrial geomagnetism. That alone made him a prime candidate for the initial Saturnian mission, which is why General Newey kept him on Titan. However, he hated fieldwork. All such technical tasks annoyed him in an elemental way, like chewing gum with a fragment of aluminum foil embedded in it. He was a scientist, not an engineer, an investigator, not a maintenance-bot. He felt he should not be headed out to Titan-Base Ksa on some rescue mission.

Colonel Rozsa and Major Singleton sat in the small, cramped cockpit of the skiff, inputting commands and watching readouts on their Heads-Up Display that floated between the semicircular console and the overhead control panels. From time to time, they would speak softly to the onboard AI via their ear-mic sets. The AI was running through a pre-flight systems checklist for the second time, while the two human pilots would occasionally glance out of the viewport in front of them. Ahead of them, through the thick viewport, the retractable hangar bay wall hung like a curtain, blocking the Titan atmosphere.

"Atmospheric engine power now reading thirty-seven thousand, four hundred eighty-two, and holding," announced the ship's AI. "Main batteries are a go; emergency battery power is ninety-seven ninety."

Singleton, watching several readouts, added, "MJS is a go."

Rozsa pushed several illuminated buttons, as she checked the display for the Manual Guidance and Navigational Controls, and the Instrumentation and Communications subroutines. "MGNC and INC are a go." She depressed another button, "Skiff-One to com-center. Do you read?"

Lieutenant Sloan's voice whispered back simultaneously in both of the pilots' ear-mic sets. "I read you, Colonel. Lock your AHS onto frequency one-three-zero-nine-seven."

Rozsa's gloved hands played over the console and its holo-screens to set the automatic homing signal to the correct frequency.

"That's affirm, Lieutenant. Linking directional coordinates into AI's GNC." As if on cue, several holo-screens in the cockpit changed as the ship's main AI began interfacing with the five mini-AIs in the cockpit.

Singleton's attention switched to a small screen on his console. The skiff's AI began generating an enhanced color-coded three-dimensional image of Titan on a small holo-monitor. As the weather data began to be added to the information already present in the small digital image, Singleton added, "Colonel, this isn't going to be an easy trip. The sub-mid-latitude wind systems are a fucking mess."

"Yeah, I know," the colonel never took her eyes off her controls, "but what did you expect given the imparted thermal energy of this event," an indicator on one of her holo-screens began to flash red, as the ship's AI whispered to her and Major Singleton.

Singleton shook his head as he worked his console and studied the readouts, "Why couldn't whatever it was had happened further north?"

"Be glad it didn't. If it had, you would be looking at another very nasty deep sea, caving adventure." Rozsa cracked a grin at the thought of the last *'adventure'* Singleton had had while diving into one of the flooded ice-cave systems on Titan.

Eight months ago, Major Singleton led a party into the murky depths of *Ciara Lacūs*, one of the small cryo-glaciokarst hydrocarbon lakes that occupied the cryotectonic depression just northwest of Xanadu. He supervised the repairs to one of the ACRPs (Automated Cryo-spelunking Research Packages) that were deployed within the deep, ethane flooded ice caves. It had been a grueling four-day mission, with himself, Lieutenant Sloan, Tech-Sergeant Tounames, Private-Specialist Wong and a Maintenance and Repair-Bot living and working out of a skiff, with one of the tiny water-ice islands that dotted *Ciara Lacūs* serving as a *dry* home base for the mission. Rozsa knew Singleton would not enjoy a similar mission.

"Colonel, weather update," it was Sloan again. "Outside winds are around twenty-nine and a half kph, but here is the bad news. TiStar-Two is reporting winds over three hundred kph from the west-southwest and climbing as you approach T-One. Global temperature is up nearly two degrees with zonal fluctuations over point one four degrees. Also, it looks like you're in for one helluva rainstorm. So heads up guys, it looks like we're going to get pissed on."

Rozsa frowned on the word *"rain."* Rain on Titan was not like on Earth and was far more dangerous. The oily yellow rain referred to as *'piss'* was made of liquid methane with a whole list of hydrocarbons and nitrogen compounds. She knew the methane rain would freeze on the skiff in large, uneven masses, and affect the craft's flight control surfaces. She also knew the atmospheric flight control surfaces of the skiff were modified and not part of the craft's original design. Like so many other things on Titan, they had been retrofitted to work in Titan's hazardous environment.

"Yeah," grumbled Singleton, his face mirroring his tone.

"Right," Rozsa muttered with disgust.

As Singleton turned back to study his three-D terrain map, he announced, "We're beginning last minute systems checks and thirty-second countdown." The major quickly scanned his console, tapped several illuminated buttons, and grabbed the control stick, protruding from the narrow panel between the two pilots.

The AI was controlling the craft, but safety regulations required a human pilot to be prepared to take over if something were to go wrong with the artificial intelligence. It almost never happened, but rules were rules.

The engine pitch rose as the skiff's propellers began to spin up to a blur, and the vessel started to tremble with subdued power, "Twenty-five seconds, and counting," announced Singleton.

Both Rozsa and Singleton monitored the onboard AI as it began to taxi the tiny craft into position. The AI deployed the ship's stubby little aerodynamic wings and began running through its last-minute status checks and system startups.

"Okay, Colonel, hangar bay Titan pressurizing." Sloan's voice came over her ear-mic, as the hazy atmosphere of Titan began a controlled bleed into the hangar bay. The bay took on a bluish-red hue as more of Titan's dense atmosphere filled the huge compartment. "Hangar bay pressurized and reading two-point six-two. Hangar bay door, opening."

"That's affirm, outer door opening." The thin wall of ceramic-carbon composite in front of their viewport slowly and soundlessly rolled upward into its narrow holding box. "Twenty seconds."

The retracting pseudo-ceramic curtain slowly revealed a murky horizon of unholy darkness and insane cold. Normally the sky was an undifferentiated orangey dark haze with only faint hints of sickly oranges, muted reds, and earthy browns. Now it was a disturbed caldron, segregated by angry and billowing clouds. The swirling masses bordered between deep red and dark purple, all backlit by a faint distant source.

Through the ghost-like holographic texts and diagrams of the HUD, Rozsa, and Singleton both stared in stunned disbelief at the low hanging clouds in the turbulent skyscape that blurred the horizon. The clouds rolled, unfurled, and consume themselves like a maniac's vision of a lava lamp from hell. They knew which combination of hydrocarbons gave the clouds their unique color, but Singleton still thought that the clouds looked like they had been in a bare-knuckle fistfight with a giant.

Below the lip of the hangar bay's doorframe, the usual dull orange ground fog had vanished, revealing a musty and irregular tangerine surface. Far below, an intensely furrowed plain was stained with faint hints of indigo and other shades of blue, that were generated by polluted hydrocarbons and other compounds. There were several dark, dry riverbeds whining their way across the icy plain like frozen snakes. A strong, mute wind blew patches of dark mist and splinters of colored ice and rock dust across the rough terrain.

Rozsa and Singleton exchanged a long, befuddled stare. The confusion of one was mirrored in the eyes of the other. Only the distant voice of Sloan broke the silence.

"Ten seconds," announced the craft's AI over the ship's com systems.

Rozsa's eyes narrowed on the holo-screen in front of her as she watched the onboard AI rev up the craft's engines.

"Prepare for launch," commanded the AI. "Five seconds, four . . . three . . . two . . . one . . . launching." At that moment, the skiff moved gently forward and upward into the dark, frozen hands of Titan.

As they climbed away, both Rozsa and Singleton surveyed the muted hills of Sotra Patera in the near distance. The soft hills of water ice, frozen ammonia compounds and meteoric rock that had been heaved into the air by cryovolcanism and the slowly shifting surface of the dynamic cryo-geology of Titan, were a wondrous sight, even through the murky atmosphere. The distorted layers and bands that were visible in the hard ice would have been quickly recognizable to any non-terrestrial glacial geomorphologist as cryometamorphism.

Singleton, who had spent many weeks hiking and climbing in those foothills of Sotra Patera with the other members of Titan-Base Lincoln, knew them well. Titan-Base Lincoln itself rested on one of these low, rolling hills at the far edge of the range. It was constructed on a vast stable plateau of pressure shaved rock and ice protruding from the slopes of Lincoln Mons, named for the cryo-geomorphologist who first mapped the area in detail, a hundred and thirty-eight years earlier.

The sun appeared as the skiff turned slowly onto its course. The tiny, dim yellow-red patch hung low on the horizon and gave no warmth or any hint of its real brilliance. Its light was cold and feeble, like the light of a birthday candle in a blackened, icy meat locker. Both skiff pilots knew that sometimes when seen in good weather, Saturn's reflected light was far brighter than that of the distant sun. Now Saturn hung extremely low on the horizon, visible clearly only to the Titan-Base Ksa complex and the T-One Drill Site.

•     •     •

Sloan turned as the com-center door opened and a well-built, dark skin man moved through the room and took a seat at the newly repaired LESAPS console. Without a word, the man's hands began to dance over the holo-screen console for the Laser Evaluation and Scanning Pulse Sensor system.

"Everything is good and by the numbers," pronounced Sloan, turning his attention back to his own terminal. "They're on course, and Major Singleton has the stick," added the lieutenant, examining the latest wind-shear data.

"Thank you," acknowledged the man in a tone that hinted at a Chakosi accent. He continued to tap icons on his holo-screen and examining the results, ignoring the young lieutenant.

Sloan glanced back at the man, thinking that Major Colin Nianta, the station's senior pilot, was feeling slighted at being left out of this important assignment. He knew from experience that he was a far better command pilot than Major Singleton or Colonel

Rozsa. However, as he sat at the console, fine-tuning his instruments, Sloan realized that the major was not upset or angry; he was simply following his orders like everyone else.

Major Colin Nianta was a shade of mahogany, with strong arms and a chest to match. Like his friend Major Singleton, his black Afro was cut short and styled very neat. However, unlike his friend, his eyes were very dark bordering on black, and they spoke of a wisdom that only time and experience could bring.

As Major Nianta popped an ear-mic set into place, his chestnut brown eyes began taking in all the scrolling data before him, as he tracked the slow, little blue dot with its informational text-box across the ghostly holo-screen. "Steve, you're looking good. Your AI is reporting that all of your onboards are green."

Singleton's reply to Nianta was broken by static, "Affirmative Major, AI reports green. Our velocity is five hundred thirty-one kph."

"That's affirm," Nianta looked around at the partially restored com-center. There were several consoles and other pieces of instrumentation that still required repair, and there was smoke damage to the walls and ceiling that still needed to be cleaned. "You're at seventeen point nine-seven percent of surface escape velocity," the major knew Singleton and Rozsa had that information displayed in front of them on their HUD, but procedures were procedures.

"That's affirm, seventeen point nine-seven percent SEV," came back Singleton.

Sloan was busy working on the new AI's prediction for possible weather conditions on the other side of Titan. The AI integrated all of the data from the few surviving surface sensors and scanning satellites in Titan orbit, and fed it to the Martino-Quinn model and spat the results out to Sloan's holo-screen. On the holo-screen, numbers and letters, and colored symbols file past as Sloan marked the screen with his index finger. Hitting a key, Sloan addressed his ear-mic transceiver, "Major, I have a revised weather update."

Nianta replied with an affirmative nod.

Sloan fingered his holo-screen, "Skiff One, I know you are not going to believe this, but now Lync is saying there's a possibility of tornado action a long your current flight line." He glanced over at Major Nianta, who was scratching his short cut

Afro. The major had developed a severe case of dandruff since arriving on Titan, and none of the doctors had been able to cure it or explain it.

Rozsa's static-laced reply boomed over Sloan's ear-mic, "Tornadoes my ass!" The young lieutenant could imagine the look on the colonel's face as she continued, "The last time Titan's atmosphere had enough energy to produce tornadoes was---"

Shaking his head, Sloan cut Rozsa off, "Ma'am, with all due respect, I know, but this AI-script for this Martino-Quinn model was originally written to model summer-fall atmosphere dynamics at the high latitudes. In spite of Professor Eastman's adjustments, it still has a problem with kinetic energy inputs and thermal transit energy flow."

There was a long pause before Rozsa responded, "Have her recheck her algorithms, and we'll keep our eyes open."

As the com-center door sounded, Sloan and Nianta turned to see Tech-Sergeant Tounames advance into the room leading a Marb and pushing a motorized handcart. The thin metal handcart was loaded with prepackaged holo-screens, rolls of fiber-optic cable, and other replacement equipment. Without any command, the Marb went to work at a wall panel, its mechanical arms moving slightly faster than the human eye could track.

The tech-sergeant gave a half-hearted wave to Sloan and Nianta as he quickly took stock of the situation in the com-center. "Just starting round two," he smiled. Dry, but in a dirty and ruffled uniform, Tounames immediately opened a panel in the wall closest to the door and started to examine the condition of the circuits within. Removing a small power-screwdriver from his equipment-laden toolbelt, he started in on the mechanism within the wall as Nianta and Sloan returned to their tasks.

Just as the com-center door was about to reseal, it opened again admitting a slim, raven-haired woman. Carrying a load of small boxes stacked to her chin, the woman acknowledged Sloan and Nianta as she moved to Tounames. It was obvious to Nianta and Sloan that in spite of the Captain's insignia on her uniform, Captain Tonja Aamodt was playing day-laborer for the tech-sergeant.

Placing the numerous carbo-plastic containers on the floor next to Tounames, the captain added in a strong, but not unfeminine voice, "This is everything on the list you wanted."

"That's great. Thanks." The tech-sergeant wasted no time in tearing into one of the smaller boxes and removing a black and gray module wrapped in bubble plastic. Tounames nodded as Captain Aamodt walked away, "Could you start opening up those consoles?"

With a thumbs-up sign, the captain moved off into the room, as Tounames subtly took in the view of her backside. The tech-sergeant, like the other men on the station, loved the way the captain's uniform pants always seemed to hug her hips, giving her buttocks a tight form. Even now, in a soot-covered uniform, he thought that the way her bulky toolbelt hung low on her hips, actually accentuated her shape. However, the tech-sergeant was well aware that Captain Aamodt was probably tougher and better at living and working in the depths of deep space than most of her larger, stronger male companions. She was a well-trained member of the Titan exploration team, with degrees in non-terrestrial glacial geochemistry and exotic isotope mineralogy. In addition, rumor had it that she was not a half-bad skiff and hopper pilot. Tounames turned his attention back to the wall control panel.

"I was talking to Eastman before we left," Singleton's voice was starting to break up over both Sloan's and Nianta's ear-mics. "It's a long shot, but I refuse to believe all this is just from the transit energy imparted into the atmosphere. Could T-One have drilled into some type of compressed cryo-geothermal pocket?"

"I wouldn't bet on it," replied Nianta.

"I doubt it as well," announced Captain Aamodt from across the com-center. "All of the cryo-geothermal pockets were mapped decades ago. You can check with Professor Yee, but none of them could have produced this type of event. We are too far out from summer for the rainfall to interact with the warmer salinosphere or even any of the alkanofer to produce hydrocarbon fumaroles, and surely none on this scale." She hesitated and then added coldly, "assuming that is what T-One was working on. I wouldn't rule out some revolutionary Geothermal-Ion power system for Titan."

There was a pause from the other end of the comlink, then Major Singleton replied in a burst of chaotic noise and mild static, "I hear you, Captain. However, I don't want to rule out an impact event. We've seen this kind of effect before. Do you remember about three years ago, the hailstorm? There was a cometary impact down in Kalseru Virga, at the same time there was an upset in Saturn's magnetic field. The particles from the comet nucleated, forming the hail event."

"Colonel, there hasn't been any comet or asteroid alert in our vicinity in the last two weeks," Sloan interjected as he typed in a long series of commands into his holo-screen. After several seconds, he was rewarded with a new screen full of information. "Looking at the data before the event, there's no indication of a rogue comet or asteroid in our vicinity."

As Sloan started to go through the more historical data on Titan, Captain Aamodt leaned in over Major Nianta, "How's the mission going?" She smelt of burnt carbo-plastic and hot wires, and black soot was conspicuously present under her jagged fingernails.

"So far, so good, but I wish I were flying," Nianta looked up into Aamodt's green eyes. They were swollen and pink, almost blood-red with irritation. "Steve is holding his own, but if the weather turns bad, they may have to go sub-orbital."

"He can handle it," smiling, Aamodt's eyes scanned the holo-console in front of Nianta.

"I hope he doesn't have to," Nianta frowned. "That event kicked a dogshit-load of fine debris high up into the main haze layer. If he has to take her higher than three hundred kilometers, he's going to have problems. The skiffs handle like a limp prick that high in the atmosphere."

Aamodt gently whipped her black hair around behind her back and leaned in closer to Nianta. She wanted to tell him that Singleton could fly more than just unfeeling machines, and could handle a great deal more than some sub-orbital maneuvers. Not to mention, he never had a limp prick. However, she knew that he probably already was aware of the situation. Relationships, especially purely sexual ones, were somewhat hard to hide on an isolated station like Titan-Base Lincoln.

"Major!" Tounames called from the doorway, several circuit boards, and colored wires hanging from the wall. "The environmental controls are online again, but I had to work around a few things and take some secondary and tertiary systems offline."

Nianta acknowledged the engineer with a grin and a nod, then turned back to Aamodt as Sloan began quietly speaking to the skiff again.

All of a sudden, everyone's PDI beeped with a general interlink message from Tech-Sergeant Yoshida. It stated that the interlink system was back online.

As Tounames was about to reply to the message, the whole room began to vibrate. Everyone froze and looked around anxiously as if waiting for someone to say something, but no one did. As the low shuddering dissipated, Lync announced in its fake empathy voice that the station had just experienced a magnitude five point two-five Titanquake and that no new damage or system failures had been detected.

"I am getting a bad feeling about this," whispered Aamodt, nervously checking her PDI on her forearm. "We shouldn't be having aftershocks this strong, so long after the initial event." She keyed in a request for information and examined the schematic of the Saturnian system that appeared on her PDI. With a look of confusion, she noted all of the current gravitational influences on Titan.

"What can we do?" Nianta asked, then added flatly, "Leave?"

"Please tell me now if we're thinking about leaving, and not a week from now, after I work my ass off trying to get this place back together," Tounames checked the repair list on his PDI and moved to a blackened and silent terminal across the room. "Oh, and by-the-way, one of the secondary systems I had to disconnect was the emergency hydraulic release for the door mechanism."

"Unless these quakes start to get worse, I don't think you're going anywhere." Aamodt was still frowning, knowing the tech-sergeant and his pet Marb had their work cut out for them.

"You can wait on the hydraulics," added Nianta.

Tounames nodded, "Yeah, we have time to get to the non-essential systems later."

Sloan smiled, and Nianta snickered at the tech-sergeant's understatement, but neither man gave voice to their thoughts. The two men just went back to monitoring the progress of the skiff, as Aamodt joined Tounames and the Marb in their attempts to repair the fire-damaged terminals.

After the skiff moved beyond the LESAPS's horizon, Nianta joined Tounames, Aamodt, and the Marb in making repairs to the com-center. They continued to converse about what was going on for nearly an hour before Lync announced the receipt of a message from the Outer Systems Command. Checking, Sloan noted that the audiovisual signal was prefix coded for General Newey's eyes-only, and had been routed to his office immediately. The news did not make Sloan smile.

•  •  •

Lieutenant LaRocque's legs were cramped in the tiny auxiliary AI-compartment in the rear of the skiff. The closet-size room was dark, lit only by the lights of the huge semi-circular console loaded with keyboards and hard-monitors. LaRocque was preparing the skiff's AI to interface with what he expected would be a heavily damaged or wholly inoperative Titan-Base Ksa's AI-system. Knowing that Titan-Base Ksa was transmitting an emergency disaster signal, LaRocque reasoned that if Titan-Base Ksa's AI were functioning it would be trying to communicate over the same frequency as the emergency signal.

That is when LaRocque noticed the second signal.

It was very skillfully hidden in the emergency disaster signal, like spyware in an image file. The surprised lieutenant doubted if anyone, who was not looking for it would have found it. Moreover, he discovered that the hidden message was also coded. Working with the skiff's AI, LaRocque attempted to decipher the mysterious embedded signal, but after an hour and a half of focused work, he sighed and hit a button on the keyboard in front of him. "Colonel? LaRocque. That embedded transmission is definitely a sophisticated multimodal harmonic."

"Can you decipher it?" Rozsa's reply through his ear-mic set.

"I don't know. It's very complex, like some kinda hyper-dynamic Chinese puzzle-box. Everything I've tried so far has only shown me what doesn't work. I'm about to change the AI's sub-operating system, so you'll see a caution-warning light on the main AI. I'm going to try a variant on the Kardashev-Doyle Information Theorem. It is a hyperbinary cipher, based on atomic masses and a Gaussian-bitwise unfolding routine. But with the limited resources of the onboards, it's going to take some time to run, and it's going to eat up a lot of the AI processing power. Some of the systems may be slow in responding."

After an unusually long pause, Rozsa's voice inquired, "Why don't you let Lync do it back at the base?"

LaRocque chuckled, "I don't have anything else to do on this little trip. Besides, on the off chance, it's an AI-parasite, I can deal with it here easier than if Lync got infected, back at TBL."

"Well, Good luck," but her voice did not sound hopeful. "Just don't infect our systems."

A broad smile flashed across LaRocque's face as he added, "I won't."

"We're three hours from touchdown." Colonel Rozsa's voice was tight and had an edge to it.

"Right," LaRocque tapped the button again and went back to work. He played with the AI via the keyboard and hard-screens in his little workspace. He and the ship's AI tried several different combinations of ciphers and LaRocque watched the results develop on the small hard-monitor.

As time passed the skiff ride began to get bumpier and more unsteady, and LaRocque could tell they were entering rough weather. An hour after Rozsa alerted everyone to secure themselves in their seats; the skiff's AI rewarded LaRocque with a series of words. It was a short, ominous sentence, which confused and frightened the lieutenant. He just stared at the words. He read them over and over again, but could not understand them. As he read, he could feel his pulse beginning to race and the sweat starting to form on his forehead. As he bounced around in his seat, he read the first sentence of the message for the fifth time.

The sentence read, **"Warning! Extreme Danger…"**

# CHAPTER FIVE

Lieutenant General Newey sat motionless and pensive, as the message from the Outer Systems Command re-played. His office felt extremely empty and lonely, the Intelligent-conference table more massive than usual. It was the second time in under two hours that Newey had watched the two-dimensional image of Commissioner Damien Marshall on the holo-screen. Sitting through the message once had been bad enough for Newey, but sitting through it twice while Professor Eastman was informed about the covert nature of the Titan-One Drill Site was like a toothache that would not go away. He could see in her eyes, that as soon as the message ended, she was going to lay into him.

Newey had known Commissioner Damien Marshall from the early days of the Amalthea-Jupiter installation. Back then, the Commissioner was the installation's provost-officer, and Newey was a newly promoted Division General, overseeing the installation's refit, and construction upgrades. In the fifteen years since Amalthea-Jupiter, Newey had grown not to like or trust the man. He had learned that the commissioner was far *too* good a politician to have *real* friends and that there was a fine line between Marshall's friends and his enemies. The man was too ambitious, too quick to place blame, and too quick to steal credit for Newey's liking. On the other hand, he did like and even trust, Professor Lori Eastman.

Professor Eastman was seated across the Intelligent-conference table from General Newey. She sat stone-faced as she watched the dark skin commissioner relay information and instructions to both General Newey and herself. She forced herself to be quiet, waiting to put forth her questions. However, she really just felt like exploding in the general's face. Staring at the moving image of the distant UESA commissioner made Eastman angrier and angrier with each word that fell out of the man's mouth. She and most of the personnel on Titan-Base Lincoln had been kept in the dark about what was really going on at the Titan-One Drill Site and Titan-Base Ksa.

Now she knew! She knew why the entire Saturnian system had been evacuated. She knew why General Newey and Colonel Rozsa had been brought in, and why she had been removed as Commander of Titan-Base Lincoln. To her credit, she was not alarmed, frightened, or even surprised. However, she was angry, and she wanted to hit something! How could they have kept something like this a secret? How could they make decisions like these? She had hoped that humanity had evolved beyond this kind of unsupported paranoia and fear of the unknown. Again, events had dashed her hopes.

Eastman had to watch highly qualified personnel be shipped out and in most cases placed into lower positions without any logical explanation. Now she knew the real reason, even though she still did not like it. However, she knew it would do no good to argue. She would bite her tongue, buy her time, and wait. Nevertheless, this transmission from the Outer Systems Command worried Eastman. It was not the things the commissioner said, rather it was the things he did not say. The questions he did not ask that made the alarm bells go off in the back of her mind.

Looking at the man's narrow face on the holo-screen, Eastman reconsidered an earlier opinion and agreed with it again. *Yes, the man's eyes were indeed too close together, and he squinted far too much for her liking.* Commissioner Marshall was one of, if not the best, baby kissing, double-talking, wife swapping, son-of-a-bitches that she had ever met. However, none of that mattered now.

"…and Rick, I wanted you to know that an emergency relief mission is being put together at this very moment. I can't give you an estimate at this time, but I just got word that both the Taj and the Onakea are being re-tasked and sent out to Saturn. Now, I know what you must be thinking, and you're right. The Taj and the Onakea were both scheduled to perform deep survey missions below the ecliptic. The Taj is at Eunomia-Fifteen, and the Onakea is less than a day from Three-Eighty-Seven-Aquitania. Even if we can get them re-fitted for an emergency support mission in a week, it will still take them about three to four weeks to get out to you."

*Welcome to deep space exploration,* thought Newey, his face expressionless.

"Now, you are authorized to utilize your emergency evacuation vessel if you choose to. However, the condition of the extrasolar craft at the T-One Drill Site and the status of the TBK facility and personnel must also be determined prior to any evacuation. If T-One and TBK are *end-of-mission,* you must secure as much of their scientific and technical data as possible, and relay that data directly to Professor Lau Kam Yang at the UGE's Institute for Advanced Technologies' Applications at Vishniac, Antarctica. She will be coordinating all data you transmit. You will not, under any circumstances notify any other departments or agencies of the presence of EBE's on Titan, without clearing it through me or the head of the Outer Systems Command, Commissioner-General Kefira Tran at the United Security Forces installation on Eunomia-Fifteen..."

Marshall's narrow brown face was unemotional as he continued to issue instructions to Newey. The general could tell by the look on the man's face that Marshall was already considering all his possible options. Marshall, no doubt had the Main Asteroid Belt deflection posts on high alert, and priority messages were probably already flying back-and-forth between Earth, Mars, the Main Asteroid Belt, and Callisto-Jupiter. Because of the current positions of the Jupiter system, relative to the Saturnian system, the bodies of the Main Asteroid Belt were actually closer travel-wise than Jupiter and its satellites.

"...all transmissions to me, the OSC, or Professor Yang are to be coded alpha-blue with a beta three prefix and sent only over secure comlinks. You are not to respond to any queries that are not properly coded with the appropriate prefix. Your station's AI is receiving the necessary alpha-blue coded prefixes and autonomous instructions, now. It is being ordered to transmit the backup data sets stored on your secure servers. Now the touchy part," he paused as if looking for the correct words. "Please notify Professor Eastman and all Frontier Authority personnel that they are now under the authority of the United Security Forces

Command. That being said, they are all now subject to the provisions under the United Security Forces Act of twenty-four seventy. This includes USFC emergency order number twelve."

The commissioner paused again as a very attractive brunette with green highlights handed Marshall a workslate, indicating something of importance on its display. Marshall sighed heavily and continued, "Rick, if you find it necessary to terminate your command, please follow the published procedures in the operations manual, under the section outlining biological disasters and environmental contamination." The image showed Commissioner Marshall reading the workslate and tapping several icons as he continued, "As I indicated earlier, your department heads may receive instructions from Professor Yang or members of her team. However, all communications from FA personnel have to be cleared by you, Professor Yang, Commissioner Tran, or myself. I'll update you as soon as I know anything. Good luck." The image of the Commissioner abruptly faded and the screen filled with frequency, coding and transmitting strength data.

"Fuck me, I need a drink," belched Eastman, looking sour.

The general snickered as he got up and walked over to a small cabinet. He retrieved two small glasses and an almost full bottle labeled: *America's Finest Straight Bourbon*. Returning to the table, Newey half-filled both glasses and slid one over to Eastman, spilling only a little of the amber liquid.

"Did he mean," began Eastman, motioning toward the holo-screen and picking up her glass. "What I think he meant?"

Newey sat the bottle down and after taking a swallow of his drink, he replied in an unmotivated voice, "Yeah. He meant to activate the station's self-destruct system." He stood, facing Eastman. "It should yield an explosion, producing just over five hundred tetra-joules." He knew she knew this already.

Eastman drained a quarter of her drink and just stared at the general. From her expression, it was evident that words had escaped her.

"It should be sufficient to vaporize about thirty percent of Sotra Patera. T-One and TBK have similar systems in place," finished Newey.

Professor Eastman shook her head in disbelief. She was aware, as was all of the senior staff on the station that the self-destruct system was nothing more than a series of subroutines in

Lync's primary operating system. The subroutines would essentially deactivate all of the cooling systems in the station's primary fusion plant, causing it to overload, overheat, and explode. *At least,* she thought to herself, *the commissioner had not mentioned the Worldfall protocols.* "Do you think T-One activated their self-destruct?"

"No, because T-One's AI would have sent out a general alert warning of the auto-destruct, and there is no radiation signature in the atmosphere indicating a high-yield detonation of that type."

Eastman frowned with a nod, sipped her drink and added, "When the fuck were they going to let the rest of us in on this little secret?"

Newey returned the nod but remained quiet for half a minute. He took another sip of his drink, and thought before he spoke, "Okay, here is the truth of it," he leaned into Eastman, his eyes boring into hers. "You know T-One was one of the first permanent installations on Titan; its mission was to investigate Titan's natural resources as part of the colonization of the Saturnian system. The initial geological survey of Menvra indicated that the meteorite that produced the crater might have been rich in ruthenium, palladium, and a host of other important metals. However, what you didn't know, and very few do, is that after ten years of planning and test borings, they didn't find a meteorite."

"They found this extrasolar craft," Eastman finished Newey's statement for him.

"Yeah, and operation Quadriga was started, and about three years ago they got a team down to it." Newey started to slowly circle the table, gently tapping the side of his glass with his index finger. "That's when the security-cover story phase of operation Quadriga began, and the low-level evacuations started. Because what they found was a ship of some kind built by extrasolar biological entities, EBEs, and based on the ice stratigraphy and various radiometric dating techniques, the craft arrived here about a quarter of a billion years ago."

"Why didn't they tell us about this operation Quadriga?" Anger was creeping into Eastman's voice as she tasted her drink again, "why the fucking secrecy?"

"Not my call." General Newey stopped circling the conference table and paused for a second. "It was only about a year ago, that they actually got access to the interior of the craft."

"And what did they find?"

Newey paused again. Even though he was a senior level United Earth Space Administration officer, the classified report he had been given on operation Quadriga had been heavily redacted. Even with significant details blotted out of the joint Outer Systems Command, Frontier Authority, and United Security Forces report, Newey got a sense of what was discovered and its importance. Of what he did know, he was not sure how much he should share with Eastman. "The craft was still partly functional." He saw Eastman's face morph into stunned surprise, "Yes, I know. Even after a quarter of a billion years, buried under twelve and a half kilometers of ice, a lot of the ship's systems apparently were still functioning."

Eastman sat up in her seat. "What type of technology did they find? Who are they? Where are they from?" she was animated, her graying red hair quivering. "Have they been back?"

The general stopped her with an upraised hand. "General Pan couldn't give me too many details, but she told me to imagine what a tenth-century monk would think if they were suddenly dropped into the middle of a modern megaplex or state-of-the-art analytical laboratory. That is what Desiree said it felt like when she first walked through the craft."

Eastman knew Lieutenant General Desiree Pan was Newey's counterpart at Titan-Base Ksa. "What did Theo Vance have to say?" She knew Professor Vance personally. He had initially been in command of Titan-Base Ksa, and like her, he had been replaced by a UESA general, in his case, by Lieutenant General Pan.

"Professor Vance's reports are classified. However, from what I could piece together from talking with Pan, Vance and others, that craft was on some type of terra-forming mission."

"Terra-forming?" Eastman took another gulp of her drink. "And the equipment is still active?"

"Some of it is," Newey as well took a hard gulp of his drink.

"By all the divinities," whispered Eastman.

Newey and Eastman had read the required documents outlining the potential socio-economic, political, religious, and psychological implications of contact with a technically superior, extrasolar entity. It had been one of those boring, annoying documents you were required to read and sign-off on, as part of becoming a commander or administrator. Now she knew why it was required.

"Are they still here?"

"Don't know."

Eastman twisted her face in confusion. "If they are terraformers, they should be coming back?"

General Newey sipped his bourbon and formulated an answer. After nearly a minute he replied, "Since we first were able to listen to the stars we thought we were alone. Sixteen hundred years ago, when the major religions on Earth came to the realization that we were not the center of the universe, they still hung on to the idea that maybe some deity had created the whole thing just for us." Newey returned to his seat at the head of the conference table but continued to stare at Eastman.

She still sat stone-faced, drink in hand.

"When microbial life was discovered in the subsurface, and polar ice of Mars and Earth-like worlds were being discovered orbiting other stars, the majority of people still believed we were the only complex life in the universe. When macro-organisms were found swimming around under the ice of Europa, then on Enceladus, our collective social ego got another blow."

"Get to the point," Eastman barked, she could feel fear in her heart.

"When the Second Dark Ages ended in the mid-twenty-third century, and we started moving out into the solar system, the first radio signals from another civilization were detected and confirmed. A civilization, two thousand light-years away orbiting Cygni-Kepler-Eleven, a star twice as old as ours, with a civilization that had developed radio technology about the same time the Goths were invading Moesia, and starting to take apart the Roman Empire."

Eastman started to interrupt the general, but he halted her with an upraised hand. "So we are colonizing and terra-forming our own system. We have shown little concern for the native organisms on Mars, and we can already see the ecological damage we are doing to the Europian environment."

Eastman looked lost, jiggling her head in confusion, "And?"

"What if those EBEs were following the same model? There were macro-organisms on Earth a quarter of a billion years ago, and these EBEs tried to wipe them out but stopped for some reason. What if they come back and want to finish the job?"

"That's absurd," Eastman scoffed.

"Is it?" Newey waved her off. "Using the revised Drake-Ishimura equation and what we know about the percentage of potentially habitable worlds in our part of the galaxy, we calculated the number of civilizations more advanced than us, within a radius of ten thousand light-years, at over fifty. We've found two, why? If those guys on Cygni-Kepler-Eleven are two thousand years ahead of us, technologically, why are they not here already? In two thousand years from now, we should be out there."

Eastman paused as it started to dawn on her what the general was getting at.

"Could another civilization be moving through the galaxy, terra-forming worlds, wiping out the existing lifeforms, either as a prelude to colonization or just to keep the competition down?" He studied Eastman as she drank her bourbon.

She did not reply for a long while, then she whispered, "The devil in the dark."

"What?"

"The devil in the dark hypothesis," She repeated, draining another quarter of her glass. She reached over with a trembling hand and poured herself another drink.

"Precisely," the general nodded. "The UESA, based on the evidence that has been found at Menvra, believes that this thing came to our solar system to either terraform the inner planets for colonization or wipe out all existing life to limit competition."

Eastman did not know what to say or do. She wanted to stand up, but her legs felt weak. She took another sip of her drink but thought she was going to throw up. "Proof?" was all she could get out without being sick.

"I'm not that far up the food chain, but Vance hinted at that was what he believed. It sounds totally plausible. Look at the geologic evidence, at least for Venus and Earth," Newey took the bottle of bourbon and topped off his glass.

"What else do you know about these EBEs?" she sipped her drink, wanting more information. "Why did they stop what they were doing?"

"I don't have a clue. The UESA has two working hypotheses; one, their craft malfunctioned, and they couldn't complete their mission and ended up crashing here. Or someone or something stopped them before they could complete their mission and the wreckage ended up here." He leaned into Eastman. "Anyway, some of the experts at the UESA think it is even possible that this craft or whatever it is was left here intentionally. They believe, based on the absence of advanced civilizations, that this may be some kind of booby trap."

"Could that be what caused this event?" Eastman stared at Newey with concern still burning in her eyes. "Did the guys at T-One set it off?"

"Don't know, but what I got from talking with Pan over the last couple of months was that her team had discovered that the craft's power systems were fully operational. They also discovered something else that made Professor Vance worry."

Professor Eastman perked up. "What did they find?"

"She wouldn't say, and I wasn't going to press her on it."

There was a minute or more of dead silence before Eastman chuckled nervously. "Theo Vance is a good scientist. He wouldn't get worried unless he found something inside that craft to make him worry."

Newey gestured with his head, "I don't know."

"What about the UESA or the OSC? Did they indicate anything that might support a devil in the dark hypothesis?"

"No." The general was getting frustrated.

Eastman did not say anything, but it was apparent that her mind was working.

"Now I know this is a lot to take in all at once---"

"No dogshit," snapped Eastman.

"Now, the experts and the higher-ups want to keep this under wraps until they know what we are dealing with. You know there are enough religious cults hanging around to turn a discovery like this into an object of worship, and that is the last thing humanity needs."

Immediately Eastman thought of the Earth-Firsters and New Dawn terror-cultist groups. They would latch onto something like this and use it to justify a return to organized and deified religions. "If this thing crashed here a quarter of a billion years ago, it couldn't be from any of the nearby star systems. Any clue about where it's from?" Her voice was hoarse and cracking.

"I don't know," Newey leaned back in his chair. "I'm not

in the loop on any of that. Once the craft was identified, protocols were initiated. Ksa and Lincoln were the closest and largest bases to the T-One site. Everyone else in the entire Saturnian system was moved out, and a cover-story and security lockdown was put in place. Colonel Rozsa and I were told, along with Professor Watkinski, who came in with us."

"What about the other newbies? Do they know what's going on?"

"The ones assigned here, no." the general leaned forward again, "They are here for specialty support, just like you. But, I am sure all of the TBK newbies are aware."

"Why did they keep some of us here and deport the rest?" questioned Eastman.

Newey raised his glass in salute to her. "You and the remainder of your original team are still here because someone believes you would be useful to this project."

The door beeped for attention, and a woman's voice requested admittance, but the general just glanced at the timepiece built into the conference table and said nothing.

Eastman too ignored the office door buzzer. "So what is your part in this mess?"

The general did not reply. He just stared at Eastman for nearly a minute, then finally added, "Same as yours, support staff." The man adjusted himself, hinting that what was coming was an uncomfortable topic. "Based on Marshall's orders, and since we don't know what happened at T-One, I'm going to assume it is connected to this extrasolar object. I am going to inform the entire station of what is going on at T-One."

Eastman sensed that the general was being less than truthful, but she did not want to press the topic just yet. "I think it's a good idea and overdue."

Newey shook his graying head.

"Well I, for one, can't believe any intelligent, spacefaring civilization could be capable of anything like the devil in the dark scenario." The professor had some more of her drink.

Part of the general wanted to smile, but emotion just could not get across his old, bearded face. "We'll find out when Rozsa and her team report in, but in the meantime, I'm going to bring Doctor Reierstadt in on this first. Given the loss of Zapollo and the conditions being what they are, and given our remoteness, I want her input. Also, I'm going to ask her to keep a closer eye on the staff."

The door buzzer sounded again.

"She's good, that's why I wanted her on my team."

"I read her file, that's why she is still here. Come in," spat Newey automatically as he disengaged the privacy mode on the door.

"One other thing," Eastman peaked in the direction of the still closed door before she spoke. "Isotopic measurements put the date of formation of both Saturn's rings and Iapetus' equatorial ridge at about a quarter of a billion years."

The general and the professor just locked eyes as the hydraulic mechanism sounded, and a large woman, tapping at her forearm PDI walked into the general's office. She wore a pressed and sharply arranged blue and gray UESA pseudo-uniform.

Doctor Barbara Reierstadt, the station psychologist, carried a workslate in one hand and a mug of amber liquid in the other. Eastman did not move, but simply looked Reierstadt over, scrutinizing her shoulder-length black hair and solid frame. The psychologist looked like an inspired child gymnast, whom puberty had destroyed all hopes of athletic glory. As the door closed behind Reierstadt, Eastman turned back to examine Newey's face.

"You wanted to see me, General?" Reierstadt's voice was smooth and cool like a singer of poetic jazz. She took a seat, one chair removed from Professor Eastman, giving her some space.

"Thank you, Doctor. I know you are probably already addressing how the crew is dealing with this event and the loss of Private-Specialist Zapollo," Newey looked straight into her gray eyes, "but we have another potential problem that I want you to monitor."

Doctor Reierstadt looked from the general to Professor Eastman and back, curiosity growing in her eyes.

"What I am about to tell you is classified information, and I want your input on how I should break this news to the rest of the base's personnel."

The woman indicated her understanding, already starting to look uncomfortable.

"The explosion at T-One," Newey glanced to Eastman before he continued, "well it most likely involved a manufactured object of extrasolar origin."

Reierstadt's artificially tanned face went void of expression. Ten seconds went by before she broke a smile and added, "What?"

"This is classified information," Newey emphasized his point by ramming his right index finger into the tabletop. "A craft of extrasolar origin was discovered at the T-One site, buried under several kilometers of ice at the bottom of Menvra crater. I want to make sure that panic does not take hold. Especially after the event we just had."

Reierstadt cleared her throat loudly before speaking. "I know this is highly unlikely, but are you fucking with me?"

Newey and Eastman exchanged a glance, and both began to speak at once, but Eastman halted, and Newey continued. "No, it's real, and that is the kind of reaction I want to forestall. The Outer Systems Command and the UESA both are aware. But, until Colonel Rozsa and her team report back, we have no way of knowing if this is a result of the Extrasolar Biological Entities."

"Aliens," Reierstadt's confusion was growing by leaps and bounds, but the artificially tanned Slavic features of her face hid it well, "by all of the Divinities."

The general took a deep breath, reached over, and typed a few icons on the Intelligent-conference table. For the third time, the message from Commissioner Marshall played. For the second time, Newey watched as one of his staff squirmed in her seat at the details of the message.

When Commissioner Marshall's message was completed, Newey broke the silence in the room. "Doc, you now know what I know," Newey continued to search the woman's face for a hint of fear, but found none, only confusion, "but we're under orders."

There was a long silence as Reierstadt looked to Eastman for confirmation, then looked back to the general, "Okay, what do you want me to do?"

"Help me formulate a way to break the news to the staff, and keep an eye on the staff as usual." ⸺

"I'll keep a tighter watch on the crew." A second later Reierstadt's expression shifted. "Wait a minute, is that why everyone was evacuated?"

"Doctor, the UESA is trying to avoid panic and wild speculation," began Newey. "You are a psychologist and know how limited information can quickly morph into rumor, then into fear, then outright hysteria." Newey adjusted himself in his seat.

"Remember about twenty years ago, a shipload of miners and their families were emigrating from the Mercurian colonies to Pasiphae-Jupiter. A day after they got out of cryosleep, half the children started getting a fever, and tiny red blisters started showing up all over their bodies. What happened?"

Reierstadt and Eastman traded a look, but neither answered as the general continued, "First it was thought to be Desert Fever, then the Shreveport-E virus, then the Red Death of Mars. As the OSC was about to order a transport with twelve hundred men, women and children *permanently sanitized,* they discovered it was only a relatively harmless strain of avian-pox. Misinformation, rumor, and panic will get you killed."

"I get it. We need to move slowly on this and not jump to conclusions," Reierstadt added flatly.

Newey continued to scan the psychologist's face, looking for something unexpected. There was nothing.

"Okay," Reierstadt's gaze moved from Newey to Eastman and back. "I'll throw some words at you in a half hour or so. You can write an announcement around it."

Out of the corner of his eye, Newey caught the change in expression on Eastman's face. "I want to keep Lori in the loop on this as well. After I make the announcement, let us know if anyone starts showing signs of unusual stress." He sat surveying both women. "In spite of what you might think, I do read your psych reports every month." He paused with a grimace, trying to choose his words carefully, "When this news becomes public, I want to know who may not deal with this information well."

"Captain Arroyo, among others, has been showing signs of PDD, which is Persistent Depressive Disorder, for the last three months, and you know he still has issues with PTSD and...."

Newey halted the doctor with a raised hand, "I am aware of the old situation Doctor, but now I am more concerned with this new one. Whatever happens, we are going to be facing weeks of very long days, filled with investigative work and repairs. I'll need everyone at their best or out of the way."

"We'll stay on top of it and keep you informed," announced Eastman standing up, indicating that they should move to the door and leave.

Doctor Reierstadt started to speak, saw Eastman's gesture, and thought better of it. She too stood, hovered an uneasy moment, then gave the general an affirmative nod, and headed out the door with Eastman. As the door was closing behind them, Newey could hear them start a polite, but forceful conversation that was cut short as the door sealed shut.

Exhausted, the general softly grumbled under his breath with disgust and age. He leaned back and sat motionless in his chair watching the images slowly change on the walls of his office. There was a group picture of Newey, Marshall and several other senior OSC and FA officials back at the Amalthea-Jupiter dockyard.

The fatigued general stared at Commissioner Marshall's face. All the time, he wished he knew what was really going through the man's mind. *What could really be going on with Titan-Base Ksa?* He felt much older than his sixty-nine years as he tapped out several commands into the holo-screen hovering in front of him, and brought up both the solarnet and the flight plans of all known spacecraft in the outer solar system. He quickly scanned the readouts, occasionally typing in a security code or some mundane password. Eventually, he was rewarded with a further listing of all of the OSC vehicles between the orbits of Mars and Saturn, and all of the OSC updates for the region in question. He was going to see for himself if the Taj was at Eunomia-Fifteen and the Onakea was about to arrive at Three-Eighty-Seven-Aquitania. To his surprise, he confirmed the status of both ships and their missions.

The solarnet images played across both the tabletop holo-screen in front of Newey and the large wall-monitor situated in the far wall diagonally from the general. The solarnet broadcasts were the solar-system-wide news and information service. It was received and eagerly watched by practically everyone, from miners and farmers to engineers and administrators, in every inhabited nook and cranny of the solar system. The general hoped that if anybody reported something out of the ordinary happening on Titan, the solarnet would pick it up and report it.

The news anchor of the solarnet broadcast was a heavyset, very attractive Nordic looking woman with short wavy blond hair, lifeless blue eyes, and an ever-present grin. Her fixed smile and soft flowing words were almost too pleasant for the general, reminding him of the AI-generated receptionists one finds in every Hospital Receiving Room and Product Showroom, in every megaplex back home.

As time passed, the general divided his attention between

the never-ending news broadcast, Lync's status reports, and his composing of the announcement to the station of extrasolar entities on Titan. Occasionally a news item would catch his attention and Newey would stop what he was doing and watch the broadcast.

One news item that caught his attention was on the massive eight point eight earthquake and aftershocks that followed the eruptions of two of the three peaks in the three Sisters range, on the North American continent. Newey's grandparents had once owned a house at the base of the once picturesque mountains that were located in the state of Oregon in the North American Commonwealth. The commentator talked about and related the uptake in seismic activity to the removal of glacial ice from Antarctica over the last thousand years. As images of destruction filed by, the commentator was equating the disaster to the loss of the Morabito-One ecosphere on Io, six years ago.

*How amazing,* the general thought, *that in this day-and-age of AIs, gravity generators, nanotechnology, smart-drugs, interactive holographic VR, fusion-ion power, and interplanetary space travel, we still could not accurately predict seismic activity or the weather on a planet more than thirty days in advance. We can predict the exact position of any object in the known solar system, at any time, down to the nanometer, but couldn't calculate the precise moment of a volcanic eruption, nor the exact time of a baby's arrival. Some things,* he reasoned, *will always be a mystery.*

Another news report that he watched with interest was on the ongoing labor riots in Scopas, Oskison, Mark Twain, and Chao Meng-Fu ecospheres on Mercury. The newswoman related the rioting to last month's decision by Merc-gov to increase the numbers of AI-mining equipment and limit the number of human workers in the deep Monazite and Wakefieldite mines. Production in the metal smelting facilities of Oskison, Mark Twain, Ahmad Baba, and McCauley ecospheres was down sixty-three percent. The unrest on Mercury was delaying shipments of samarium to Mars, neodymium, vanadium and other rare earth elements to Earth, and impacting terraforming schedules, manufacturing, and construction projects from Mercury to Jupiter.

Still, with her annoying smile, the young woman introduced several short vid interviews with labor leaders from Venus and the Asteroid Mining Colonies. The news anchor predicted that even if the miners on Venus and in the AMC did not stand with the Mercurian miners, there would still be shortages of Rare Earth Metals for months. She predicted a subsequent drop in economic productivity across-the-board and a slowing of growth until the crisis on Mercury was resolved. As the woman, seemingly without taking a breath, launched into another report, the general leaned back with a sigh and glanced at his chronometer, *forty-seven minutes before the surface team reaches Titan-Base Ksa.*

Newey fumbled through his jacket pockets for a cigar. A minute later, he produced one, a little bent, but intact. It was not a *real* cigar, as *real* soil grown tobacco was much too expensive, even for a lieutenant general. The last time he had a *real* cigar; it was back on Callisto. Commissioner Marshall had given Newey two *real*, soil grown handmade Maduros. One he smoked immediately, the other he was saving for the announcement of the discovery, along with a bottle of two-hundred-year-old single-malt scotch whiskey. However, for now, he would have to smoke the cheap cloned, machine processed, chemically treated cigars and the *less* than America's Finest Straight Bourbon.

The general lit his cigar, poured himself some more bourbon, and turned back to the newscast. Running across the top of the screen was a flashing data stream. The SWAM Service (Solar Weather and Monitoring Service) was announcing the likelihood of a level five, solar eruption event within the next twenty-four to fifty hours. The crawl along the top of the screen announced the outposts, planets, and installations most likely to be affected by the CME. Saturn and its satellites were the eleventh to march along the top of the screen.

Newey expected the coronal mass ejection would most likely be accompanied by a powerful, negatively charged magnetic field and hard EM radiation. He blew out a slow, large cloud of blue-gray smoke and glanced at his chronometer again. Knowing the time-delay for the broadcast and the approximate seven-hour travel-time to Saturn for such a CME, he shook his head sadly.

He noted the date and time on the holo-screen, Monday, January first, twenty-nine-fourteen, five-fourteen GMT-EC (Greenwich Mean Time-Earth Calendar). *What a way to start a new year, and can this day get any fucking worse?* He thought with an audible groan. Just then, Lync announced that an alpha-*red* coded transmission had been received with a *delta one-one* prefix. It was from UGE Senior Senator Anna Robinson, chair of the UESA oversight committee.

Newey's head dropped. It was a message from a very influential United Governments of Earth senior senator, which did not have the proper code nor prefix for him to respond too.

*Yes,* he thought, *my day can get worse.*

# CHAPTER SIX

"This is insane!" bellowed Major Singleton struggling to handle his controls. "We are in a bad place here!"

Dark and cold shards of ice, with the hardness of carbon steel and the velocity of a slapshotted hockey puck, raced past the cockpit windows of the tiny skiff as it edged closer to the Titan-Base Ksa installation. A look that spelled out *serious concern* was written all over the faces of the two pilots. Not just because the extremely high winds were trying to force them into the side of the large, dark and silent structure that was Titan-Base Ksa, but because of how Titan-Base Ksa appeared through their viewports and on their monitors.

The skiff's AI was working hard to match a color-coded three-dimensional frame overlay of the installation with the distorted image drifting by in the viewport. The superimposed outlined projected by the HUD shifted and rotated as geometric shapes tried to match up with the moving image in the viewport. Identification markers appeared, flashed, changed, disappeared, and reappeared, as the chaotic scene in the viewport slowly shifted as the skiff orbited the remains of the base.

Through the viewport, the entire northwest corner of the installation appeared to have collapsed in on itself. Each of the five levels of the complex had been mashed in and twisted violently. It looked as if an angry footballer had kicked in the side of a wet cardboard container. Thousands of small, bright flashes flared to life and then were carried away by the high winds.

"Can you make out the auxiliary landing pad?" barked Major Singleton, not taking his eyes off of his controls. He was now in the role of command pilot. "Lidar and Geomapper are useless!"

"I got a visual on the roof landing pad on the last pass," replied Colonel Rozsa from the co-pilot seat. "It looks in good condition, but lots of debris." Rozsa cursed under her breath, as the lifeless voice of the skiff's AI warned of a systems overload.

"We're burning out the stabilizer systems," announced Major Singleton, hiding his fear and handling his controls as best as he could. "This thing isn't designed for hurricanes," his voice tensed as he fought the pitching ship.

"Take us in, Major."

Singleton wrestled the control stick with one hand and used the other to work his other flight controls. "The wind'll take our maneuverability!" The major's voice was calm as he hit the image enhancers on his multispectral terrain scanner and hoped for a better portrait of the ship's surroundings.

Without warning, a sudden gust shoved the craft downward. Through the cockpit viewport, the mutilated structure of Titan-Base Ksa rapidly loomed dangerously close. Both pilots quickly averted their eyes, not wanting to see just how close they were to disaster. They glued their eyes to their consoles and mentally pleaded for a lucky break.

"The structure is creating contrary vertical drafts all over the place," barked Rozsa. "Crosswinds are measuring at fifty-five plus."

Suddenly an icon on the major's holo-screen turned red and began to flash. "Number two's intake heating coils just blew!" he shouted over the warnings of the ship's AI. "Main stabilizer is overloading!"

The colonel did not reply as the pitch of the engine's hum began to waver, and the entire craft began a slow, vibrating roll to starboard. A sharp alarm sounded denoted by the AI's voice informing them of an engine manifold problem that was beyond its abilities to correct. It instructed the pilots to take immediate action.

"I'm deflating main bag!" screamed Singleton, as he began venting gas from the aerostat and fighting the sudden loss of control. The cockpit alarms changed tone and pitch again as the skiff's AI matter-of-factly, and in technical terms, announced that the ship had entered into an aerodynamic envelope that winged aircraft pilots would have called a Stall.

The skiff began to drop out of the dark tortured sky above Titan-Base Ksa like a mortally wounded bird. From the rear of the craft, they heard several panicked shouts filled with dread as the ship rolled sideways.

Singleton corrected the roll and deployed the landing gear. "Gear down and locked. Touchdown in three...two...one..." An unexpected adrenaline surge and the ship's AI conspired to make Singleton jam the control stick forward faster than he intended. He instantly yanked it back, but it was too late. Singleton looked up at the AI-enhanced image of the landing pad, and his heart skipped a beat. "Oh fuck."

In the low gravity, the skiff slammed hard against the frozen surface, bounced once, before coming down a second time and sliding a short distance across the landing pad. The violent landing generated both solid and liquid debris, which in the fearsome wind, quickly froze, the unnatural gale taking the material away to some dark, distant part of Titan.

Inside the skiff, stomach muscles tensed and microcircuitry flashed into useless ash, as the sound of shorting wires and hissing gas was drowned out by the wail of sirens. The main lighting system wavered and failed, as the tiny emergency lights flickered to life. Rozsa and Singleton both had known better landings.

"Colonel, are you all right?" moaned Singleton, trying to refocus his vision on his controls. His head had ricocheted off the side of the cockpit, and he still felt the blow just above his ringing left ear. All of a sudden, he felt something wet and warm on his face and knew almost immediately what it was. However, at present, he had more important concerns. His console displays were flashing and blinking at him as he began securing his controls. The more he looked, the worse it got, his eyes were everywhere on the console at once, trying to follow too many warning lights and signals of impending catastrophe.

Rozsa slowly leaned back in her seat, a look of pain on her face. "Yeah, I'm still here, I think. How is our atmosphere?" She looked over at Singleton with blurry vision. Her right arm throbbed from the elbow to the wrist, but she knew it was not broken. "Check your head." The wet blood on Singleton's face reflected the console lights that were screaming for attention. Noticing smoke in the air, Rozsa quickly refocused and gave the console and HUD holo-images her attention.

"Forget my head." Singleton's hands were moving rapidly over his controls. His eyes tried to read all the cockpit displays at once. "No fire. Pressure looks good, but I'm not sure of anything at this point."

Following several loud crackles, the sirens faded out, but the hissing and popping of rapidly moving gas and shorting circuits continued. The colonel leaned back and with a few short coughs surveyed the smoky cockpit. Half of Rozsa's holo-screens were dark, and her hard-monitors displayed the snow of dead channels. However, the displays that were still functioning told her more than the faint ghostly whispers of smoke. All of a sudden, it dawned on her that there was no soft-spoken AI-voice issuing forecasts of doom from her ear-mic piece or the cockpit speakers. That was definitely not a good sign.

Finding the communications system down, Rozsa yelled back to the rear of the skiff. He was looking for signs of life, and requesting a status check. There were a couple of 'We're okays!' more or less in unison, but nothing much else. Rozsa and Singleton ran several quick system checks, then they attempted to contact both Titan-Base Lincoln and Titan-Base Ksa, but their communication system only fed them static. Finally, Singleton unbuckled himself with a series of spasmodic coughs. "I'll go check on the others."

"You'd better check your head," ordered Rozsa, unbuckling herself from her seat, ignoring the thin veneer of settling gray smoke.

"I'm fine," voiced Singleton, climbing out of his seat and for the first time, in the muted gravity, noticing the ship was at an acute angle. "This ain't good."

"And you just figured this out?" Rozsa tapped out several commands on the few still functioning holo-screens on the HUD. "Make sure Arroyo is okay, we're going to need him."

Singleton just shook his head in response as he climbed out of the tilted cockpit and down the ladder to the central area where the others were seated. The ship was listing at an uncomfortable angle, which was only made bearable by Titan's weak surface gravity.

The major surveyed the ramshackled scene with mixed feelings. Several small storage lockers had popped open, and numerous small and large items had been tossed around the crew compartment of the skiff. Part of the major was relieved as he saw that all of the passengers were alive and relatively uninjured. However fear was crushing the relief because he did not know if that situation was about to change.

The group all moved with purpose, but all looked stunned and a little lost. Pulgar was helping Arroyo unbuckle himself as the two wrestled with the jammed quick-release on the engineer's seat harness. Tech-Sergeant Al-Yuzwaki and Professor Yee battled with a broken duct that was spewing white clouds of gas from an overhead rack. There was bright red blood and gray-white vomit all over Yee's mouth and on the front of his e-suit.

"That's only reprocessed helium and nitrogen from the primary buoyancy system, we're okay. There is a manual emergency flow regulator beneath access panel Three-C, near the ladder." Arroyo indicated the small, nondescript access panel behind the ladder, as his seat harness buckle gave way. Without missing a beat, he moved out of his seat to help Al-Yuzwaki and Yee.

Singleton turned his attention on the closed panel, focusing on getting at the hidden regulator valve within. Trauma-Specialist Lebowitz, looking shaken, but otherwise okay, quickly moved onto an overhead compartment, breaking out several color-coded emergency kits and a large med-kit.

"I take it we crashed." ventured Yee, his nose bleeding and sour smelling puke covering the front of his e-suit. "What the hell happened?"

"Hotshot pilots, I wonder if the ESTSB knows about the Major?" Arroyo had an undertone of anger in his *Japotinian* accented voice.

"The Earth Space Transportation Safety Board gives anybody a license to fly these days," announced Rozsa, climbing down the ladder slowly and stiffly. "But you don't need a license to be blown down in a freak storm." She quickly scanned the compartment, still slowly flexing her right arm. She needed to know the extent of the ship's damage, and she needed to know it yesterday. A slight haze from the smoke and gas was hovering in the compartment, and she hoped her cockpit readouts were correct, and it was not a combustible mixture.

"I didn't think Titan's atmosphere could get so dynamic," commented Yee as he glanced over at Rozsa. When it was apparent that no reply was coming from the colonel, the professor turned back to the billowing white clouds in front of him and continued to help Al-Yuzwaki tape the fractured duct. Captain Arroyo was already checking the other pipes and conduits running along the wall.

"Pulgar, go check on LaRocque, see if he's okay. Arroyo, the AI is out, and I need a complete damage report, ASAP." The colonel suddenly slammed her left hand against a bulkhead, momentarily losing her temper at both herself and their situation.

"I think we are on batteries," Arroyo added, observing the compartment lights and functioning data screens, "better start with the main buses." He had a wall panel off and was deep into the microcircuitry and colored wires in seconds.

Lieutenant Pulgar nodded her understanding as she moved toward the rear of the compartment; making eddies and swirls in the layer of white mist hanging in the main area of the skiff.

With the med-kit open, Trauma-Specialist Lebowitz was quickly assessing Major Singleton at the bottom of the cockpit ladder. Noting no serious injury to the major's head, she turned her attention to Professor Yee. "How does your nose feel?"

Yee wiped his nose on his e-suit sleeve and snorted, producing a small mass of clotted dark blood. "Great," he sighed looking to Lebowitz, then Major Singleton.

Trauma-Specialist Lebowitz produced two small polycotton plugs and pressed them up Yee's nostrils. The trauma-specialist knew from the expression that flashed across Yee's face, that *real* cotton would have felt much better in his sore sinuses, but *real* cotton costs far too much to be wasted on something as meaningless as a nosebleed. With a smile, the Trauma-Specialist began to assess Professor Yee's condition.

Lieutenant Pulgar went through the hatch at the other end of the main area, as Rozsa, rubbing the back of her neck, moved to help Singleton. The popping of the damaged circuits and the hissing of escaping gases started to subside, as somewhere an air purifier kicked in with the clatter of moving debris.

A few minutes later, as Arroyo headed up to the cockpit to check the damage, Pulgar returned supporting a staggering Lieutenant LaRocque by the arm. If it were not for the one-seventh gravity, Pulgar would not have been able to guide LaRocque any place, let alone into a seat. Trauma-Specialist Lebowitz moved in to investigate LaRocque's condition, "Excuse me," flashing an apologetic smile at Pulgar.

Rozsa took in LaRocque's dazed and confused appearance. In spite of his barely coordinated movements, he appeared to be more or less uninjured. "How is he?" the colonel indicated LaRocque, as she continued to survey the scene around her. Mentally, she was working out an alternative mission plan.

"He'll be okay in a minute," Lebowitz pronounced over her shoulder, nodding to Pulgar who was standing next to her.

LaRocque looked at the blurred form of Pulgar and felt like his stomach was going to erupt up through his mouth. He would have felt better swimming laps in a stormy sea with a bad hangover. He smelt lilacs mixed with smoke and ozone and realized it was only Lebowitz's perfume.

The medtec forced a gel-cap into his mouth then broke a small capsule under his nose. The smell turned the inside of LaRocque's nostrils, and the back of his throat, into fire as he coughed and choked. His vision cleared, and the ringing in his ears stopped almost immediately, as he came back to full consciousness. Within a minute, the world was back in focus, and his nausea disappeared.

Lebowitz waved the broken capsule in LaRocque's face again, but this time he objected. "That's enough!" LaRocque gagged, knocking her hand away, "I'm good, really."

With a smirk, the trauma-specialist acknowledged Pulgar. Smiling, Pulgar leaned in and kissed LaRocque on the forehead.

"Sit here for a while; I need to check the others." Lebowitz vanished up into the cockpit, trekking after Captain Arroyo.

"Can you function enough to help me with that?" Rozsa indicated a bank of dark hard-monitors.

LaRocque looked at Rozsa with a smirk and a thumbs-up sign. "I'm with you, just give me a second."

She smiled back at him and returned the thumbs-up sign.

As LaRocque pulled himself to his feet, Rozsa removed a small tool pouch from the inside of the open access panel. Together, the two started working on the mass of non-functioning equipment. They poked through the melted wires and blacken microcircuitry that use to be high-powered electronics as if it was an unpleasant meal. However, as they worked, it quickly became apparent that the majority of the damage was superficial. Nevertheless, there was some damage that caused both of the officers to gasp and sent their pulses racing.

"I managed to decipher some more of the buried transmission," announced LaRocque, inspecting a microcircuitry board that looked like a well-used, greasy barbecue rack.

"It changes nothing." Rozsa continued to catalog the mass of burnt wires and cook circuit cards. She did not look at LaRocque, and her voice was very low, practically a whisper.

"Given our current situation, don't you think it would be better---"

"I think we need to assess the situation and determine if anything here really does pose a danger." She glanced around to see if anyone was listening, "No offense, but I would like it if Lync or someone else checked your results before we go pushing the panic button. For all we know, it could be some known biological hazard. It could even be a misunderstanding of some kind." She did not believe what she just proclaimed any more than LaRocque.

"No fucking way," whispered LaRocque, his blue eyes flashing anger and his Venusianized accent underlying his words. "You and I both know that a message like that wouldn't go out without command authorization." He stared at Rozsa, moved closer to her, and lowered his voice even more, "You, and the General, haven't been straight with---"

"Lieutenant!" the authority in Rozsa's voice told LaRocque the conversation was over. "I am ordering you to keep your mouth shut about this. First, let's see what our conditions like, then we'll check the weather. After that, I'll decide if we should move into the station and investigate." With that Rozsa went quiet, and turned back to her work.

LaRocque stared at Rozsa a moment, taken aback by the colonel's apparent hostility, "What about getting to T-One?"

She said nothing. The colonel went back to work as if she had not heard the lieutenant. He too went back to work on the delicate microelectronics.

For the next thirty minutes, the skiff crew worked to maintain the systems that were still functioning on the battered craft and bought some order to the crew compartment. They re-stowed the jettisoned items back into their storage units and compiled a list of the systems that were not functioning. The team noted all the systems that could be made to function again with a minimum of effort. At least the life-support systems were functioning normally.

"Okay, the maneuvering thrusters are pretty bad off, but I think I can fix'em with a little luck," Arroyo's voice was cool, direct and to the point, as he read from the small display on his PDI. "However, the number two pressure pumps for the main bag is more of a problem, I think the motors shot. Two of the three main APUs blew. It must have caused a voltage surge because a lot of the circuitry in the secondary hull got cooked. The main electrical bus is showing a nonlinear under-volt, which means there is an intermittent short someplace." He gestured at the opposite bulkhead, "Almost all of the AI-flight control circuits are burned out, but the manual systems appear to be okay. The main drive engines look okay; there are a couple of minor heater coil leaks. But, the main stabilizers look frozen over. I'll have to go outside to be sure, besides as hard as we hit, I would like to check the landing struts and the propeller mounts as well."

"And if the struts or propeller mounts are damaged?" Rozsa's face mirrored everyone else's on the downed skiff. She looked and felt as if her account was overdrawn, and she was three months behind on the payments for her living quarters.

A smug expression washed over the engineer's face. "Here's the good news. There is an auxiliary flight deck directly under us with at least five to ten skiffs in it. Even if every skiff on the flight deck is destroyed, there is a maintenance shed with all the parts we may need."

"See, you are useful," Rozsa turned away from the sour look Arroyo gave her and looked to Pulgar seated with LaRocque, Trauma-Specialist Lebowitz, and Professor Yee, "Pulgar, your bad news?"

"The main high-gain transmitter is shot. I might be able to do something with the emergency transmitter if the antenna is still intact. I think we are squawking an ELB, but I can't be sure."

"Please check on that Emergency Locator Beacon." Rozsa rubbed the back of her neck, taking a deep breath. Her arm had stopped hurting, but her neck still ached. "LaRocque," she hoped he had better news.

"The main AIC is salvage scrap," answered LaRocque,

looking glum as he felt his headache coming back. "But if necessary I can pull parts from any skiff and have us back up in five, six hours."

Rozsa did not respond. She called up a color-coded schematic of Titan-Base Ksa on her PDI embedded in the sleeve of her e-suit and studied the image. Professor Yee had used the functioning scanning equipment and the recorded scanner data they collected while circling the installation to get some idea of the condition of Titan-Base Ksa.

Based on Yee's analysis and Captain Arroyo's opinion, it was highly improbable that any of the fifty men and women on the installation had survived. The structural damage appeared total; there were only faint, random EM emissions, no contact with the station's AI or any of its personnel. The only thing they could detect was the station's emergency beacon.

As Colonel Rozsa considered their next move, a lively discussion began to develop regarding what they should do next. Captain Arroyo, and Lieutenants LaRocque and Pulgar wanted to wait for the Outer Systems Command to send in a better-trained, better-equipped team. Tech-Sergeant Al-Yuzwaki, Trauma-Specialist Lebowitz, and Professor Yee pointed out that it was their duty to search the base for survivors. Major Singleton was more or less, sitting on the fence. It was Colonel Rozsa's mission, and he would back her decision. Personally, he, like Yee, Lebowitz, and Al-Yuzwaki, thought it would be worth it to continue with the mission. Colonel Rozsa listened to the thoughtful deliberations, weighing both sides, but as the volume and energy of the conversation increased to the point of outright argument, Colonel Rozsa halted the debate.

"Alright," she began, her tone emotionless, but firm. "Given the condition of the station and the lack of voice communication with any of the TBK personnel, we can assume there are no survivors. However, we have to confirm that fact. Also, we need to secure any data TBK has on the possible cause of this event. Captain, I want you, Pulgar and LaRocque to sweep the station west to east, top-down. Then assuming you find no survivors, get to the flight bay and work on getting us out of here."

"That's affirm," coughed Captain Arroyo checking his own e-suit's PDI.

"If you find a flyable ship, we take it."

The captain just nodded his understanding to Rozsa.

Major Singleton, working on his e-suit's PDI glanced over at Al-Yuzwaki, who was just grinning to himself. It was hard to determine if the big tech-sergeant was grinning out of disgust or excitement. As their eyes met, both Singleton and Al-Yuzwaki knew where Rozsa was going next.

Rozsa continued, "Major, you and Professor Yee, Al-Yuzwaki and Lebowitz will come with me. We'll break into two groups; Major, you, and Yee will take levels four and three. Al-Yuzwaki, Lebowitz, and I will take level one down to two. We'll all sweep south to north since the heaviest damage is on the northern end of the station." She scanned the faces around her and saw more than she wanted to. "Worst thing that can happen is Nianta gets to rescue us, and we get to listen to him remind us of it until we get off this frozen ball of dogshit." She faked a grin.

No one else was smiling.

"If we don't report in, in a few hours, the General will have someone out after us." Rozsa surveyed the faces of her command once again, eyeing for trouble.

Several wanted to say something, but none did. LaRocque and Pulgar looked to Major Singleton and Captain Arroyo, hoping that one of the senior officers would say something to challenge the colonel. They were surprised that neither man did. It was unlike Arroyo not to say something, and both lieutenants just sat bewildered at the captain's silence.

Colonel Rozsa, seeing the concern still on the faces of LaRocque and Pulgar, added, "Anyone have a problem?" She stared at LaRocque, daring him to mention the transmission.

He did not.

There was a round of silent stares, but no one verbalized anything.

"Then let's get to it," finished Rozsa, as she moved to get started.

The others looked at each other one last time with apprehension, then proceeded to carry out the colonel's orders. They all gathered their gear and cautiously donned their e-suit helmets. They proceeded through their e-suit's AI's safety checklist, and manually double-checked their e-suit systems.

As they moved toward the small airlock hatchway, Major Singleton stepped in front of the group. "You all know this, but I am going to remind you again, especially now. With a low grav, denser than Earth atmosphere and unusually high winds, we could easily be taken away by the wind. I want everyone tethered, with one hand on the line at all times, understood?"

There was a round of affirmative nods then they stepped into the small decontamination-airlock chamber. It was very small, and they had to pass through in groups of twos and threes.

The group hated the extra delay but knew it was necessary. Even though Titan's environment was hostile, it was still possible to cross-contaminate with Titan's ecosystem. The simple organisms' native to Titan could easily be killed off or forced into some neo-evolution, swapping RNA with viruses and bacteria from elsewhere in the solar system. That would screw up hundreds of years of biological research.

As the outer hatch slid aside, a hail of carroty-gray dust and colored ice interspersed with droplets of a clear-yellow oily liquid spun and whirled around the eight with a roar. Stepping out of the skiff, Rozsa was practically carried away by the force of the wind. Looking up at the sky, she hoped that the weather would improve, but she doubted it. The tortured sky that greeted her was a vision of some madman's nightmare. Barely visible through the moving cloud deck was a large disk, painted in broad bands and narrow swirls of light brown, dying yellows and angry pinks. The disk stared down on them like the unblinking eye of a giant cyclops.

Each of them had seen the great ominous eye of Saturn before and under far better circumstances. At more than eleven times as large as the moon as seen from Earth, each knew that the distant gas giant hovering over their heads was no threat. As the twisted and demonic clouds momentarily obscured its cold stare, the eight cautiously proceeded down the ladder leading to the debris-covered surface of the auxiliary landing pad. They all understood that the great and distant planet that watched them gave no warmth, no comfort, and little light to their frozen home.

Standing at the foot of the short ladder of the skiff, the group slowly and silently observed the destruction around them. The shattered remains of cargo containers and Marbs were spread all over the crumbled landing area. A heavy wind that sounded like an angry animal pulled and pushed at them. With an atmosphere two and a half times as dense as Earth's and a surface gravity close to one-seventh of Earth's, moving around on Titan was like operating at the bottom of a twenty-five-meter deep wave tank, with its agitation set to max. The urine colored droplets of oily rain froze on contact with the suited figures and flaked off like dry, dead skin with each movement of their bodies. It reminded Rozsa of Nianta's dandruff.

The cold, unpredictable surface was something Colonel Rozsa, Professor Yee, and Trauma-Specialist Lebowitz were not use to dealing with on a regular basis. Yee and Lebowitz very rarely ventured on to the surface of Titan. Even more rare, would they have to leave the comforts of a transport. Major Singleton, Captain Arroyo, Tech-Sergeant Al-Yuzwaki, and even Lieutenants LaRocque and Pulgar had more experience on the surface of Titan. However, they were not accustomed to Titan's environment acting like a mad dog out for blood.

Fighting the screaming wind, Rozsa activated her e-suit's PDI and indicated the direction to move. However, before any of them had done any real work, the strain of fighting the unusual wind and rain had already exhausted nearly all of them.

There was a flash of lightning and the deep-throated growl of thunder that rippled out in all directions. The lightning made a rainbow of bright colors in the dark sky as it propagated across the gloomy, charry-colored atmosphere. Atmospheric electrical discharges were extremely rare on Titan, and only Major Singleton had seen it before. None of the others had known Titan's atmosphere to be so active. It made Singleton and Al-Yuzwaki very nervous. Even Colonel Rozsa was having second thoughts about proceeding with the mission. She hoped that the entry hatch was intact and functional as she led her seven companions in the direction her PDI pronounced the main entry hatch should be.

As lightning flashed blood-red in the mournful sky again, fear and apprehension erupted in everyone as muffled thunder echoed off the gently sloping terrain of Ksa. They all felt as if the storm were stalking them, like a hungry animal waiting to strike.

# CHAPTER SEVEN

Lieutenant Wai-Mun Fung was growing depressed and tired. She had spent the last five hours with Tech-Sergeant Yoshida and half a dozen Marbs performing repairs on the sub-engineering level. For roughly the whole time, Yoshida had talked and mumbled, recalling and rehashing the events that led to the death of Private-Specialist Zapollo. With the flood waters drained, the extent of the damage could be seen, and it was very extensive. Equipment and machines that would normally have only required maintenance once a year now needed substantial repairs. From where she sat, Lieutenant Fung could see several Marbs working on other large machines and sections of the massive piping network of the sub-engineering level.

The thermostats on the level were malfunctioning, and the temperature was down around seven degrees Celsius. Feeling the cold, Fung wanted a hot shower and some warm food. She knew she could make an excuse to leave the despondent tech-sergeant to finish the repairs on the huge electrical transformer units all by his lonesome, but she also knew that that would only serve to depress the man further.

Fung's caramel tinted eyes slowly glazed over as she sat under the dim ceiling lights and passed tools and equipment to Yoshida. Both the lieutenant's attention span and enthusiasm had suffered from the seesaw ride of conflicting emotions she had been through in the last day. Her emotional state had gone from being a victim of fear and confusion to suffering from the effects of loss and survivor's guilt. That was what Yoshida's problem was. It was obvious, and as soon as she got a chance, she would inform Doctor Reierstadt. She, on the other hand, just wanted back the peace and quiet of her regular routine.

Tech-Sergeant Yoshida was hidden inside the enormous electrical transformer unit. The large machine just had its electromechanical guts pulled out, repaired, and put back in by the tech-sergeant and Lieutenant Fung. The tech-sergeant's sorrowful voice was little more than a muffled echo coming from somewhere deep inside the inactive device. Occasionally the engineer's hand would flop out of the massive device accompanied by a request for something.

Just as Fung got herself comfortable again, Yoshida's hand popped out of the machine once more requesting something, "I need a one point five compression-straight-stop."

Fung reached into the nearby parts case and pulled out a small oval handled valve. It was not what Yoshida wanted. Muttering under her breath, Fung fished around in the case a second time, finally producing a slightly larger valve. "Here you go." The heavy suggestion of Mandarin in her voice was unmistakable.

As the engineer's hand vanished back inside the device with the requested part, he continued to lament about Private-Specialist Zapollo. Just as Fung was about to tune Yoshida out again, he started to complain about Captain Arroyo. More than complaining, Yoshida was practically blaming Zapollo's death on the captain.

Since arriving on Titan with General Newey's replacement team, Fung had heard rumors about Captain Arroyo. She had overheard fragments of conversations between the longtime members of the Titan-Base Lincoln staff. Arroyo was a personnel problem, even before the order was given to evacuate the Saturnian outposts. Since then, it had become worse. Arroyo was a good engineer, one of the best she had ever worked with, but as weeks turned to months, the captain seemed to lose his commitment to his job and the mission. She and most of the others on the station knew the captain's history, and she also believed that the man should never have been assigned to the Saturn mission in the first place, let alone allowed to stay on for this special support mission. Now, Tech-Sergeant Yoshida was all but accusing the captain of negligence in the death of Zapollo.

Once again, Yoshida stuck out a greasy hand from inside the transformer, requesting another instrument. Fung reached into the large tool case and handed Yoshida a small multi-functional device. "If the Capt'n had only listened to…"

Fung sat back against another large piece of equipment, making herself as comfortable as possible. She continued to listen to the tech-sergeant as she called up and examined the electrical transformers schematics on her PDI, mounded on her jacket forearm. She knew the other large electric transformer unit for the waste reclamation system had to be repaired as well. "How come a Marb isn't handling this job?"

"There is a lot of exterior work that needs to be done," Yoshida's voice suddenly lost some of its sadness. "Better a Marb working out there for ten or twelve hours than one of us."

Fung smirked. "I see your point. Did you replace the LBA?"

"Yes, and you can turn on the power," ordered Yoshida, pulling his muscular body out of the machine, his blue and gray UESA pseudo-uniform jacket covered in grease stains. Surveying the face of his superior, who was now just his assistant today, he asked, "Mind if I light up, ma'am?" He was already fumbling around in his pants pocket.

"Only if you share," smiled Fung.

"Break time." Yoshida produced a pack of hemporettes and a small gold battery powered lighter. He lit it up, took two long drags on it, then passed it to Fung.

Fung took the lit item and pressed it between her teeth as she got up, the back of her short black hair sticking to the side of the purifier. Leaning over to the machine Yoshida was working on, she slowly and with apprehension, activated the massive device. As the motors and mechanisms of the thing slowly came to life, a small grin slowly spread across Fung's face, "Nice." She puffed away on the hemporette.

"Thanks, L.T., you're not half bad as a mechanic yourself," Yoshida smiled as he tried to brush the dirt off his soiled uniform. The gesture was more out of habit, then for its effectiveness, "and how about passing it back now?" He liked Fung, she was the only person on the station who would do Tai Chi exercises with him, and like him held a fifth-degree black belt in Aikido. Even though he thought she was attractive in her Keikogi, he knew she was a devout lesbian and had no interest in him outside of an exercise partner, subordinate, co-worker and, hopefully, a friend. She was a semi-quiet loner most of the time, but he had seen her toss back a few drinks with the rest of the station's personnel. He was also aware, like everyone else, that this strange assignment bothered her. He also suspected that as part of General Newey's replacement team, she knew more about what was going on than she was admitting.

From conversations, he had with Fung, Yoshida knew that the lieutenant was not a people person, by any stretch of the imagination. Growing up in the foothills of the Himalayas, in the province of Yunnan in the Democratic Union of Asian States, she had developed her introverted tendencies at a very early age. As a teenager, when her school was on break, she would take, sometimes, weeklong hikes among the conifers and high mountain lakes of the region. Now in her late twenties, she looked, acted, and sounded every bit the rough mountain woman.

Fung smiled at Yoshida, as the transformer hummed steadily and the pungent smoke drifted around the two. She handed the smoldering hemporette to him as she heard the distant clank announcing the entry of someone into the sub-engineering level. "Hope that's Tounames so we can grab some lunch," added Fung, turning at the sound.

"Yeah, well before we go I do have to fix that intake flex coupling," he pointed at the massive apparatus behind Fung. "It blew and coated the UV inhibitor." Yoshida exhaled out a cloud of smoke as he slid the hemporette to one corner of his mouth, and eased past the woman, moving to the other purifier.

Moving aside, Lieutenant Fung glanced in the direction of distant footsteps. They were just audible over the background sounds of the Marb repair and reconstruction work. "I checked it; the UV inhibitor is going to have to be replaced." Her voice held all the excitement of a ten-year-old being forced to clean their bedroom. "Let Tounames do it."

"Yeah, well it shouldn't take that long," Yoshida replied, passing the shrinking hemporette to the lieutenant. As a member of the surveying team, with degrees in both cryoplanetary geology and low-temperature geotechnical engineering, Yoshida knew Fung would be more of a help with the repairs than most of the others.

He remembered the early conversations with Fung, hearing about how she had learned the basics of geology and engineering, watching her hydrogeologist father and civil engineer mother maintain the Meili-Bitahai aqueduct system. It was also where she met, married, and divorced her first and only wife. She was the main reason Fung joined the UESA, took up the art of Aikido, and asked for a duty assignment out at Jupiter.

Voices could be heard approaching from out of the distance, accompanied by the sounds of shoes on wet plastocrete, Fung handed Yoshida back the remains of the hemporette. Trading glances, Fung and Yoshida both knew that in spite of the drainage pumps, there were still several small puddles of standing water that needed to be dealt with.

From around a large gas-separator appeared Tech-Sergeant Tounames with Private-Specialists Zuverink and Wong in tow. Immediately Specialist Wong caught the attention of Lieutenant Fung. Private-Specialist Hiroshi Wong, like Fung, was part of Newey's team.

The young private-specialist was barely twenty-one with bright brown almond eyes that looked older than his age would imply. The young man was physically small with long black hair that was always tied into a ponytail and was always seriously in need of a cut and a wash. Rumor had it that he slept in his uniform most nights and only changed his clothes once a week. Those chronic facts and others habitually annoyed Fung and most of the other officers on the station.

It was excruciatingly obvious that in most parts of the inner solar system, the private-specialist would have been arrested for having an *anti-social lifestyle*. In the mid-twentieth century, he would have been labeled a *Hippie*. During the *Great Awakening* of the twenty-third century, after the Second Dark Ages ended, he would have been called a *Greenchild*. Now he would have simply been sentenced to a year in a re-education facility.

The members of the station also knew that the only reason he was allowed to roam the installation in such a disheveled manner was that he was also the exploration team's only Cavern Expert, a dangerous job even with POVs (Psytronics Operated Vehicles) and ideal conditions. During a previous tour of duty, Wong saw more of the cave systems under the surfaces of Titan, Iapetus, and Rhea than any other human being, alive or dead.

Hiroshi Wong had grown up in and around the karst terrain of Herzegovina in the ECU (European Common Union) and learned to negotiate caves and tunnels working on his family's fungus plantation. With the untimely death of the young man's father a week after arriving back at Titan, Colonel Rozsa was forced to order Wong to have weekly sessions with Doctor Reierstadt, in order for him to deal with the emotional stress. She had put him on antidepressants and was monitoring his behavior. Wong's progress was slow, but his work did not suffer. Because of that, his skill, and the difficulty of getting a replacement for him, the general overlooked the young man's personal and professional shortcomings. Both the general and Fung knew there was time to straighten him out, assuming he did not de-list after this special assignment.

"I knew it! I just knew it!" Tounames exclaimed, shaking his head. "I told them, you two were probably lighting up down here."

Zuverink dropped the tool case she was carrying and leaned against a structural support pillar.

"New recruits?" inquired Fung, still looking over the two private-specialists.

"Wong and Zuverink are here to help Mitsu and me with the repairs. The old man wants to see you, Major Nianta, Capt'n Aamodt, and Professor McGilmer in the com-center right away." Tounames' voice was worn-out as he watched Wong drop down next to Yoshida. The young private-specialist's eyes stared at the hemporette hungrily, as Yoshida took a long drag and slowly passed it to Wong as if he were handing the younger man something precious. Tounames just watched the exchange and shook his head sadly.

"Why didn't he just call me over the interlink?" Fung watched as Yoshida gingerly blew out a thin blue cloud of smoke that wafted among the small group like a gaseous amoeba.

"No clue," Tounames started accessing his own forearm PDI, checking a set of engineering drawings regarding piping in the sub-level. "I do know it has something to do with Skiff-One."

Wong took a drag on the smoldering hemporette and coughed up the smoke. He had not used hemporettes in the last month because he was trying to curb his use of the substance with the assistance of Doctor Reierstadt. However, the last few hours had been rough, both physically and emotionally.

"Hey," continued Tounames, still focused on his PDI and not noticing the growing look of concern moving across Fung's face, "did anybody check the reactor in the last hour? Lync is reporting that one of the helium-three cooling chambers has a temperature caution light. We'll need to manually step down the Deuterium pumps."

Fung was suddenly alert, "What about Skiff-One?" She ignored Tounames' question as she quickly lost her growing level of intoxication.

"I don't know. Demitri came tearing out of the com-center," explained Tounames, seeing the look of concern spreading across Fung's face. "He said the General wants you and the others now, and he looked worried."

"You didn't ask why?" The lieutenant's Mandarin accent punctuated her growing concern.

"The guy just headed off," Tounames looked up and followed several colored pipes along the ceiling, ignoring Fung's anxiety at what he had just said. "He looked worried, and given the dogshit that has been happening around here, I was not going to stop him, to ask."

Fung clapped Tounames' shoulder, as she dashed by him and trotted around the gas-separator. Tounames looked after her, then forcing some enthusiasm into his voice added, "Let's get to work. Yoshida, Zuverink will help you. Wong with me, we'll check out the helium cooling units."

Wong passed the hemporette back to Yoshida as he moved to Tounames. As the two men began discussing the helium cooling units' schematics on Tounames' PDI, Yoshida killed the remainder of the hemporette, then he got to work on the silent purifier with assistance from Zuverink.

As Tounames and Wong disappeared from Yoshida's sight, he overheard Tounames wonder aloud about what was going on in the com-center with the skiff and were their comrades in trouble.

Zuverink too overheard Tounames and Wong's exchange as they moved off. Her thoughts, like Yoshida's, were on the mystery unfolding in the com-center. As she was about to make a comment to Yoshida regarding the situation on the station, another large tremor rumbled through the sub-engineering level. It was quickly followed by Lync announcing that the station had experienced yet another aftershock. As something nearby shorted out with the sound of angry electricity, Lync proclaimed that the quake was a magnitude four-point five-seven and that no new damage or system failures had been detected.

Zuverink and Yoshida exchanged a long concerned look.

•  •  •

The gentle notes of Mozart's *Eine Kleine Nacht Musik* played softly in the background as Doctor Reierstadt ate her mid-day meal in the empty, stark white cafeteria. She sat alone among the ten large circular tables and fifty gray chairs that were spread around the large room, patiently waiting to be used by the station's personnel. Even before the evacuation, it was only on very rare occasions did the entire station's company eat together in the cafeteria as a group. On official UGE holidays, such as Pioneer's Day, Ancestor's Day, Memorial Day, the days of Thanks and Forgiveness, and The Seven Days of Worship and Remembrance did the entire crew assemble. The Outer Systems Command personnel dressed in crisp, clean dress uniforms, the UESA scientists in sharp civilian attire. They would celebrate the holidays and eat a formal dinner together. Sometimes, on birthdays or other such anniversaries they might have a party in the cafeteria, but most of the time no more than eight or ten of the station's personnel would eat at one time.

Reierstadt looked up from her meal as she felt the tremor move through the room like a ghost with an upset stomach. She instantly looked to the front wall of the cafeteria, which was a huge flat-screen monitor. There was nothing, the screen was blank, and that was rare. It usually had something on it, for even though it was rare for the station members to gather in the cafeteria, Lync would generate images of wilderness settings or natural scenes of Earth or Mars or display solarnet updates from civilization. Now it was blank and flat gray.

Doctor Reierstadt turned at a sound from the back of the room. Surveying the area, she noticed the remains of the long forgotten party and the serving table that the aftershock had displaced, sending a metal tray crashing to the floor. There were no Marbs available to clean up the interrupted New Year's Eve party, and no one had thought to return the food trays to the autochef. The autochef, with its five food dispensers and their individual holo-screen controls and tray returns, occupied the back wall of the cafeteria.

The doctor gave half an ear to Lync's announcements, as she continued to fork the synthetic creamed garlic potatoes and sea-peas into her mouth. Knowing that the two canine chops in front of her had probably been processed and frozen five years earlier or that the sweet blue rice-bread was closer to algae than rice, did nothing to suppress her appetite. Everything on her compartmentalized plate looked fresh and real, thanks to the culinary magic of the autochef.

Bits of food stuck to her upper lip for a fraction of a moment before she would wipe them away, she was in a hurry. She was preoccupied with her work, not to mention that the food on her tray was, in fact, quite good. Reierstadt ate fast and continued to work on her operational plan, formulated around what General Newey had told her.

The psychologist glanced nervously at her chronometer. She had a schedule all worked out, with sit-down visits planned for everyone from General Newey right down to Private-Specialist Wong. She wanted to document as much as she could on everyone, especially on those already having problems. It was not because she was devoted to her work, but because it was the first time since arriving on Titan, she actually had something outside of the normal routine to observe and study. At best, she felt she could get one or two good scientific papers out of the mess, especially if it involved extrasolar entities. At worst, it would make for a very long, boring report to the UESA and Frontier Authority.

Reierstadt keyed her PDI and read thru her last test results. Everyone on the station had shown some signs of stress during their time on Titan, but all were within acceptable levels. All, that is, except for two individuals, who were outside the acceptable range. As indicated by the previous months of test results, Private-Specialist Wong and Captain Arroyo were both showing levels of stress above their projected norms. Reierstadt also had access to everyone's personnel files, and she knew the reasons behind the unusually high-stress levels had more to do with personal histories than it had to do with their current assignment.

Private-Specialist Wong's stress was three point nine times

above his projected levels for the short period of time he had been on Titan. Worse was Captain Arroyo, who registered at five point eight times his projected norms for accumulated stress. Reierstadt knew that Wong's problems were directly related to the sudden death of his father, just prior to the start of this assignment. He had been extremely close to his father. On the other hand, Captain Arroyo's problems were due to his last duty assignment, and of the horrible disaster that ended it.

Nine years ago, an explosion and fire destroyed the asteroid research station Sisyphus-Three. The disaster almost cost Captain Arroyo his life and did take the lives of sixty-three of his friends and coworkers. The captain and eight other severely burned and injured survivors, suffered for fifteen days in the burnt out installation, with very little food, water or heat, and no medical supplies. Lying trapped in the freezing, debris-filled space for more than two weeks, suffering from cold and second and third-degree burns, had laid the foundations for a classic case of post-traumatic stress disorder in the captain.

Just as the third movement of the Mozart piece was beginning, the cafeteria's pneumatic door sounded. Major Nianta and Doctor Tan entered the room shoulder to shoulder, talking intently. Both Nianta and Tan glanced around the brightly lit space, a look of concern and suppressed anxiety painted across their features. As the door hummed closed behind them, they nodded to Reierstadt in unison, and she returned the gesture. Continuing to talking briskly, Nianta's Chakosi accented voice rung off the empty tables and white walls like a metal coin, as he and Tan made their way to the autochef.

For a moment, Reierstadt was surprised to see Major Nianta, believing he was in the com-center. He was wearing a heavily insulated gray-black e-suit, not the standard station duty clothing. The major looked totally out of place among the gray chairs and empty tables, not just because of his bulky environmental suit, but because it clashed with the worn blue baseball cap covering his cut afro. The slightly soiled blue souvenir had *ANNAPURNA* printed across it in dirty white letters. As far as she knew, the hat had practically never been washed in nearly seven years. He considered it his good luck charm, ever since he flew co-pilot on the Annapurna test vehicle over seven years ago. Doctor Tan had suggested, half-jokingly, that his dirty Annapurna souvenir was the cause of his persistent dandruff.

The Annapurna had been a prototype craft designed to test an experimental faster than light drive system. Even though the matter-antimatter powered spacecraft shattered velocity records for both manned and unmanned craft and reduced the *real* space-time dilation by forty-seven percent, it still did not live up to expectations. The mission did, however, get Major Colin Nianta into the official history text.

Doctor Ning-Jing Tan or NJ, as she was called, wore a neat and tidy uniform, accentuated by her shoulder-length black hair and firm, shapely figure. Like most of the human species, Doctor Tan's ethnicity was varied. It was obvious from her eyes she had mostly Asian ancestry, but the coffee hue to her citrine complexion suggested some African or Native Australian bloodlines as well.

Doctor Tan was the station's chief general physician, which meant that she handled the procedures the autodoc was incapable of handling, which was not much. UESA regulations required that at least one human medical officer be stationed on all registered ships and outposts. Titan-Base Lincoln technically had four medical officers, since Doctor Tan had three qualified medical technicians under her.

Since arriving on Titan with General Newey's party, Doctor Tan had not had to practice her trade. She expended most of her time checking monthly physicals, assisting with laboratory experiments, writing and reviewing research papers, and handling minor scrapes and scratches. However, after the excitement of the quake and the death of Private-Specialist Zapollo, Reierstadt knew the woman had to be very busy.

Reierstadt unobtrusively observed the couple, as they got their trays and took seats at the table furthest from her. As they began eating, they continued to converse in low tones. The psychologist was well-trained in reading body language and experienced enough to know when something was wrong between two people. She knew that the two were engaged in a serious sexual relationship, but she also knew that the two were upset about something, and the whispered conversation between the two had nothing to do with physical or emotional relationships.

As the psychologist continued to subtly observe the major and the doctor, she wished she were better at lip-reading.

Reierstadt found it instructional that Major Colin Nianta, who had been at Titan-Base Lincoln for years had apparently become seriously involved with Doctor Ning-Jing Tan, one of Newey's people.

For a long time, she watched the two out of the corner of her eye, as she continued to eat her own food. Reierstadt subtly made notes, both mentally and on her PDI. To her surprise, she heard her name called. Looking around, she saw Professor Eastman moving into the room, the door closing behind the middle-aged professor.

With the lively tempo of the Rondo of *Eine Kleine Nacht Musik* flowing softly through the cafeteria speaker, Eastman acknowledged Nianta and Tan then looked back to Reierstadt. "Barbara, I was looking for you," began Eastman as she walked to one of the autochef dispensers at the back of the room. She mumbled in her request and waited, surveying the room, taking in the locations of Nianta, Tan, and Reierstadt.

Reierstadt with a face full of food, spluttered "More bad news?" As an afterthought, she deactivated the display on her PDI.

Eastman looked at her in cold silence. A moment later, her tray of food arrived with a mug of dark liquid. After making her way to Reierstadt's table, and sitting across from the psychologist, she began again. "I have a few ideas about reporting procedures." Lowering her voice, she glanced at Tan and Nianta, making sure they were not listening to her. The two were still deep into their own conversation. Leaning into Reierstadt, she added, "After thinking it over, I think you need to know…"

# CHAPTER EIGHT

The eight were glad to be out of the wind and the slick, oily rain. However, the inside of Titan-Base Ksa did not relieve their anxiety. Several faint emergency lights were functioning, as they entered the remains of the auxiliary hangar deck. The place was of older construction than Titan-Base Lincoln, made of heavy duroplastic and dark metals mined from Mars and the Asteroid belt. According to their e-suits, it was cold inside the complex, and the atmosphere was hydrocarbon-rich nitrogen with only traces of oxygen. With the illumination being unnervingly low, the group was glad to have their e-suits and wrist search-beam lights. They helped in discerning the unbelievable devastation that surrounded them.

Broken glass, bits of metal, duroplastic and insulation along with ice crystals covered the floor. Large duroplastic beams, sections of insulation, and lengths of piping hung from the shattered ceiling. The sound of each footstep of the group, crunching, and crackling, echoed in the stillness of the darkened hangar deck. Intermixed with the rubble were large, out of place and overturned equipment, small tools, and half-folded construction beams. Colonel Rozsa immediately recognized the folded beams as part of the station's superstructure. That meant to her that the station might no longer be structurally sound.

"The Harlem system is still functioning," noted Tech-Sergeant Al-Yuzwaki over the e-suit communication system. He was playing his wrist-light around the inside of the structure like everyone else. "They still got normal grav."

"That means the main reactor's still hot," added Captain Arroyo, pointing out the part of the structure that had collapsed. He could see mist and darkness through the gaps.

"Okay," spat Colonel Rozsa ending the chatter before it got started. She turned to face Singleton. "Major, I think I am going to scrap my initial plan. Instead of conducting the sweep with me, I want you, Arroyo, Pulgar, and LaRocque to check out those two skiffs." She shone her wrist light on two skiffs at the opposite end of the hangar deck. "See if either one of those is still operable. If one can fly, I want you to prep it. If that is the case, Arroyo, I want you and LaRocque to see about opening the flight deck outer door. Be careful moving the door, it could bring the flight deck down on top of us. Pulgar, get on the long-range comms and see if you can give TBL a status update."

There was around of affirmative mutters and nods.

"And if they can fly we'll start working on the least damaged one," added Singleton.

"Good. Yee, Al-Yuzwaki, and Lebowitz, you come with me." Rozsa swung her light over to a closed hatchway labeled: **AIRLOCK # 81**. "We'll conduct a search, one level at a time."

"That will take more than twice the time," commented Major Singleton. "If everything is a go with the skiff and the door, do you want me to take---"

"No," Rozsa cut Singleton off and moved her wrist-light across the ceiling and walls. They and others in the group did the same. "I didn't like the looks of the structure when we landed, and now that I'm inside I like it even less. Just wait for orders understood."

"Yes, ma'am," answered Singleton in his e-suit helmet.

"The e-suit comms seem to be working okay in here," behind their faceplates, Rozsa surveyed the illuminated faces of her command. "We'll check in every thirty minutes. If for some reason we find ourselves out of communications with you, we'll head back. Unless the General himself overrules me, you are not to come after us, unless I call for you. Understood?" She stared at Major Singleton.

"Crystal."

"Forget trying to get to T-One, just get back to TBL." Rozsa motioned toward the closed airlock hatch. "Let's get to it."

The group of eight separated into two smaller groups of four. One group led by Major Singleton moved off to the right, towards the two parked skiffs. The second group, led by Colonel Rozsa continued straight ahead, towards the closed airlock.

Colonel Rozsa studied the hatchway as she approached it. The LED display on the airlock hatchway control panel was dark. "Okay, this may be a snag in my plan."

Tech-Sergeant Al-Yuzwaki moved in front of the colonel, seeing the problem. "Let me see what we've got." He squatted down before the panel, examining the controls. Al-Yuzwaki, using a tool taken from his belt, pried away the LED touch-pad facing, and its underlying thermal protective layer. He studied the wiring, calling up a tech manual on his e-suit's forearm PDI. Despite the largeness of the gloves and smallness of the circuitry, Al-Yuzwaki set to work on the tiny innards of the control. His gloved fingers deft and deliberate in their movement, he patched over and bypassed ruined circuitry, "There is no power on this side, but there's power from the airlock backup systems."

"Can you open it?" inquired Rozsa, peering over the tech-sergeant's shoulder.

"Give me a minute," he was working furiously at the open panel. After a long moment, the control panel came to life as the hatch began to move with the sound of hydraulic motors and scraping metal. "That should do it," announced Al-Yuzwaki.

What the four saw behind the hatchway, they expected. The inner airlock hatch was open and past it was a black hole sprinkled with distant lights. There was no noticeable pressure change as the airlock hatch opened, and that little fact told them that most of that section of the station was exposed to Titan's environment. It meant that anyone not in an e-suit in that section was dead.

Turning to her group, Rozsa scanned each of their faces. "We are likely going to encounter deceased T-One personnel. Anyone not up to this, speak now?" She was staring straight at Professor Yee.

The professor met the colonel's eyes and declared, "I'm good," his Afrikaan accent clear and hard.

"Sure?" pushed Rozsa, not wanting a problem from the man.

He gave an energetic affirmative hand sign. No one else

voiced a comment or response.

"Okay, watch your step," instructed Colonel Rozsa, moving forward through the hatchway. Behind her came Professor Yee and Trauma-Specialist Lebowitz with Tech-Sergeant Al-Yuzwaki bringing up the rear. In the beams of their wrist-lights, pools of liquid stained the floor and lengths of pipes and bushels of torn fiber-optic cable and wire dangled from the missing ceiling panels. Shredded sections of flexible conduit jetted from the ruptured walls and hung limp like huge dead worms.

"If anyone survived, they'd be in the cafeteria, med-bay, or the two disaster shelters," announced Trauma-Specialist Lebowitz, her wrist-light scanning the corridor in front of her.

"We should also check hazardous storage and bio-containment," offered Al-Yuzwaki. "They were designed to survive a catastrophic structural failure."

"Agreed," was all Rozsa answered as she led her group deeper into the destruction that was the Titan-Base Ksa installation.

They moved in a single file, a meter and a half apart, steadily creeping down the eerily empty corridor. No one said a word, but wrist-lights and eyes kept moving. The sound of their breathing somehow made the dark passage even more unsettling, more claustrophobic.

The group passed an elevator, its doorway bowed inward. It was obvious the lift was not working. A few paces beyond the damaged elevator was an open doorway labeled: **STAIRWAY # 6.**

Moving into the stairway, with her small party behind her, the colonel looked over the railing down the stairwell. At a number of places down the spiraling staircase were flickering emergency lights, fighting to stay bright.

"First disaster shelter is on level three," announced Rozsa. "Watch your step," she commanded as she started down the stairs. That is when Rozsa spotted the first group of frozen bodies.

The bodies ranged in color from pale blue to dark purple, depending on their ethnicity. Some of the victims appeared to have died quick, while others seemed to have fought death to the last. After a brief exchange, Rozsa and her team continued down the staircase, stepping over and around body, after frozen body.

For close to three hours, Colonel Rozsa, Professor Yee, Trauma-Specialist Lebowitz and Tech-Sergeant Al-Yuzwaki searched the lower levels of Titan-Base Ksa. They climbed through wrecked section after wrecked section, and all they found was death and destruction. The first two disaster shelters they checked were empty. Apparently, no one had time to reach the safety of the shelters before death overtook them. They encountered a few undamaged corridors, but most had collapsed. Doors that were damaged were pried open, and sealed compartments were carefully checked for signs of life before they were opened. All they found were groups and piles of frozen bodies.

All of the Titan-Base Ksa personnel that Rozsa's group either had met or had worked with in the past were dead. Most knew death had come for them. They showed signs of asphyxiation before they froze, but most died quick, flash freezing rock solid within a minute of being exposed to Titan's environment. Some of the bodies were in conditions that obviously indicated that the blast had killed them before the cold or the atmosphere could do the job. Virtually all of the victims had the emotions of unpleasant death preserved on their ghostly, discolored frozen faces.

What seemed to trouble the four more than the numerous bodies they encountered was the shifting force of gravity inside the station. In one corridor, it was Earth normal, the next it was Titan normal, the next it was something between the two. Al-Yuzwaki speculated that the HARLEM system was damaged or the power distribution conduits for the system were failing.

In the silent cold and gloom of the deceased station, the four recorded vid images via their e-suit cams. All but Professor Yee made commentary on the disturbing images around them for their reports. Tech-Sergeant Al-Yuzwaki noted details of the station's damage, Lebowitz commented on injuries and manner of death of the station's personnel. Colonel Rozsa issued commands and asked her team questions she knew a board of inquiry would also ask. Professor Yee, however, crept along with the group, hardly speaking. Every few minutes Trauma-Specialist Lebowitz or Colonel Rozsa would ask the geophysicist how he was doing. He would reply with some type of short, sharp response.

By the time the small group had managed to make its way down to the laboratory section of the base, small stalactites, drip curtains, and small soda straws of multicolored contaminated ice were hanging from the edges of dark holes and openings in the ceiling and walls. Occasionally bits of dust and falling debris would catch the beam from their e-suit lights, and flash them a bit of color for an instant before disappearing again into the icy darkness.

Rozsa, Yee, Lebowitz, and Al-Yuzwaki moved cautiously through the area housing the biosciences laboratories. The section had little pressure-blast damage, but from the appearance and conditions of the equipment, and the dead laboratory personnel, the environmental seals had failed. Supercooled nitrogen had apparently poured into the section, just fast enough to let lab personnel know that they were going to die. Lebowitz thought the lab looked as if it had been upgraded since the last time she had been in it. There was more and newer instrumentation in the place. The interior of the biochemistry labs, even in the cold and dark, looked newer than the facilities at Titan-Base Lincoln.

That is when they encountered the door.

•　　　•　　　•

Major Singleton and his party discovered, after a thorough inspection, that the two Titan-Base Ksa skiffs, located in the auxiliary hangar deck, had more damaged than the one they had arrived in. He immediately ordered Captain Arroyo and Lieutenants Pulgar and LaRocque to scavenge whatever parts they could from the Titan-Base Ksa skiffs and the area of the auxiliary hangar deck. He wanted their skiff operational by the time Colonel Rozsa and her team got back.

Within an hour, Lieutenant Pulgar had managed to get their skiff's transmitter working and had contacted Titan-Base Lincoln. Major Singleton gave General Newey a status report on their current situation. He also relayed the fact that Colonel Rozsa and her party had found nothing but bodies and wreckage, and that she was still searching for survivors. The only message they got back from General Newey was to make regular reports and standby for further instructions.

Major Singleton, Captain Arroyo, and Lieutenants Pulgar and LaRocque worked hard on the repairs to their skiff. The repair work helped take their minds off of the fact that Titan-Base Ksa was now little more than an ice-shrouded tomb. They worked in silence with a minimal of words. The numerous, technical tasks kept their brains busy and away from the unpleasant thoughts that fought to invade their conscious minds. The repairs were not the greatest; nevertheless, they were the best they could accomplish under the circumstances. It was obvious that the little craft had taken a beating, but with hours of hard work, sweat and some luck, it would be flyable, at least according to Arroyo.

After the first two hours of working on the complicated and complex repairs in near silence, healthy speculation began to fill the stale air of the small ship. The numerous comments and counterpoints regarding the events that brought them there began to be bandied back and forth between them. However, it only served to spice up the simmering pot of fear and apprehension.

"It's probably all some security force's covert operation that ran into trouble," babbled Arroyo, not even trying to sound convincing. "I wouldn't be surprised if an SF rescue and recovery team touches down while we are out here."

Ignoring the Captain, LaRocque closed the microcircuitry access panel he was working on. "Are we done yet?" he inquired with an unenthusiastic sigh. He wanted to mention, during their conversations, the hidden message he had discovered in the Titan-Base Ksa transmission. However, Major Singleton had forbad it.

"Yeah, we are set to go," added the captain as he closed an overhead panel above LaRocque. "For now, all we can do is wait."

"So we can take off if we need to?" inquired Singleton.

Under normal circumstances, Captain Arroyo would not have cleared the ship to fly, at least not without another fifty or so hours of repairs, replacement parts, and equipment checks. "That sealant needs a few hours to set properly, then we can try the main buses."

"Can we fly?" asked Singleton again, this time with frustration in his voice.

The captain looked the smaller Singleton up and down, and replied, "We can try," his accented voice seasoned with a hint of challenge. "I don't know if the buses are going to hold. There could be scorching in areas I can't get to; in that case, we are fucked."

"What about the bag? Will it re-inflate?"

Arroyo knew the main gasbag for the dirigible would re-inflate without a problem, but at the moment, he just felt like aggravating the major. He just shrugged.

Singleton just shook his head and turned to LaRocque, "Is the AI up and running?"

LaRocque continued to frown and shot back, "In dummy mode."

"Can it get us home or do we need Colin to fly another skiff here and pick us up?"

LaRocque almost broke a grin when he replied, "If the other repairs hold, the AI can get us home. What I meant by dummy mode is that the old AI's neurotronic network got fried. It would take about twelve to fifteen hours to imprint a new neurotronic network on to this skiff's AI."

"Did you try running a restructuring algorithm on the subsymbolic form network, in the higher logic?" inquired Pulgar, injecting herself into the conversation.

"Of course I did," snorted LaRocque. "I am currently running a Solomonoff-Hirokawa smoothing routine to prevent AI-dementia from occurring."

Pulgar and LaRocque launched into a long technical discussion that left Major Singleton behind after the term *multilinear rational neurologics* was used. However, all the ramblings concerning algorithms and mathematical theorems involved in AI-operating systems gave Singleton an idea on what they could do to pass the time and relax.

"I get it," interrupted the major.

There was a moment of uncomfortable silence as the two officers stared at one another. Singleton walked over to a storage cabinet, opened it, and removed an object. Moving to a small table in the cabin, he slammed down a deck of playing cards. "Anyone for a game of Prime Numbers?" The game was simple to play and required only a good memory and little mathematical skill. It had been invented by the first lunar construction crews' centuries ago and had over time become a mainstay among the bored minions across the solar system.

Glancing at the thin deck of playing cards, Pulgar smirked. "Whose deck is this?" She picked up the pack of cards. The deck of playing cards was pornographic in nature. It had small, nude figures that moved in the most erotic ways.

LaRocque and Arroyo both burst into laughter as Singleton chuckled, "That's been in here for nearly three years, ever since Tommy Conti did that mission with those archaeologists, you remember?"

"Yeah, the ones that pulled that old probe from the bottom of Aztlan," added Arroyo, "over by the northwest edge of Elba Facula."

Pulgar continued to grin, as she stared at the liquid crystal animated holograms on the faces of the cards. She remembered that long ago story, the now gone Lieutenant Conti told about the three weeks he spent with the four techno-archaeologists below the surface of Aztlan, looking for a twenty-first-century probe called *'TALISE-TWO.'* They spend two weeks looking for the ancient probe and a week digging it out of the soft muck at the bottom of the shallow hydrocarbon sea that was Aztlan.

If she were not so close to the edge of total physical and emotional collapse, Pulgar would have been aroused by the silently moving and fornicating figures. She did find the images interesting, as she watched them do all sorts of things that were barely in the range of human decency and physical ability.

Major Singleton transferred some of his personal music that had been stored on his PDI to the craft's AI data storage unit. Singleton was a connoisseur of ancient music, especially of the mid to late twentieth century North American musical form called *Rhythm and Blues.*

Arroyo, Pulgar, and LaRocque sat down on the floor and dealt out a hand from the deck of cards. The music that flowed out of the small cabin speakers was some archaic tone that Singleton said was popular in the late nineteen-seventies on Earth. To the others in the small cabin, the music sounded slow, offbeat and mildly chaotic, like a band playing together for the first time, and using the wrong instruments to play the tune they were attempting.

As the major joined them on the floor, the music reminded him of secondary school, relaxing with his friends watching ships takeoff and land at the local transportation hub. The music made the ship cozy, and as time passed and the card game progressed, none of the four even noticed as it changed from one mellow, soulful piece about Georgia being on someone's mind to a light vocal-instrumental regarding someone's distorted dream of going to California.

"I think they found some old Titan lander from seven, eight hundred years ago, and its fucking reactor blew-up on them."

Pulgar paused to glance at Arroyo, who was both, reading his hand and listening to her, and eyeing Major Singleton.

"No," began Singleton. "I think T-One discovered some extrasolar asteroid that had some biologic material. I think they detonated a fusion device to prevent the spread of contamination." He glanced at LaRocque, making sure the younger man did not comment.

"No radionuclides in the atmosphere," offered Arroyo. "This close to that kind of detonation and the detectors would be screaming." He was aware from the briefing back at Titan-Base Lincoln that no radiation had been detected.

"Well," began the big captain, still studying his cards, "I know Tonja still has a fifty-three-year-old bottle of small batch, wooden-barrel, straight Tennessee bourbon, if this whole evacuation, special mission thing turns out to be about some buried extrasolar spacecraft, we are celebrating."

LaRocque stared at Major Singleton but said nothing.

"Do you know where she got that," inquired Pulgar taking in the major's dark face. She knew bourbon aged in *real* wooden barrels was very expensive and in very short supply, especially this far from North America.

"When she made Capt'n," Singleton began, "her brothers sent her a care package containing the bottle. She's supposed to make it last until she makes General." The smile on the major's face widened as he continued to stare at the cards in his hand. He wondered if the people depicted on his playing cards were real or AI-generated. Probably not, he concluded, thinking of the number of pulled muscles and sprained tendons one would get performing some of the acts depicted on the cards.

"How did they afford it?" Pulgar cut-off LaRocque before he could begin.

"One brother is a Dreamweaver, and the other is a high-up in Wein-Tao Pharmaceuticals." Singleton like everyone knew that dreamweavers were highly skilled neuro-entertainers. Dreamweavers could control their dreams for recording, and after AI-enhancement could be sold as high-end fantasy vacations that could seem like weeks or months, but were in actuality only one night of sleep.

"In all the time I've known Tonja," LaRocque's face morphed from one of unhappiness to surprise, "She never mentioned that one of her brothers was a Weaver."

Pulgar sat with her mouth opened in stunned silence. "You know she never mentioned that to me, and we've known each other how many years, now?"

"Who likes to talk about their wealthier siblings," Singleton grinned. "Did you know Tounames' family back on Earth, co-owns one of the biggest cybernetics firms in North America?"

"That I did know." Pulgar dropped a card and took another from the top of the deck. She just studied her hand.

The conversation stopped for a long while with only a few words here and there, as needed to keep the game moving along. As the game progressed and time passed, the three of them slowly became aware that the inside of their ship was starting to reek of old sweat, gold solder, and burnt carbo-plastic. The odor reminded them of moldy old athletic shorts. They were aware that the air-conditioning and ventilation systems were working at minimum power, and there was little they could do about the slowly growing stench. At least not until the main electrical system was back online.

"We haven't heard from the Colonel in a while, you think we should check in with them?" Pulgar inquired aloud. She had sixty-eight, with cards that depicted a variety of very strange acts involving several well endowed muscular men and three very busty women.

LaRocque looked up from his hand, "The Colonel said if they lost contact, they would head back." He had a winning hand. He needed ten to win. "That signal is what still bothers me." LaRocque had long ago lost interest in the perversions taking place on the faces of the playing cards. However, he wanted desperately to talk about the warning message he had discovered in Titan-Base Ksa's disaster signal. Deep down he was worried about Colonel Rozsa and the others.

"Well, a disaster signal isn't exactly a smiley face for someplace warm and cheery," Major Singleton was staring at Lieutenant LaRocque.

"Anyone wants a hit?" Captain Arroyo put his hand down and picked up the deck. He had fifty and knew that even if he got a three, he still could not win the game. He too was losing interest, not just in the erotic images, but also in the game itself.

Pulgar looked at Arroyo, astonished at his lack of concern. "Aren't you worried about them?"

"I'm not worried. The Colonel isn't due to check in for another fifteen minutes. If they ran into a problem, they would have called. If the Colonel couldn't call and couldn't raise us, she'd head back. They're well trained and experienced."

LaRocque forced a grin, "I'll take one."

Arroyo flipped LaRocque a card. "King," he paused to study the holograms on the face of the upturned card. It showed a bleached blond woman with blue and red highlights, and firm breasts, dressed in a pink plasto-leather bodysuit. She was pouring what appeared to be hot oil over a dark skin Asian-looking man, who was tied to a bed with a camel restrained in his mouth.

LaRocque laid down his cards, "Prime number sixty-seven." He looked over at Pulgar. She was still looking at Arroyo. "That makes it seventeen-forty-one, which is prime number two-seventy." He flashed a smirk.

Pulgar just continued to stare at Arroyo.

"Come on Ariel, ease up. I'm sure they're fine," LaRocque reached for Pulgar, his fake grin morphing into a fake smile, like that of a slick politician. "They are not stupid."

Pulgar looked to LaRocque, unemotionally and very cold. Then she turned her attention to the cards in her hand. "Hit me!" she barked with anger just barely detectable in her voice.

Arroyo dealt her a card.

"Prime number seventy-one," she threw down the four jacks, three sixes, queen of hearts, and the three she was just handed. "That makes my total one thousand seven hundred forty-seven, which is prime number two-seventy-one. I win," she got up from the floor and moved off angrily.

Sorely, Arroyo splashed the deck of cards down on the small table, "I quit." As a new piece of antique music began to play, the captain looked around almost hungrily, searching for something entertaining. He needed to keep the colony of anxiety ants that were tunneling at the back of his mind from spilling out of his eyes. For an instant, his wandering gaze fell on Pulgar climbing the ladder to the cockpit. The captain grinned, even in an e-suit; Pulgar still had a shapely figure. Then Arroyo caught himself, he knew LaRocque and Pulgar had been, to use an old expression, *sampling each other's DNA* for several years now. "Hey. I'm hungry," Arroyo announced with a widening smile, as he stood up and stretched. "You guys want something to munch on?"

LaRocque followed the captain to his feet, his eyes staring after Pulgar, "I could use a bite." He walked over to the foot of the ladder.

Still smiling, Arroyo rubbed his hands together and called after Pulgar, "Ariel! Would you like something to nibble on?"

"No!" came back the bitter, terse reply.

Arroyo's grin faded at the lieutenant's tone, but he shrugged and went through the hatch at the end of the main section. LaRocque forced a deep breath and headed up the ladder to the cockpit. He had seen that look on Pulgar's face before and knew what to expect.

"Lieutenant!" Barked Major Singleton in a commanding voice, stopping LaRocque. "Don't forget yourself." That comment drew a long stare from LaRocque.

There was a wordless exchange between the two officers, then LaRocque climbed up the ladder and into the cockpit.

Pulgar was sitting in the copilot's seat, staring out the cockpit viewport at the dark ice and dust blowing through the Titan atmosphere. The dim lights from the console seem to enhance Pulgar's beauty. The soft curves of her face and the sheen of her hair reminded LaRocque of ancient images he had seen of women, who were selected for their beauty and sex appeal to advertise commercial products for large companies. He smiled as he took in her face. *Real* beauty had not changed in over half a millennium.

"Come on," LaRocque took the pilot's seat next to her, "Of course we're worried about them, but worrying doesn't help anybody." Even in the stale air of the cockpit, LaRocque thought he could smell Pulgar's personalized perfume again, lilacs and morning glories spiked with a mild extract of Pulgar's own pheromones.

Pulgar leaned back in the chair and sighed, "Alain, what is going on here?" Her voice was grave and low. "Ever since the evac, nothing has made sense. Who knows what we're walking into out here?"

As the wind and weather outside the skiff made itself heard in the cockpit, LaRocque leaned over and took her hand. "I know this is all very mysterious," he watched her eyes, wanting to help her. "But the OSC and the newbies had to have a very good reason for keeping us in the dark. It's not like this is our first time working under *need-to-know* only orders."

Pulgar stared at LaRocque as if he just turned purple. "Yeah, that's not scary at all. We've already lost one person."

"We'll be fine." LaRocque was hoping that what he was saying had some truth in it. "It was probably some type of secret bio or chemical research," by sheer force of will, he held a smile on his face, trying to reassure Pulgar. "Maybe they found some under-ice ecosystem that holds the secret to eternal life."

Pulgar just stared at LaRocque, dumbfounded.

"Come on, if it is bio or chemical, Colonel Rozsa and the others will be safe enough in their e-suits."

Pulgar looked at him with a deep sadness in her teary eyes. "But suppose it's something else, something we can't even imagine."

LaRocque's tone changed, "Like what?" The smile slipped, and concern washed over his face.

"I don't fucking know!" exploded Pulgar, pulling away from LaRocque, "If I knew I'd do something about it!"

"Okay! What do you think we should do?" Her outburst had raised his anger, and he knew the conversation was going nowhere fast, "We have our orders, and we can't do anything right now, but wait!"

There was a heavy silence for half a minute as Pulgar just stared at LaRocque with watery eyes. "I've just got this queer feeling that something's wrong. I haven't had a feeling like this, in all of the time we've been on Titan." Several tears flowed down her cheek in a long, wet line. "I know something bad is going to happen. I can feel it."

LaRocque moved out of his seat and hugged her, "Hey, in five minutes or so the Colonel is supposed to check in," he looked at his chronometer. "And if she doesn't check in, I am sure she will head back or have one of the others move back into comms range."

Pulgar tried to smile but failed. She was concerned that if Colonel Rozsa and the others did not check in, General Newey would order them to go look for them. She feared that if they when searching, they would find something else, something her mind would not let her visualize.

"Come on, let's go eat," LaRocque wiped the tears from her cheek with a smile. "The Capt'n may eat all the freeze-dried kelp and cheese sandwiches and drink all that great tasting artificially flavored grape concentrate. You know the one they say taste almost like GE'd stuff."

This time the smile made its way onto her face, "I hate kelp."

He flashed a disarming fake Parisian smile, "I know you hate kelp, but you love cheese." They both laughed. Outside the viewport, the storm appeared to be subsiding, and inside the archaic music continued with a tone about someone getting married in a chapel of love.

After they left the cockpit, they rejoined Singleton and Arroyo, who had returned from the tiny storage compartment. He had retrieved twelve packets of artificial crabmeat bars, six packets of genetically engineered blueberry rice with artificially flavored chipmunk gravy, and five packets of genetically enhanced banana-milk concentrate.

"What, no kelp and cheese?" inquired LaRocque, smiling at Pulgar, who was cheerfully beaming back at him.

"I was going to ration it out," Arroyo looked put out. "The kelp and cheese sandwiches are the best tasting food packs on this thing. I really like that stuff. It would make a good meal for the Colonel and the others when they get back."

Pulgar knew Arroyo was not really saving food for later. The skiff was stocked with enough survival rations to keep ten people alive for two weeks, so she knew the three of them were in no immediate danger of starvation. She did, however, chuckle at the ingredients listed on the foil packages of food. Was there really such a difference between *genetically engineered, genetically modified, and genetically enhanced*? She knew it was all grown in an AI-controlled food processor. However, in spite of that, she still wanted to know what brominated vegetable oil was doing in a banana-milk drink.

As they ate the freeze-dried food bars and drank banana-milk concentrate, the conversation moved from minor repair work needed on the skiff to possible alternate mission scenarios, and finally to childhood experiences and family members. All of them noticed, but none of them mentioned the obvious. Colonel Rozsa and her team had not made contact as scheduled.

LaRocque talked about his school-days in the tunnel systems on Venus and about his friends in his adolescent years and early twenties. He was very careful, with Pulgar sitting next to him, to avoid mentioning any of the herds of women that marched through his youth. However, he did tell several funny stories about his eccentric Russian great-grandmother and his Vietnamese great-aunt who both worked construction in the old Mid-Atlantic mining colonies, and could not get along with each other.

Apparently struggling to hold back her fear, Pulgar talked at length about her father and siblings, and her school adventures.

Captain Arroyo, checking his e-suit's timepiece every few moments, talked about growing up in the aqua-farming town on the shores of the Argentinian-South Atlantic Seaway, his work, and very surprising to Pulgar and LaRocque, he talked about the Sisyphus-Three disaster. Both of them had only heard him speak of the incident once before, and never in any detail. The talk of the Sisyphus disaster had slowly drained the pleasure out of the light-hearted conversation like air out of a stuck balloon. The captain, sensing too late, what he had done, changed the conversation and began talking about *Jai alai* matches among the college teams in the South American Commonwealth.

Soon they got tired of the talking, and the conversation began to slowly fade into silence. Pulgar dropped off to sleep, and Major Singleton dialed down the volume of the music to barely audible. He and Lieutenant LaRocque then went up to the cockpit to check the communications systems and attempt to contact Colonel Rozsa. Captain Arroyo took out the deck of cards and started playing Chinese solitaire. He was all but drained, and he wished to sleep, but his mind kept drifting back to the Sisyphus-Three disaster. Every time he closed his eyes for more than a minute, he would see the burnt and blood covered faces of his former Sisyphus companions. The smells in the cramped damaged skiff reminded the captain of his Sisyphus nightmares with their stench of oily and rank boiling carbo-plastic and burning flesh.

Suddenly Major Singleton's voice exploded from the cockpit speakers. He was announcing that he had just re-established communications with Colonel Rozsa, and she needed assistance, and she needed it now!

# CHAPTER NINE

General Newey and Lieutenant Sloan sat two seats apart from one another at a console in the com-center. Both looked worn-out and beat. Sloan was sporting a days' growth of stubby facial hair, and Newey's gray beard was in need of a trim. Sloan sat leaning back in his chair, feet on the semi-circular console next to an empty coffee mug and the remains of some food in a travel container. He was nodding off with his wrist PDI displaying the text of a law book entitled: *Inner System's Criminal Penalties and Punishments Associated with the Possession, distribution and/or Sale of Band or Illegal Materials, Substances or Electronic Media.* The young man's half-conscious mind drifted around thoughts of the various punishments associated with his illegal distraction. He never knew that some banned VR-Games carried a criminal penalty of chemical sterilization for just their possession.

Newey was nearing the end of a station update he was transmitting to the Outer Systems Command. It would be the last clear transmission he or anyone else on the station would be able to send for the next fifty hours. A large coronal mass ejection had sent a torrent of EM static and hard radiation racing across the inner solar system towards deep space. The massive burst of electromagnetic energy would soon scramble communications between Titan and the inner solar system for at least two days, if not more. The general was not worried for he knew they could up-link with their EET in orbit. Using its high-gain antenna and long wavelength transmitter, they could relay a message to the Outer

Systems Command via the numerous secure relay satellites within the orbit of Jupiter.

"...the complete recording of Robinson's message and my response is also included," continued Newey. "The rest of the data will be transmitted in fifty-three hours, plus or minus thirty minutes. Colonel Rozsa and her team are en route from Titan-Base Ksa and should be here within an hour. She has secured materials from TBK that appear to have originated from the object located at the T-One Drill Site. A full report will be transmitted by Colonel Rozsa and the members of the surface team, after re-acquisition of the carrier signal." The general glanced over at Sloan, who was now fast asleep and gently snoring. "It will be relayed via the Tolstoj, Mercury - Valhalla, Callisto comlink with a beta three prefix." He looked first at his PDI chronometer, then at the chronometer embedded in the console. It read: **02 MIN 07 SEC TO L.O.S.**

"Two minutes to loss of signal, once again, station data set Nine-Fourteen-C is being transmitted on sub-channel two on this frequency. AI-telemetry is encoded on sub-channel three. This is Lieutenant General Richard Newey, Commander Station Titan-Base Lincoln, over and out." He hit several icons on a holo-screen and surveyed the sleeping Sloan and the small screen of the man's PDI. He grinned to himself as he read several paragraphs. *Someone won't be playing virtual-combat games again,* thought Newey as he tapped the dozing man, "Go get some sleep."

Sloan, rubbing small crusties out of his eyes, sat up. "Yes sir, thank you, sir." Stretching like a cat, the young man deactivated his PDI, got up, and left the com-center. Sloan's loud yawn was cut off by the sound of the pneumatic door closing behind him.

The general watched the door close behind the groggy lieutenant. Rising slowly, he drifted around the com-center, checking systems and inspecting readouts. He checked his shirt pockets for a cigar and found none. He wished he had a cup of coffee to wash the stale plaque taste out of his dry mouth.

Lync made a long-winded announcement to the entire station, which echoed down empty corridors and bounced around quiet rooms. The data feeds from both the inner solar system and the numerous remote probes scattered around the Saturnian system were now completely unreadable, due to solar wind activity. Based on data it had received and its own analysis of the solar wind flux, Lync predicted that the communications network would be offline for fifty to fifty-two hours.

Newey half heard the announcement. He was too occupied checking his PDI to pay much attention to the now too familiar soft artificial voice. The exhausted officer was busy seeing if a Marb were available to bring him a cup of coffee and a cigar. There were none. They were all still occupied with critical station repairs. As he considered linking to one of the station's personnel and having one of them bring him some coffee, the LESAPS console unexpectedly beeped for attention. Lync instantly announced the detection of Skiff-One on the edge of the LESAPS-Titan horizon.

Newey quickly ordered Lync to bring up the LESAPS holo-display, and instantly a tiny dark blue dot with its identification tag and vital information appeared on the transparent screen. The terrain surrounding Titan-Base Lincoln highlighted in shades of yellows, greens, and grays. Newey reached over and hit an icon on the holo-screen. "Titan-Lincoln to Skiff-One, come in."

There was no reply.

"Titan-Lincoln to Skiff-One, come in."

Through a blast of static came Rozsa's voice, "Skiff-One to TBL, we read you." The colonel's voice sounded like she was speaking from inside a deep fryer cooking wet, cold meat.

"Colonel I can barely read you," Newey's voice rang with relief. "EM interference is spiking. What's your status?"

"We're good. Weather is still making flying difficult. The package is still stable," A bit of whistling radio noise broke into her transmission along with the sizzling and popping of EM static.

"Affirmative Colonel, we'll have everything ready for you by the time you land."

"I am formally requesting level-one bio-containment," Rozsa's voice sounded hollow and had a reverberation to it that made her sound genuinely distant.

"That's affirm Colonel. I'll get back to you in a minute." Newey hit a holo-screen icon and bellowed hoarsely, "Attention. Everyone attention, Skiff-One is on final approach. We are going to emergency alert condition two. I repeat we are going to emergency alert condition two. The following personnel get your heads up and your asses moving. Nianta, up to the com-center, Major Singleton may need assistance with approach and landing. Yoshida, Tounames, and Fung prepare to standby for a CFM on or near the hangar bay. Aamodt, Wong, and Brauer suit up and standby at the hangar deck airlock. Costello, Watkinski, McGilmer, Tan, and Garcia report to the bio labs and prepare to receive hazardous materials. Let's consider this a level-one biohazard." The general switched back to the skiff. He hoped that Yoshida and the others had gotten some rest in the last couple of hours. It was hard enough to respond to a Crash-Fire-Medical Emergency in an environment like Titan's, but to do so exhausted was impossible and dangerous beyond belief. "Colonel, we're getting ready."

"That's affirm, TBL. We'll be there in approximately twenty-seven minutes," Rozsa's voice had a hint of apprehension.

The image of the skiff on the LESAPS screen moved steadily closer to the station, as the glowing neon blue ID tag indicated. The symbol for the skiff dropped and climbed, sped up and slowed down in an undecipherable pattern. It looked as if the pilot had never flown a skiff before, and this was their very first time at the controls. Newey, in his mind's ear, could almost hear the abnormal whine of the skiff's engines as it fought against the unnatural headwinds.

Without warning, the com-center door sounded, and Major Nianta exploded through the barely open doorway at a dead run. "How are things?" asked the out of breath major, hopping into the console chair as Newey vacated it.

"They're ten minutes out and not doing well at all."

"Lync, direct all the flight data on Skiff-One to my workstation, please," Nianta hurriedly tapped out a series of commands on the holo-screen. He was already a mass of concentration and focused energy.

General Newey immediately turned his attention to the task he was hoping to avoid, but now knew he had no choice. He tapped two icons on his forearm PDI and called up a statement he had prepared hours ago. Hitting several more icons on the device, Newey connected himself with the station's internal communications system and took a deep breath. "Attention everyone. Attention!" his voice boomed over the room speakers and out of Major Nianta's PDI speaker. "This is Lieutenant General Richard D. Newey; Commander of Titan-Base Lincoln. I have a very important announcement to make. Ten years ago…"

•　　　•　　　•

Captain Aamodt thoughtfully scrutinized Private-Specialist Wong and Medtec Brauer as they completed donning their e-suits. Aamodt eyed every movement and examined every action of the private-specialist and the medtec with all of the concentration of a talent scout at an audition. The dark gray e-suits, thought Aamodt, did not quite fit the décor of the sterile white room that was the preparation area for the hangar bay's decontamination-airlock.

As the captain scanned the two younger team members, she held some reservations about the blond Medtec Susan Brauer. She thought the young, well-built woman was too smart and ambitious to be a medtec. Brauer had demonstrated on several occasions that she was as capable and as knowledgeable as any of the doctors on the station. *Why was she only a medical technician?* Aamodt could not discover any reason why Brauer did not qualify as a medical doctor, and that fact bothered the captain on a regular basis.

Medtec Brauer was one of General Newey's replacement personnel, and for a young woman on a remote and relatively isolated station, she rarely spoke to anyone, including Aamodt. They never really had a conversation for more than five minutes, even after she had been on the station for several months. The only things that Aamodt noticed about Brauer was that the woman had cold, brown eyes that seem to watch everyone, and she appeared to take great efforts in being polite and professional to everyone. In spite of Aamodt's suspicions, the two women got along fine.

"Wong, check Brauer's suit," ordered Aamodt, wanting the medtec's e-suit doubled checked.

Wong, in the middle of checking his helmet seal, immediately stopped and followed the captain's instructions, knowing that Brauer did not have as much time in the e-suits as he and Aamodt. He did not spot any problems with the medtec's e-suit. "You're good. Confirm with your suit AI." Wong gave Aamodt a sharp thumbs-up sign, his face expressionless, a match for the medtec.

"Is it true?" Brauer's voice was coarse as she sealed her e-suit. Cool, plastic tasting air flowed over her face as she continued, "Did Major Nianta win the pool? Did T-One really discover EBEs?" Suddenly her e-suit's AI began to announce the condition of her e-suit in a voice that was far more mechanical than Lync's.

"You heard the General's announcement, same as me. I guess we'll find out in a few minutes if he was fucking with us." Aamodt looked back at the entryway hatch to make sure it was closed, then she tapped the sleeve of her e-suit. "General, this is Aamodt in the Ready Room, how long before Skiff-One arrives?"

"Three minutes, but don't enter 'till after the initial decontamination," Newey's disembodied reply came back through her helmet speakers. "I have you on monitors."

Aamodt waved at the tiny surveillance camera in the far corner of the Ready Room ceiling. "Let us know when. Ready Room out," she tapped her sleeve's interlink again. "Okay, let's have a seat. This is going to take a while."

Aamodt and Brauer both sat on the bench in front of the e-suit storage unit, and the double row of shelves holding e-suit repair kits and other emergency equipment. Wong paced back and forth, nervously rubbing his gloved hands together. His mind was racing through different scenarios on what could possibly happen when the hatch to the hangar deck finally opened. He knew his job well, but this was something just a little beyond his job description. He craved a hemporette or a drink because that itchy feeling was slowly growing again along his nervous system. However, he knew he must never say anything to anyone about it. If he did, he knew he might find himself in a re-education or de-tox facility, his career, and future shot.

"Will you sit down, I'm getting dizzy watching you," begged Brauer.

"How can you be so calm? There's an extraterrestrial---"

"Hey!" objected Aamodt loudly, having been born in one of the lunar colonies. She took her lunar heritage seriously and, like most non-Earth-born, did not like the term *extraterrestrial*. She knew some anti-society types used the word *extraterrestrial* as a derogatory term to refer to non-Earth born humans. The term *extraterrestrial* carried all of the same hatred and prejudices, as some ethnic slurs did in the nineteenth and early twentieth centuries.

Wong remembered to be *socially correct*, even though he honestly did not mean any insult to anyone who was not Earth-born. "Excuse me, an extrasolar lifeform is about to land in the next room? We are about to make history." As if to emphasize Wong's words, the illuminated red: **DANGER HANGAR DOOR OPEN** Warning light-sign came to life over the hatchway that led to the hangar deck. The automated safety lock slammed home on the hatch with an audible clank.

"Who says I'm not nervous? I'm just as nervous as you are, but walking back and forth like some backstreet Bangtail isn't going to help much."

Wong shot a hard eye at Brauer, "Just shut up, will yeah please." He continued to pace the small room.

"Both of you shut up and consider that an order," commanded Aamodt as the red illuminated sign switched over to **HANGAR DOOR CLOSED - DECONTAMINATION IN PROGRESS**. "Aamodt to Colonel Rozsa we are in the Ready Room and ready to assist you, awaiting decontamination."

"That's affirm Captain," replied Rozsa's matter-of-fact voice over the com system.

"We've got fifteen minutes," announced Aamodt.

Time passed, and no one in the Ready Room spoke. Every few minutes Lync would announce the time to the end of the decontamination cycle, and the results of the scan of the biofilters for the system. All was going as expected. Colonel Rozsa would conduct a voice check every few minutes even though Lync was monitoring their vital signs, along with General Newey in the com-center and Doctor Tan in the med-bay. Ten minutes into the decontamination cycle, the three in the Ready Room ordered their e-suit AIs to run a diagnostic on their suit systems, as they mentally readied themselves.

As their individual e-suits made an audible report on their suit systems one by one, Aamodt was focused on the moment with the concentration of a demolitions expert, handling defective explosives. Brauer's mind was laser-focused on her job. Wong just wanted to be someplace else.

At the two-minute mark, Aamodt stood up and went to the hatch, all the while eyeing Wong. The private-specialist appeared nervous, granted if the general were correct, this was major history in the making, but Aamodt knew that Wong was better trained than his behavior implied.

"Okay." Brauer stood up and joined Aamodt and Wong. "Are we ready for this?"

"Ten to one this turns out to be something else," spat Aamodt, her eyes playing over the Ready Room, inspecting the place even though she knew it was in perfect order.

It went eerily silent in the room, as the safety lock on the entry hatch sounded loudly as it moved out of the way. The warning sign burning brightly above the hatchway rapidly went from **DECONTAMINATION IN PROGRESS** to **ALL CLEAR TO PROCEED**. Each of the three gave their fellows a questioning glance, but no one said anything. There was nothing to be said, they could feel it in the air like the early morning chill on the day of a big autumn parade.

"Captain, standby," Lync's announcement startled Brauer and Wong, as it sounded over their e-suit com systems. "You are cleared to enter the hangar."

Brauer signaled her readiness. Wong stared at the hatch a minute then gestured her readiness.

"Okay, here goes nothing," Aamodt took a deep breath and pressed the **HATCH OPEN** button.

Something big and loud exploded out from behind the hatch as it moved aside. It snatched up Aamodt with a scream, sending Wong and Brauer diving backward in terror.

"You fucking asshole!" shouted Aamodt, banging Arroyo angrily on the top of his helmet. "What the fuck are you doing? This isn't a damn joke!"

Arroyo dropped Aamodt as he fell against the side of the hatchway, laughing like a lunatic. Behind him was Colonel Rozsa, Major Singleton and the rest of the skiff crew, all but Lebowitz and Pulgar were laughing.

"We knew you guys would be a little on edge, but that was too much!" roared Arroyo. His laughter was on the verge of being uncontrollable and had an unhealthy quality.

Captain Aamodt cursed, then she attacked Arroyo as Wong and Brauer realized what was happening. Instantly Rozsa, Singleton, and LaRocque forced themselves between the two captains. Medtec Brauer, her brown eyes bulging with outrage as she too started in on Arroyo. Wong, his embarrassment turning to anger, followed Aamodt and Brauer's led and joined the assault on Captain Arroyo.

Rozsa and Singleton looked at each other as Newey's voice frantically boomed in their helmets and in the Ready Room, "What the hell is going on? Report! Someone report!"

"Should we let them have him?" inquired Singleton, struggling to control the grin on his face.

"Under normal circumstances, yes, but," Rozsa, knowing that the general was monitoring them, pushed both sides apart, forcefully. "Okay, enough! Break it up! The fun is over!" She stared at Arroyo's unshaven face through his helmet faceplate. The man looked out of control, and she suddenly found Captain Arroyo's laughter a little uncomfortable.

"Enough! You heard the order!" shouted Singleton, stepping up and assisting the colonel, pushing Aamodt and her team back. "Settle it later!" The look on the shielded faces around him were all unnervingly serious.

Captain Aamodt and the others backed off. "Vincent, I've had it with your fucked up attitude. I'm going to stick my foot so far up your ass the next…" Aamodt broke off in the middle of her comment and settled down a little as Yee and Al-Yuzwaki appeared out of the hangar. For the first time, Aamodt noticed that all the members of the skiff crew had travel-packs and large specimen bags slung over their shoulders. Each of the bulky burdens had some type of *Hazardous Materials* or *Biohazard* emblem affixed to it.

"Aamodt, somebody tell me what the hell is happening there?" the general's voice sounded like he was about to bust a blood vessel.

The angry captain waved at the ceiling camera, followed by the others. "It's just Vincent being an asshole again, sir." Aamodt stared at Arroyo with hate in her eyes.

"Now is not the time for this!" Newey sounded as angry as Aamodt appeared, "Get that stuff into containment ASAP. Costello and McGilmer are waiting for you."

"In the skiff are more, non-biological materials," added Rozsa.

Aamodt paused, surveyed the exhausted faces of the group behind their helmet faceplates, and with a frown stuck up an angry gloved finger. "It's true? T-One discovered---"

Rozsa cut her off, "Not now Captain. You and Wong get that material down to the labs."

Singleton, staring at Aamodt's face behind her helmet faceplate smirked, "You know you're beautiful when---"

"We haven't got time for this shit," this time Newey's voice sounded more annoyed than angry as it boomed through helmet and room speakers alike. "Aamodt, you, and Wong get the rest of the materials out of the skiff. Take whatever specimens they have in there to the labs. Then I want the two of you to prepare a preliminary damage assessment of the skiff. I'm canceling the CFM."

Rozsa was already moving toward the inner hatchway, "Brauer, you escort the Capt'n and Wong down to the labs after they collect the rest of that stuff."

No one articulated their thoughts as Rozsa, and her group moved out of the Ready Room. Wong looked over at Captain Aamodt with confusion spreading across his young face. Aamodt just stared at the departing skiff crew as if they had just urinated on her foot.

As the group moved out of the room, heading off towards the laboratory section along a sealed route, Rozsa explained to Newey over her helmet intercom what was happening.

• • •

Three women hastily inspected equipment in Biological Sciences Laboratory Number One. All three were outfitted in bloated, rubbery white biohazard protective suits. Professor Jira Costello, who appeared in charge, systematically checked her instruments. Like most frontier authority scientists, she was painfully thorough, looking for the slightest problem or anomaly. Her green eyes did not miss a tool, panel, console, or holo-screen. She even double-checked her biohazard protective suit. The suit and transparent helmet made the tall, slim woman, and her two similarly dressed companions, look like old fashion biochemical workers of centuries ago. She had even lowered the temperature in the lab to a hundred and fifty below and replaced the atmosphere with nitrogen.

Costello's lab looked much like the other two biological sciences laboratories on the station, which were themselves similar in design, construction, and layout to the other twelve science laboratories. Each bio lab was connected to its neighbor by a dual negative pressure airlock system, which was monitored by the station's AI. Each bio lab had similar arrangements of storage cabinets, hard-monitors and holo-screens, but was loaded with very different analytical equipment. All three bio labs had an AI-scan platform and motorized worktable arranged along the centerline of each of the brightly lit ovoid shaped rooms. Bio lab number two was set up to study microorganisms; bio lab three was equipped with instruments for genetic mapping of non-terrestrial species. The lab Professor Costello was currently working in was set up to investigate non-terrestrial macro-organisms, and to conduct experiments on the large aquatic organisms that lived in the sub-ice water environments of Enceladus.

Professor Jira Costello was an exoviro-geneticists and Titan was her first long-term research assignment. She was on Titan to study the molecular heredity of the chemosynthetic organisms that inhabited the hydrothermal vents, deep below the frozen surfaces of Mimas, Enceladus, and Tethys. She had been born and raised in Camerino, Italy not far from the Chienti River in the European Common Union. Graduating from the ECU National University at Milan with degrees in molecular and genetic paleo-biochemistry, she attained her Ph.D. in low-temperature synthetic-biochemistry. As a post-doc and research assistant with one of the big pharmaceutical conglomerates, her professional career was going nowhere fast, when she joined the Frontier Authority. She had only been a member of the FA for only two years when she was chosen to come to Titan.

"Jeannet, you ready?" Professor Costello looked around the lab, one more time, before Colonel Rozsa, and the others were supposed to arrive. She, like everyone on the station, was monitoring the skiff team's progress over the station's interlink system.

The other scientist in the lab was Professor Jeannet McGilmer. She stood just inside the doorway, still looking a little apprehensive as if she were having second thoughts about what was going to happen.

Professor Jeannet McGilmer stared at Professor Costello with concern in her brown eyes, but she kept her thoughts to herself. McGilmer, at just over one point four meters in height and forty-seven point three kilograms, was the most petite person on the station, even before the evacuation. However, her lack of physical stature was more than compensated for by her professional achievements. Having earned three different Ph.Ds. in the field of biology before she was thirty, Professor Jeannet McGilmer was Titan-Base Lincoln's resident xeno-microbiologist, specializing in developmental xeno-microbiophysiology. After drawing a questioning stare from Professor Costello, McGilmer responded with a quiet, "I'm ready."

"Garcia, you ready?" inquired Costello as the hum of the pneumatic lab door sounded.

The third woman in the lab was a young, dark-haired medtec. Miyo Garcia turned away from the console as Rozsa came through the door. "I'm ready," the medtec's Spanish accent drew the attention of Arroyo, as he entered the room behind Singleton.

Miyo Garcia was the station's senior medtec. As she surveyed the burdens that Singleton, Arroyo, and Yee were carrying, she realized her professional plans had changed. She knew that she would qualify to be a full medical doctor by the time this mission came to an end, assuming she got passing marks from McGilmer and Tan. Now, she knew that she would be made an M.D, and maybe she would even get a good position back home in Baguio.

Miyo Garcia was a proud Filipino, born and raised in the island's main seadome of Baguio. Even though she looked and sounded native Central or South American, her father was a full-blooded Filipino and her mother a Mindanaoian, from the Philippine State of Mindanao in the Democratic Union of Asian States. She did not mind being mistaken for Central American. It only bothered her when a fellow Filipino made the annoying error.

"Colonel, Major. Where are the extrasolars?" Costello looked questioningly past Rozsa.

Singleton and Arroyo, both sweating and breathing heavily, smiled and glanced in Professor Yee's direction. "Well, it's like---"

"What happened?" It was clear from the harsh tone of her voice, and the way she cut off the major, that Professor Costello was very disappointed.

Rozsa's arms quivered as she held up a specimen bag. The change from Titan to Earth-normal gravity had turned their hefty burdens into nearly backbreaking loads. "It's in these bags." The others indicated their bags as Rozsa looked back at Yee. "It had a little accident. It'll all be in the report."

"It appeared to have been frozen solid, the cryogenic chamber it was in was damaged, and when we tried to retrieve it, it shattered," explained Yee, moving over to Costello.

"It was dead already," added Rozsa. "The guys from T-One found it."

"Wonderful," she exclaimed. Costello could see the sweat pouring down Yee's face through his e-suit helmet visor, and she could hear the combined faint hums of the e-suits of the skiff team. "Put the pieces on the table," instructed Costello, pointing to the bare worktable under the scan platform that was suspended from the ceiling.

Rozsa and the others opened up the bags and unceremoniously dumped out the still frozen pieces of the extrasolar onto the lab table. As the jumbled pieces hit the table surface, some crumbled further with a sound that reminded Costello of a dozen pairs of shoes falling down a flight of stairs. Each tiny portion of the shattered extrasolar figure had bits, and pieces of the inner lining of the bag stuck to them.

"Oh," uttered Costello, McGilmer, and Garcia softly in unison. In silent astonishment, they all stared at the chaotic pile of crumbled pieces that were spread across the worktable. It was the skiff team's first look in normal light at what they had found and brought back. All in the room felt suddenly cold as a light vapor rose from the table.

Staring at the puzzle on the worktable, they began to identify what appeared to be familiar looking anatomical parts, a tooth here, part of a leg there, and all of it so cold that the air surrounding the pieces was beginning to condense. The liquefied atmosphere was running off the mass of parts to form shallow pools on the table. The pools of clear liquid bubbled and boiled their way back into invisible gas.

"This is amazing," Costello looked bewildered, her thoughts racing at a billion kilometers a second. She tried to stop the sudden grin that swept across her face but failed. They were going to make history, and they were going to be famous.

"Well, I'm glad you like it," Rozsa finally announced, "cause, assuming there is enough water available, we're going to take some showers, get some hot food and some much-needed sleep."

Costello quickly came back to reality, "After all of you go through direct decontamination and medical screening for level-one biohazards. NJ's waiting for you, she'll perform the physicals."

"Oh, dogshit!" Rozsa shot a hard eye at the professor, "Fuck you and your decontamination. We've been smelling each other's sweat for---"

"Orders Colonel, you know the protocols regarding a level-one biohazard," the tone in Costello's voice, and the manner in which she turned her attention back to the lab table, told Rozsa that the professor did not care about anything she had to say regarding anything. Costello obviously wanted Rozsa and her team out of her lab as soon as possible.

"Let's go, people," Rozsa led the others to the door. "The sooner we get this over with, the sooner we can get some rest," she hated medical examinations, especially the rubber glove part.

"Hey, be careful it was frozen down to around absolute zero," informed Yee, turning toward the doorway. "Also, we collected T-One's research and recorded a dogshit load of images of our own. You might want to go through T-One's data before you start in on our guest."

Costello nodded, shaking her long brown curls inside her protective suit. Not looking away from the table, she half-heard Yee and knew they had plenty of time to wade through the date and the vid images.

As Rozsa and the skiff team left the lab, Costello exhaled loudly as if relieved of a burden. "Okay, Miyo scan through Rozsa's vid-cam data for an image of this thing before they did whatever they did to it. Jeannet let's see what we've got here." She paused for a moment, then activated the vid and data recorders. "Some Deep Kockers and a large skeins."

Medtec Garcia hovered over the worktable for a moment, surveying the remains with a look of both revulsion and fear. As McGilmer moved to a nearby instrument table and removed two pairs of the requested tools, Miyo Garcia left the room to do as Professor Costello had requested.

Handing one set of tools to Costello, the two scientists started moving pieces of the thing around on the worktable.

"What a mess," announced McGilmer, staring at the shattered pile of frozen body parts that were spread all over the worktable. "This is going to be like putting together a jigsaw puzzle."

"Well, hopefully, they took images of this thing before they fucked it. First, let's see what we can see, then we'll see if there is anything we can do with it." Costello did not sound optimistic, nor did she appear anymore hopeful through her transparent helmet. "Turn down the lab temp as low as you can, I don't want this thing thawing out just yet."

McGilmer typed out a few commands on a holo-screen. "Okay, let's get started."

The two biologists were captivated by the remains before them. They both worked in near silence for almost an hour, until Medtec Garcia returned to the lab with a look on her face that caused the two scientists to stop what they were doing.

As the pale and stunned young medtec approached Costello and McGilmer, her expression instantly reminded both professors of the moment they had been informed of Private-Specialist Zapollo's death. Indeed, they both thought the medtec was about to tell them of the death of someone else from their team. Then she showed them an image on a workslate. It was an image of the unbroken thing that now laid fragmented on the lab table.

For a full minute, the three women just stood and stared at one another and the image of the thing on the workslate. They then immediately contacted General Newey and Professor Watkinski and showed them the image. The conversation that ensued was brief but energetic. Finally, General Newey and Professor Watkinski ordered the two professors to continue with their work.

For the next four hours, Costello and McGilmer worked unceasingly on the strange collection on the table. The two women had Lync scan all the fragments and generate three-dimensional images of the pieces. Based on the images taken by Colonel Rozsa, and her team, they had Lync slowly re-assemble the fragments on a holo-screen so they could follow it as a guide. It all looked to Medtec Garcia like it was some bizarre board game. She had never seen anything so frightening, and deep down prayed she would never see anything like it again, especially alive. Even the best realistic, AI-generated monsters created for the holographic vids did not scare her as much as the thing on the table. Deep down she knew that her fear could distinguish between AI reality and *real* reality, and the thing on the table was definitely *real* reality. It reminded her of the deep fear she had experienced once as a child when she was cornered by a large and angry dog.

After most of the pieces had been reassembled, Professor McGilmer and Medtec Garcia left bio lab one to conduct an analysis in the microbiology lab. As Garcia followed McGilmer out of the room, she glanced back at the thing taking shape on the worktable, and thought to herself that all of this was going to make all of them extremely famous.

Assuming, that nothing went wrong first.

•  •  •

Colonel Rozsa and the other members of the skiff team sat shrouded in thin, paper-like outfits in the small decontamination chamber. The room temperature was just cool enough to make their metabolisms work at keeping them warm. Lync monitored their vital signs, skin moisture, and tone, plus the room's bio-filters. The vigilant machine looked for the minutest signs of organic or other contaminants in their systems. Every thirty minutes each had to give a microliter of blood and every hour each had to give a urine sample so Lync could chart and monitor their metabolisms for anything that might threaten the health of the station. Doctor Tan reviewed Lync's results every hour. She also conducted detailed and uncomfortably invasive physical exams on each member of the skiff team at random intervals.

The eight members of the surface team watched, with growing boredom, a situational comedy on the room's holographic vid player. The comedy series was popular throughout the solar system. It dealt with the life and times of Sir Isaac Newton. However, the waiting group was not in the mood for a historical comedy, no matter how funny. They all worked on reports using their PDIs and workslates, and they made meaningless small talk, avoiding the topic of Titan-Base Ksa and the unburied dead still there.

Occasionally someone would attempt to tell a story about some adolescent experience or past duty assignment that all in the room had heard before. The stories were usually as boring as the first time they had heard them, but everyone, for the most part, was polite. They all knew why the person was attempting a personal story. However, in the middle of someone's story, Arroyo would interject an off-color joke that no one found funny.

In between work, bursts of fake laughter from the vid, and old stories, they would theorize about the nature of what they had found, and what it might all mean to them, and to humanity as a whole. Nevertheless, as time passed, both Rozsa and Singleton watched Arroyo with growing concern as the man began to talk more and more, telling inappropriate stories and making inappropriate comments. Finally, after several near arguments between Pulgar, LaRocque, and Arroyo, Colonel Rozsa commanded the captain to get some rest, even if he was not tired. Pulgar and LaRocque, for the most part, sat quietly next to one another and halfheartedly worked on their reports and listened to the uninteresting room chatter and vid dialog.

After two hours of random boredom and report writing, Yee, Lebowitz, and Singleton all grew tired of the situation and the pointless babble. Each curled up into their own little crude, fetal-like protective sphere, and tried to get some rest on the sterile white recliners. Rozsa, Pulgar, LaRocque, and Al-Yuzwaki continued to make light conversation, all the while, keeping an uneasy eye on Arroyo and secretly watching the wall chronometer, counting the minutes.

While the eight members of the skiff team were counting the minutes until they could be released, Medtec Brauer decontaminated all the items that the skiff team had brought back with them from Titan-Base Ksa. Brauer then took the items that were obviously not of human design to Professor Eastman and Private-Specialist Zuverink for analysis.

Professor Eastman, employing Lync began to study the various unknown artifacts in detail. She was not an engineer or a techno-archaeologist, but she could handle Lync and the scanners. To her, it was like playing detective. It was all just a matter of asking the right questions, at the right time.

On orders from General Newey, Zuverink fed all of the data, recorded reports, and technical information gathered by the skiff team from Titan-Base Ksa into Lync. As she did, she kept an eye out for any reports by General Pan, the Commander of Titan-Base Ksa, or Professor Vance, head of the Titan-Base Ksa's scientific investigation team. She was to contact him at once if she encountered anything to do with either of these people.

During the five hours of reconstruction, decontamination, and analytical investigations of the materials brought back from Titan-Base Ksa, General Newey had ordered Fung, Sloan, Yoshida, and Tounames, along with Doctor Reierstadt to all get some sleep. Each gladly took a long quiet rest in their separate quarters. However, Doctor Reierstadt had a difficult time trying to sleep. She spent an hour tossing and turning in her bed before she decided to take a pill to help her drift off to sleep. The fact that the deceased men and women of Titan-Base Ksa had become the first humans in recorded history to have physical contact with extrasolar intelligences, somehow troubled her.

Of all the people of the station who were asleep, only Lieutenant Fung dreamt. She was running nude through a strange forest at night. The unfamiliar woods were bathed in cold blues, ember reds, and pale yellows. It was as if a bright, multicolored full moon was rising, but it was not a moon rising into the strange night sky, it was a galaxy. An enormous barred-spiral galaxy, seen almost face on, as it rose up over the trees in front of her like some great glittering eye. The light from billions of stars reflected off the frost covered leaves of the huge trees surrounding Fung. Some of the oddly shaped foliage appeared well over a kilometer high.

She stopped running and noticed that somebody or something was coming toward her out of the darkness. It was her ex-wife, naked, with goosebumps and erect nipples from the cold. She was shouting at her in a strange language. It was not modern Mandarin or regular Cantonese, nor was it Standard English or any combination of the three. However, by the tone of her ex-wife's voice, Fung could tell that she was trying to communicate something important to her. From nowhere, a look of terror swept over her ex-wife's face, as she began to back away. Fung turned around to look behind her and felt a sharp pain in her lower back...

She woke up! Her room was dark, and her bed was damp with sweat. She felt as if something terrible was going to happen.

# CHAPTER TEN

"I guess that does it," Costello finally announced, as she moved the last piece of the massive form into place. There were half a dozen smaller fragments left over that Costello and McGilmer had not been able to place, but for the most part, the thing on the table looked roughly the way it appeared in the images taken by Colonel Rozsa and her team before it had been shattered. However, now it looked more like a three-dimensional jigsaw puzzle covered in the thick frost of its own self-generated microclimate. The bluish-white frost coating the fragments acted like glue, holding the strange pieces together like some preschooler's art project. The whole surreal mass was centered in the middle of a supercooled puddle of liquid air that bubbled like a cauldron as it converted back into cold gas.

"By all the Divinities," Garcia whispered as waves of sickly cold gas flowed off of the frozen nightmare before her. The sheer presence of the otherworldly looking object on the lab table sent shivers down the senior medtec's spine. The cold that radiated off of it made her feel like she had entered an icy meat locker, and she found herself, unconsciously trying to keep a respectable distance from the table.

"I doubt if any Divinity you want to believe in created that," grimaced Costello as she placed the pile of leftover fragments on a tray and sat them next to the reassembled form.

She too was obviously troubled by the appearance of the thing. The fog rising from it did nothing to lessen its ominous demeanor. *A classic image of the devil* thought McGilmer. It reminded her of a twisted and eroded statue of a gargoyle she had once seen somewhere on Earth.

The frozen entity on the lab table appeared to be an upright, quasi-humanoid form just under three meters in length. The form was large, dark, and demonic in appearance and its skin had a coarse texture like that of very rough sandpaper. With the cold blue-white mist wafting around it, Professor Costello immediately thought of Shiva, the destroyer in Hindu mythology. Indeed, it looked to Costello like some monstrous blend of Shiva and Lei Kung, the Duke of Thunder from Chinese mythology. In the image taken at Titan-Base Ksa, the lifeform appeared to span one end of the color spectrum from black to dark olive green, now it was light gray, colored with frost.

During the reconstruction, Costello and McGilmer realized that the figure's four-armed muscular body was clothed in a material that did not behave like either a synthetic or metal, at the temperatures and conditions it was currently under. Stepping closer, McGilmer noticed that the material covering the creature's four arms sported what looked like an insignia. In the workslate image, they were clearer and not crusted over in frost. The four images were of a large black and white galaxy set above a solar system with seventeen planets. The insignia looked tiny set against each of its massive arms. A light stream of transparent liquid flowed and bubbled down the sides of the body of the ominous looking statue, as the three women in the room stared transfixed.

If McGilmer was correct in her assumptions, it had a number of small, multi-faceted, insect-like eyes set in small armored sockets that ran down both sides of what should be its head in four columns. If they were eyes, they would give the creature total peripheral vision. Each of the numerous tiny complex eyes was glassy, rough, and edgy like fragments of black quartz crystal. Two chains of raised pinholes began on either side of its face from where a nose would have been on a human's and proceeded to encircle its head in a boney ridge, bisecting the rows of eyes into four upper and lower columns. On either side of its head, next to the last column of eyes were two long, gill-like structures. McGilmer speculated that the structures could be used for respiration. Costello thought they could be ears. Neither professor was willing to wager their careers on their guesses. "*El diablo de mis padres?*" Garcia frowned as if she had just read Professor Costello's mind.

Costello looked back at the senior medtec, "Well, I hope not." She read the holo-screen on the side of the lab table. The temperature of the frozen form was now negative two hundred and sixty-nine degrees Celsius. Its weight was over four hundred kilograms. However, what caught the doctor's attention was the reading on the particle detector. The strange form on the lab table was beginning to show signs of radioactivity.

Costello activated the interlink system built into her protective suit, "Kostya? This is Jira; please join us in bio lab one. We have something interesting for you to see."

"I've got plenty of interesting things to look at already," the reply came in a voice that was both enthusiastic and tired, "but I am on my way."

"Lync, run a BLIS on the lab seals, and confirm our bio-containment," ordered Costello, still staring at the table's readout. "Jeannet, this thing's showing signs of radioactivity."

"Bio lab one seals are at one hundred percent integrity, there is one hundred percent positive pressure, and no unidentifiable compounds or organisms have been detected. No identifiable pathogens are present in the lab," informed Lync's disembodied voice.

Professor McGilmer and Medtec Garcia moved passed one another, as Garcia went to a lab counter and activated a small device. McGilmer moved to examine the lab table's holo-screen.

"I'm detecting an emission of fifty-four millisievert." Costello punched out a set of commands on the table's holo-screen. The reply flashed back over the tiny hard-monitor, "According to the scanners the radioactivity is increasing logarithmically with the temperature." McGilmer and Costello just stared at one another as if a waiter had just delivered them the wrong meal.

Garcia, her task completed, waited uncomfortably. She just stared at the horrific mass on the table. Suddenly the lab door sounded, and in rushed Professor Watkinski. The professor was clad in a protective suit with a similarly dressed Doctor Tan following close behind.

"What have you got?" Watkinski asked from inside his biohazard suit.

The three women in the lab surveyed the ghostly pale Professor Kostya Watkinski. Garcia always thought the freckled faced geo-microbiochemist looked more like a bookish intellectual, even more than Professor Yee did. *It must be the look for Ph.D. graduates from MPIT*, thought Garcia.

Watkinski's already bloodshot blue eyes were screened behind the face-shield of his bio-protective hood. The edge of the uncombed mop of copper red hair was stark against the white of his protective suit and bland skin. His pale skin tone was apparently a genetic trait. A week after his arrival at Titan-Base Lincoln, as part of General Newey's group, Watkinski had shown McGilmer, a family image. He was apparently a native of Earth, living in Khantia-Mansia, URR (United Russian Republics). The man's wife and three daughters were all redheads, physically fit, but like the professor, unnaturally pale, practically albinistic.

"Kostya, this thing's showing signs of radioactivity," informed Costello, noting the reactions of both the geo-microbiochemist and Doctor Tan, as they caught sight of the body on the table.

Tan felt a wave of ice water wash over her and down her back to tingle the base of her heels. The thing on the table scared her in a primal way that she did not understand. All she could do for a long moment was stare, frown, and whisper softly under her breath, "Oh my Divinities," the Cantonese accent strong in her voice.

Professor Watkinski also stared blindly at the table in amazement. In all of his forty-four years, he had never thought he would see anything so demonic in real-life. His scientific and intellectual curiosity was peaked, but his survival instincts wanted desperately to kick into high gear. "*Bozhe moi*," he moaned in a voice not quite too low to hear. "It looks remarkably like the Hindu Goddess Shiva."

"Yeah, accept Shiva is much prettier," added Tan, still staring hard at the table.

"It's dead," McGilmer could sense the fear in her coworkers, "you don't have to worry. We took out its batteries." The audible sound of atmospheric gases boiling away from the constantly forming puddles on the table did nothing to help Watkinski or Tan feel any better about what was before them.

"I wish we had found batteries," Costello corrected McGilmer's useless attempt to ease the growing feeling of uneasiness in the room, "at least something would have been familiar." Everyone standing around the assemblage on the laboratory table had the same unconscious apprehension. There was some deep-seated fear of it, like some timid animal that had just gotten the faintest odor of a fierce predator.

Watkinski looked over at her, "Congratulations Doctor Frankenstein." He was not trying to be funny, and there was no humor in his voice. "You've created..." his voice trailed off to silence as he looked at the aberration on the lab table. He added coldly, "The destroyer of worlds."

Garcia coughed out a nervous chuckle, but no one looked. There was dead silence in the room for almost a minute.

"Did you do a body form chart?" Tan still could not force her eyes away from the thing.

"Yes, and I have Lync working on a genomic sequence map and running an analysis for amino acid structures. We'll build a database profile for cross-referencing, as well as for a tissue typing study." McGilmer surveyed Tan and Watkinski, both still looking like they were in a state of shock. "Also, I have Lync searching for nano-and micro-organisms and parasitic forms. They should be completed in an hour or so."

"Good," Tan noticed the readout on the side of the lab table. "So, did Shiva's ugly brother here, get contaminated?" she continued to frown.

Costello looked at the table's little holo-screen, "I would assume so, the reading is now fifty-five millisieverts." She looked at Watkinski and Tan, just as the two of them moved closer to the table, in unison. "The reading is up one-hundredth of a point in the last few minutes."

Watkinski looked carefully at the re-assembled mass on the table, as cold condensed air continued to flow off the frozen unnatural statue, forming clear evaporating rivulets. "What's the temperature? Has it gone up?" He noted the rising mist swirling above the table.

"Yeah," answered Costello, her tone was all uncertainty. "It's up thirteen degrees since the last time I looked."

"Jeannet, think we should warm it up a little bit." Watkinski pretended not to notice the stunned looks he got from McGilmer and Garcia.

"My thoughts exactly," grinned Costello as she slowly circled the lab table. She re-examined every minor detail of the icy form as if she were about to purchase it for a great deal of hard currency.

McGilmer thought it was a bad idea, but gave her approval.

"Lync raise the temperature of the specimen on the lab table slowly," ordered Professor Watkinski.

McGilmer and the others instinctively backed away from the lab table, "Our hard work is going to fall apart as it melts."

The scan platform, protruding over the lab table through the drop-ceiling, slowly started to emit an orange light. After a few seconds, the light slowly darkened to a reddish hue. The puddles of liquid air on the table began to bubble and boil away with increasing vigor, transforming back into colorless gas. Several of the frozen fragments of strange tissue began to slump to the tabletop as bits of the specimen bag lining, that were stuck to them, slowly began to slide away from the various pieces. After another minute, a dull white, milk-like fluid began to ooze slowly out of the spaces between the bits of unfamiliar material.

There were a series of unexpectedly loud beeps followed by the voice of Lync. "Bio lab one atmospheric monitors are detecting increased levels of sulfur dioxide, sulfur monochloride, carbon monoxide, carbon tetrachloride, hydrogen sulfide, and tellurium hexafluoride. It is recommended that all personnel in bio lab one maintain level-one protective protocols." Lync repeated its message.

"Okay, Lync, stop the heaters," instructed Watkinski, eyeing the white substance. "Let's see what we've got."

The light from the scan platform faded, but the mass continued to thaw. "Heaters are powered down," replied Lync.

The others advanced on the table, silent and wide-eyed, as Lync repeated its announcement concerning the gases appearing in the lab's atmosphere.

The once neatly reassembled form on the table was now a semi-organized oozing mess. Strangely, it reminded Doctor Tan of a mound of vanilla parfait with way too much fruit and berries.

"Miyo, I want a five-milliliter syringe with a sixteen gage," Costello's voice was devoid of emotion as she carefully examined the odd white fluid.

Garcia sat down the small device she was holding, then moved to the instrument cabinet, all the while keeping her eyes on the activity at the lab table. She still could not make herself look away from the table for longer than the briefest of instants.

"Make it two," Watkinski had an expression on his pale face as if he had ordered a well-done shiitake mushroom-tofu steak and gotten a raw and rancid llama tongue instead.

Garcia nodded.

"What is this? Blood?" questioned Watkinski, his racing mind reflected in his tired face.

"I don't know," imparted Costello, quickly surveying the group. "Jeannet, what's the temperature?"

She checked the reading, "A hundred and forty-four below. The radiation level is still rising. It's now twenty-seven hundred and thirty millisieverts."

"It looks like semen to me," noted Garcia as she handed both Costello and Watkinski a large gauge syringe. No one commented on the medtec's observations as the two professors began withdrawing some of the white fluid. The computerized syringe measured the amount of liquid being collected on tiny digital indicators.

"I don't think its blood. Unless this thing's blood can flow at minus a hundred and---"

Without warning, one of the creature's reconstructed legs moved. The shriek that Doctor Tan let out as she jumped back twanged everyone's nerves and sent a wave of cold adrenaline racing through everyone's veins.

"What is it? What happened?" Watkinski instantly moved his hands away from the table as if it had sprouted teeth and developed a mean bark.

"It moved!" shot Tan, keeping her distance from the table. "The leg, it moved."

Professor McGilmer sighed with a flood of relief, "Relax, I did it." She held up a probe-pin.

The tension level in the lab dropped a notch as everyone sighed a breath of relief. They all could feel the adrenaline flowing through their veins and their hearts pumping in their chests as if they all had had too much, really strong espresso.

"Next time, let someone know," spat Tan as she approached the table again.

"Sorry, I was just checking for---"

"Okay Jira, I'm going to run a quick and dirty on this with the GC and Mass Spec," informed Watkinski, talking over McGilmer. "NJ, help them with the anatomical work up. Make sure you get tissue and fluid samples from a variety of body locations. You know the drill. Lync, I want a ten-ten workup performed on these samples, plus a full scan for polyproteinal and genomic structures."

"Yes, Professor Watkinski," acknowledged AI.

"And don't forget to do a complete NMR on all the tissues," added Watkinski, as everyone calmly surveyed their colleague. Finally, Costello gave her 'yes' and everyone went to work.

Watkinski took his syringe full of white fluid to one of the chemistry laboratories. There he injected his syringe filled with the milky liquid into the gas chromatograph-mass spectrometer and monitored the device as it performed its analysis.

• • •

In another laboratory, an exhausted Private-Specialist Zuverink was uploading the information stored on the data clips brought back from Titan-Base Ksa by Colonel Rozsa and her team. There were two and three-dimensional still images, vid and multi-spectral scanner images, written and oral reports from scientist and technicians alike. Analytical data and test results were also stored on the tiny, fingernail-size storage devices. Hundreds of zettabytes per clip, and there were dozens of clips, not to mention the memory tabs from a dozen workslates.

As Zuverink watched the flow of data, she noticed one data clip had a series of encrypted files on it that were different from the others. Bored and curious, she had been running LaRocque's deciphering routine on the encrypted files. Apparently, the first few words of the transmission were the easiest to decipher, like the pictograms on an ancient international sign. Even if you could not read the words, you got the meaning of the message.

For the better part of an hour, Zuverink sat watching the multitudes of odd, unreadable symbols march up the holo-screen, the symbols relaying no useful information to the sore-eyed woman. Then just as the drowsy young woman was about to contact the com-center and ask to be relieved, the symbols began filing by in a continually changing pattern of ancient Semitic, Chinese, Bengali and binary characters. Finally, after a moment of lightning-like activity by Lync, the vid image of a brown skin, hazel-eyed man in a standard-issued UESA pseudo-uniform appeared and began to talk, as information scrolled through a small window in the vid image.

It took Zuverink a few moments to realize what she was looking at and she excitedly activated her PDI and keyed the interlink system. "General Newey, this is Zuverink in the AI-lab. I think I have found what you and Professor Eastman wanted."

General Newey's image appeared on Zuverink's PDI. "Let me see what you've got." Newey sounded tired and busy.

Zuverink keyed several images on both her PDI and the AI-controls she was using. "These look like Professor Vance's Reports." Zuverink's voice had an edge to it as she watched the vid, and saw the expression on the brown man's face.

There was an awkward pause before the general replied, "Stop what you are doing, and wait until I arrive. I'll signal Lori, and we'll be there shortly." Zuverink's PDI made an audible beep as Newey disconnected.

In spite of General Newey's orders, Zuverink continued to watch and listen to the hazel-eyed man in the vid for a few more minutes. Her enthusiasm and joy at being able to decrypt the dataclips slowly began to drain away, as the realization of what the professor in the vid was talking about dawned on her. Her apprehension quickly turned to cold fear as the true meaning of what she was hearing and seeing began to sink in.

She knew they were in real trouble.

# CHAPTER ELEVEN

Newey was tired, and every wrinkle and furrow in his gray face reflected his exhaustion. He considered the faces of the five scientists and Colonel Rozsa, who were all gathered around the Intelligent-conference table. He had ordered all of them to his office to review and discuss the data concerning the materials returned by Rozsa and her team. All seven had active holo-screens in front of them, the Intelligent-conference table projecting images, diagrams, and equations. Lync had produced an analysis of most of the data collected from Titan-Base Ksa, along with the incomplete results of the laboratory work performed on the dead extrasolar lifeform. None at the conference table seemed to like what they were seeing.

The general sat quietly at the head of the table. He still yearned for some sleep or a cigar but settled for some black coffee. He had only skimmed through the document on his holo-screen once. The document was a very complicated summary of the information discerned from the mass of materials brought back from Titan-Base Ksa. However, one thing was very clear; Titan-Base One had discovered something that was potentially very dangerous. Worse was the fact that the extrasolar lifeform Rozsa's team had retrieved from Titan-Base Ksa may not be as dead as it appeared.

Professor Eastman was seated at the opposite end of the conference table from General Newey. She occasionally glanced away from the documents she was reviewing and surveyed her coworkers. Her emotions seesawed between anger and fear. Professor Yee, whose expressions mirrored Eastman's, looked paler than usual. He was reading the ghostly text moving in front of him. Every few seconds he would touch his face as if each new paragraph spoke of the unexpected death of a loved one. Professor Watkinski, seated next to Yee, sat erect and alert. He was using both hands to move and manipulate holo-images around in the air before him. The redheaded geo-microbiochemist's face was emotionless as his eyes followed the images. Professors Costello and McGilmer were leaning into each other whispering, pointing at, and manipulating the information before them. They were both excited and scared at what they were seeing. Colonel Rozsa just sat and surveyed the people around her, calmly scanning the faces and expressions of those seated at the table. Every few minutes, Eastman's and Rozsa's eyes would meet and lock. Both women were not pleased with the situation.

"So General, do you want to tell us why we were not informed about what was going on at T-One sooner?" inquired Professor Yee, his almond eyes moving from General Newey to Colonel Rozsa to Professor Eastman and back again.

Newey leaned into Yee. "Knowing about extrasolar lifeforms in other solar systems through radio transmissions or from spectral scanners launched nearly five hundred years ago is one thing. To have them walking around in our backyard is another." He saw the look in the professor's eyes and leaned back. "The UESA thought it was better to investigate the craft, figure out what this thing was and have answers to the questions that were going to be asked."

"What did Vance find that caused him to embed that warning message Lieutenant LaRocque discovered?" inquired Professor Costello, staring hard at the general from her place at the conference table.

Newey shook his head and peered over at Colonel Rozsa. "You read the message; I thought it was clear."

"Yeah, clear and cryptic," exclaimed Professor Watkinski, sarcastically, "like a glass of cheap Mercurian Miner's vodka."

"Lync," General Newey addressed the station's main AI. "Please read the encrypted text Lieutenant LaRocque discovered embedded in the T-One distress signal."

149

The lifeless AI spoke. "Warning! Extreme danger! Titan-Base One has recovered a vehicle of extrasolar origin. This vehicle and its cargo are to be considered extremely hazardous and could pose a serious threat to human life. Level-one biocontainment should be enacted for all of Titan, and implementation of the Worldfall protocols should be considered as a possibility."

The general, Colonel Rozsa, and Professor Watkinski all shifted uncomfortably in their seats at the mention of the word *'Worldfall'*. All of them seated at the table knew that the Worldfall protocols were more than merely activating a station's self-destruct system. It essentially meant cooking the surface of an entire world with high-yield thermonuclear devices from orbit. It had never been done before in the near thousand years of human space exploration. Of the seven times, a thermonuclear sterilization procedure had been invoked, it had been done to an isolated station or plague ravaged colony on some asteroid or moon. Never had it been done to an entire planetary body.

"So when did they find this thing again?" inquired Professor McGilmer.

Newey was too tired for this. "You heard my announcement, and you've seen Professor Vance's summary report. This craft was initially thought to have been a deposit of heavy elements from some asteroid impact. Ten years ago it was identified as a craft of extrasolar origin, then it was decided to extract the craft from the bottom of Menrva crater." Newey saw the expression change on the faces of McGilmer and Costello. Watkinski, Eastman, and Rozsa just sat silently and waited. "When T-One finally got access to the craft, the decision was made to evac everyone from the region of Saturn."

"What? The UESA didn't trust us to keep the find quiet?" asked Professor Yee.

Rozsa flashed a grin towards the man. "With five thousand plus personnel out here, it would have been kinda hard to keep a thing like that secret for long."

"She's right," supported Professor Eastman. "Someone would have mentioned it to someone back home, and the secret would have been out."

"And that's a bad thing?" questioned McGilmer.

"You know there are religious cults that would use a discovery like this for their own ends." Eastman peered around the table. "Those so-called neo-modern deified religions are re-washed hangovers from before the Second Dark Ages."

"Okay," General Newey loudly knocked on the Intelligent-conference tabletop. "Before we get too far off track, let's move on. After the evacuation, General Pan, who was an experienced construction manager, and myself were selected to take command of the two nearest installations to where this craft was located. Since Professor Vance was one of the best techno-archaeologists around, he was tasked with leading the investigation into this vehicle."

Motioning at her holo-screen, Costello added, "This is what they found?" A holographic image of the extrasolar vehicle was now rotating slowly in front of her, as technical data on it scrolled by. The craft was bizarre in form, looking much like a flowering Texas Amethyst Sea Holly.

"Yes," replied Newey.

"If they knew this thing was dangerous, why didn't they tell us?" blasted Professor McGilmer. "If we knew, we would have taken steps."

"According to this, Vance and his people only got access to the craft's interior about a year ago." Colonel Rozsa stepped in to stop Costello from responding to McGilmer's comment.

"Is that why they went to radio silence?" asked Yee.

No one spoke for close to a full minute, as they continued to examine their holo-screens.

"Yes," Newey finally replied. "It was protocol."

Professor Yee stuck his hand up as if he were in primary school again. "Have we access to the data TBK downloaded into our secure servers?"

"Access to that data is one of the things I have asked for," responded Newey. "Commissioner Marshall will have to authorize Lync to grant us access."

"Great," muttered Costello.

"So based on this information," began McGilmer, getting everyone's attention again. "This thing crashed here two hundred and fifty million years ago, and has been buried at the bottom of Menrva since?"

There was still an uneasy quiet.

"Yes," replied Watkinski finally, tapping a holo-control, and removing the transparent screen in front of his face.

"So what I need to know is, is this assumption of the T-One investigation team correct?" added Newey, staring at Watkinski.

Professor Yee cleared his throat loudly and looked to Eastman, who gave him a subtle nod. "We obviously don't have complete information, but all indications point to---"

The general cut the geophysicist off, "Yes or no?" He was still looking at Professor Watkinski, even though he was addressing Yee.

"Yes," injected Professor Eastman. "We both knew Theo Vance a long time."

"I knew him from several of my advanced courses in grad school," added Yee, grimly.

Newey glanced at Rozsa, who sat stone-faced. "So this thing came here a quarter of a billion years ago to terra-form."

"Bio-form," corrected Professor Watkinski, leaning forward. "It's a more complex and invasive type of terraforming. Professor Vance's team believed, and I agree, that this thing came here to bio-form several of the planets in our solar system."

"Why?" questioned Professor Costello.

Everyone abruptly looked at her as if she had just become rudely flatulent.

"Prelude to colonization," added Rozsa, matter-of-factly.

Eastman deactivated her holo-screen. "If you look at section ten point two of Lync's summary of the data, it seems this device began its initial," she looked to Watkinski before she continued. "Bio-forming activities on Venus and Earth, then for some reason came out here to Saturn."

Yee typed a few icons on the Intelligent-conference table, and a large diagram appeared above the center of the table. It was two detailed geological time scales of both Venus and Earth. "A quarter of a billion years ago on Venus was the beginning of the CTA period, or Clotho Tessera-Ashton period. It correlates to Earth's Permian-Triassic. Both planets underwent severe volcanic upheaval; on Earth, it led directly to the extinction of somewhere around ninety-six percent of all the species on the planet."

Eastman snickered, "We lovingly refer to it as the Great Dying."

Yee saw the change of expression on the general's face and added, "Yeah. On Venus, according to radiometric dating, the planet basically reset its geologic clock around this time. The place could have been like Earth a quarter of a billion years ago, then the volcanism hit the reset button."

No one said anything for a long moment, as what was had been discussed sunk in, then Professor McGilmer spoke again. "There is some very controversial evidence that appears to indicate that Venus could have been more like Earth six hundred million years ago than it is today."

Again, an uneasy quiet settled on the room.

Colonel Rozsa broke the silence. "What about the thing we brought back?"

"Looks like it is some kind of biomechanically, engineered organism," answered Professor Costello.

"Based on the information obtained by the T-One team it's a biomechanoid of some type," Professor Watkinski's voice was smooth and cool but had an edge to it that made Newey and the others even more uneasy. "If this thing is natural, I for one don't want to see the world it evolved on."

Rozsa looked to General Newey and found him staring at her.

"This makes no sense!" exploded Eastman, "If this thing was terraforming---"

"Maybe they---" began Costello interrupting Eastman, only to be interrupted herself by Professor Watkinski, as everyone at the conference table began to talk at once.

Instantly everyone was felled silent by the general's rapping on the Intelligent-conference tabletop with the knuckles of his tightly clenched fist. "Alright people, let's just stay focused on what we know," ordered Newey, bringing the group back to the central topic. He surveyed the group again, "Okay, now Professor Watkinski, what about this biomechanoid? The thing in the lab, what is it?"

"Well, Lync is still working on the data," he looked up the table at Eastman, "but based on what this preliminary report appears to be saying, I think we've discovered something incredibly fascinating."

"That part I already figured out, Professor." Newey's voice rang with sarcasm as he looked to Colonel Rozsa. He fought the urge to explode at the frustration he was feeling toward the group of scientists.

Watkinski ignored the general's remark and continued, "Our large friend in the lab is not dead, or at least what we would consider dead."

Eastman glanced up at Watkinski and noticed Newey looking at her. Their eyes met, and she instantly sensed his apprehension.

"Is there brain activity?" asked Newey.

Watkinski looked to McGilmer, and the small woman began. "Physically it is undifferentiated, meaning that it does not have distinct internal organs. There is nothing that looks like muscle or tendons or anything that could be a heart or brain or bones---"

"Wait a minute," Eastman stepped in, "I saw that it has arms and legs and features on its head that---"

"There is absolutely no difference between a structure that looks like an eye and a structure that looks like a finger," McGilmer paused at the sudden groan emitted by Colonel Rozsa, who was watching her intensely. "Its cellular structure is like a spider's web, in the shape of..." her voice broke off into silence.

"On a molecular level," started Professor Watkinski, "It is unbelievably intricate and a true work of art. A number of the molecular bonds are a unique type called Agostic interaction. There are internal, caged molecules that appear to function almost like some kind of pseudo-nucleotide sequence. They are linked together in ways that are very reminiscent of hyper-complex organic hydrocarbons, with very flexible bonding angles."

Rocking forward in her seat, Professor Costello added, "The molecular units seem to behave like a quasi-genetic sequence."

Watkinski looked to Costello for approval as he continued, "Jira, please correct me if I am wrong, but the genetic sequence, if you what to call it that, is composed of four strands."

Costello leaned in again and entered a command into the Intelligent-tabletop, and the holograms of the geologic columns were replaced by an image of a strange nucleotide sequence. In a tightly packed mass of intertwining molecules, the whole structure resembled nothing more than the capital Greek letter Sigma with two-inverted capital A's, connected at the top and base. The whole bizarre structure was extended in three dimensions. "The strands of this pseudo-genetic sequence are composed of ten building blocks that are very different from any known nucleotide sequence. As you know, all earth-based life has a DNA built with four nucleotides constructed around two strands in a double helix. Europian based life, like the fish species, Ponto-Carliodus Saganai, has two strands of DNA constructed of six nucleotides."

"I think this thing is a truly engineered organism." Watkinski paused to look around the table. He only saw growing confusion on the faces of his colleagues. "The DNA material is uniform throughout its system. It forms larger structures similar to cells. However, the gross functions of these," he paused, looking for better terminology, "*synthetic* cellular structures are more like some type of highly advanced nanites." He called up a new hologram and flipped it to the center projector of the table, replacing the DNA image.

Newey closed his eyes and with an annoyed shake of his head growled, "Meaning?"

"Meaning, that it is able to repair, adapt, or replace any of its gross structural features, almost like enhanced stem-cells." Watkinski paused to survey the faces at the table, "On a macro scale, I would not be surprised if we were to cut it in half, we didn't end up with two smaller versions of the same creature." He let that sink in before continuing, "Now, based on what we can understand so far, those advanced nanites can manufacture and repair any part of the thing on a molecular level. However, it can do it with an efficiency on the order of around three hundred percent."

"Now let's forget for a moment that I have two master's degrees in engineering and construction management, and am a Lieutenant General in the UESA with forty plus years of experience dealing with weird dogshit here in the outer solar system." Newey's voice stank of sarcasm with a hint of irritation, "Explain this to me as if I were an expert in twentieth-century graphic illustrations." Newey's attention was fully focused on Watkinski. "And please speak slowly, and use small words."

"Yeah," added Rozsa, her concentration split between the general and Watkinski.

Professor Watkinski half smiled, "Its cellular units, if you want to call them that, behave in a manner very similar to the way our NER, MMR, BER function."

"What are they?" asked Newey obviously growing annoyed at Watkinski.

"Sorry. NER, Nucleotide Excision Repair; MMR, Mismatch Repair; BER, Base Excision Repair, together they act like molecular Marbs, basically keeping our DNA from degrading. Now, and this is a Lync generated conclusion, these cellular structures have a sort of collective intelligence that allows them to rewrite important sections of their own DNA sequences, similar to the way an autonomous AI can rewrite sections of its own operating system to cope with unplanned situations."

Everyone just glanced around dumbfounded, not believing what he or she was hearing.

"The nanites that make up its system are on the order of twenty-four nanometers. The Denver virus, which is the smallest known circovirus, measures only fourteen nanometers across."

Everyone shifted uncomfortably at the mention of the Denver virus. They all knew about the highly infectious agent, a few first-hand. It had done to sections of Venus and Mars what Smallpox and Bubonic plague had done to medieval Earth but in an eighth of the time. The Denver virus was one of the deadliest pneumonic super pathogens ever to burn its way through humanity.

"The gross structure of the fluid in its body is similar to that of quantum-Teflon, but with some very unusual electromagnetic properties. The closest substance I've seen that behaves like it is a superfluid, like an ultra-cold, fermionic gas at a temperature of about point two nanokelvin," concluded Watkinski.

"If this thing actually turns out to be alive, it will add a whole other biochemical tree to the Szostak-Talkingwaters-Oglesby Arboreal model of life." Costello smiled, knowing that if she and McGilmer could work out this little evolutionary puzzle, their professional futures were made. Assuming, of course, someone on Professor Vance's team had not already solved it first.

"If it is alive," Yee adjusted himself and mentally made a note to brush up on his low-temperature quantum biophysics. "How does it process energy? How does it consume raw materials?"

Costello jumped in as Lync announced a Titanquake, but no one in the room felt it. "The initial indications are that its systems can absorb a wide spectrum of electromagnetic energy. Also, it is able to breakdown or tear apart most molecular bonds. They can reassemble them and make copies of itself."

"Make new nanites?" questioned Rozsa.

"Yes," responded Costello, her green eyes surveying the group at the table. "Very---"

Newey cut her off with an upheld palm and addressed Professor McGilmer, "Any chance of these nanites infecting us?"

"Not likely." injected Watkinski, stopping McGilmer's reply. He glanced around the table looking for professional support and finding it on the faces of Eastman, Costello, and even McGilmer. "Lync predicts a one in eleven point two quintillion chance of infection."

"The fluid and tissue samples we collected," informed Costello, "seemed to go dormant once separated from the host by more than a meter or so."

"Dormant?" queried Eastman.

"Like I said before, the thing's not dead." There was another long pause filled with more silent exchanges of confused looks. Finally, Costello added, "We know this is hard to understand, but based on what we think we know, this thing is a machine constructed using the guidelines of a biological organism."

Professor Watkinski followed up on Costello's comment. "It is also equally valid to say it was some kind of biological organism, whose biochemical evolution closely resembles that of a molecular machine."

There were several irritated grumbles from around the Intelligent-conference table, but no one openly voiced an opinion.

"Based on all the science we know," Watkinski slowly shook his head, "either possibility is valid."

The general flashed a concerned expression and added, "Any chance of bacteriological or viral contamination?"

"We have detected four bacteria strains and nine viruses," answered Professor Costello with a smirk. That little exchanged suddenly produced a similar grin on the faces of McGilmer and Watkinski. "All of which are of known type, and the most serious of which is the Type B Crowlius Coronavirus. Commonly known as, the Crowley's Cold virus," they all knew from experience that, even with the most advanced decontamination methods available, numerous common bacteria spores and viral agents were lying dormant inside their sealed electronic equipment, and mountains of supplies and provisions, just waiting for a warm body to come along.

The general looked physically relieved at her answer, "I like that, but keep an eye on it please." Newey turned his attention back to Watkinski, "Kostya, what else can you tell me about this thing?"

"Well, Vance and his team found several of these inside the craft, inside some type of cryo-chamber. The one we bought back was the result of their first attempt to revive one of them." Professor Watkinski paused a second as he took in the faces of the group, then he added, "Apparently they were preserved in a perfect vacuum and at zero Kelvin, no molecular motion whatsoever." He paused again, looking to Colonel Rozsa, waiting for a comment, but none was coming. "That is why it shattered when the Colonel's team tried to remove it from its container."

"How many are still on the craft?" Rozsa wanted to know.

"Thirteen others," responded Newey, drawing looks from the others at the table. "What else do we know about this thing?" The general settled back in his seat and ignored the looks he was still getting from around the table. "Did the TBK crew figure out where the craft originated?"

"No," Professor Yee straightened himself and leaned forward, "but Vance and his team believed, based on what little they could figure out, that this thing was probably from a level seven or eight civilization on the Cormier-Arlin scale."

"Excuse me, but I don't know that scale?" interjected Professor McGilmer.

"It's a theoretical comparison scale for civilizations," Professor Eastman still eyeing the general with suspicion.

Yee continued to answer the question, "It was developed in the early twenty-fourth century after intelligent signals were detected originating from outside our solar system. The scale has been modified since then. On the Cormier-Arlin scale, the ancient Mesopotamian societies would be about a level one. Eighteenth-century European societies would have been a level two; late twenty-first century Japan or India would have been about a level three. We live in about a level five society now."

"What is the highest ranking?" Newey inquired, scanning the faces of both Yee and Eastman.

"Level twelve," Eastman answered coldly. She sensed the concern in the general's voice. "A level twelve society would have the ability to manipulate time and space on a sub-quantum level, have nearly instantaneous transportation capabilities and have the power to slip dimensional bonds and visit other parts of the multiverse. Basically, they would have the ability to play what most societies would consider a true deity."

"And these guys are from a level seven or eight society?" the tone of the general's voice spoke volumes more than just his words.

Yee nodded, "Yes. A level eight civilization can travel at high multiples of light speed without worrying about time dilation effects, construct Dyson spheres, and bio-form whole planets for colonization."

"Wonderful," spat McGilmer.

"I have a question," interrupted Eastman. "Why didn't their comrades come looking for them?"

There was a moment of silence, then Yee answered, "Maybe they did come looking for their friends. Maybe they saw the conditions of the inner solar system at the time, and didn't find any signs of their exploration, and declared it a loss and moved on to the next system?"

There was no reply, and everyone just scanned their neighbor at the table until Eastman nodded her approval.

Professor McGilmer, considering in turn, each person at the table, added, "So what are we going to do about it?"

"What do you mean?" Costello stared hard at her coworker.

"What I mean is, our friend out there," began the professor, pointing at the office door, "is slowly, but steadily re-assembling itself like someone hit the '*solve all*' icon on a jigsaw puzzle." She stared at Newey.

"For the moment, nothing," General Newey's voice was flat and devoid of emotion.

"I agree." Watkinski fell back in his chair, obviously relieved. "This is history in the making."

"General, you've gotta be joking," exclaimed Eastman. Everyone, except Watkinski and Rozsa, where taken aback by Eastman's tone. "This thing is dangerous!"

"I'd like to point out that most of this is just speculation on the part of Lync." Watkinski tapped the Intelligent-conference table with the fingers of his left hand. "Vance's people studied this thing and its craft for essentially a year. The answers are locked up in Lync's secure servers."

"Yes, all we have to go on is this preliminary report and a few dozen vid-reports on some dataclips. I don't think we have enough information to take action. So, for the moment we wait," the general, sized up the surrounding faces. "We'll transmit a report to the OSC and wait until their experts give us some direction."

"General, I believe I am qualified to work on this," informed Professor Watkinski, "this is why I was assigned here, remember?"

"Why exactly are you guys here in the first place?" inquired McGilmer, voicing a question that had been floating around Titan-Base Lincoln since General Newey and his people arrived.

Newey did not answer Professor McGilmer's question immediately. He just surveyed the expressions of Professor Eastman, Colonel Rozsa, and Professor Watkinski. "I am here to help in the relocation of the extrasolar craft to a more controllable facility. The Colonel is here to assist me. Professor Watkinski---"

"I am to oversee biological containment and environmental protection," blurted Watkinski, cutting off the general.

"What about Fung, Wong, Al-Yuzwaki, Zuverink, Tan, Brauer, and Lebowitz?" inquired Professor Costello, very suspicious.

"They're young, bright, and capable. Given an opportunity like this, they won't question orders too much." The general explained, eyeing Professor Eastman. "The staff that was left in place, which includes all of you, are here because you were the best people available. You know Titan; you know T-One, you know TBK, and you all have experience." Newey's eyes quickly swept the faces of the group and returned to Eastman, "For instance, Major Nianta is familiar with our most advanced spacecraft. His expertise as a pilot may prove necessary."

"So what are you experts going to do?" The tone of Eastman's question was an obvious challenge to the general.

"This situation is beyond anything that was foreseen," Newey quickly glanced at Rozsa then back to Eastman. "Right now we are going to go on the assumption that this thing is not an immediate threat, but---"

"I think we should let it thaw itself out and re-assemble," Watkinski's face was morphing into a mask of anger, his voice ringing an octave higher, "If it regains consciousness, we could learn so much about it."

"If this thing were to wake up, we don't even know how to communicate with it," added Eastman.

"Do you think we can communicate with it?" Newey directed his question to Watkinski.

The redheaded professor shrugged. "That might be a question you might want to ask your AI and communications people."

"Do we know if the TBK guys figured out a language translation matrix for these beings?" asked Costello, "Assuming they have a language we could understand."

There was a quick round of blank stares. No one had gotten that far into Lync's report to answer that question.

"Lync," called Newey to the room ceiling. "Are there any indications that the TBK team translated the EBE's language?"

The station's main AI's reply was swift. "Yes, however, based on the data I have at hand, Professor Vance's team was able at best to translate one word in ten."

"Lync, do you have access to any of TBK's work on the translation matrix?" asked Eastman.

"Yes," came back the disembodied AI. "Professor Verdibello's laboratory notes were among the data retrieved by Colonel Rozsa."

Eastman and several others at the table pictured Professor Yanina Verdibello with her constant smile, bright green eyes, and two hundred and one-centimeter stature. She was one of the tallest and smartest women Eastman knew. It saddened her deeply to see that an image of the woman's frozen body was among the thousands of images collected by Colonel Rozsa and her team.

"Lync begin constructing a translation matrices based off of Professor Verdibello's notes," commanded Newey.

"Yes, General."

"We are making an assumption that it wants to talk?" Eastman looked to Watkinski and Newey for an answer, a hint of distaste in her eyes. "I think it is a bad idea to let this thing wake up. At least, not until we get some idea as to what it may do once it is awake."

"I don't agree," voiced Costello, staring down Eastman. Each could feel the other's eyes burning into them like hot knives. "I think a lot could be gained by letting it recover, especially if you want to know if it is a threat."

Professor McGilmer asked, in a harsh voice, "What if this thing wakes up and wants out?"

Professor Watkinski adjusted himself in his seat. "Given what we know about its physiology already, I don't think we could stop it."

"And that is the exact reason, we should stop it from re-assembling," blurted Eastman.

There was a long silence, as everyone took stock of their neighbor's face and the level of growing concern that was spreading around the table.

"Why not just keep it frozen and---" Yee was cut off.

Several others started to interject, talking over one another with a growing level of animosity, which only served to underscore the level of divisiveness spreading through the group. Only Colonel Rozsa remained quiet. She just continued to read her holo-screen without comment.

"People! Please!" the general cut everyone off. "I need to hear from each of you if we are all to get through this in one piece. Now, Professor Yee, you were about to say?"

"What about keeping it frozen," he met the look from Watkinski. "At least until we get directions from the UESA." Watkinski pushed the holo-image away from him in anger as Yee continued, "I personally believe the labs available on Mars or the lunar surface would be far better equipped for this type of study."

"We can't stop it," Watkinski fired, "We can't generate temperatures in the bio labs low enough to stop it from re-assembling. We can only slow it."

"We could remove several of its larger pieces," suggested Yee

Watkinski just stared at Yee a moment, then shot, "That is the dumbest thing you've said!"

Yee popped up out of his seat. "Fuck you!" he screamed at his colleague as all the scientists at the table began shouting at one another again.

Newey slammed his palm against the table with a boom and the room when silent. "Until I get some firm instructions from the OSC or the UESA," Newey growled, "It's hands off! We'll keep its temperature as low as possible, but we are not going to remove any pieces or inhibit its reassembly in any way until we are ordered too."

There was a long moment of silence as everyone waited for someone to challenge the general, but no one did.

Professor McGilmer raised a hand as if she were back in school. "Excuse me General, but what if our visitor does pull itself back together, and decides to take a walk. What do you propose we do, assuming that it doesn't like the décor of our lovely home?"

Everyone was already staring coldly at Newey.

"If this thing does fully re-assemble itself, how long do you think it'll be before it wakes up?" It was clear by the tone of his voice that Newey was holding back his anger with great effort.

"Assuming it does wake up."

Watkinski, Costello, and McGilmer all shrugged in unison. Watkinski finally added, "I guess it depends on its nanites?" He activated another holo-screen and began typing in a series of commands. A second later, a three-dimensional color graph appeared and began to rotate. "Well, Lync predicts anywhere from two and a half hours to three-point two-seven weeks."

"That's fucking helpful," spat Eastman.

"If this thing wakes up, is it going to recognize us as intelligent beings or is it going to try and complete its mission?" inquired Rozsa, surveying the professors at the table.

Professor Watkinski stared hard at General Newey before answering the colonel's question. "It is from an advanced civilization. Of course, it will recognize us as fellow sentient beings."

"If it was willing to destroy all life on Earth two hundred and fifty million years ago," began Eastman cautiously, "I don't think sentient beings are a concern for it. Earth was littered with self-aware creatures back then."

"Yeah," snickered Watkinski, "with the intelligence somewhere between a chicken and a house cat."

Before Eastman could respond, Newey stopped her with an upraised hand, "I think you all should continue your research and continue to build a useful database from the information already collected." The general quickly scanned the group and settled his gaze on Eastman. "However, let me say this again. No one is to touch the extrasolar lifeform, biomechanical device, whatever you want to call it, without direct authorization from me, in person. Clear?"

No one replied.

"If our guest gets up, which I doubt, we'll have to be ready for it," Newey paused. "We'll have Lync monitor it around the clock, and try to narrow down that prediction. If we see any indications that it's regaining consciousness, we'll take some kind of action."

"What kind of action?" Echoed both Watkinski and Eastman simultaneously, their voices heavy with suspicion.

Newey ignored the two professors. "In the meantime, we'll stay alert and take some precautions, just to be safe. For now, I want everyone to get some sleep," he was mostly referring to himself. "And again, until further notice, no one is to touch that thing."

There was silence and disheartened glances from the group.

"Lori, you and Kostya setup the protocols for a monitoring program with Lync. If no one has any more questions or comments, you are dismissed. Colonel, I need to speak with you."

Each member of the group deactivated their holo-screens and stood up in unison, and filed out of the office chatting politely with each other, but with vigor. Costello surveyed the general and Rozsa a moment then moved out. Colonel Rozsa remained behind.

After the door closed, Rozsa looked at Newey, "Do you really think that thing is going to wake up?"

Newey exploded at the colonel like a mother catching her three-year-old playing with a running power-saw, "What the fuck were you thinking?" He moved to stand less than a meter from the shocked colonel's face. "Why the hell didn't you wait for instructions before bringing that thing back?"

"You know damn well we were on a short count out there!" Taken aback by the general's hostility, Rozsa yelled back and did not give a centimeter of ground. "Communications were spotty at best, and we were out there burning consumables like twentieth-century America. I didn't know," the angry colonel began counting off on her fingers as Newey moved to his desk, "if the skiff was going to fly again. I didn't know if that fucked up weather was going to get any worse. You said you wanted as much info as possible, *'I want hard facts when I explain this mess to the OSC,'* these were your exact words!"

Rozsa followed Newey to his desk and continued, "We know a dogshit-load more now than we knew when this mess started, and---" the colonel's face was turning red and bright pink.

"Granted," Newey cut her off as he produced half a cigar from his top desk drawer, "but you went too fucking far. You sure as hell shouldn't have brought back that thing without my direct orders."

Rozsa went to speak but was stopped again by the general as he lit his cigar. "LaRocque informed you that the transmission was a fucking warning of some kind, and both Professor Yee and Major Singleton---"

"Yeah, but---"

The general put up a hand to silence the colonel. "Commissioner Marshall is re-tasking the Taj and the Onakea," He inhaled deeply from his cigar and blew out a plume of gray smoke. "He's sending them out here. Both ships can be outfitted with nuclear delivery systems within a week, and be out here in a month."

"Sir, I honestly doubt that they---"

"I have a message from a senior UGE senator, which I can't answer because it wasn't coded with the correct prefix."

"Let me guess," the colonel closed her eyes and appeared to ready herself, "Senator Robinson, chair of the UESA oversight committee?"

With a grin, the general produced a whole cigar from his desk drawer and held it up for the colonel.

She declined.

"She'll contact Marshall, and he'll handle her."

"I agree," Newey's expression told Rozsa that it was the end of her protests. "But the thing is, how are we going to keep this ball of dogshit from blowing up in our faces?" the general produced a new cloud of smoke from the cigar.

"First, keep this thing from coming together for as long as possible," Rozsa understood that the general had vented his anger and was now back to handling business. "Second, send a team out to the craft and investigate the incident that led to T-One's destruction."

"Yes," The general got up and started pacing around the room, rubbing the back of his neck. "But I am going to wait on sending a team to the T-One drill site. We don't know how many people T-One lost out there. I am not going to send anyone out there until Marshall or someone above him orders me too."

"I would at least have a team in place," added Rozsa calmly. "Odds are fifty-fifty they want us to at least dispatch a recon party. Get some fresh up close and personal data on the site."

"Okay, we put a team on standby," Newey moved to a cabinet, retrieved a bottle of America's Finest Straight Bourbon, and grabbed two glasses. "But given what's happened, we might get access to the T-One data that's on our servers." Newey, talking around the smoldering cigar, poured himself and the colonel three fingers worth of the amber liquid. "You ever hear of the Devil in the Dark scenario?" He quickly flicked the column of growing gray cinders into the ashtray on his desk and repositioned the cigar in his mouth.

Taking the glass of bourbon, the colonel's complexion turned a shade paler. "Yeah, but that's only a theory."

"Gravity is a theory, evolution is a theory, light is a theory," Newey took a swallow from his glass and poured another. "This is a hypothesis."

"But super powerful aliens, knocking off---"

"What do we have here, Colonel?" The sarcasm hung in the air like the pale smoke of his cigar. "An EBE from a highly advanced civilization, which may have been responsible for changing the course of evolution in our solar system." As he walked over to the wall, the smoke trailed after him like a ghostly amoeba. He stared blindly at the picture of the earth and moon until an image of Mars and one of its orbital stations replaced it. "I've been working out here among Jupiter and Saturn too long and seen too much." Newey turned to Rozsa, and both stared restlessly at one another for a full minute, as the general puffed away on his shrinking cigar.

"Assuming that---"

Newey interrupted the colonel by activating his forearm PDI and calling for Captain Arroyo. There was no reply, but just as the general was about to signal the captain again, Arroyo's voice came through in a slow dry, sleep-laden tone.

Newey tapped the device. "Captain, sorry to have to wake you, but I have a special assignment for you."

"What is it, sir?" From the sound of Arroyo's accented voice, he was suddenly very awake.

Staring at Rozsa, the general pronounced, "I need something we can defend ourselves with, in case we have a problem with our guest."

"Sir, do you mean weapons?" Arroyo's calm, but surprised voice boomed out of the tiny speaker.

"Yes."

"What kind of weapons?"

The ease at which Arroyo took the news bothered Newey on a subconscious level. "I just want you to put together a safety net for us. Use whatever you need to, but don't cause a panic by talking about weapons. Oh, and Captain, I would like something useable in about three hours." The general deactivated the unit, cutting off Arroyo's reply.

"General Newey," began Lync's disembodied voice.

"Yes, Lync," the general and Colonel Rozsa both knew what the AI was going to say before it spoke. "The manufacturing of weapons by OSC personnel is strictly prohibited by law. It is in direct violation of the UESA charter, and the---"

"Lync, as a Lieutenant General in the Outer Systems Command, I am invoking emergency Security Forces act number eighty-one. Authorize voiceprint; Newey, Richard D. Rank, Lieutenant General, position, Commander Titan Base Lincoln, Saturn System. Authorization code; September Two-Nine, Alpha, Brooklyn, Jillian. Confirm?"

There was a pause that immediately drew the attention of both officers in the room. The AI rarely paused. After what seemed like a whole minute, Lync replied, "Confirmed, awaiting secondary access code."

Newey looked at Rozsa.

She downed the remainder of her drink in one large swallow. Grimacing, she cleared her throat and pronounced, "Authorize voiceprint; Rozsa, Karen R. Rank, Colonel, position, executive officer Titan-Base Lincoln, Saturn System. Authorization code; February one-eight, Whiskey, Reagan, Hypatia. Confirm?"

"Second access code confirmed."

"Lync, remove security restrictions on manufacturing and production units for Captain Arroyo, and inform him," ordered the general with a smirk.

"I will comply," was all the AI offered.

Neither the general nor Colonel Rozsa spoke for a few minutes. Rozsa poured herself another large glass of bourbon and waited for Newey to say something. When it did not look like the general was going to speak, she did. "Sir, do you think Arroyo should be the one making weapons?"

"I know, but he is the senior engineer," moving back to his desk, he finished off his drink and poured another. "Until Reierstadt declares him unfit, he's in charge of engineering."

Rozsa went quiet.

"With the temp as close to absolute zero as we can get it, Lync predicts that this thing could take up to two weeks to re-assemble itself. After that, we don't know how long it will take to regain consciousness, assuming it does ever wake up." The general rubbed the back of his neck again, and stared at Rozsa a long second. "We'll set up an around-the-clock watch schedule." He indicated the office door. "I don't want any of our very educated friends there, alone with it. Only uniform personnel, make sure that they all have had the SF's VR-weapons training. Put us in the rotation too."

"What about Tan and Reierstadt, and the medtecs?"

Newey blew out another long, large, quiet plume of smoke from his nostrils as he again contemplated Rozsa's question. "Yeah, I don't think anything is going to happen too soon. For now, put Lebowitz on first and have Reierstadt relieve her in four hours." He chewed the end of his cigar. Newey's PDI beeped for his attention, and he tapped the device. It was a direct interlink communication from the com-center, "Yeah?"

"General, this is Sloan," began the young man's voice over the device's tiny display. "I just detected something odd."

Newey pulled the cigar from his mouth, "What?"

"Well, sir, it appears Lync transmitted an encrypted message." Sloan's voice sounded strange, and he looked unsettled to Newey. His Venusianized, neo-central European accent was timid. "The transmission was sent out through the high-gain antenna, then routed through the EET's main AI."

Newey peered over at Rozsa, not surprised, "It's okay, Lieutenant."

"Yes sir," there was an uneasy pause. "It was a bit strange since we are still in comms blackout, and nothing was scheduled, and no notification was made."

"It's okay Lieutenant," Newey deactivated his PDI. "Lync just informed the OSC and the SF that I have invoked eighty-one. They'll know something is wrong."

"Yeah," coughed the colonel, looking back at the general's old bearded and worn face, "Something that requires us to be armed."

The two officers continued to stare at one another in silence.

# CHAPTER TWELVE

Doctor Tan stood in the doorway of Major Nianta's quarters, her long, thick black hair draped over her shoulders, flattering her smiling, but tired face. "You busy?" she asked in a tone that suggested anxiety as she strolled into the major's quarters uninvited, the hydraulic door sliding shut behind her with a hum.

Everyone's quarters were built around the same floorplan, only the layout and number of rooms varied. Major Colin Nianta, being an officer had a wide living room-office area, a large lavatory with a spacious shower, and a large bedroom with a huge bed and walk-in closet. The smart-walls were the same blue-gray neo-plastic composite as else were on the station. Numerous embedded picture blocks and a few modern acrylic art paintings spotted the living area. Several reproductions of ancient oil canvases from impressionist artists from the nineteenth and early twentieth-century hung on the walls like real antiques in a museum.

"A little," replied Nianta, seated at a small smart-topped desk equipped with a holo-monitor. Next to him sat a compartmentalized plastic tray dirtied by the remains of a meal. Soft music was playing in the background. Sizing up Doctor Tan as she moved into the room, Nianta instantly could tell something was wrong. He flashed a smile and added, "What's going on?"

"Are you kidding me," she scoffed, "I'm supposed to be resting, but I can't sleep. All I keep doing is thinking about that thing in the lab. What are you doing?"

"The Colonel wants me to put together a recon mission

out to the T-One drill site," he tapped a few commands into his holo-screen and shoved two images off the page he was working on. "Want to come along; I'll need to bring someone from medical?"

Tan slowly wandered up behind Nianta as he sat at his desk. "How long are you planning to be out there?" She grabbed him and began to firmly massage his broad shoulders. The man's strong muscles were tight.

"Depending on the conditions," he uttered, the massage felt good. "Two to four days."

"When are you leaving?"

The man closed his eyes. "Whenever I get the word," he took his hands off his desk and let his arms hang down by his sides. He could smell Tan's perfume, enhanced by her own body chemistry.

Noting the tray on the major's desk, Tan inquired, "What did you eat?"

Nianta grinned with his eyes still shut. "The autochef says it was pan-fried lionfish, over lemon-flavor grits with a side of asparagus."

"Sounds good."

"I think the autochef needs to be checked," The major's voice was laced with pleasure. Tan's kneading of his shoulders and neck was slowly guiding Nianta towards nirvana. "I think the fish tasted more like muskrat." The music changed to some popular piece from a couple of decades ago.

There was a minute or so of Nianta softly moaning with pleasure as the doctor continued to loosen his stiff neck and back muscles, then Tan blurted, "You'll need to be careful." She was now working her thumbs into the muscles of his shoulder blades. "Have you seen the EBE yet?"

"Only Lync's reconstruction."

"Well, I've seen it with my own eyes," Tan could feel her level of anxiety spiking. "It's a fucking nightmare."

The major could feel Tan's anxiety as well. Even through his uniform shirt and undershirt, he could feel Tan's short, but sharp fingernails dig into him. It felt distractingly good, arousing him. "Hey, I think you could use a drink." He moved away from his desk chair and took her hand. It was soft, warm, and moist, just as usual.

"Make it a double," she added as she followed him to a center table in the room.

Nianta stared into her eyes a moment then moved to a small cabinet set in a wall of the main living area. He retrieved a bottle of single malt Mars Blue Scotch, and two short glasses. "After that explosion, I don't think we have much to worry about." He handed Tan a glass and poured her a drink, filling the glass to the brim with the inky fluid. "And the one Rozsa's group brought back is in pieces."

Tan sipped her drink, then said, "You don't know?"

Nianta tilted his head slightly. "Know what?"

"That, whatever it is, they brought back with them from T-One is re-assembling itself in bio lab-one like some fucked up, AI children's auto puzzle."

The major stared at Tan for half a minute then he tasted his drink and added, "I am assuming the Colonel and General Newey are aware of this?"

Tan took another long sip from her glass, twisting her face a little with the action. "General's orders, hands off for everyone."

Nianta could tell that this was what was upsetting Tan, and preventing her from resting. "If this thing puts itself back together, do you think it will wake up?"

All of a sudden, Tan appeared visibly distressed. "I don't know. We sealed it in a cryo-chamber and lowered the temp as low as the system would go."

The major studied her a moment. The woman he had come to love was afraid, tense, and tired. She obviously did not want to be alone and was too tense to sleep. He took a leap of faith and blurted out, "Do you want to sleep here tonight?"

Tan took a step back and looked the major up and down for a moment, then replied with an expression that Nianta could not translate, "No I don't want to sleep! I just want to be with you for a few hours and forget what I saw in the lab today!"

They both sat their drinks down on the table, and for a few seconds, they just stared at one another, transfixed, each revving themselves up for what they both knew was coming. Then they attacked.

It had been three, maybe four days since the last time they had enjoyed each other's carnal pleasures. In the first frenzy of the moment, they tore at one another, all the while moving towards

Nianta's bedroom. There was neither the need nor the desire for subtlety as the two of them peeled off each other's uniforms, leaving a trail of discarded clothing all the way to the bedroom.

Panting with uncontrolled passion, Nianta struggled to catch his own breath, not wanting to miss a single kiss, a single taste of her now sweaty body. He mumbled some erotic words of passion as Tan dug her fingernails into his back and bit his right ear. She was beyond words as she placed her hands behind his neck and pulled him down towards the bed, on top of her. Kissing him furiously, she whispered the only words her desire ravaged mind could muster, "Come on, you fucker." She bit the major's shoulder as he entered her with force, taking her breath away for an instant.

Doctor Tan rocked her hips back and forth as if fighting the writhing major on top of her. Nianta moved his hard bare buttocks, gleaming with sweat, rapidly and with force between Tan's equally sweaty legs. He undulated on her, gathering momentum, pushing himself deeper. The steady moaning of Tan and the grunts of Nianta were only drowned out by the wet thopping sound of sweaty muscular flesh on sweaty muscular flesh, and the three-hundred-year-old musical piece now playing in the background.

Suddenly without sign or words, Tan rolled Nianta off of her. She spun onto her belly and bounced up onto her knees, issuing a profanity-laced order to the major. He did not hear the doctor, but knew the move and mounted her from behind, grabbing her smooth, pale hips and thrusting. A moment later, the doctor was face down in a pillow, clawing at the bedding and whispering encouragement to the major. Their intellects were gone; their minds had defaulted to basic animal instincts. They moved and worked in united ecstasy.

Five minutes and the two changed positions again, pillows and blankets falling to the floor. Now Tan was on top of the major, riding him as if he were a two-wheeled motor machine navigating rough terrain. She whispered hot passionate words to him as he fastened his mouth around her right breast. They wrangled that way for minutes, each putting as much effort and momentum as physically possible into the act. Without warning, Nianta lifted Tan off of him and into the air. He dropped her down on the bed next to him, rolled back on top of her, and started again. He needed to release himself into her but needed her to release herself to him.

After ten more minutes of lovemaking, their movements were rhythmic and continuous. Their actions grew faster and faster until a moment of convulsion hit Tan, and her back arched and only her shoulders and heels pressed into the bed. Nianta felt her and could not hold himself. Grabbing her slick buttocks and grunting, he blurted an expletive, pulling her rigid form closer. For a moment, they squeezed one another, gasping for air as they released each other in a series of spasms of painful pleasure.

They collapsed and lay still for a long moment, then the major moved off the doctor, beads of sweat running down his dark back. Tan adjusted herself, pulled a thin blanket off the floor and over the both of them, and snuggled closer to Nianta. Again, one piece of music ended, and another began. This piece caught the major's attention. It was *Remo Giazotto's Adagio in G Minor for Strings and Organ*. He knew both the smart-bed and the station's AI understood what sex was and both were programmed to accommodate it. The smart-bed did what all smart-furniture does; make the person using it as comfortable as possible. Lync had made the room warmer, darker and the music more in tune with how they were performing the act itself. Nianta grinned to himself and started to order Lync to change the music when Tan commented how soothing it was.

He let it play.

Doctor Tan lay on her side with her legs intertwined with Nianta's. Studying his onyx face, she softly stroked the major's muscular arm. As the longing and mournful melody played, she noted the recent scratches and fingernail marks on the man's arm and chest. She hoped the bottle of dermal spray in the drawer of the nightstand was still useable. However, she knew it would not be the first time someone walked into the med-bay with cuts, scratches, and bruises from energetic sex.

They laid quietly for a minute, listening to the soft music. Nianta surveyed the naked woman next to him; his right arm half-covering her body, his hand resting on her moist, smooth inner thigh. "What do you think this all means?"

Tan was still taking in the contours of the man's black body. "I don't know, but I have a really bad feeling about this. We shouldn't let that thing re-assemble itself like that. Who knows what it could do. Maybe---"

"Have you spoken to Lori?"

"Yes, and until we get instructions, we are just going to have to mark time." Tan glanced at the large reproduction of a classic oil painting that was presented by one of the bedroom smart-walls. She had seen it many times since she had started visiting the major in his quarters. Given her mood and the music playing in the background, the painting caught her eye. It was a work by the twentieth-century artist Paul Cézanne entitled *Pyramid of Skulls*. "Why do you have that particular painting?" She pointed at the piece at the center of the smart-wall.

Nianta glanced at the painting, fighting and losing to keep the frown from his dark face. "I don't want to talk about art, I want to---"

"Come on," she sensed something. Nudging him, she pressed the question. "Out of all of the art that exists, why did you choose that ghastly thing?"

"My prints help remind me of my humanity." He pulled her closer to him, "for instance the Allen Freelon work next to my desk, the *Gloucester Coast*, reminds me that we cannot explore the wider ocean by standing on the rocky shores of home."

Tan caught Nianta's weak attempt at distraction. Her apprehension that sex had relieved started to creep back into her mind. "No, that one. Why that particular one?" she continued to point at the painting.

Nianta studied the dark image, a pile of three human skulls facing outward with a fourth in the background staring toward the sky. He did not verbalize his thoughts for several seconds, then he turned to Tan and offered. "It'll spoil the mood."

She frowned and pulled herself up to look into his eyes. "Tell me."

He stared into her soft brown eyes a second, then barked at her, not quite with anger. "That Cézanne reminds me that no matter what you do or how careful you are; death awaits us all."

Tan instantly pulled away, as an icy chill washed over her.

•　　•　　•

Captain Arroyo had only been asleep for less than an hour and a half when General Newey called him. It had taken him nearly that long for his restless mind to fall asleep. When he was asleep, his dreams were filled with the ghostly-burnt faces of long-dead coworkers and friends. Distorted images of his last skiff trip were clouded with the distant memories of the smoke and flames of the Sisyphus disaster. Through it, all was the overwhelming sensation of claustrophobia. To him, it felt like being buried alive in a small cramped box, deep within the humid darkness of warm damp earth.

After washing his face in cold water and downing two of the pills Doctor Reierstadt had prescribed, Arroyo acknowledged the message from Lync that informed him that he had unrestricted and unlimited use of the three-dimensional manufacturing equipment. It took Arroyo approximately one minute to realize what the AI's message meant. He immediately activated the large holo-monitor embedded in one of the smart-walls of his quarters.

Arroyo sat down on the edge of his smart-bed, "Lync, do you have any designs for weaponry?"

"No," came the machine's terse reply.

"Do you have images of weaponry?"

"What types of weaponry are you interested in seeing?"

Arroyo thought about the question a moment. All of the real weapons carried by individual members of the security forces or any of the civil militias were of the non-lethal type. The engineer, all of a sudden, realized that outside of knives and other cutting tools, there were very few lethal weapons in human society. The only deadly projectile weapons that anyone ever got a chance to use were in illegal VR-games. Simply possessing an illegal weapon was a mandatory PR (Personality Reconstruction) sentence. Unless, however, you were under twenty years of age, in which case you were looking at five years in a local Re-Ed facility. "Weapons that are the simplest and fastest to manufacture, that require little training to operate, and that are the most lethal," he finally answered.

"All weapons other than nuclear or particle-beam-based weapons fall into those categories," its North American Midwestern accent somehow becoming more pronounced.

"Weapons similar to the types used by the security forces in their lethal weapons VR-training scenarios. I want individually portable projectile or beam-based weaponry," stated Arroyo.

"Projectile or beam-based weaponry?"

The captain thought about the question a long moment, then said, "Start with real weapons that are depicted in VR-training scenarios, graphic vids, and illegal VR-games. Also, show me any historical vids where these weapons are used." Arroyo already knew that most of the vid that he would see would be from the Antarctican Resources War. The Resources War had been the last and bloodiest war in the long history of human warfare. The war along with its aftermath, commonly known as the Second Dark Ages was the last time lethal weapons were mass-produced by the human race. That last bloody gasp was a critical pivoting point in human history. The captain chuckled to himself as images of weapons began to appear on the smart-wall holo-screen. *Maybe we are at another turning point in human history*, he thought silently.

"I must warn you," Lync's fake voice hinting at concern. "Most of the images are extremely graphic."

The large man coughed out a single mocking laugh, "I've lived worse. Begin."

Scenes from ancient documentary vids began to move across the smart-wall, detailing the devastating weaponry used by men, women, and in some cases children, in combat situations from seven hundred years ago.

Twenty minutes into the ceaseless carnage and soulless narration and description by Lync, Captain Arroyo got up from the edge of his bed and poured himself a large, clear glass of Tequila. He had played illegal and graphically violent VR-games as a young man, but he understood that it was not real. However, the historical images he was now watching were real. Those were *real* people fighting, killing and dying. He didn't feel sick, but he did not feel wealth either.

Keeping an unhappy eye on the smart-wall, Arroyo downed his drink and poured another. Cursing under his breath, he looked away from the smart-wall as a woman and child were both turned into a faint cloud of dark pink mist, and shreds of flesh covered clothing by, what Lync described as a standard JPH twelve point seven-millimeter projectile fired by a Jones-CheyTac M-Seven-Hundred Spitfire mini-gun. Lync continued to describe the projectile as a nano-processor controlled, steering vanes equipped, projectile that was able to adjust its trajectory mid-flight in order to stay on target when the flight path had been altered by uncontrollable variables.

For nearly another hour, historical vids of people engaged in armed conflict assaulted Arroyo's senses. Helmet cam vids showed in horrific and gory detail what high velocity, metal projectiles could do to human flesh and bone. From the long-vanished jungles of Central Africa and South America to the blood-soaked, bomb-cratered concrete urban landscapes of North America and Europe; Captain Vincent Arroyo took notes on his PDI.

Arroyo tried very hard not to think of how much some of the scenes of burnt out structures, blood, torn flesh, and shattered bone reminded him of Sisyphus. He could almost smell the odor of cooking human flesh and hear the cries of agony from Sisyphus. Several times Arroyo winced and turned away from the scenes of bloody, close-quarters combat in the ice trenches of Antarctica, thinking to himself, *'What sick, perverted, morally corrupt belief system could con people into doing that to other people?'* After only four minutes of watching vid taken by snipers during a battle in the ruins of an Asian temple, Arroyo ordered Lync to turn off the smart-wall holo-screen.

Visibly shaken, Captain Arroyo went into the smart-bathroom and took several more pills. Coming out of the bathroom, he sat down at his desk and called up the controls to the molecular three-D printers down in the main machine shop, in the sub-engineering section. Manually entering commands, he gave the machine instructions to begin making weapons. He realized that he was probably the first human being in six hundred years to order the manufacturing of personal weaponry that was lethal.

He contacted Yoshida and Tounames, and after a quick conversation, he got dressed and headed down to the sub-engineering level. Once there, he met up with Yoshida and Tounames, and the three got to work on their assignment. In the dim sodium lights of the sub-engineering level, they soldered wires, cut pipes, welded metal, and retrofitted microelectronics as if they were preparing for a war.

•     •     •

Trauma-Specialist Lebowitz sat in the bio lab doing an AI-generated three-dimensional crossword puzzle. She had been writing a report, but had grown tired of the endless document, and turned to the puzzle for relaxation. She liked phonetic puzzles, especially ones with science or medicine as the main theme. The raven-haired medtec had done thirty of the words and definitions when she got stuck. She could not figure out the ten-letter word for a magical procedure by which the cause of a particular event or the future is determined. Finally, in frustration, she quit.

With boredom and loneliness beginning to take their toll on the young medtec, Lebowitz wandered around the lab in her protective suit for over an hour. She checked readouts and AI settings and slowly began to realize she was becoming hungry. Thoughts of *a plate of Cameroon style fried celery with a side dish of spicy cheese dipping sauce, and a bowl of capybara drisheen* began to drift around in her head like one of those holo-retina projected, talking advertisement-signs one encounters in a megaplex. She knew, however, it would be about another hour before she would be able to eat anything. Her duty shift still had a ways to go.

The bland-colored lab radiated isolation and timelessness, as she fought the feeling of being the only living thing in the universe. It dawned on her that she was paying more and more attention to the translucent canopy that shielded the remains of the extrasolar lifeform, situated on the laboratory's worktable. She was subtly glancing at it as she moved around the room, keeping an eye on it, and she did not know why. It was not as if the assemblage of strange parts, hidden in the trapped cloud of cold white gases within the sealed canopy was calling to her, but it was something. *Something is wrong? Something is different.* She thought to herself, as she looked closer at the worktable. Scanning it carefully with brown eyes that reflected both mental fatigue and curiosity, she did not discern anything out of place or abnormal. The holo-screen on the side of the table displayed various measurements of the exotic lifeform. Its temperature had risen to sixty-three point four Kelvin, and its radiation level was up to five thousand millisieverts, but the graph of its EM signature showed that its emissions in the gamma rays spectrum were decreasing. The canopy appeared secure, and nothing looked out of place. She moved closer still. "What the hell...?" bewildered at what she saw, Lebowitz stepped closer.

Through the dense fog inside the canopy, the startled medtec could just make out a white, fleshy, veiny membrane that covered the numerous broken fragments of the extrasolar biological entity. The thin covering of the EBE instantly reminded Lebowitz of raw tripe. Beneath the white membrane, the broken pieces of the extrasolar creature had apparently moved closer together. The spider web of veins that covered the membrane pulsed with opalescent colors.

She tapped out a series of commands on the table's holo-screen, twisted her face in disbelief and said, "Lync, please confirm. Report status of the specimen on worktable?"

The station's main AI responded in its usual cold monotone voice, "Five point eight percent rise in biochemical activity in the last sixty minutes, temperature risen fifteen point two degrees in the last sixty minutes, paired production of positrons up three point four percent in the last---"

"Thank you, stop report, and continue monitoring," Lebowitz turned with a start as her PDI beeped for attention. With her heart racing, she answered it.

"I'm just checking to see how things are going," Major Singleton's black face was a welcome and comforting sight to Lebowitz.

"Oh, things are great," she glanced back at the table. "Our new friend is putting himself back together, real quick," a chill ran down her spine as she momentarily saw the outline of its face through the veiny membrane and translucent canopy, "I'm expecting it to ask me for a beer and a blowjob any time now."

For an instant Singleton's tone was light as he replied, "Everyone likes a good B and B," then she saw the wave of concern sweep across his face on the PDI's tiny screen. "Are you sure?"

"Oh yeah," Lebowitz kept watching the worktable as she fell into a chair. "Man, I want to be out of here. This thing is beginning to give me the creeps."

"Does it show any signs of life?" concern had quickly become heavy in the major's accented voice.

Lebowitz could see and hear the level of Singleton's concern ratchet up. She replied with a forced grin, "No, and if it did I don't think I'd be staying around."

"It's been almost two days since we brought that thing back," there was more than a hint of anger in Singleton's voice. "I don't like the idea of that thing reassembling itself. But the only thing we can do is try to slow its progress."

"Well, it isn't working very well. Besides, look on the bright side, its things like this that make careers. You'll probably leave here a full Colonel, Major."

The image of the major turned, and there was the sound of talking in the background, then he turned back. "Yara, Captain Aamodt just came in to relieve me. Doc Stadts should be relieving you soon. Keep an eye on that thing, and be safe."

"Sleep tight," Lebowitz chuckled, knowing the situation.

Taking Singleton's place at the other end of the comlink, Aamodt appeared and added very warmly, "I think very few of us are sleeping knowing that thing is on the base."

Lebowitz grinned as Singleton said something to Aamodt, just out of reach of the omnidirectional microphone. She could not quite make it out, but she had a very good idea as to what it was, "Tell the Major we should all sleep together for safety." There was a burst of laughter from the other end of the PDI speaker as Lebowitz turned at the sound of the room door opening.

Doctor Reierstadt strolled in, clad in a protective suit that looked as if it did not quite fit her properly. As the two just stared at one another for a moment, Lebowitz noticed the digital notepad the doctor was carrying in one hand.

Reierstadt finally acknowledged the medtec with a wave as she moved into the room. The psychologist actually liked Trauma-Specialist Medtec First Class Yara Lebowitz. Lebowitz was another of *Newey's Newbies*. Reierstadt had taken note of how Lebowitz's toned body and firm breasts, which were just a little too large for her frame had caused a stir when she first arrived. The young, brown-eyed, Yemen-Arabian woman had caused some initial posturing by the younger male members of Titan-Base Lincoln. The psychologist also noticed how that changed as soon as they got to see her as a committed and determined colleague. Lebowitz was one of the most qualified medical professionals Reierstadt had ever met, especially for a twenty-three-year-old fresh out of Callisto's new Tornasuk College of Modern Medical Sciences.

"Doctor Reierstadt just arrived," announced Lebowitz. "I'm glad to get the hell out of here, besides I gotta piss like a camel."

"How's our visitor?" Reierstadt gestured toward the cold canopy with the notepad, as she moved to Lebowitz.

"Biochemical activity is up," the young medtec frowned as she looked back at the lab table, "So is radioactivity. I'm no physicist, but there is something weird about the emissions spectrum."

"Great. Leave Kostya and Jira a message about it, and if I were you, I'd copy the General and Lori." Reierstadt did not like the idea of being alone with the encapsulated thing on the table any more than the young medtec. Looking at it, she shook her head slowly, "I don't want to jinx Zuverink, but I hope this thing doesn't do anything on my watch."

"Zuverink?" blurted Lebowitz and Aamodt, simultaneously.

"I thought the General was next up?" inquired Aamodt's distant voice.

"She has a short watch after this," Reierstadt informed both Lebowitz and the disembodied Aamodt. "She's taking the first thirty minutes or so of the General's watch, while he checks out something or other."

Lebowitz got up from the seat as Reierstadt slipped in behind her. "Well, I'm going to get some food, take a shower, and get some sleep." She patted Reierstadt on the shoulder, "Lync is recording into main DSU seventeen. The lab's AI and automated data recorders are running in mode C and using secondary DSU fifty-one, eighty-eight."

"Hey Doc, if you need something, give me a buzz," Captain Aamodt added from the PDI.

"Will do Captain," Reierstadt surveyed the consoles and holo-screens and gave Lebowitz a thumbs-up sign, as the interlink channel on the PDI went dead.

"Good luck, Doc," a smirk was plastered across the young medtec's face as she moved to the doorway.

Reierstadt unhappily glanced back at Lebowitz and gave a faint wave as the lab door closed behind the departing medtec. As the notes of the working door hydraulics died away, the lab became painfully quiet. Except for the barely audible hum of the room's ventilation system, and the air processor unit of Reierstadt's own protective suit, the lab was as silent as a morgue.

The psychologist stared at the slowly turning clouds inside the canopy and the barely visible white skin-like material the fog was attempting to conceal. After a long moment, she sighed deeply and mumbled under her breath something about this not being in her job description. She then turned her attention to the electronic notepad. Reierstadt continued working on a report she had been writing regarding the current mental and emotional state of General Newey and Captain Arroyo.

Just as she was getting comfortable in her work, there was a series of muffled sounds like something heavy falling onto a thick-carpeted floor. The sound was followed almost immediately by Lync's monotone voice. "Unknown poly-telomeric structures detected in primary monitored specimen. Fluidic behavior is now in violation of the Stokes-Einstein relation."

Reierstadt turned around and scanned the canopied worktable and the lab, but everything was in order. The door was closed, and no one other than herself was in the room. Lync repeated its last statement and went silent.

The sound came again, faint but sharply irritating, like that of a metal fork being forcibly scraped across a slate walkway. However, this time the sound was long and drawn out, and Reierstadt froze.

It stopped, and its sudden absence caused Reierstadt's heart to skip a beat.

Fighting back panic, Reierstadt got up, and as slowly and as cautiously as a cat stalking a bird, she reluctantly crept toward the source of the noise. The worktable at the center of the lab seemed to be the only thing in the room. With her eyes ablaze and her hands trembling like a hardcore caffeine addict, she approached the cold, hi-tec sarcophagus.

Through the swirling mist beneath the canopy, she saw what was making the eerie sound.

# CHAPTER THIRTEEN

Captain Arroyo was talking vigorously as he and General Newey moved along a row in the sub-engineering level. Yoshida and Tounames followed the two men closely, as they weaved around massive machinery and passed occupied Marbs. Arroyo rambled on, bouncing from the technical problems associated with getting some piece of equipment back online, to Doctor Reierstadt's attitude towards him, to finding parts to finish his latest assignment. Newey just kept walking next to the man, listening quietly with an expression of subtle concern.

Sergeants Yoshida and Tounames, both still wearing dirty uniforms and sporting grimy toolbelts, said nothing. It was plain to anyone observing them, that the two non-commissioned officers were not at all pleased. They had been with Captain Arroyo the last few hours and had watched his mental state slowly grow more unsettled. They were both genuinely distressed and planned on bringing their concerns to the general as soon as possible. For now, they let Arroyo prove their case for them.

The four halted in front of what resembled a long narrow blockhouse, constructed of gray plastocrete. It looked out of place, sitting there surrounded by the vast array of pipes and machines of the sub-engineering level. It had an old-fashioned hinged metal door with the words: **Hazardous Material Holding Room # 16** stenciled on it, above several red, warning pictograms. Arroyo opened the door and led the way inside, still talking. Yoshida and Tounames grimaced at one another and followed Newey and

Arroyo into the small room.

The interior of the narrow room was not what the name on the door indicated. The drums, containers, and canisters of dangerous materials that were customarily stored there were gone. General Newey immediately recognized the two portioned stalls and tables as a firing line. The place had been transformed into a makeshift weapons testing range.

"Well, here they are sir," Arroyo indicated a number of familiar objects on the firing line. There were several larger devices on the gray plastocrete floor near the stall. "Given the fact that even though all of the OSC personnel have been through the Security Force's VR-Weapons training course, none of us has ever used a *real* weapon, let alone ever constructed one. Given that, this is the best we could do." The captain pointed over to one side of the room, past the two unhappy sergeants. "I looked at what worked best at killing, but was simple to operate and light-weight."

Next, to a short arc of black syntha-leather couches, three long racks were half filled with reproductions of ancient firearms. The weapons were of two types and dated from the late twenty-first and twenty-second centuries. Even though they looked like antiques, they were in actuality re-constructed and re-engineered replicas that used modern microelectronics and composite materials.

Yoshida went to interrupt Arroyo and Newey, but Tounames quickly grabbed him by the arm and motioned for him to stay calm. The man appeared on the verge of exploding.

"Show me your stuff," Newey looked down the firing range at the marked and numbered walls. The lines that ran along them gave the elongated room an appearance of greater length and more space than was actually the case. Barely visible along the striped walls were a newly installed array of micro-motion sensors and holo-emitters. Newey knew that the motion sensors were there to track projectiles as they travelled down the makeshift firing range in pursuit of targets generated by the holo-emitters.

Arroyo surveyed the five sleek, ancient looking, but heavily re-engineered shotguns and five handguns. He randomly selected one of the dark gray and black shotguns from the counter. He loaded a magazine full of shells into the weapon with such force it startled Newey. "We made the housing and most of the parts with the three-D printers. We basically redesigned and rebuilt the guts of the thing from scratch." He rotated the weapon around in his hands. "I kept the same outer design, but it functions more like a coilgun."

Newey's expression faded a bit as he looked over the weapons. "I was hoping for laser-based weapons."

"I would have liked to use the cutting and welding lasers, but the hand units are too small for me to do anything with, and the big, high energy plasma plate welding units are too heavy for one person to carry around the station." The captain cocked his head oddly, and added, "Unless you want to tune down the Harlem system a notch?"

Newey made a negative gesture with his head.

"Well, if we had more time, I'm sure we could put together some comparable to the EM phase weapons, like the ones you see in illegal VR space games."

Newey slapped a hand down on the man's shoulder with a grin. "It is what it is, Captain. Continue."

Arroyo smiled and continued. "There's no chemical propellant and a minimum of moving parts. It functions much better than the real thing. In case you don't recognize it, it's an ancient Jones-Benelli Magnastar Model AL-sixty coilgun. It dates from the mid-twenty-second century."

"I remember this one from VRG-Texas Hold Up." Newey had *virtually* used the weapon decades ago as a college student, playing a violent and illegal VR-game about lawlessness and random violence in the Dark Age's refugee slums of Southlake, Texas.

Arroyo worked the action of the weapon expelling an unused shell, "It works in both pump-action, single shot mode, and semi-automatic triple-action mode." The captain held up the heavy metal and composite weapon in one hand and passed a black metal coilgun projectile to the general for his inspection. "It fires an eight-point eight-nine millimeter, kinetic energy SIAP projectile."

"What's a SIAP projectile?" asked the general, slowly examining the huge dark slug. He would have preferred something like a laser pulse rifle. He had used and seen them in dozens of VR-games and sci-fi-action vids, but he was also intelligent enough to know that even a paperclip could be deadly if used properly.

"Standard issue all-purpose projectile. It is very similar to the AA-fourteen light armor piercing, anti-personnel projectile used in the Antarctican Resources War. However, our materials are better, but it's the same design used centuries ago. Ours has nickel alloy shear-away casings surrounding a boron carbide barbed slug. All powered down the barrel by a DeLuca ninety-nine micropulse-rated, homopolar generator with a hundred megajoule output." Arroyo paused with a psychotic grin, "The projectile itself is designed to shred a soft target and knock a hole in a hard one."

"So they'll fire out on the surface?" questioned the general, knowing the answer.

"Yeah, or in hard vacuum for that matter," Arroyo continued to smile, "and at three-meters, it'll take a camel's leg completely off at the hip."

"No dogshit?" marveled the general, sitting down the SIAP projectile, picking up one of the weapons, and examining it.

Arroyo shook his head, "No dogshit."

"Oh, by the way, sir," Tounames interjected, "all of this is extremely illegal. Are we cleared to do this?"

"We're good," Newey was still entranced with the weapon in his hand. Like everyone in the room, he had only held a firearm in VR.

"If it isn't," the proud captain waved his arm over his homemade arsenal, "This'll get us all life in a re-education facility if we're lucky and PR for sure if we are not."

"Yeah, or become a live art act in some theme park in Antarctica," Newey sat the weapon on the countertop. "Just how I wanted to spend my retirement, believing I am a live-artist named Monique Jergens from Bangassou, UNSA." The general flashed a grin at the memory of a young female officer under his command who had been convicted of poisoning her domestic partner. The woman had been sentenced to Personality Reconstruction. He later learned by accident, that she had been renamed Monique Jergens from the Unified Nation States of Africa, who was employed as a live art model at some theme park in Boehner, Antarctica.

Arroyo ran his hand along the cold, black death machine, "I doubled the original muzzle velocity to well over twenty-four hundred meters per second," he paused and glanced back at Yoshida and Tounames. "The only problem is that in semi-auto mode, the magnetic flux compressor overheats and causes a de-gaussing of the SCMs. So you only get a three projectile burst, then you have to wait two seconds for the system to re-initialize."

Arroyo fingered the safety and toggled the action switch to '*S*.' "Plus it has a standard laser-sight." He hit the small rubber nipple next to the trigger guard to activate the green sighting laser.

"Lync, activate sporting clays, multi-targets, single shooter," announced the grinning captain, "Now!"

Immediately a series of yellow and black circular targets appeared very near the group and rapidly moved away in several different directions. "Watch your ears," Arroyo commanded as he aimed the weapon down the range at the fleeing targets and fired. Upon leaving the barrel, the metal projectile produced a dull muzzle flash as its surface instantly became red-hot due to air friction. Even with the sound absorbent properties of the plastocrete walls, the hypersonic projectile ripping through the sound barrier echoed like the crack of a whip in an empty mansion.

Lync tracked the discharge from the weapon down the firing range, measuring its mass, velocity, trajectory, and rate of deceleration seventy-two thousand times a second, then it fragmented one of the holographic targets into a hundred tiny holographic bits. The projectile exploded on impact with the back wall, the kinetic energy of the small piece of nickel alloy and boron carbide blowing a *real* hole in the plastocrete the size of a North American watermelon.

"There is still some recoil, but it's nothing compared to what it should be," Arroyo calmly deactivated the targeting laser and toggled the action back over to '*A*.' He then proceeded to fire into the new targets down the range.

The Jones-Benelli Magnastar was no longer a single shot weapon. It produced an intermittent burst of metallic thunder and cobalt-blue lightning in groups of three, which immediately got everyone's full attention. In nine seconds, the captain had pumped all thirteen remaining rounds from the under-barrel magazine into and through the holographic targets. He only missed three.

"I guarantee if you hit somebody with this, they ain't getting up," he winked at the general with a sharp nod, as he fingered the weapon's safety and returned the killing machine to the countertop. Noting the damage to the far wall beyond the floating targets, Arroyo picked up one of the semi-automatic handguns, "We also reproduced these old Glock-Whelan L-seventy-seven slug-throwers." He released the ammunition clip from the butt of the black carbo-plastic weapon. The smooth, lightweight weapon was a replica of the standard issued sidearm for most of the combatants of the Antarctican Resources War.

"I've seen these in that VR-game that Lieutenant Sloan plays all the time."

Arroyo nodded an affirmative to the general. "It holds seventeen, nine-millimeter rounds in the magazine and one in the firing chamber." He slammed the magazine back into the semi-automatic pistol, chambered a projectile, and fired at the new target on the range.

The two rounds that exited the weapon from the single squeeze of the trigger did as much damage to the holographic target as the coilgun blast. "Yoshida used a gel-oxy, solid fuel propellant to give the ammunition a punch. They are basically the same type of rounds used in the Antarctican Resources War, except ours are a nickel-carbon alloy. The rounds have high penetration power, even after going through some intervening material, like say an e-suit. They'll expand on impact and cause extensive damage to a soft target." The captain tittered a sick, stomach-turning sound that was devoid of humor. "They are definitely one shot, one stop."

The general did not reply as he surveyed the spent handgun cartridges on the floor. What could he say? The captain had done precisely what he had been ordered to do.

Arroyo secured the handgun as Yoshida removed his fingers from his ears. He muttered something that only Tounames could hear, and the man smiled at his friend's comment.

"How many of these did you manufacture?" Newey asked.

Arroyo indicated the space behind the couches, "Six Glock-Whelans, and seven of the coilguns."

"What else did you come up with?" Newey had noticed the other objects that were not coil or handguns.

"Well, Tounames modified two of the portable ice-melters." Arroyo picked up a bulky rifle-like device with a long black pressurized gas-fuel cylinder secured in its frame. "He tightened the firing radius and increased the heat output, with the aid of some old-fashioned compressed butanol and hydrogen peroxide. It's up to about three thousand degrees, which makes them very dangerous in or out of the station." He stopped and looked hard at Newey, then added, "If we have to use any of these weapons inside the station, make damn sure you know what is behind your target. At the right range, any of these weapons can take out a wall or viewport. No one fires one of these," Arroyo indicated the ice-melter in his hands, "near or at a viewport. Even though the viewports are made of Thermo-Transplastic, they can't stand up to a three-thousand-degree temperature differential."

Arroyo moved the device in his big hands so the general could see some of its modified features. "And outside, because of the partial pressure of methane and the compressed hydrogen peroxide in the fuel, there is the possibility that they could ignite the atmosphere around the nozzle."

Newey snickered uncomfortably, "How much of an area?" He knew that if things got so out-of-hand that they had to use any of these weapons, igniting a few square meters of Titan's atmosphere would be the least of their problems.

"It depends on atmospheric conditions, half-meter up to ten meters." Arroyo motioned to the two sergeants, "I was going to have one of them test these things outside, later."

"Anything else?"

"Only this," Arroyo sat the ice-melter down and picked up what looked like a hollow metal tube with a molded handgrip and several other odds and ends added on to it.

"What is it?" The general had an idea but wanted to be sure.

"They used to be called recoilless rifles," answered the captain proudly. "This one is based on something called the Norinco-Phnom Four. It was an antitank weapon employed heavily by Chinese Coalition Forces during the Resources War." Arroyo suddenly stopped and surveyed the general. "Do you know what a *Tank* was, sir?"

Newey appeared put out by the question. "Yes, I know what a *tank* was, Captain."

"Good, cause I don't think you'd want to use them inside the station, but Yoshida whipped up a couple of rockets just in case. We also tinkered with a couple dozen seismic survey charges, turning them into small but powerful thermo-kinetic charges. Basically, we made thirty-five high yield hand-grenades."

Newey let out a slow whistle followed by a grin, "Very good. You weren't playing around."

"You didn't say play around, sir," Arroyo sounded too happy. "And you wanted insurance in case that *whatever-it-is* we brought back from TBK has friends?"

"Something like that," whispered the general.

Behind the general and Captain Arroyo, Yoshida whispered something in Japanese and Arroyo shot a hard eye at him. The captain had understood what the man had said and had not liked it.

"Captain!" Newey got Arroyo's attention back. "Let's save it for another time." The general activated his forearm PDI. "Attention everyone, attention," his voice poured out of the captain's and the two tech-sergeant's PDIs. "In groups of three, starting with Colonel Rozsa, and Majors Singleton and Nianta, and proceeding in descending rank order, I want all OSC personnel to report to the sub-engineering level, Hazardous Material Holding Room number sixteen for special instruction." He tapped a few other icons on his PDI and added, "Colonel Rozsa?"

This time the general's voice did not exit everyone's PDI.

"Sir," the colonel's image appeared on the small screen of Newey's PDI.

"I want our people to get familiar with our new weapons. Have everyone do some target practice. No less than one hour for everyone. Since we don't have a VR-training scenario, grab that VR-game of Sloan's and have them each play a few of the scenarios using similar firearms. Clear?"

"Yes, sir. I'm on it," was all Rozsa articulated before she and the general ended the conversation.

"Tounames! Yoshida!" boomed the general, "As the staff shows up, walk them through these. Distribute this stuff to our people. If any of the Frontier people show up, send them away, my orders."

"Yes sir," as all the two tech-sergeants replied in unison.

Newey turned to Arroyo, "Fine work, Captain, but now I need for you to get some rest."

The big captain shrugged, "Sir, I'm fine---"

"That's an order, Captain, no arguments." The general's voice rang heavy with authority as he shifted his glare back towards Tounames. "Sergeant, take this," he tossed the man the weapon he was holding. "Make sure we have enough ammunition."

"Yes, sir."

●　　　●　　　●

Doctor Reierstadt had been nervously watching the extrasolar entity in the bio-lab for hours. She had reported the changes to both Colonel Rozsa and General Newey, but she was merely told to continue to monitor it, and she would be relieved as soon as possible.

When Private-Specialist Zuverink, in her protective suit, walked into the lab unannounced, Reierstadt was both stunned and relieved. Zuverink had a workslate in her gloved hand, and one of Arroyo's new weapons in a holster strapped to her hip.

"Sasha, I'm glad you're here," Reierstadt looked as nervous as she sounded. "This thing is scaring the crap out of me." The doctor waved the younger woman over. Noting the sidearm attached to the private-specialist's leg, the psychologist's level of anxiety spiked. "What the fuck is that!" She indicated the weapon.

Zuverink slowly moved to join Reierstadt, "The General got authorization for us to have real weapons." The older woman cautiously moved away from both the approaching private-specialist and the thing on the worktable.

"Weapons? Where the fuck did weapons come from?" Reierstadt looked and sounded confused and frightened. "I wasn't told there were weapons on the station!"

"Whoa, Doc," Zuverink instantly slowed her approach and put up her hands to reassure the psychologist. "Calm down. It's all right, the General got authorization to have Capt'n Arroyo make them. It's all documented and good."

"You know how to use that?"

"Been playing violent VR-games since I was seventeen, been through the required security forces-urban combat training sim, but never touched a *real* weapon until about thirty minutes ago."

Reierstadt did not voice a response to the private-specialist.

"What's going on with our guest?" Zuverink answered her own question as she moved up to and peered through the gray-white fog inside of the canopy.

The pale membrane was tighter now, almost form-fitting the extrasolar entity, like a layer of melted cheese over the four-armed form. The vein pattern was pulsating with a rainbow of colors. Waves of luminous fluid were rippling back and forth along the veins, as if in slow motion.

"Did you inform anybody?" the private-specialist was still scanning the scene underneath the canopy.

Reierstadt exhaled. "Yeah, but the General just said don't interfere with it until he gets here." She seemed to relax a bit. "Professor Costello doesn't think it's going to wake up for at least another week."

Zuverink surveyed the cocooned body; she could just make out the limbs of the thing. It appeared to her that both legs and one arm had reattached themselves back to the torso, and the other arms and head were within centimeters of the torso. "Yeah, well that'll be way too soon for me," she retreated to a small table and sat the workslate down.

Reierstadt nodded behind her suit visor. "Good, you got other work. It will keep your mind busy and off our friend there."

"Well, I'm going to watch a vid first."

"I'd recommend a romantic comedy or a musical."

"Nope," Zuverink grinned, "Classic horror."

Reierstadt twitched and added, "You've got to be kidding?"

"Nope," Zuverink shook her head, "can you think of anything more appropriate?"

Reierstadt smirked as she walked over to the console and snatched up her workslate. Still grinning, she turned toward the door and spat coldly, "I think I'll be going."

"Aren't you going to at least stay until the General shows up?" Zuverink quickly moved in front of the hurrying doctor, blocking her path.

"No. That's quite all right," she answered, pushing past the nervous private-specialist. "In spite of what Jira says, I've had quite enough of our friend there for now. Besides, I'm not a fan of horror vids, and what are you worried about? You've got a weapon," the doctor indicated Zuverink's sidearm. "I didn't have dogshit."

"I'm not worried."

"Good. Lync is recording into main DSU seventeen, and the lab AIC and automated data recorders are running on mode C and using secondary DSU fifty-one, eighty-eight." She paused, then added, "The General will be here in an hour or so, good luck."

"But," was all the slender private-specialist could utter as the doctor walked out of the lab, the door slid shut behind her with a hum that Zuverink thought sounded final, "*Netikelis!*" She spat at the closed door, a Lunarized Lithuanian accent making a brief appearance. She surveyed the covered worktable and the rest of the quiet lab, resting her hand on the butt of her Glock-Whelan.

Sighing, she did a round of the lab and manually checked the data recorders and monitors, then she moved to the small table, where she had initially deposited her workslate. She carried it over to the control console, pulled up a chair, and activated the device. The small screen came to life with the title: **TALONS**, in big red letters.

Zuverink sat back to watch the two-dimensional version of the twenty-six-year-old AI remake of a two-hundred-year-old holographic movie. All she needed was the roasted pine nuts and a darkened room. She could not eat roasted pine nuts, and she did not turn out the lights.

She may have been twenty-three and experienced in dealing with the cold unknowns of the outer solar system, but she was still a little girl at heart. As Lync made an announcement about another Titanquake, she sighed with annoyance. Almost as a reflex, she called out, "Lync, audio announcements off."

Lync's voice died in mid-sentence.

At first, Zuverink watched the vid uneasily. She glanced back at the worktable every now and then, but eventually, she settled down to watch with interest the scary monster vid about a creature called "Talons." by the people in the story.

As time passed, the thought of the creature on the worktable, getting to know the creature in the vid, struck her as funny. That idea made her smile, but for some reason, she felt her smile swiftly fading, and her body trembling with an unexpected chill. She heard some primitive voice deep down inside of her subconscious screaming at her, telling her that something was wrong. At first, she thought it was the scary vid and her situation that made her feel uneasy. Hearing a faint sound, she first thought it was from the vid, but it was not. She halfheartedly glanced back at the worktable and froze. The canopy was open, and the worktable was empty.

The extrasolar entity was gone.

# CHAPTER FOURTEEN

General Newey and Doctor Reierstadt talked for nearly half an hour in the chambered vault that was the locker room and decon area for the laboratory sections. Their conversations focused mainly on the mental health of the crew, especially that of Captain Arroyo. He related his impressions of the captain's behavior in the sub-engineering level and the comments that Yoshida and Tounames had made regarding Arroyo. Newey ordered her to examine him as soon as possible. She agreed that his description of Arroyo's behavior was disturbing and that she would get him evaluated immediately.

After Reierstadt left the dressing room, Newey smoked the remains of a cigar he had in his uniform pocket, knowing fully that he was violating station protocols by doing so. However, it was his station, and no one would comment on it to his face, and besides, who was to know. He then stripped and stored his wrinkled uniform in a locker, took a quick, chemically active decon shower, then proceeded to put on a protective biohazard suit. He then went through a mild exterior decontamination, unholstering and exposing his Glock-Whelan and its ammunition to the decontamination agents.

In the middle of General Newey's decontamination cycle, Lync's voice suddenly came over the small chamber's speakers. "Bio lab one monitors are no longer operational. Last recorded data indicates that the monitored extrasolar sample's activity level increased sharply during the last thirty seconds of data collection.

The extrasolar form has relocated from primary laboratory workstation. No other data available." The AI's monotone voice was accompanied by the text of its audio message scrolling across the general's tiny PDI screen.

Newey did not hear Lync repeat its message. Concern exploded in his mind as he tried to contact Private-Specialist Zuverink over the PDI's interlink.

There was no response.

He was about to contact the com-center when Lync's voice came over the room speakers again. This time it was announcing a failure in a number of bio lab one's critical systems.

"Lync, discontinue General announcement of bio lab one system failure," instructed Newey. He activated a direct interlink channel to the com-center, "Aamodt?"

The station's main AI went silent just as Captain Aamodt's voice answered the general over his PDI.

"Can you contact Zuverink in bio lab one?"

"No sir," came her calm reply. "I tried the second Lync announced the system's failure, and it showed up on my screens. I can't get the lab monitors up either."

"I'm in decon and will be there in a few minutes, standby," the general's voice and demeanor were both fighting to stay calm and restrained. "Don't alert the others. I don't want to worry them unnecessarily."

"That's affirm," Aamodt's voice was still composed, but had an understandable edge to it.

Rechecking his sidearm and ammunition, the general's mind was racing with possibilities as he sat quiet, but alert in the decontamination chamber. *Had the extrasolar creature arisen earlier than expected? Had the thing moved and the young private-specialist panicked and done something rash? Could it just be a systems failure of some kind? Should he alert Rozsa and Singleton?* He hoped that his scientists were correct and that the extrasolar would wake slowly, giving him time to call for assistance. However, with Lync's alert and no contact with Zuverink, the situation was already looking grim. Nevertheless, he knew he could not just jump to conclusions, everyone was spooked enough already. When the decontamination procedure was completed, he headed for bio lab one at a dead-run.

As Newey entered the bio lab, he froze. Disastrous wreckage, bathed in an unfriendly gloom greeted him. Most of the ceiling panels were missing, and overhead lighting panels were smashed and dangled lifelessly in the still air. There were occasional small, white-hot flashes of light, the product of arcing electricity from the mangled wires hanging from the missing ceiling panels. All of the cabinets and table drawers were open, and their contents were strewn about the floor as if a horde of unruly children had been searching for hidden candy. Amidst all of it, there was smashed electronics everywhere. Eerily an untouched workslate sat on a table, still playing some vid. Ironically, Newey recognized the vid as an old sci-fi from years ago. Then it struck him, Zuverink was nowhere to be seen, and neither was their guest.

Newey slowly drew his Glock-Whelan from the old style velcro holster, a replica of those used in the late twenty-first century. "Zuverink?" his hand trembled as he brought the semi-automatic pistol up into a modified isosceles shooting stance, just like he learned in the VR-Training vids. The hydraulics of the lab door sounded louder than usual as it slowly slid shut behind him.

There was no reply as he advanced into the lab, "Zuverink, report!" He could feel the increase in his heart rate, like the gradual ramping up of a drum-roll, as fear generated beads of cold sweat began to slide down his armpits. "Sasha?"

Still, there was no reply.

"Sasha! Answer me now!" Newey could feel his gloved hands growing sweaty as his suit's air-conditioning unit kicked into overdrive. Cautiously, the general rounded the worktable with its open canopy and discovered the reason why Zuverink gave no reply.

She was on the floor; or rather, all over the floor.

The mangled remains of the young private-specialist lay in the center of a massive pool of dark blood. Her protective suit and uniform were all but stripped off of the oddly twisted body. The butchered woman's internal organs lay all over the lab floor like some sick work of art. Newey had not expected to see something so graphic and overwhelming as he stared at the scene before him. The sight of the dead woman's, excrement-covered intestines instantly reminded him of a freshly gutted animal.

Stumbling back, Newey noticed there was partially clotted blood slowly dripping and oozing from the ruined drop-ceiling. The nauseated general found himself being grateful for the protective ventilation of his biohazard suit. Memories of the foul odors that came from ruptured human intestines exploded into his consciousness, as he fumbled for his PDI. "Comscenter!" Glancing back, Newey noticed that the private-specialist's Glock-Whelan was on the floor next to her. From the position of the weapon's blood covered slide, he knew that the weapon had been fully discharged, its magazine of nickel-carbon slugs emptied.

"Aamodt here," The woman's reply signaled she was still on edge.

"Captain, listen very carefully. Zuverink's dead---"

"What!" interrupted the stunned captain, "What happ---"

"Just shut up and listen!" Newey was breathing as if he had just sprinted the first ten kilometers of the Martian New Year's Marathon. A dozen different scenarios were running through his head, and all of them ended badly. "I want you to have Lync lock all the doors, to be opened on voice command only. Then I want you to bring the station to emergency alert condition one. Inform everybody that our visitor, guest, whatever you want to call it, is alive and running around loose. Order everyone to the cafeteria then you get down there."

"Yes sir, but---"

"Did you get that?"

"Got it, but---"

"No buts just do it!" shot Newey, deactivating his PDI. Through an act of willpower, the general slowly, and with his Glock-Whelan at the ready, began searching the darkened lab, just in case the extrasolar entity was still hiding in the shadows, waiting to spring on him.

The unexpected sound of Lync's calm voice startled Newey, almost causing him to discharge his weapon.

As the general slowly swept the dimly lit lab, he calmed himself. Then he decided that even armed, it was probably not the greatest of ideas to be looking for their visitor alone. He cautiously backed up to the lab door, expecting the thing that killed Zuverink to jump out at him at any moment.

However, nothing did.

Turning to face the door, he took a deep breath and commanded, "Door open." The general felt the sudden surge of adrenaline as the lab door slid aside, but there was nothing. Newey rushed out into the corridor and looked both ways, sweeping the hall with the Glock-Whelan. Only the empty passageway and bare walls greeted him.

"Door close," he started toward the locker room as the lab door slid closed behind him. As he headed back to the locker room, thoughts of how the situation was getting out of hand raced through his mind. Scenarios and hypotheses danced through Newey's conscious mind, then it hit him. He had lost another person under his command in less than three days. The general was promptly struck with anguish and pain. However, to his surprise, he realized he was going through a normal decontamination routine, his brain running on autopilot. Years of routine and training were simply old habits, and hard to break, in spite of the exhaustion and grief.

•   •   •

The monotone alert from Lync only confused the half-asleep staff of Titan-Base Lincoln. Captain Aamodt's frantic voice, which was uncharacteristic of her, only added to and served to heighten people's confusion and fear. She told them that the extrasolar lifeform was up and about and that it was dangerous. Aamodt informed them that the station was at alert condition one and that all of the doors on the station were now only operating on voice command. The captain started to inform them that Zuverink had been killed, but thought better of it. She did not want to start a panic, but knew that the tone of her voice had already done the damage.

Colonel Rozsa hopped into her clothes and almost forgot her shoes. She panicked for a moment when the door to her quarters failed to open, but remembered the captain's statement and ordered the door open. Flustered and confused, she raced to the cafeteria at a dead-run with the Glock-Whelan in hand. The colonel found herself peering down adjacent corridors and into open doorways, as she nervously made her way to the cafeteria.

Major Nianta, with a Jones-Benelli coilgun, went to Doctor Tan's quarters. Together, Nianta and Tan headed for the cafeteria, both asking each other questions, which neither had answers too. They met up with LaRocque, Pulgar, and Sloan on their way to the meeting. Nianta, LaRocque, Pulgar, and Sloan nervously escorted Tan the rest of the way to the cafeteria, their loaded and ready weapons leading the way.

Lieutenant Fung was startled by the figure in front of her when she opened the door to her quarters. The projectile she involuntarily squeezed off narrowly missed Professor Watkinski's right foot. The crack of the Jones-Benelli coilgun in the empty corridor surprised both of them, as the SIAP projectile ripped a basketball-sized chunk of composite material from the corridor floor, centimeters from Watkinski's foot.

Stunned and bewildered, the two looked at one another and the new floor-window to the deck below theirs. They shouted at each other as if they were in a crowded college bar. It only added to their growing fear when they realized that the only noise was the sound of their own heartbeats, pounding in their ears. Watkinski, sweating and breathing heavy, looked as if he was having a heart attack as he and Fung moved down the corridor, headed for the meeting area.

All in all, the cafeteria was a mass of blind confusion. Accented voices reverberated off the pale walls as Doctor Reierstadt stood near the edge of the growing circle of people, taking in the interplay of primal fears and deep-seated emotions. To her, it was textbook responses, like those akin to a parent in a busy megaplex, who suddenly realized that their toddler was missing, or a scrapyard worker, who bumping against a piece of running machinery, realizes that it was a high-powered laser cutter and the safety shield was missing.

The growing sense of panic was especially evident when Newey rushed into the cafeteria, and everyone wanted answers at once. They were all shouting questions at him, looking wild-eyed and scared like caged animals in a fire. An outsider would not have believed these were all highly trained professionals and not a mob of terrified parents at some primary school disaster.

"Quiet! Damn it! Quiet!" The general waved his weapon in the air angrily. "Quiet!" The voices in the room dropped to a low rumble as Newey took a deep breath and calmed himself. "Now everyone, sit down, shut up, and listen!" There were still a few whispers as everyone found a seat. Most had dressed in a hurry; some donned wrinkled uniforms, while a few others wore disheveled civilian clothes.

"Okay, everybody now listen," Newey, the Glock-Whelan still in his hand, stood in front of the group with the huge flat screen hard-monitor behind him. "That thing that Colonel Rozsa and the skiff team brought back from TBK. The thing T-One's crew found on the extrasolar craft, well, it's alive and running around here someplace. It's extremely dangerous."

"How dangerous?" interjected Professor Lori Eastman, cutting off the general. She wanted the details.

"Extremely, fucking dangerous!" he spat angrily staring at Eastman. "It killed Zuverink!"

There were several sharp gasps as a wave of shock rippled around the room. There was instantly a lot of mumbling among the twenty-three seated in the room. Only Rozsa and Singleton noticed the change in Newey's voice that hinted at fear.

Doctor Eastman exploded, "I told you! We all warned you, but you didn't listen! We explained---"

"Okay Lori, you've made your point!" Rozsa sharply cut her off. "The important thing now is how are we going to handle this?"

Reierstadt's face was a mask of shock and confusion. "I left her alone," she lamented softly under her breath.

"The General had that watch," whispered Trauma-Specialist Lebowitz from within the group, her tone accusing.

Everyone in the assemblage had their eyes on Newey, their panicked expressions mirroring the fear in their hearts and their desperate need for safety and security. "Professor Watkinski, you, and Professor Costello finish your analysis. I want to neutralize it without having to kill it. Al-Yuzwaki I want you to escort them down to the labs. Once they are secure, get back up here."

"Arroyo, I want you to take Tounames and Wong down to sub-engineering and pick up those modified ice-melters and that little noisemaker of yours. Grab those modified survey charges." Tounames tried to interrupt the general, but he waved him down. "I know we can't use the charges because of the possibility of further damaging the station." The expressions on both Tounames' and Yoshida's faces turned decidedly gloomy at the general's comment. Newey pressed on, "Captain if it comes to it, I hope you are a good shot with that recoilless gun of yours?"

Arroyo did not reply. He looked dazed and ill as if he had just found the severed remains of a hairy and bloody testicle filled scrotum, at the bottom of a bowl of gumbo he had just been eating.

"We have as much hope of stopping this thing with

these," scoffed Watkinski, "as an early hominid had of stopping a thunderstorm by throwing rotting fruit at it."

The general looked to Rozsa, who was staring at him. "When Arroyo and his team get back here, we'll form search parties. We'll hunt it down."

"Yeah," uttered someone under their breath, but loud enough to be heard.

Tounames, Yoshida, and Al-Yuzwaki all glanced knowingly at one another and nodded. The three tech-sergeants were all thinking the same thing.

"The rest of you, stay in twos and threes. Pick someone's quarters and stay there." Newey surveyed the group, "Captain Aamodt, assign everyone with a weapon to escort the science staff someplace safe, and then I want them back here, ASAP. The rest of you stay calm, and stay in touch." He looked to the ceiling and added, "Lync. I want everyone to check with you every thirty minutes. Someone doesn't check-in; notify me, Colonel Rozsa, and Majors Singleton and Nianta, immediately."

"A check-in schedule for all base personnel has been set," replied Lync's voice, "with a time interval of thirty minutes."

"Thank you, Lync." Newey took in the group. "We'll all be okay."

Professor McGilmer snickered, "Easy for you to say, and Lori was right."

The general kept talking, "We're going to search this place and find our visitor. Hopefully, we can communicate with it."

Singleton and Nianta glanced at each other as the unarmed Singleton stepped forward. "Let's assume the death of Zuverink was an accident or misunderstanding, and we try to talk to this thing, but it doesn't want to play nice-nice and talk things over like reasonable people? What then?"

As if to answer the major's question, Lieutenant Pulgar, who had been inspecting her Glock-Whelan, suddenly slammed home the full magazine and chambered a projectile with such a loud sound that the room fell silent for a moment. She toggled the safety.

"Sir, you know how big this place is?" Lieutenant Fung knew that the general was aware of exactly how big the station was and how huge the task was he was asking them to perform. "It'll take forever to search everywhere."

"Just over eight hundred cubic kilometers of living space," added Tounames. "Not counting storage units, ventilation ducts, maintenance---"

"Kill it," growled Arroyo, staring blindly ahead. "Blow its motherfucking brains out." Everyone could see that he was shaken, and his thoughts were centered more on revenge, than their current situation.

Newey and Reierstadt surveyed the large captain and then glanced at each other. "Okay, let's get to it," ordered Newey.

As everyone got up, those who had tasks to complete got moving on them. The others muddled around the cafeteria as if they were afraid to leave each other's company. Reierstadt had apparently recovered from her initial shock and had moved next to Captain Arroyo, talking to him softly. Newey noticed her immediately.

The general waved Tounames and Wong over to join him. "You two watch him," keeping his voice low, he indicated the huge captain talking furiously with Doctor Reierstadt. "I need calm heads. He might blow this thing away, and I want it alive."

Tounames acknowledged the colonel, as Rozsa join the small circle of men. "Sir, I'm not one of his biggest fans, but I agree with the Capt'n. Why don't we just kill it?"

"Because, one," the general thrusted up an index finger. "This is one of the biggest scientific discoveries in human history," he put up another finger. "Two, we need to try and communicate with it before this really gets out of hand." Newey added a third finger to the other two, "and three, based on what I've seen of this thing, I'm not one hundred percent sure we can kill it with these." The general indicated his weapon.

The last part of the general's whispered statement registered on the neighboring faces like a positive cancer screening. Tounames looked back and forth between Newey and Rozsa for a long minute, not sure what to say or do. "Yeah, I'll look after the Capt'n." The tech-sergeant, looking down caste, walked off towards Arroyo. Wong hesitated for a second, then halfheartedly saluted, and followed after Tounames.

"Be careful," muttered Rozsa, under her breath. The colonel and the general exchanged a knowing glance and moved on.

Professors Watkinski and Costello cautiously left the

cafeteria, headed for their laboratories accompanied by Al-Yuzwaki. The tech-sergeant, led the way, the Glock-Whelan held low, the safety off. As he and the two scientists moved along the empty corridors, he realized for the first time just how quiet the station truly was.

Armed with the Glock-Whelans, Sergeant Tounames and Private-Specialist Wong, flanking the unarmed Arroyo, left the cafeteria as a group. The dull-eyed captain appeared to be mentally somewhere else, as he cautiously led his small band toward the sub-engineering level to retrieve the recoilless rifle and the three modified ice-melters. Surprisingly none of the three men was as afraid as they had been initially. Private-Specialist Wong actually felt safe in the company of the two physically larger men. It also did not hurt that he had smoked a hemporette prior to receiving the alarm from Aamodt.

In the cafeteria, Newey slowly surveyed the faces of those still in the room. A few glanced at him sideways, and for a moment, he thought he could feel their eyes gnawing at him, quietly accusing him of something awful. It did not matter; he had an unpleasant task he needed done. Before he could speak, Doctor Reierstadt strolled over to him.

"As soon as he gets back I'm going to take Arroyo down to the med-bay and up his dosage of the antipsychotic, antidepressant that I have him on already," whispered Reierstadt into the general's ear, keeping an eye out for anyone who could overhear her.

Newey looked annoyed as he whispered back, "Just keep him under control." He then turned his attention back to the group in the room. "Lync, have two Marbs clean up the remains of Private-Specialist Zuverink in bio lab one. You know where her body goes."

"In the works General," replied the disembodied machine, "My condolences for your loss."

"I am going to need a volunteer to oversee this, anybody up to it?" There were a few exchanges of sad and nervous glances; no one stepped forward to volunteer.

The emotionally drained general knew that would be the response. He surveyed the group for a moment and settled on McGilmer, pondering her, then he asked, "You ever play any VR-games using firearms?"

She flashed a surprised expression that disappeared instantly. "*Grand Zombie Apocalypse Five: The Mars Outbreak* was my favorite VR-game when I was an undergrad."

Newey wanted to chuckle, but he was too drained. He flipped the safety on his Glock-Whelan and tossed it to McGilmer. "You and Brauer oversee the bots taking care of her."

McGilmer started to ask a question but discovered her own answer to the question as she glanced at Doctor Tan. "Okay." She looked to Medtec Brauer, "Susan, you going to keep me company?" The two women motioned to one another and moved out on their unpleasant task.

"Okay, listen up. We're going to find our friend," informed the general, addressing those who remained in the cafeteria, "Fung with me, Rozsa, you, and Yoshida. Nianta, you, and Aamodt pair up. Singleton, you and LaRocque," Newey paused a second. "Lori, when Captain Arroyo and the others return, tell them to break up into two-person teams and start a search. Have them start back down in the sub-engineering level and work their way up to level one. Tell them to check everywhere, ventilation ducts, access tunnels, storage units, crawlspaces, everywhere. We're going to start at the first level and work our way up to the hangar deck."

Doctor Eastman produced a concerned look. It had not escaped her notice that the general had referred to everyone in the last half hour by their last name, except her. "You are aware that we are unarmed in here?"

"Pulgar and Sloan have weapons, and you should be safe in here as long as you all stay together. Arroyo and his crew should be back in a few minutes." As if to punctuate his statement, he tapped his wrist PDI's tiny chronometer's display.

Major Singleton glanced at Captain Aamodt. She winked back at him with a reassuring smile, even though he sensed the same apprehension in her as in the others in the room.

"Lieutenant Pulgar, Professor Yee. After Captain Arroyo returns, please escort the medical staff to…" he trailed off, lost, as he looked around puzzled. "Wherever they need to be, then get up to the com-center and hold down the fort."

"Right, but I got an idea. Why not use Lync's internal sensors to track this thing?" asked Yee, as almost everyone in the room immediately seemed to be surprised. "Couldn't Lync detect motion that isn't one of us?"

Newey and Rozsa glanced at one another. "A lot of the internal sensors are still down. Lync can locate us because of our PDTs, but unless this thing moves into an area where the sensors are still functional, we're blind." Newey knew the personal data transponders system and Lync's all-seeing sensors would have been of great help.

Professor Yee's eyes bounced between the officers. "How long would it take to get Yoshida and those guys to restore the system?"

"Weeks," Newey glanced at his PDI impatiently.

"What about using the portable scanning units we've got?" suggested Colonel Rozsa. "It's got enough radioactive isotopes in its system to be detectable by the station's internal sensors."

"The scintillation detectors aren't sensitive enough for in here," Newey indicated the room's walls and ceiling. "The composite materials used in the construction of the station screen a hundred percent of the alpha and beta particles, and about eighty-one percent of any Neutron, X, and gamma-ray emissions. I doubt if there is anything to detect."

"Plus there's got to be ten thousand low-level radioactive sources scattered around this place," added Yee.

Doctor Tan walked up to the small group, "Sir, a word in private."

Everyone in the small circle looked at their neighbor then stepped away, leaving Tan and Newey alone. "Everything all right, Doctor?"

Tan snickered at the absurdity of the question, then asked, "Why did you send Professor McGilmer to take care of Zuverink? That's a medical issue?"

"NJ, you are the only real medical doctor we've got, and I don't want to risk important assets on a simple clean up." Newey knew the second he said it, that it was the wrong thing to say. He hurriedly glanced at his PDI's timepiece, "Sorry, we got to get moving here. That was all to it." He instantly moved toward the doorway, leaving Tan staring after him.

Major Nianta moved in next to Tan as the general joined Fung in the doorway to the cafeteria. The major and the doctor embraced. "Be careful," Tan whispered.

"I'm always careful," his forced smile turned dark as he

added, "I asked Ariel to watch out for you."

Tan's reaction bordered on anger, "I don't need some Divinity-forsaken baby-watcher! I---"

"No!" The major halted Tan. "You are listed as critical personnel, and you are part of the Frontier Authority, not the Outer Systems Command. So, unlike the chief engineer, you don't get to go into harm's way unless it's absolutely necessary." She tried to speak again, but he stopped her again. "I have to go, love you." He kissed her deeply on the lips and moved past her. He patted Pulgar on the shoulder while eyeing the weapon in her hand.

Captain Aamodt tossed back Nianta's Jones-Benelli that she had held for him while he spoke to Tan. He made sure the safety was on as he and the other members of the search team gave one last good luck gesture to the group in the cafeteria. They then left the room.

Doctor Tan and Lieutenant Pulgar looked at one another, concern on their faces as Professor Yee and Lieutenant Sloan began an energetic conversation. Yee wanted to use the station's fire detection system to search for the extrasolar lifeform's radiation signature. That is when Lync made an announcement.

"Attention, I am detecting an unauthorized and unidentifiable electromagnetic pattern attempting to access station systems. The pattern does not conform to any known AI-parasites or network spiders. I have isolated holo-terminal GH-Five in the greenhouse."

"Lync enabled level-one defensive protocols." It was LaRocque's voice booming out of every console and PDI speaker in the room.

"I have enabled all level-one defensive protocols for all isolinear-pathways for my neuro-network."

Everyone in the cafeteria just stared at one another, dumbfounded and silent.

# CHAPTER FIFTEEN

Tech-Sergeant Al-Yuzwaki and Private-Specialist Wong were both stunned as they examined the large open pressure door that led to the brightly lit greenhouse. Both men knew that the greenhouse, like the cafeteria, med-bay and gymnasium was one of the designated disaster safe-zones on the station. If the station were to sustain severe structural damage, any of those sections could maintain the survivors for six months with its own power, food, and life support systems. The massive, alloyed pressure door they were looking at was designed to be one of the strongest barriers on the base. The deformed dull metal had a number of long, jagged slashes in it. Each gash went straight through the two-centimeter thick nickel-chromium-based alloy and curled the dark metal back like the peel on a banana.

Just inside the greenhouse door was a console with several hard-monitors and a number of holographic ones. The console had been gutted, electronic bits and knots of fiber-optic cable and hair-thin wiring were spread all around the destroyed console. To the men's surprise, two of the holo-screens were still functioning, displaying meaningless gobbledygook.

As Al-Yuzwaki and Wong stood in the doorway of the enormous enclosed garden, they surveyed the vaulted ceiling with its artificial bluish gray sky and holographic clouds. They could smell the numerous natural aromas in the air that included Mountain Pine, Orange Blossom, Venus Cave Lavender and

Champlain Shrub Rose, among others. However, the two men kept their modified ice-melters held at the ready and their eyes searching.

The tech-sergeant looked at Wong's face and saw worry written there. He activated his PDI and tapped the interlink system. "General this is Al-Yuzwaki. Wong and I are in the greenhouse. Our friend is here all right."

"Are you sure?" Newey's voice was unemotional as it came out of the tech-sergeant's forearm-mounted device.

"Yes, sir. It looks like it may have been trying to access some of the station systems," Al-Yuzwaki read the stenciled ID on the damaged door, "It looks like it ripped through pressure door GH-One, and tried to get access through terminal GH-Five. It could still be inside the greenhouse."

"That's affirm. Singleton and LaRocque are sweeping through the gymnasium and pool area now, moving towards you. Arroyo and Tounames are moving through engineering. I'll have them move up toward the Living quarters, and cut this thing off. Colonel Rozsa and Tech-Sergeant Yoshida are near the cafeteria and are moving towards you now. Fung and I are in Corridor-B, section two, level three and are working our way back toward the living areas. If you find it, don't threaten it and don't fire unless you have to, acknowledge."

"That's affirm," Al-Yuzwaki indicated to Wong for him to start moving. "We are moving into the greenhouse." Both men were aware that the corridor that had led them to the greenhouse was almost a straight run from the science section.

"Be careful. Stay in touch and good luck, Newey out."

As the two men slowly began their search for their strange intruder, they began to navigate around the various plants that grew in the five-meter thick layer of enriched soil. They knew that besides the station's biologists, who conducted experiments on the genetically engineered food crops, the romantically involved couples on the station also came there to spend time immersed in the lush greenery. The couples would lay and play among the hundreds of natural and genetically engineered trees, bushes, and flowers.

In areas that were not planted with uniform crops, the reddish-gray soil was visible. The material had been imported from Mars, enriched, and fortified with semi-organic matter from the

Titanian surface. Most of the soil was carpeted with thick genetically engineered blackish-green grass and clumps of flowering plants. Wong remembered when General Newey's team arrived on Titan and saw the greenhouse; General Newey told them how fortunate they all were. On most of the planets and satellites of the inner solar system, people would have to wait on a list for months in order to spend a single day in such a beautiful climate controlled nature park. They were truly fortunate to have one available at any time.

Tech-Sergeant Al-Yuzwaki, like everyone else on Titan-Base Lincoln, was a frequent visitor to the greenhouse facilities. However, he came there not for romance or science, but to tend his personal crop of North American *appeaches*. He loved the genetically engineered fruit that was a cross between the Cortland apple, and the Freestone peach, which he believed was healthier than the processed, prepackaged fruit the autochef spat out. He loved tending the short, thick-trunked *appeach* trees, which gave him some quiet downtime that reminded him of his youth in northern Europe.

For half an hour, the two men slowly and silently moved through the lush and exotic vegetation. Intense concentration radiated from both Al-Yuzwaki and Wong as they eyed the high branches of every tree, and examined every stand of bushes as if each plant could be concealing a mortal threat. Again, they had to check in with Lync, the seventh time since beginning their search. Still, there was no sign of their unwanted guest, only a lone maintenance-bot confronted them. The machine, undistracted was patiently working alone on some piece of machinery that stood next to a dwarf almond tree.

Al-Yuzwaki addressed the bot by its unit number, stenciled on its multi-armed, barrel-shaped frame, and asked did the unit see or detect anything out of the normal. The machine, in a pleasant voice, replied it had detected several tearing metal sounds one hour and eleven minutes ago, and an unidentifiable shape moving through the stand of bamboo. Al-Yuzwaki, motioning Wong towards the stand of tall bamboo trees, wished the Marb with their dumb-down AIs had a more developed sense of curiosity.

Wong, with the ice-melter at the ready, moved through the small patch of tall red bamboo. Uneasily he smiled, "Like what my father used to say, it's what you can't see, that'll kill you. I've found that to be all too true."

"Well hopefully this thing can't become invisible," Al-Yuzwaki heard a faint metallic sound and whirled around in a sudden panic as Wong brought his ice-melter to bear on the strange noise. Both men stood facing the source of the sound.

A set of steal wind-chimes, hanging from a tree branch, moved lazily in the breeze.

The two men smiled, and Wong nervously lowered his weapon and added with an anxious chuckle, "This is getting ridiculous."

"You're damn sure right about that," Al-Yuzwaki batted at the wind-chimes as he moved on, "Let's keep going." The tech-sergeant, followed by Wong, continued slowly across the micro-forest section of the greenhouse, heading towards the opposite pressure door. Neither man lost focus, in spite of the beauty of their surroundings, as they continued to stealthily advance across the vast woodland area.

Emerging from a cluster of green and brown Yam trees, they moved across a small grassy area studded with fruit bushes. Approaching the next pressure door, they noticed it was mangled in the same fashion as the door on the opposite side of the greenhouse. The control console mirrored its counterpart on the other side of the domed ecological conservatory; it too had been violently ripped apart.

The two men exchanged a knowing look as Al-Yuzwaki activated his PDI. "General, Al-Yuzwaki here, we swept the greenhouse, and it's gotten through pressure door GH-Two and is in section two. It could be moving towards the living quarters or down towards engineering."

"That's affirm," the general's voice was still calm. "Continue your sweep towards the living quarters."

Unexpectedly Wong made a gesture with his hand indicating he wanted to rest. Al-Yuzwaki nodded his approval. "General. Wong and I are going to take five, before proceeding."

"That's affirm, but stay sharp, Fung and I are moving toward you. We'll link up in the area of the living quarters. Newey out."

The two men moved to a nearby strawcherry tree and flopped down on the grass, but kept an eye on the open doorway. Wong took out a hemporette and lit it in the glowing igniter of his ice-melter. After taking a long drag on the hemporette, Wong passed it to the bigger, older man.

Al-Yuzwaki inhaled the pungent blue smoke and blew it out the corner of his mouth. The strong odor of the hemporette made the perfume of the flowering plants even more aromatic in the tech-sergeant's nose. Looking over at Wong, he smiled. The younger man was poking his index finger into the soil between clumps of grass. *It must be nice to be able to forget your worries so easily*, thought Al-Yuzwaki, shaking his head and puffing on the burning hemporette.

Wong always found it astonishing that something that felt so real could be so fake. He was amazed that the greenhouse, which served as their reminder of humanity's natural environment was created from materials so foreign. That the things and structures that made-up the station were born of elements from as far away as Mercury, and as close as the nearby islands of Fensal and the ice dunes of Xanadu. In his mind, Wong marveled at the knowledge that gigantic drifting chunks of rock halfway between Mars and Jupiter had been destroyed to make humanity's habitats in the dark and cold of the outer solar system. It was a sobering thought to think that the enormous treasures of minerals and metals throughout the solar system had waited billions of years in the vacuum of space, only to be harvested and made into things for the benefit of humanity.

Looking up through the branches of the strawcherry tree, Wong surveyed the artificial sky. It was another perfect fake day, in the perfect fake paradise. "We've been searching for nearly three hours." He noticed the ripe strawcherries on the tree and had a flash of memory. It was of the chocolate Martian raspberry cake from the New Year's Eve party. To Wong, with all that had happened in the last few days, the party seemed like it was a million years ago. "Where could it be?"

"How the fuck do I know!" fired Al-Yuzwaki. "Maybe it left! Maybe it got bored and had its friends come get it. Maybe, if we're lucky, it crawled into a storage unit and died!" The tech-sergeant exhaled a cloud of blue-gray smoke and passed the hemporette back to Wong.

"Sorry! Didn't mean anything by it," Wong surveyed Al-Yuzwaki's face and saw his own frustration. He stood up, placed the half-smoked hemporette into the corner of his mouth, and shimmied up the first couple of branches of the strawcherry tree. There he began to quickly pick and pocket several handfuls of the dark-red strawcherries.

"I just don't like this hide-and-go-seek dogshit. I'm not going to get any sleep with this fucking thing wandering around." Al-Yuzwaki's tone was angry, but he kept their surroundings under surveillance for sudden movements or sounds.

Wong jumped out of the tree, passed the hemporette to Al-Yuzwaki, and slumped on to the well-manicured grass. Blowing out a long column of smoke, he laid back and began popping strawcherries into his mouth. Silently he thought of Zuverink and Zapollo. He thought of how each had died, and whether or not the situation they were in would get any worse. He had liked Zuverink and could relate to her more than the others. Zuverink and Zapollo had shared the same rank as he, sitting at the bottom of the station's command structure, and now he was the only private-specialist on the whole of Titan. Shaking his head with the thought, he missed Zuverink and Zapollo, especially Zuverink. They could talk freely without self-consciousness or worrying about being put in someone's report. He really missed her, as he missed his father.

There was an announcement by Lync regarding a seismic event, but both men ignored it. Lync must have been performing another round of check-ins because it annoyingly asked for each of them in turn.

After both of them had replied to Lync's inquiry, Al-Yuzwaki turned to Wong, hemporette in hand and an annoyed look on his face. "Let's finish our sweep, kid." He stood up, tossed the remains of the hemporette away and headed toward the wrecked pressure door. "I want to find this motherfucker."

"Yeah, so do I," moaned Wong as he stood and put the remainder of his strawcherry harvest back into his pocket.

•  •  •

"Fuck it!" screamed Lieutenant Pulgar at the holo-screen in front of her. She had been working remotely on the station's internal scanners for hours, trying to re-establish the system. Having no luck, she was growing frustrated at the near useless system, and the seemingly endless check-ins with Lync. Both she and Doctor Tan were becoming frustrated with the lack of news regarding the hunt for their visitor.

As she looked across the room at the reclining Doctor Tan, who had become her temporary roommate, Pulgar took in her humble, but comfortable quarters. She was a little embarrassed by the clutter spread across both nightstands on either side of her large, neatly made smart-bed. There were four black syntha-leather chairs arranged around the room with two small tables, two large glass cabinets displaying knickknacks and personal items, and a large desk with an AI holo-screen.

From her seat in front of the holo-screen, Pulgar could see across the room into both the large sterile white bathroom with its walls covered by smart-mirrors and the large walk-in closet next to it. At the moment, the large smart-mirrors in the bathroom slowly scrolled her morning-reminder board and reflected the rest of the bathroom fixtures. The small screen that normally displayed her favorite news and entertainment shows from the inner solar system now flashed: **Unusable Signal**.

Looking into the open closet revealed a small room stocked with duty uniforms and an assortment of civilian clothes, all neatly arranged on hangers. There were also two sets of dress-grays, one dull yellow insulated flightsuit, and standing isolated and unobstructed at the rear of the closet, an emergency e-suit and a large, yellow and red disaster kit. The emergency e-suit and disaster kit were both ready for use in the event of a station-wide disaster.

"Come watch the vid, I think a good part is coming up," Doctor Tan sat on the floor on the other side of the room, her back against one of the black syntha-leather chairs. She was splitting her attention between the digital workslate in her hand and the old holographic vid playing on the smart-wall's entertainment screen in front of her.

Pulgar sighed as she scanned both Tan and the hologram, "What the hell are you watching?"

"The Eyes of Space," Tan smiled but did not look up from her workslate. "Believe it or not it's a documentary on USVs and EBEs. It was in the main entertainment system."

"What's a USV?" The second Pulgar asked the question she remembered with a frown.

Tan's grin widened, "An unidentified space vehicle."

Pulgar's flash of a smirk signaled her disbelief, as she moved to join Tan. "Why in the name of all the divinities are you watching this?"

"Curiosity, don't you want to know if anyone else has ever met our friend and his buddies before?" The doctor's smile wavered and faded, "Besides, I couldn't rest if I tried." Tan looked up at Pulgar, "this keeps me from worrying about…" she hesitated an instant, then said, "this mess." She tossed the workslate to the floor and took a sip of coffee from the mug sitting next to her. Even though the coffee was hours old, the temperature-controlled heating unit in the mug had kept it warm.

Pulgar looked at the doctor, somewhat surprised at her comment. She knew she really wanted to say Major Nianta's name. "I know what you mean. All I can think about is getting the fuck away from here." At the last moment, Pulgar decided to sit on the bed rather than on the floor next to Tan.

The doctor, coffee mug in hand, moved to the chair near the bed, and sat stone-faced, staring at the smart-wall. The two women remained quiet a long while, watching the vid, but neither really seeing it nor following the narration.

"You know that one way or the other, our assignment here is over," Pulgar broke the silence. "You have any idea about what you'll be doing next or where they are likely to send you?" She was aware that the doctor was as career driven as anyone else on the station and that she would probably be head of UGE or UESA Medical before she was sixty-five.

Tan chuckled and looked over at Pulgar, sitting on the bed. "In the short term, I have some research I want to publish, and I'd like to get back to Earth for a year or so and have some outside time and breathe some real outside air."

Pulgar smiled, but like most people who were born and raised away from Earth, she felt that *outside air* had too many unpredictable qualities. She felt that being in the open without a protective suit was unnatural and unnerving. She had only been to Earth twice, and both times, it had taken her weeks to get used to that eerie sensation of *unprotected openness*, like being the only naked person in a crowd.

"Long-term, I have a few projects I am working on," her expression morphed, "and before you ask, yes, they involve Colin. He and I are close, and he's even mentioned children," her expression changed again.

"That sounds *interesting*," Pulgar's tone reflected the look on the doctor's face.

"He is a traditionalist. He's a good man, great in bed," Tan flashed a grin, "I think he'd make a good father, but this deep-space dogshit has got to go."

"Marriage?"

"Possibly," smiled Tan.

"I hear it's still popular on Earth and Mars," Pulgar smirked again. "You remember Capt'n Callwood? She was on the surface team. She did the marriage thing, even dropped her birth last name for her husbands."

"Now that is just dogshit crazy," scoff Tan, "I can see birthing one or two children, but my name is my name. You?"

"Fuck no! Besides most places require you to have a permit to have a child, and I never filed for one when I turned sixteen."

"My parents made sure I got mine on my sixteenth birthday," grinned the doctor, uncomfortably. "But I don't know if I can stand walking around with an abdomen acting like a slowly inflating buoyancy bag of a skiff, for ten months either."

"Yeah, me with some cranky little crumb snatcher wanting a nipple in its mouth every five seconds." Pulgar shook her head in disgust and grunted, "No fucking way." The lieutenant was not convinced that childbirth was right for her.

Pulgar and LaRocque had talked about a long-term partnership, but like her, LaRocque had his own professional ambitions. LaRocque was a good man and probably a brilliant one as well, but she was not entirely sure he was the right man for her. Pulgar knew LaRocque had a barely suppressed desire for the affections of other women. When LaRocque would have too much to drink, especially in their first year on Titan, he would flirt with any woman within arms' reach. Then he would put on an e-suit, go outside with a pair of makeshift wings and flap around in the thick atmosphere and one-seventh gravity like some prehistoric bird screaming, *'No gravity! No gravity!'* Only after he crashed into one of Professor Eastman's aerosol ionization experiments and broke his back, did Colonel Rozsa put an end to his off-duty flying.

"I do think Colin is the one I want children with," continued Doctor Tan. "His only downside is that he can be too laid back sometimes, and he has let a lot of great assignments slip through his fingers, like commanding an Eris-Dysnomia mission."

Gesturing slowly with her head, Pulgar added, "Yeah, I know he got offered an Eris-D mission."

"Who turns down an assignment like that?" Tan raised an eyebrow at the thought. "Granted, he has already put himself in the history texts, twice."

The two women traded a blank stare, "I'd think that would be a better opportunity for a man like him than being here. Of course, he wouldn't be here for five years if he didn't think it would do better for his career than some deep space mission." She looked back at the vid, as a sinister melody began to play. The vid's narrator, in an eerie tone, began to describe a particularly chilling encounter between a group of geotech workers and a USV, inside Artemis Chasma, near Venus' southern pole. "Besides, he probably saw your image in the group of current TBL personnel and fell in love with you, straight away."

The two women laughed in unison. "I do think he'd be a good father," Tan added looking Pulgar up and down with a grin. "After this mess with that…that, whatever the fuck it is, you could probably write your own pass, get a position anywhere. You don't need a childbearing permit on Mars."

Pulgar shifted her position, "Yeah, but Alain has that stupid male gene. You know the one, if I can't fuck it, root for it, or kill it; I don't want to know about it, that gene." She continued to grin. "I remember you telling me about some old classmate of yours at the University of Somalia? You almost married him."

A broad, gentle smile swept across Tan's face. "Yeah, but we were both very young," she acted as if she were watching the vid, but her mind was elsewhere. "Thaddeus Bahadur, use to call him Teddy Bear, was in my advanced cranio-surgical recitation. One thing led to another and…" the doctor broke off, her smile growing even wider.

"For me, it was a cadet named Fouad-Michael Yamaguchi. We were at the UESA's Stebbins-Birkhoff lunar facility," Pulgar chuckled as she remembered her ancient romance. "He was tall and muscular, and had one of the thickest, longest---"

There was a loud, dull thump.

Startled, the two women stopped and looked at the holographic vid on the smart-wall. The vid images were of two e-suited persons working quietly at a rock outcrop on the surface of Venus, the vid's narrator calmly describing the men's actions.

It came again, a sound like a large sack of wet sand landing on a hard surface.

The two women turned toward the room's doorway in confusion, as something hard hit it for a third time. The carbo-plastic of the door slowly began to deform inward with an ear-piercing screech, as something big and powerful began to split the material. Several long dark green objects appeared through the carbo-plastic and moved slowly downward and outward, unzipping the barricade like the skin of an orange. A second later, a dark, muscular appendage punctured the remains of the door, and began to slowly, but forcefully rip the door open with a sound that was muddled with the scream of the door's protesting hydraulic motors.

Pulgar and Tan fought to control their growing panic, as they immediately began scanning the room, searching for a means of defense against their intruder. Tan, remembering her PDI, put the device to her lips. "General, Colonel, anybody, that thing is breaking into Pulgar's quarters." Tan's voice was low and even, and remarkably controlled.

There was no reply.

Pulgar remembered her Glock-Whelan among the clutter on her nightstand, but it was too late. The hydraulic motors of the door failed with a lioness-like roar, as the destroyed barrier gave way in a violent spray of hot sparks and red hydraulic fluid. The two women ran to the far side of the room, as the massive, dark creature appeared to flow into the room. Pulgar instantly noticed that the thing maneuvered with a gliding motion as if the station's Earth gravity were only a fraction of its normal environment. The four, highly animated arms of the thing gave it an almost spider-like appearance as it advanced to the center of the room.

"Tan! Stay away from it! We are on our way!" The general's voice exploded out of both Tan's and Pulgar's PDIs creating a strange false echo. LaRocque's voice was on the heels of the general's but was immediately cut off by Major Nianta's voice, which was himself cut off by the general. "Attention! Everyone! Our visitor is in the living quarters' section, Lieutenant Pulgar's quarters!"

"We are trapped General," whispered Tan, her eyes never wavering from the thing in front of her. With her PDI held close to her mouth with a trembling arm, she added, "It's between us and the doorway."

The strange and exotic lifeform appeared to be staring at the two terrified women, a number of its multi-faceted, black, insect-like eyes rotated toward them. The rest of its eyes were all moving in different directions. Its eye's movements reminding Tan of images she had seen of the extinct creature called a chameleon. There was an explosion in the holographic vid, and instantly, the extrasolar was next to the smart-wall. It moved unbelievably fast for its size, and both Pulgar and Tan were shocked by its speed.

It remained next to the smart-wall for several seconds, then it seemed to refocus its attention back on the two women. The women were taken aback when it unexpectedly made a series of sounds that, for a second, confused them. The sounds were like words, but in a language, neither woman recognized. The next series of sounds the entity produced was sharp enough to hurt their ears and base enough to be felt in their torsos.

"Maybe if we make a run for it?" suggested Tan, her voice a low, quivering whisper. It was not clear if she was speaking to Pulgar or into her PDI.

"No way, it would be on us in a second," Pulgar kept her voice low as she studied the arachnid-like gargoyle in front of her. Its muscular system outlined under the skintight jumpsuit it was wearing. The soft movements of its multi-jointed arms and fingers and the gentle movements of its head suggested to the lieutenant, a female gender. However, its insect-like eyes and reptile-like appearance scared Pulgar deeply.

The extrasolar entity apparently heard the soft exchange between the two women and shifted its position. As it slowly began to advance, it lowered all four of its arms, but that did nothing to lessen the growing fear within the women. Through its partially open mouth, Tan noticed its sharp, serrated teeth, black and deadly. It reminded her of blackened shark's teeth.

"Pulgar, Tan respond!" The general's voice had an edge to it as it came out of the PDI's tiny speaker.

"Go, sir," whispered Pulgar, still eyeing the intruder.

"We're entering the corridor outside your quarters." Newey sounded as if he were running, and there was a muffled voice in the background talking to him. "Give me a picture."

Both women activated the micro-cams in their PDIs. Out in the corridor, the general examined the real-time vid-images of the inside of Pulgar's quarters. "We are now outside the door, and I have a good view of it."

The two women practically collapsed with relief but were immediately tense again as the extrasolar with unnatural speed, repositioned itself between the women and the entrance. The things movements were so swift that it was difficult for the women to follow.

"It knows somethings up," whispered Pulgar, trying not to alert their unwanted guest.

It made a high pitch shrill, and for the briefest of moments looked confused and appeared to Tan as if it were trying to understand what they were saying. "It knows you're at the door," the doctor's voice was barely audible as she and Pulgar sunk back toward the open closet, both women holding their PDIs as if to fend off the nightmare. The thing took note of their movements, and appeared to ready itself, teeth showing.

"Pulgar, listen. Get in a corner and get down. Fung and I are coming in on the count of three!" The general's voice was incredibly loud as it came out of both PDIs.

Pulgar and Tan glanced at each other and noticed that they both were sweating, "Affirmative, on three." Pulgar was always amazed at how fast beads of sweat could form on a person's forehead, as she and Tan backed into the closet.

There was a pause that seemed like an eternity, then came the general's count over the interlink system, "Slowly, on the count of three. Ready, one… two… three."

General Newey slowly moved into the doorway, empty-handed. The extrasolar lifeform did not react but was obviously focused on the general. The two calmly stared at one another, as Newey slowly advanced into the room. He began speaking to the thing in a low, calm voice, the way one would talk to a lost child or a scared animal.

The EBE did not respond.

Moving slow and cautiously, Fung appeared behind Newey. Her Jones-Benelli was held high, its emerald laser-sighting beam zeroing in on the extrasolar.

The EBE reacted with lightning speed. With a high pitch screech that shattered several glass items around the room, it batted Newey out of its way like a bothersome insect. The impact sent him flying across the room onto and over the bed.

Fung only saw the general vanish from in front of her, and a dark blur suddenly in her face. She did not even center her sighting laser before pulling the trigger of her coilgun. The thunderous, semi-automatic blast hit the creature dead center in the chest area. The blast lifted her attacker off its feet and sent it halfway across the room. It slammed into a glass cabinet, shattering it explosively. By the time the limp form landed on the floor, Fung had her targeting laser centered on it, but the thing did not move.

Pulgar and Tan popped out of the closet expecting anything. Spying the general riving in pain across the room, Tan instantly rushed to the man's side. Pulgar seeing their intruder sprawled on the floor let her head collapse against the nearest wall with relief.

Fung, still alert and in a security force's shooting stance, slowly advanced on the motionless form, her targeting laser not wavering a centimeter from the creature's head. She noted the small puddle of white fluid growing under the fallen thing and realized that it was its blood. With the muzzle of the coilgun less than half a meter from the thing's head, she kicked it as hard as she could.

Nothing happened.

"I knew if one of us popped it once we'd get the fucker," smiled the elated lieutenant, "Hot damn!" She fingered the safety on the weapon and relaxed as she surveyed the room.

"I think his shoulder's fractured," announced Tan after quickly examining Newey, "may be his collarbone as well."

Lieutenant Fung turned to Doctor Tan, "I'll get---" There was a dull thud like that of a heavy syntha-leather bag dropped onto a wooden floor. Fung's expression changed from one of joy to one of shock. *"Cao ni niang,"* she coughed, looking down at her stomach, *"wangbadan."* The stunned and paralyzed woman tried to speak again, but nothing came out of her open and quivering mouth.

As the creature rose from the floor, its razor-like fingers tore downward through Fung's back with the sharp sound of tearing cloth. The strike had severed Fung's spinal cord, several of her organs and diced her intestines, which all spilled out onto the bedroom floor in long sections with a wet, sick sound. The lieutenant's body slumped but did not fall, as the EBE's powerful arm held her up like some bizarre ventriloquism act.

Pulgar stared at the scene for a second before the odor of Fung's innards brought a wave of terror to her. It washed over her as she shoulder-rolled over the bed and scrambled to and out of the room door.

Doctor Tan paused and surveyed the new situation. She was alone with an injured man and facing a nightmare. She looked into the dying eyes of Lieutenant Fung, she looked at the abomination standing behind her deceased co-worker, she looked at the general who was glaring back at her with a face that reflected death, and she looked at the handgun strapped to the general's thigh. Almost instinctively, she moved toward the door, snatching the Glock-Whelan out of the general's holster. Reaching the entrance, she turned and emptied the entire magazine in the direction of the extrasolar lifeform.

The EBE was suddenly on the room's ceiling, and the Glock-Whelan rounds sailed through Fung's body, tearing out red chunks of flesh and pearly white bits of bone as they continued on into the smart-walls and furnishings behind her falling body.

"Run!" screamed Newey in agony.

The EBE emitted a sharp sound and was instantly on the floor again. Tan bolted out of the room and dashed down the corridor screaming in a combination of English and Cantonese, her control and reasoning skills slipping.

The angry intruder paused for the briefest of moments.

Before he knew what was happening the thing had the general by his left ankle, hanging upside down over the edge of the bed. He wailed in pain and tried to move, but it was hopeless. The thing seemed to study him, the way a mantis studies a butterfly, just before it eats it. Then, unceremoniously, it dropped Newey and was out the door.

As the panic-stricken Tan rounded a corner, she collided with Al-Yuzwaki and Wong. "It's right behind me!"

"What?" asked Wong, confused.

"Where is the General?" inquired Al-Yuzwaki, his adrenaline level spiking.

"Wai-Mun is dead! It's fucking right behind me!" was all the terrified doctor could get out as she moved past the men, practically tripping over her own feet.

As Al-Yuzwaki stepped around the corner with Wong on his heels, he called back over his shoulder. "Where are the General and Colonel Rozsa?" As if in response to his question, the EBE rounded the opposite corner. The three came to a dead stop and stared at each other for an uncertain moment.

Wong felt like he had been staring at the motionless intruder for an hour. He noted every line, every small color change, and every bizarre feature of the unknown form before him. He thought the creature's numerous insect-like eyes, inhuman as they were, looked like there was a mind at work behind them. Then he heard the tech-sergeant.

"Burn'em up!" Al-Yuzwaki shouted as he and Wong both fired their ice-melters.

The two streams of pale blue flame engulfed the creature in the center of the corridor. An unearthly howl began as the barely visible extrasolar nightmare flailed wildly in the hellish shower of fire. The ear-splitting screams of the creature sounded like someone was castrating small animals without anesthetic.

Shivers ran up and down the spines of both men, as the thing appeared to randomly bounce off walls, floor, and ceiling, in a vain attempt to escape the flames. Sections of the suspended ceiling crashed to the deck in a fiery mass, further engulfing the creature in multicolored flames and huge, brightly colored cinders. Waves of heat washed back over Al-Yuzwaki and Wong forcing them to retreat several steps as they continued to unleash their ice-melters on the extrasolar entity.

After what seemed like an hour to the two men in the corridor, the hellish screams and nightmarish groans of the extrasolar creature died away, leaving only the roar of the ice-melters. There was no movement in the flaming remains of the corridor except for collapsing rubble, quickly being consumed and converted to ash by the blazing inferno.

"We got it!" shouted Al-Yuzwaki over the roar of the ice-melters, as the flames washed up the corridor. In unison, the two men terminated their fire.

The flames clinging to the walls began to burn themselves out, as the two men became aware of the wail of the station's fire alarm and the monotone voice of Lync announcing the fire they had started. Al-Yuzwaki looked to the ceiling for the fire-suppression system, but it appeared to have been welded into the charred remains of the damaged ceiling. He also noticed that the light levels in the corridor were quickly dropping, due to both the billowing clouds of dark smoke and the destroyed ceiling lighting panels. What remained of the ventilation system was working hard to remove the thick smoke from the corridor through damaged and rattling grates.

The thing was an unrecognizable flaming mass slumped against a corridor wall. Mounds of burning debris melted or turned to ash all around it, as thick black clouds of smoke continued to fill the corridor. The EBE did not move or exhibit any signs of life. Sparks popped off the charring remains like exploding coals from a campfire. There was a faint sound under the wail of the alarms and Lync's voice. Wong thought it sounded like bacon sizzling in a hot pan.

"Okay," coughed Wong, as he stared wide-eyed at the still burning mess. "I think we can call this one well-done." His eyes burnt and his nose was filled with the rotten egg smell of cooked sulfur, but all he could do was stare mesmerized at the scene before him.

Finally, after a minute, the two men exchanged a knowing glance as the thick dark smoke clinging to the ceiling slowly rolled in both directions along the corridor. Bending low and waving settling smoke out of their faces, both men began to smile at their victory.

Al-Yuzwaki activated his PDI, "General, this is Tech-Sergeant Al-Yuzwaki in Corridor-C, level two, section two, we got our friend."

There was no reply, but before Al-Yuzwaki could repeat his call, Colonel Rozsa's voice boomed out of his device. "Sergeant, we are moving to your location!"

"Affirmative, Colonel. Wong and I fried our guest, but the corridor has taken heavy fire damage, and we have no fire suppression and little ventilation."

"Lync is dispatching Marbs!" From the sound of Rozsa's voice, through the screaming alarms, Al-Yuzwaki could tell that she was running, "We'll be there in a minute!"

"That's affirm!" He disengaged the interlink connection. "You stay here! The Doc and I'll get some emergency gear just in case the fire starts up again!" Al-Yuzwaki looked around for Doctor Tan.

She was gone.

Wong's smile faded a little as he coughed again,

"Respirators would be nice! Who knows what's in this smoke!"

"Nothing that doesn't cause cancer!" answered the tech-sergeant, still wondering about Doctor Tan. As he turned and headed back the way they had come, two Marbs spun around the corner. One was the Marb he and Wong had seen in the greenhouse.

"Where the hell did NJ go?" inquired Wong stepping out of the way of the Marbs, frowning and waving the dense clouds.

Coughing and hacking, Al-Yuzwaki added, "I'd better find her." Then he disappeared into a dark wall of smoke, Private-Specialist Wong looked back to survey the busy Marbs and study the smoldering and motionless mass on the floor.

Both the station's fire alarm and the central AI's voice died abruptly, leaving an eerie quiet. In the dim light of the charred corridor, Wong slowly approached the blackened remains. The heat radiated off the remains of the walls and ceiling, and the stench of sulfur and burnt carbo-plastic stopped him.

The young private-specialist retreated to the bend in the corridor and plunked down. Glancing back uncomfortably at the working MARBS and the charred mass embedded in the quickly dying embers, he hoped that the general would not want them to return to Titan-Base Ksa and get another.

# CHAPTER SIXTEEN

Colonel Rozsa and Tech-Sergeant Yoshida, racing to the site of the demonic engagement came upon Tech-Sergeant Al-Yuzwaki desperately struggling to keep Doctor Tan and Lieutenant Pulgar apart. The two women were yelling at one another, trying to get at each other. Tan kept switching between English and Cantonese, looking as if she wanted to rip out Pulgar's throat.

"What the fuck is going on?" Rozsa was both angry and confused.

"She left the General and me." screamed Tan once again breaking into Cantonese and lunging at the lieutenant, "*Say Baht Poh!*"

Pulgar shouted over the doctor, "Wai-Mun was dead, the General was out of commission, I had no weapon…"

"What do you mean, Fung's dead?" Rozsa interrupted Pulgar by grabbing her arm and spinning the lieutenant around to face her.

"She's dead! That thing tore her apart like a piece of soggy toast and took the General out with a swat of its arm," yelled Pulgar, her attention moving between the major and the doctor.

"The Lieutenant ran," Tan's angry voice held a restrained fury that was directed solely at Pulgar. "She was supposed to protect me, and she left us to that thing."

"What happened?" asked Rozsa nervously eyeing both women, "Doctor?"

As Tan began to explain what had happened, Rozsa

directed the small group to continue moving back along the corridor, towards Wong's location. As they made a fast trot, Pulgar and Tan eyed each other angrily as Tech-Sergeant Al-Yuzwaki added the details of his and Wong's encounter with the thing. Pulgar and Yoshida sighed with relief at Al-Yuzwaki's description of the creature's fiery demise, but Rozsa and Tan did not relax. They had seen the data on their visitor and knew it could still be a threat. The anxiety level only increased as Rozsa tried and failed to contact General Newey over the interlink system.

As the five got closer to the site of the fiery battle, the air grew steadily thicker with black and brown smoke, and the smell of molten carbo-plastic. Rounding a curve in the corridor to a darkened T-intersection, they entered the shadow-filled corridor where the engagement had taken place. A dozen steps in and the group came to an abrupt halt. There, in the faint light and ghostly shadows of still smoldering embers, they saw the remains of two Marbs. The machines had been torn apart, right down to their wheelbase, and among the wreckage was Private-Specialist Wong, the young man lying face down on the debris leaden floor. Both Wong's ice-melter and the extrasolar lifeform were gone.

There was a long apprehensive moment in the silent burnt out corridor, as the five stared at the darkened scene before them. With the reality of the situation sinking in, Doctor Tan moved to the fallen private-specialist as Rozsa, Yoshida, and Al-Yuzwaki readied their weapons.

"Doc?" Rozsa's eyes wanted to look at Wong but would not move from the fire-damaged corridor before them.

"His neck's broken." In the dim light, Tan could see the broken vertebra in Wong's neck, acutely pushing up under his discolored skin. On the back of his head, there was a large patch of torn flesh, covered in rapidly clotting dark blood. The young man's black ponytail had been violently ripped from his scalp and was missing. Under the dead man, among the debris were the remains of several crushed strawcherries.

"We didn't run into it, so it either went back through the living quarters' section or," the major indicated the other branch of the T-intersection, "down Corridor-D. You two check Corridor-D," Rozsa motioned the other way, "we'll check on the General and Fung. When help gets here, we'll sweep back towards the greenhouse, but be careful it took his melter." She eyed the nervous looking Al-Yuzwaki and Yoshida, the burnt sulfur smell starting to make her eyes tear.

"No. Wait?" began Yoshida surveying the situation and not understanding it. "It took his melter? How does this thing know what it is, or how it works?"

Colonel Rozsa eyeing the passage in front of them replied, "If it can crew a spacecraft capable of crossing dozens, if not hundreds, of light-years, I think it can figure out how an ice-melter works."

"Colonel," Al-Yuzwaki indicated Wong's body on the floor, "what about the kid?"

"There's nothing we can do for him now," Rozsa's voice was unemotional. "We'll have to take care of him later. You two get moving."

Yoshida looked at Al-Yuzwaki and found him staring back, a mixture of concern and fear quickly spreading across his sweat-stained face. The two sergeants were thinking almost the same thought, as they began to advance back up the corridor toward the intersection. It was obvious they were in no hurry to find their unwanted guest.

"Ladies, let's go find the General."

"That won't help much," spat Tan, indicating Rozsa's weapon, as she and Pulgar joined the colonel. "I shot it and so did Wai-Mun, much good it did both of us." Her voice still had an edge to it that sent a subtle message to Pulgar.

Only the upraised hand of the colonel stopped Pulgar from commenting. With a quieting nod, Rozsa and the two other women cautiously stepping over blackened debris proceeded to Pulgar's quarters. As they moved along, Rozsa contacted majors Nianta and Singleton via her PDI's interlink and gave them a quick rundown on their current situation. While talking to the two majors, the colonel came to the realization that they were in serious trouble. Their weapons appeared useless in defending them, and now two more of their comrades were dead.

As they approached Pulgar's quarters, they could smell the aftermath of the battle, the pungent aroma of human excrement laced with the heavy odor of fresh blood. Inside the room, they found Lieutenant Fung lying in a puddle of dark blood and gross chunks of pink and gray tissue. General Newey was sitting in a chair, feverishly trying to reload a Glock-Whelan with one hand.

His face was ash gray and covered in sweat; his right arm lay limp next to him and looked dislocated. The man's left hand trembled as he fumbled with the semi-automatic pistol pinched between his knees.

Instinctively Doctor Tan moved to the struggling general. After quickly giving him a once-over, she made a makeshift sling for the man's arm with one of Pulgar's bed covers. She then reloaded the general's weapon, as Pulgar grabbed the forgotten Glock-Whelan off of her nightstand and retrieved Fung's fallen coilgun. Rozsa ordered Pulgar into the corridor to stand watch. She nodded and reluctantly moved back outside the shattered bedroom doorway. Bobbing nervously around the entrance, the trembling lieutenant was terrified. She knew that if the creature did return, she could not hope to stop it.

• • •

Sergeants Al-Yuzwaki and Yoshida moved slowly and stealthfully down the corridor, all the while being hyper-vigilant for the slightest of movements. Neither man thought what the two of them were doing was a good idea. It had become obvious that Al-Yuzwaki's ice-melter and Yoshida's coilgun were both of little use against their mysterious intruder. Fear danced through their heads as every sealed doorway narrowed their search.

"You think it went down E or F?" Al-Yuzwaki tightened his grip on his ice-melter as the two of them stood nervously at the new intersection in the corridor.

"Unless the fucker kept going straight," Yoshida motioned up the corridor with his Jones-Benelli.

Al-Yuzwaki gritted his teeth and motioned with his head, "Why in the name of all the divinities did they design this place like a fucking maze?"

"They didn't design it. Your friendly, all-knowing AI designed it," the engineer tried to grin, but it manifested itself as a sickly twitch, "based on some dogshit psych theory about mental alertness and problem-solving."

"Like fucking rats running a maze?" snorted Al-Yuzwaki peering back the way they had come. Even though the air temperature was comfortable, he found himself still sweating and his hands clammy.

Sirens started to wail throughout the corridor as several of the hall lighting panels began to flash yellow caution lights. Lync's voice followed the caution lights announcing a breach in airlock Two-K on level two, Section-L.

"*Chikushoo!*" Yoshida heralded, as he and Al-Yuzwaki began to run up towards airlock Two-K.

As they approached Section-L, Al-Yuzwaki responded to Colonel Rozsa's interlink message regarding Lync's alert and their status. Ahead they saw a lit sign, which read: **AIRLOCK # 2-K AHEAD** and noticed that the yellow caution lights had been replaced by red warning lights. The two peered at one another as they sensed the sudden drop in temperature and the pungent, irritating smell of benzene and rotting methane. They knew what that odor was and that being exposed to it for more than a few moments was lethal. It was Titan's unhealthy and unpleasant atmosphere.

As the two men slowed, they continued to hesitantly advance up the corridor, surveying the conspicuously marked airlock hatch at the far end. It was closed and apparently untouched, and there was no sign of their unwanted guest. Approaching the hatch, they noticed that the airlock system warning light was flashing both red and yellow. The outer hatch was open, and the inner hatch was locked.

Yoshida quickly scanned the keypad and made sure the emergency locks were in place for the inner door, as he tried to seal the outer one. It would not close.

"It's outside," bellowed Yoshida, peering through the viewport in the airlock's inner door, seeing only the cold, empty chamber beyond.

"You think that thing can survive outside?" Al-Yuzwaki thought it was a stupid question the second he asked it. "What the fuck are we going to do now?"

"How the hell am I to know?" Yoshida's voice was low and confused.

Al-Yuzwaki moved to the other side of the hatchway and activated his PDI, "Colonel Rozsa? Al-Yuzwaki. Yoshida and I tracked our visitor to airlock Two-K. That thing has gotten outside."

"Is the airlock secured?" questioned Rozsa, her voice surprisingly calm.

"Yeah, the inner door is sealed, but the outer hatch won't close."

"I'll relay it to the General and inform Yee in the com-center. You two stay there and watch the airlock. If it tries to get back inside, call me."

"That's affirm, Al-Yuzwaki out," he deactivated the interlink. "Now we wait." He fell back against the wall as he slid to the floor, relieved and exhausted.

Yoshida, keeping an eye on the airlock, joined Al-Yuzwaki on the floor. He was still feeling jittery, expecting something else bad to happen. There was a long pause, then Yoshida added, "I can't wait to get the fuck out of this place."

Al-Yuzwaki looked at Yoshida for a long minute, as if the man had just insulted his mother. "Yeah, but think about it. Zapollo, Zuverink, Fung, and now Wong will be going home in neoprene bags," the tech-sergeant's voice was stone-cold and rock-hard. "Not to mention everyone at TBK."

"Yeah, and I hope that's all who go home in a Divinity forsaken bag," fired back Yoshida in a voice that was as hard and cold as Al-Yuzwaki's.

The two men just stared knowingly at each other, the red warning lights still flashing in the corridor.

•　•　•

Professor Watkinski sat perplexed in front of the console holo-screen. The extrasolar's tissues and blood had proven to be tougher and more resilient than he had thought possible or would have believed possible, if he had not performed the analysis himself. However, scrolling across his holo-screen were the results of the first two hundred and fifty experiments conducted on the extrasolar materials. The extrasolar's tissues had survived bombardment by the entire electromagnetic spectrum. It had survived solutions that spanned the entire range of pH, and temperatures as high as twenty-eight hundred and eighty Kelvin with no effect. The nanite-like machines that composed the thing's body had survived through vacuum and under tremendous atmospheric pressures. It was fast becoming apparent to Professor Watkinski that their extrasolar visitor was virtually indestructible.

The door opened, breaking Watkinski's concentration.

Professor Costello entered quickly, looking as grave and nervous as Watkinski felt. "Door close," she barked, moving to Watkinski. "Don't tell me, nothing, right?"

Watkinski just looked at her. "The only things that affect it are extreme heat and extreme cold, and I am talking nanokelvins. I think intense pressure affects it, but I can't generate atmospheric pressures that high here. Strong electric charges appear to disrupt the communication between the nanites."

"How powerful a charge are we talking?" inquired Costello.

"On the order of a few thousand amperes," Watkinski deactivated his holo-screen and rubbed his eyes.

"What about repair rates, and levels of energy decay?" Costello looked at the ceiling and searched her mind for overlooked questions and ideas.

"The repair rates vary by several orders of magnitude. I haven't even figured out how those nanites sense damage to the coding sequence, let alone how they locate damaged areas. As for energy decay rates, each one of these little monsters uses approximately nine-point nine-five electron nanovolts of energy a day."

"Derived from where, the decay heat of the radiogenic isotopes?" she surveyed Watkinski's face, noticing he was in need of a shave.

The tired geo-microbiochemist nodded, "Oh yeah. They appear to be able to derive energy directly from both a photovoltaic process and a complicated nuclear synthesis. I'm using both the standard Carrington-Hendry microseivermetry technique and the Woods-Wortman method, but the PRIMS won't have any results for another three hours." Watkinski shook his head to clear it as he sat back. "Their main power generation system is kinda like a light-water thorium reactor, but within the confines of a few dozen nanometers. For instance, thorium two-thirty-two seems to be reacting using a thermal neutron to form thorium two-thirty-three, emitting a gamma burst."

"And, thorium two-thirty-three is unstable." Costello looked as if she were waiting for him to get to the point. "That gives you what, protactinium something?"

"Thorium two-thirty-three has a half-life of approximately twenty-two minutes, and it decays to protactinium two-thirty-three."

"You're saying this thing is utilizing the radiation emitted in the decay process?"

"Yes, but here's the interesting part, protactinium itself has a half-life of about twenty-seven days before decaying to uranium two-thirty-three. Which emits another neutron that starts the whole cycle over," Watkinski saw the look that was fast spreading across Costello's face. He wanted to grin in response, but he was too tired.

"You mean to tell me, that this thing is...." Costello paused, her face a contoured mass of disbelief, "that on a cellular level, this thing has a metabolism like an old style breeder reactor!"

"It's the thorium cycle, but you are close," Watkinski finally grinned at his friend's amazement. "Between that, and photoelectric generation, and a one hundred percent efficient waste heat recovery system, this thing can---"

"That's incredible. Can you confirm this with the PRIMS?" Costello knew that the Phased-Resonance Ionization Mass Spectroscopy analysis would be slow and time-consuming, and she was in no mood for waiting. "Can we interfere with its energy transfer?"

"All my tests come out negative. The little fuckers are fast, they form complex polymers and can apparently resurface themselves and alter their bonding agents at will. It's something like the beta-hydride elimination in Ziegler-Natta polymerization, but the chain running mechanism is unbelievably fast. I literally watch them resurface from silicon-boron to selenium-nickel oxide in a matter of minutes." He rubbed the back of his neck, "I don't even know how this thing retains its form if it is moving atoms and molecules around like this. If we ever figure this thing out, we'll be able to rewrite all the texts on everything from micro-biochemistry to quantum isotope crystallography to nanoelectronics. Crap, the article I could put together at this very moment, would win me both the Gates-Santos and the Tribhuvana prize in both nano-crystal field theory and isotope bio-microchemistry."

"How about trying a focused---"

The laboratory speaker interrupted Professor Costello as both scientist's PDI interlinks came to life with Professor Yee's voice, "Attention everyone! Attention! That sonuvabitch is outside on the surface," the professor's voice was calm but had an undertone of anger. "Our weapons and locked doors don't seem to be much of a problem for this thing. However, Colonel Rozsa is ordering a party out on to the surface after it. The General has been injured but it is not serious, but I have to inform you that Lieutenant Fung and Private-Specialist Wong have both..." There was a pause, then he added, "are both *end-of-mission*."

Costello gasped, putting her hand to her face, as she and Watkinski simply stared at one another in stunned silence.

"The Colonel wants everyone to remain at alert condition three and make sure you are in a secure location." Yee paused again as if contemplating something, then he added coldly, "Do what you can to be safe in case this thing gets back inside."

Watkinski fingered his interlink, "Fred, it is Kostya. Inform the General, and whoever else might be going after that thing, that only extremes of temperature and electric charge seem to have an effect. My preliminary report is in the system."

A moment later Professor Yee replied, "I read you Kostya. I'll pass your message along. NJ and Lieutenant Pulgar are taking the General to the med-bay. He's got some minor injuries. Reierstadt is headed there now. Brauer is on her way to join you, and Lebowitz is coming to the com-center."

"Why?" asked Costello, leaning over Watkinski.

"The Colonel wants everyone in groups of no less than three."

"Who's with you?"

"Lieutenant Sloan. He and I are working on a way to use the station's fire detection system to track our friend if it gets back inside. The Colonel said she'll be up here to join us as soon as possible."

Both Watkinski and Costello turned at the hydraulic sound of the lab door opening.

"Door close," commanded Brauer, looking ruffled as she dashed into the lab.

"Susan just arrived." Watkinski turned back to his PDI, "But this thing appears to be able to resurface and reconfigure its cellular operations in order to utilize its own waste energy. So it has a radiation signature as small as a barium enema."

"Great," Yee appeared to be talking to Sloan, whose voice was just audible in the background.

With a grim tone, Watkinski added, "So I guess you can

pass that bit of news along to the Colonel as well."

"Right," Yee's reply was flat.

A flash of realization swept across Watkinski's face as a forgotten memory suddenly surfaced. "Hey, Fred, what happened with trying to talk to this thing?"

"I don't know," Yee's exhausted voice produced a faint hint of sarcasm, "I wasn't there, but I gather it didn't feel much like talking."

"Kostya out," Watkinski switched off the interlink connection.

"So, Doc, I guess we are in a world of hurt?" Brauer had a grim expression on her face.

Watkinski and Costello looked at each other flabbergasted by the medtec's comment. They both turned to Brauer and just stared.

•   •   •

Doctor Tan sat nervously at the diagnostic console of the autodoc's medical analyzer. She carefully examined the multicolored readouts and images, as the sensors and scanners of the autodoc controlled medical analyzer drifted slowly over the injured body of General Newey. Near the main entrance to the brightly lit room, Lieutenant Pulgar sat like a dark statue in a chair, silently moving the loaded Glock-Whelan back and forth between her anxious hands. She wished she had kept the coilgun, but the colonel took it for the hunt.

Her null expression showed all of the shock, fear, and disbelief that bounced uncontrollably around her mind. A day ago, she would not have believed that she could ever get so scared or be as frightened as she was at that moment. She did not believe she could let her fear control her actions so badly, and all she saw every time she closed her eyes was the look on Fung's face.

Pulgar glanced up at a new sound and surveyed the large med-bay behind her, as it continued to hum and beep. The bulky medical analyzer, similar to the ones in the bio labs, occupied the middle of the room. It was a glorified scan table with a long illuminated scanner plate and an articulated instrument arm protruding from the suspended ceiling. There was a translucent partition separating the examination area from the hospice area with its ten beds, all equipped with monitoring units and restraining straps. The examination area itself was lined with storage cabinets and analytical workstations. The far wall was the autodoc's treatment unit. To anyone unfamiliar with the automated medical device, it looked like some bizarre, oversized ancient microwave cooking unit. The systems had been initially designed for non-medical personnel in remote locations, and as a physician's assistant in overcrowded urban settings.

"Right shoulder has multiple fractures," Tan announced to no one in particular, "Left ankle is crushed, and there is marrow leakage and some hemorrhaging as well." She deactivated the analyzer and moved to the scanner table. "Help me put him in the autodoc."

Pulgar angrily shoved the handgun into the belt of her pants and moved to aid Tan, as the doctor instructed Newey to strip. He looked at the two women hesitantly then began to undress with some assistance from the doctor.

Tan and Pulgar were helping the general into the large treatment compartment of the autodoc as the med-bay door sounded. In a smooth, fluid motion, Pulgar turned, drew her weapon, and brought it to bear on Doctor Reierstadt as she entered the room.

The dark haired psychologist stopped and stared at Pulgar, but saw only the barrel of the ancient weapon. There was a pause, then Reierstadt ordered the door closed behind her.

"How long will he be in there?" exhaled Pulgar, obviously shaken as she replaced the weapon back into her belt. She continued to stare at Reierstadt.

"Oh, about thirty to forty minutes," Doctor Tan punched a series of commands into the holo-screen of the autodoc and observed as the machine confirmed the order.

"What happened anyway?" Reierstadt advanced on the autodoc and took in the scene.

Pulgar's expression and tone changed as memories flooded back to her in a tidal wave of pain, "We were talking in my quarters when glory boy came through the door," she explained to Reierstadt, quickly glancing at Tan.

"Yes. How sweet," Tan walked over and flopped into a chair at an interface terminal. "I need a drink."

After a few moments, Pulgar added, "I could use a few."

She finally looked away from Reierstadt, but the tone of her voice hinted at the fact she was still shaken.

The psychologist mustered a grin, "After all that has happened in the last few days, I'd say we could all use a good stiff dose of Thorapin."

"Deflexidizetine is probably more in order," added Tan with a stressed smile.

Both Pulgar and Reierstadt looked at Tan with slightly surprised expressions, then Reierstadt stood flagpole straight, "NJ, in view of our current situation and with the loss of our co-workers, I think it is in the best interest of our survival that you issue---"

"Are you sure?" Tan immediately cut her off. "I don't like the idea of trying to deal with this thing with everybody as high as a geosynchronous satellite." The doctor was staring at her companions. Deep down she did not want to be medicated for anything. She knew that none of her companions would like the idea either, yet she was also aware that panic and claustrophobic fear clawed at each of them like a drowning cat.

"I'm not saying to turn everyone into mindless zombies, just a little something to take the edge off." Reierstadt surveyed Tan and Pulgar for a long moment, then added, "It'll make taking care of Wai-Mun and Hiroshi much easier, on all concerned."

Without a word, Pulgar watched the interplayed between the two doctors.

Doctor Tan got up stone-faced, and slowly moved to one of the medical cabinets. She pressed her left thumb against the tiny scan plate for the lock, and the medicine cabinet door popped open. Taking out a small white bottle, she added matter-of-factly, "Two capsules, all around. I'll keep the bottle..."

# CHAPTER SEVENTEEN

Doctor Tan just stood at the bend in the corridor leading to airlock Three-K. Despairingly she studied the cluster of people gathered there, her logic and emotions slugging it out in her head. One second she was afraid, the next angry. She felt fear, love, loneliness, hatred, and comradeship all coming and going with the speed of thought. She also knew they had to do this.

In front of the open airlock Majors Nianta and Singleton, Captains Arroyo and Aamodt, and Tech-Sergeant Al-Yuzwaki were preparing to go outside and onto the surface of Lincoln Mons, the pressure-molded ice mountain on which the station rested. They were going to hunt down their unwanted and now, much-hated, guest. Colonel Rozsa was there as well, hurriedly talking tactics and strategies with the two majors. All the while Tech-Sergeant Yoshida buzzed over each of the five suited figures, checking each of their e-suits in turn with all the care and attention of a nineteenth-century Italian tailor.

The apprehensive doctor observed all of the activity at the other end of the corridor, restlessly taking it all in for several long minutes. She focused on Nianta's dark brown face and studied his days' growth of facial hair, and the irregularities in his short Afro. So intently did she stare at the man that even at a distance, she could make out the lines and textures on his tired face. Tan knew the recent events were beginning to take their toll on him, as they were on everyone. The doctor found she was starting to develop a headache, as she shifted her attention to the other members of the small hunting party.

Of the five members preparing to go out into the cold darkness of Titan, only Nianta and Singleton had their helmets off. Nianta, Singleton, and Aamodt all wore toolbelts strung with DMX seismic survey charges modified to function as grenades, and each carried a Jones-Benelli Magnastar coilgun. Arroyo carried the metal tube-like recoilless rifle and a small, insulated pouch of projectiles. Al-Yuzwaki still sported the ice-melter.

Doctor Tan realized she had been holding her breath and exhaled with a barely audible sound. She could no longer stand her mounting tension and moved up the corridor. Approaching the assembled group, she addressed Major Nianta. "Excuse me. May I have a word with you?"

Nianta looked at the pale doctor, knowing what was going through her mind, "Sure." He handed his weapon to Rozsa and walked Tan back down the corridor, out of earshot of the others. "They told me what happened in Pulgar's quarters." He knew what she wanted and was trying to change the subject.

She stared at his face a moment, "Why are you going?"

He instantly knew his plan was not going to work. "Because, the Colonel ordered me too, besides that thing may decide it's better in here than out there."

Tan stepped closer to the major and whispered, "You're a pilot, not a mountaineer. None of these weapons have done anything, but piss it off."

He surveyed her for a half second. "I'll be fine, I know my way around on the ice, and I've been through the security forces' VR-weapons training." There was a long silent exchange between them before Nianta added, "Look after Arroyo lobs one of those things into it, we'll come back, and I'll convince Aamodt to open one of those bottles of good bourbon that she has been hoarding."

She felt her tension break, as her voice trembled, "What if you don't come back?" She stepped closer to him and stared into his weary eyes. It dawned on her for the first time that she really did love him.

He smiled, "Not going to happen, I'm the best metal-coffin tester this side of Mars," his smile morphed into a smirk at the mention of the slang term for a test pilot. "Besides you gotta die of something." He knew it was the wrong thing to say. He always picked the worst times to attempt humor.

Tan stepped back angrily. "Divinities fuck you!" Her outburst attracting the attention of Colonel Rozsa and the others, "This isn't a fucking game or some dumb-ass test flight! You can't..." She turned and rushed back up the corridor and rounded the corner, leaving Nianta with his mouth open in silence.

The major found himself unconsciously whispering, "Yeah." He halfheartedly hit the wall with a clenched fist as he went back to join the others.

No one said anything or asked any questions regarding Tan, they all knew and understood. Nianta and Singleton exchanged a knowing glance as they donned their helmets. Singleton and Aamodt also traded a look that was telling to anyone watching. Colonel Rozsa nudged Singleton as she handed Nianta back his coilgun, having observed the wordless interplay.

Colonel Rozsa and Tech-Sergeant Yoshida wished them all good luck, as everyone forced a smile. None of them felt optimistic about the hunt. They all knew that none of their weapons were having a lasting effect on the intruder.

The five glumly entered the decontamination-airlock compartment and sealed the inner hatch behind them. As the airlock's decontamination system cycled through its sterilization procedures, the atmosphere exchange process began with a burst of cold crimson gas.

No one in the chamber voiced a response. It was as quiet as an ancient library, the only sound being the hiss of moving gases within the small, quickly cooling chamber. Suddenly, before anyone was ready, the warning-light sign for the outer hatch changed. The hatch that had been damaged in the initial event days ago sputtered open to reveal a depressing sea of gloom.

The face of the mountain was dark, cold, and uncharacteristically calm. High above, the ghostly halo of the distant sun filtered through deep, dark orange clouds, giving little light to the tiny group as they moved slowly and cautiously out onto the surface. A huge multicolored aurora ebbed and flowed quietly overhead like some fluid, mute celestial animal desperately trying to reach the surface of Titan. The wind blew soft and nearly soundlessly as the five stood at the head of the ladder that led down the outside of the station.

"Man, that CME is creating one hell of a light show," muttered Nianta, taking in the brilliant display above them.

"Yeah, Saturn's magnetic field is slinging it around like a motherfucker," added Singleton.

"That had to be a level five alert for anybody inside the orbit of Venus," continued Nianta, staring at the sky. "I bet half the crews unlucky enough to be stuck in the path of this one are shitting in their suits."

"Well I'm close to shitting in my suit," announced Aamodt looking everywhere, but up, "and it's got nothing to do with a CME." She knew her own voice must have sounded just as hollow and distant to Nianta, as his voice sounded to her.

"Suit lights," ordered Singleton, his e-suit's AI activating his suit's exterior lights. He immediately noticed that a thin layer of ice had formed over his weapon. "Arroyo, I hope you were right about these things."

The big captain glanced sourly at Singleton and shook his head angrily inside his helmet. "I told you, all this stuff'll work out here." He followed his comrades and commanded his e-suit's AI to activate his suit's exterior lights.

"They'd better," added Nianta, refocusing himself and tapping the ice off of his weapon, "or we're fucked." He activated his laser-sight, and Singleton and Aamodt quickly followed his action.

"Yeah, much good these things did Wai-Mun or Hiroshi," there was suppressed anger in Al-Yuzwaki's voice. The bitter fury that he felt was visible in his blue-green eyes. He, like everyone else, searched the fog-shrouded area around them for signs of their prey. "We're never going to find it out here."

"I smell smoke," announced Arroyo, hurriedly checking his e-suit indicators.

Both Al-Yuzwaki and Nianta eyed the captain. "I smell it too," added Al-Yuzwaki. "It's in my clothes from the encounter Wong, and I had earlier." He had to force the images of the battle and Private-Specialist Wong out of his mind.

"That burnt smell is in all of our clothes," Nianta traded a glance with Singleton. "I smell it, Captain; it's nothing to worry about." He watched as Arroyo tried to relax with several long deep breaths.

"Smells like---"

"Shall we go gentlemen?" announced Singleton, cutting off Arroyo. He started down the ladder with an alert Nianta right behind him, "We'll see if we can pick up its trail outside of airlock Two-K."

"Barbecue," uttered Arroyo with an inappropriate chuckle. He started down behind Nianta, "I've been to a *real* barbecue."

Everyone instantly understood what Arroyo was referring too, but no one commented.

"Major Singleton?" It was not one of the five.

"Yes, Lieutenant?" responded Singleton, his eyes still scanning the darkness at the edge of his targeting laser.

"Colonel Rozsa ordered me to monitor you." Sloan's voice came through clearly in everyone's helmet.

"That's affirm," Singleton smiled to himself. "Turn on all the exterior lights." He pointed the barrel of his weapon down the ladder, the sharp laser light a sickly blue in the thick atmosphere.

A moment later, "And one of the old deities said, *Let there be light.*" The outer lights of the station flared into brilliance. There was nothing below Singleton on the ladder except rainbow colored ice.

"And there was light, and it was good," finished Nianta with a whisper. The pale lights on the outside of the station were all bathed in a ghostly reddish pink halo, that gave them an eerie, blood drop-like appearance. Nianta and Singleton both scanned the outside of the station, sweeping the area with the barrels of their coilguns, their laser-sighting beams cutting deep into the foggy distance.

Captain Arroyo giggled sickly then added sarcastically, "But he didn't like what he saw in the light, so he said *let it be dark half the time.*" He emitted a long, soft, unhealthy laugh that made Al-Yuzwaki's skin crawl.

The others in the party glanced at Arroyo, but none of them presented any opposition to the officer. Singleton waved them forward as the five climbed down the ladder to the icy catwalk outside of airlock Two-K. The catwalk was wide for one person but extremely narrow for a heavily armed cluster of five. The outer hatch to airlock Two-K was a mangled mess, reminding Al-Yuzwaki of the greenhouse doors he had seen with Wong.

"Okay guys," Nianta turned to the small group, toggling the safety of his Jones-Benelli Magnastar, "Let's find'em."

"Yeah, and what do we do when we find him," scornfully remarked Al-Yuzwaki, exchanging a knowing look with the others.

"Call him a bad boy and give it a swat on the hand for trespassing? Because that's about all, any of these weapons are going to do to it." The memory of his and Wong's fiery encounter with the extrasolar was still very fresh in his mind.

"Knock it off!" barked Nianta, glancing at Al-Yuzwaki.

"Tonja, you and Arroyo head that way and sweep down to Level One." Singleton pointed to the right. "We'll head this way and sweep up to the roof landing deck."

"If you see anything, call in and wait for us," ordered Nianta as he continued to scan their surroundings. "Try not to let it spot you first."

"Our suit lights will make that kinda impossible," spat Al-Yuzwaki.

"Sergeant," was all Nianta barked to quiet the younger man.

Aamodt had noted that Singleton had used her first name when he addressed her. She warmly added, "You be careful too," her voice hinting at the fear growing within her.

Singleton flashed her a forced grin, "Yeah." Without another word, they separated into two groups and moved off in opposite directions. The exterior lights were cold, giving no warmth or security to the two groups as they advanced.

Tech-Sergeant Al-Yuzwaki moved along slowly with his ice-melter at the ready, his massive frame bracketed by the two smaller majors behind and to either side of him. All three advanced cautiously in the low gravity and kept their eyes searching. The targeting beams of the two coilguns belonging to the two majors would occasionally detect an unseen object in the tangerine mist, and the three would feel a sudden surge of adrenaline. A wave of relief would then sweep over them as they identified the unknown as a mass of ice or a piece of frozen over machinery. The emotional rollercoaster ride was beginning to take its toll on their alertness as they continued to explore.

"Steve," Nianta's voice was subdued, "You think we'll get out of this?"

"I hope so." Singleton glanced behind them, "Just keep your mind on the job."

"Easy for you to say, this isn't like a crevasse field on Rhea or looking for evidence of Sastrugi on *Hotei Arcus*," Nianta thought back to how wrong his joke had been during his last encounter with Doctor Tan. "This isn't like pushing the limits of some prototype vehicle; this is one major pile of dogshit."

"I hear that my friend. I hear that." Singleton thought of the *dg*-books and VR-games he had read and played as a child. *This,* he thought *was like walking point on some frozen, chemically contaminated battlefield during the Antarctican Resources War. But this was for real.*

• • •

Captain Aamodt stayed several steps ahead of Captain Arroyo, who carried the loaded recoilless rifle. As they cautiously crept along the catwalks and porches on the outside of the station, Arroyo would sporadically mutter something, but it was not for Aamodt or anyone else outside of himself. Since Arroyo had come back from Titan-Base Ksa, Aamodt had noticed that his behavior had become more abnormal and irrational, even for him. Initially, she did not mind the low grumblings; it was reassuring to have someone human close at hand in the cold dark she was wandering through. However, as time passed, it began to trouble her that she could not understand half of what he was saying.

Several times Arroyo's random mutterings would be loud enough to be understood by Aamodt. They seemed to always involve something unspeakably nasty dealing with their intruder. Occasionally Aamodt would hear the general's or Doctor Reierstadt's name connected to a vile curse. A few times, she even made out something about smelling smoke and Sisyphus, intermixed with Zuverink's name or Zapollo. Unexpectedly, the air conditioner in her suit began to whine, and a blast of cool air washed over her face. She quickly realized she was sweating, and the flow of refrigerated air brought the pungent smell of her own sweat to her nostrils.

Now, after twenty minutes of stalking their unwanted guest in the cold and gloom of the station's exterior lights, Aamodt was starting to have doubts. Fear was beginning to win-out over courage, as panic gnawed away at the back of her mind. She began to wonder what was making her more nervous, the murderous inhuman thing running around in the dark and the cold, or the armed and apparently unstable human being moving behind her.

• • •

Nianta, Singleton, and Al-Yuzwaki all had the same eerie feeling. It was like being alone in a large house, and slowly realizing that someone else, someone who did not belong there, was silently watching you, peering at you from the quiet shadows. Worse, the person was studying you with an unfriendly eye and unnatural intentions. The graveyard silence did nothing to relieve the tension in the atmosphere. The only sounds were their own breathing, the gentle hum of their suits' environmental systems and the occasional status check by Sloan. Singleton thought it was almost humorous that everyone was breathing more or less in unison. It sounded to him like soft snoring in an echo chamber.

Nianta's mind kept switching back and forth between thoughts of the nightmare they were hunting, and thoughts of Doctor Tan. Try as he may, he could not focus on the dangers before him. Tan's words and her face kept tumbling through his mind. He had been in both dangerous situations and intimate relationships dozens of times before but never had his relationships kept him from concentrating on the tasks at hand. He did not know which frightened him more, the creature hiding in the cold gloom, or not seeing Tan's face ever again.

Al-Yuzwaki was just plain scared. Four of his friends were dead, and he was outside on the surface of no man's land, looking for their killer. A killer, who he knew was a projectile resistant, flame-retardant, nightmare from the deepest, darkest bowels of Hell. He wanted to pack his bags, fly up to the EET, and call it a mission. He knew if they left orbit today, even with quarantine and debriefing, that he would arrive back at Mars in time to catch the end of his family's observance of the old holiday of Ramadan. His parents lived in the Noctis ecosphere on Mars and would have a huge feast to mark the end of the holiday. *After this,* he thought, *we could all use some serious relaxation.*

They came upon another ladder.

"I think this leads to the hangar deck maintenance shed," informed Nianta. "I'll check it. Rather be safe than sorry." The major looked around carefully as he thought about climbing the ladder.

"We'll cover you," Singleton checked their rear. "Watch yourself, our friend's around here someplace."

Al-Yuzwaki glanced up at the bright aurora dancing a

tango in the deep sky, as low clouds and bands of pale orange fog moved inaudibly passed. He still felt like he was being watched.

Nianta started up the ladder, his weapon pointed ahead of him. He ascended the ladder slowly and carefully, his eyes scanning the pink and orange murkiness before him. As he swept the ladder ahead of him with his weapon, his targeting laser would encounter hanging ice or a rung of the ladder one second, and stream out into the distant, aurora-filled sky the next.

He went past the third level, checking to his left then to his right with the beam of his e-suit lights and the barrel of his coilgun. There was nothing. He continued on, passing the fourth level with similar results. He was approaching the maintenance shed on top of the hangar deck when something nearly tore his helmet off.

The stunned major flew out and away from the ladder with a panicked scream, his arms and legs flailing and his body twisting like an angry newborn. Nianta saw his weapon disappear into the night, as he felt himself falling passed Singleton and Al-Yuzwaki like a weighted helium balloon.

Singleton and the others could hear Nianta's static-riddled transmissions, over the voice of his e-suit's AI warning of a breach. They could hear the high pitch whine of moving gases as Titan's cold atmosphere roared into the major's damaged e-suit. Abruptly, and to the horror of his companions, the major's e-suit transmissions ended, as he disappeared into the shadowy depths below the station.

Singleton immediately wrapped an arm through a rung of the ladder and began firing his coilgun up into the mist at their unseen attacker. "Colin!" he screamed, fighting panic as he glanced back into the darkness.

Nianta was gone.

Al-Yuzwaki started downwards, but Singleton stopped him. "What about the Major?"

"He's gone!" Singleton knew it was a rocky and icy nine hundred meters to the small pluvial lake of supercooled ethane below.

Sloan, Aamodt, and Arroyo all started shouting over their helmet transceivers at once. It came out as one unintelligible scrawl, as the device tried to transmit too many voices at once.

"It's on level three or four," screamed Singleton, "I didn't see it! But it's on level three or four!" He thought, he made out Arroyo shouting wildly that they were on their way. "Colin is over the side! I think his suit's damaged!"

Singleton and Al-Yuzwaki started up the ladder, smoothly gliding upwards in the low gravity. The adrenaline pumping through their veins made a roar in their ears. Their limbs tried to move faster than their restraining e-suits would allow, as panicked questions boomed in their ears from their distant friends.

• • •

"Oh fuck," was all Aamodt could say as the large, charcoal black, multi-armed nightmare landed in front of her in a towering mass. She was in shock over the size and animation of the thing and did not notice the ice-melter it was carrying in one of its appendages.

Arroyo was stunned at the sudden appearance of their prey. He shouted, "I got it!" Then he fired the recoilless rifle.

In spite of its name, the recoil from the weapon in the low gravity took the big captain off his feet and propelled him backward not quite three meters, as the wildly aimed shell barely missed Aamodt and the extrasolar. It slammed into the far corner of the station, igniting into a massive blue-white fireball. The concussion wave from the explosion was visible in the thick, cold atmosphere as it radiated out into the dark of Titan at lightning speed, drawing their guest's attention for a split-second.

Within the station, the blast triggered klaxons and alarms on every level, as Titan's atmosphere and that of the station's violently blended together in a whirlwind of noise and debris. The station's AI instantly began closing emergency bulkheads in the engineering section. It also began issuing warnings and information about the breach in the station's structure. The outside lights of the station winked out, and after what seemed like an eternity of darkness, they slowly, as if fighting for life, pulsed back into pale pink existence.

Singleton and Al-Yuzwaki descended the ladder faster than they had gone up when they were suddenly bathed in light. "Look out!" was all Al-Yuzwaki had time to scream, as a stream of flame hit him and Major Singleton like a gust of wind in a hurricane.

Hopping off the ladder, as their attacker tracked them with

the ray of fire and light from the ice-melter, Singleton flipped left, and Al-Yuzwaki fell right. The creature, looking unreal in the glow of the ice-melter focused on Al-Yuzwaki. The searing flames engulfed the terror-stricken tech-sergeant as the monstrous form began to move.

"What's going on?" Boomed Sloan's voice, broken and distorted over the helmet speakers. "*Fick!* What's happening?"

In the low gravity, Al-Yuzwaki bounced around wildly, screaming and flailing as he tried desperately to put out his flaming e-suit. He could smell burning carbo-plastic and felt both heat and cold on his lower body. The fear of painful death loomed large in his panicked mind as he fought to stop the fire from migrating into his e-suit. He could feel the hot flames searching out and feeding on the life-sustaining oxygen, now bleeding out of his e-suit.

Captain Aamodt, her weapon on semi-auto, zeroed in on the extrasolar creature and fired at point-blank range. The coilgun rounds lifted the creature off its feet and two meters into the air. It landed upside down but held onto the ice-melter. The recoil from her coilgun propelled Aamodt backward into Captain Arroyo, who was moving to collect his lost recoilless rifle and get back into the fight. The two went down in a pile, looking like a pair of drunken acrobats.

Al-Yuzwaki was still screaming and thrashing about as if he were a fish out of water. His damaged e-suit hissed like an angry snake, as Titan's toxic atmosphere rushed into the compromised suit. The e-suit's AI spat warnings of approaching death as he fumbled with the useless controls. Neither he nor his e-suit's AI could do much to stop the disaster that was descending down on him.

Singleton dropped flat, toggled his weapon from single-action to semi-auto, and through the orange haze took careful aim with his laser-targeting beam. He fired a blast from his Jones-Benelli at their terrifying assailant. Several of the rounds struck the ice-melter's fuel tank, which exploded in a blinding flash of blue-white light and bone searing heat.

For a full three seconds, the extrasolar lifeform was a mass of colored flames, before the lack of oxygen killed the fire. The creature scrambled back to its feet and for a moment appeared to stare in the direction of Singleton, not moving. A chill ran down the major's spine, even though he could not see its eyes, he felt the inhuman glare of the extrasolar cutting through the haze and locking on to him. At that moment he froze with confused fear, the creature also glided around the damaged corner of the station and was gone.

A jumble of sounds, klaxons, and voices, all clearly audible, exploded over Singleton's helmet speakers. The sound jolted Singleton back to reality as he popped up and shouted, "Tonja! See to Al-Yuzwaki! Arroyo, with me!" then he skipped off after their fleeing attacker. Reaching the missing corner of the station, Singleton paused and stared at the black, cave-like opening. The interior was briefly illuminated by a series of arc-welder-like flashes from shorting wires and severed cables. It was hard to believe that only a minute ago, the dark and icy debris covered mess before him was part of a state-of-the-art research installation.

"What's going on?" Sloan's voice was on the edge of panic. "*Scheisse!* Somebody talk to me!" In the background, it sounded like the com-center was going crazy.

Captain Arroyo, still muttering to himself furiously struggled to reload his recoilless as he went foraging after the major. Rounding the missing corner of the station, Arroyo spied Major Singleton at the base of a ladder. Looking up, their fleeing attacker was already passed level two and climbing fast. Arroyo dropped to one knee and aimed the launcher at the dark figure on the ladder, but before he could fire, it leaped. The creature's body flattening and deforming like a bed sheet in the wind, sailed downward in a perfectly controlled slow-motion glide and landed on the outer edge of a viewport. Arroyo, taken aback by the thing's maneuver, just watched it drift down to its new position. Realizing it was getting away from him, he quickly panned his weapon to the target.

"No! Wait! You'll…" Singleton was too late; the recoilless projectile was on its way.

The high-yield rocket-propelled warhead, the extrasolar, and the Titanian atmosphere all exploded into biochem lab number three with a roar that could be heard throughout half of the station.

•　　•　　•

Professor Watkinski, who had been sitting at the holo-screen console of the positron diffusion microscope, was trying to contact the com-center when he was suddenly thrown across the lab. The force of the impact with the opposite wall shattered his skull like a boiled egg dropped from a kitchen counter. He never felt the wave of debris and deadly cold that enclosed him a second later.

Pieces of the ballistically launched thermo-transplastic from the viewport slashed into Medtec Brauer's body with all of the efficiency of a dozen, well-sharpened butchers' knives. Coughing up blood and crying, the mortally wounded medtec tried to crawl to the lab door. The cold and poisonous atmosphere combined to stop her from reaching the sealed door. The last thing she saw with quickly freezing eyes was their extrasolar intruder.

Professor Costello bleeding from multiple cuts and compound fractures desperately tried to reach the laboratory door. However, within a mere ten seconds, her frozen eyes cracked like marbles from the intense cold, and her fingers snapped off like dry twigs against the debris-covered floor. The pain of her wounds was replaced by the agony of her quickly freezing lung tissues. Asphyxiated and frozen, she did not even feel the lab door as she fell against it.

The stunned intruder got up, but one of its four arms did not. Without missing a beat, it snatched up its severed arm and bolted to the door. It batted the solidifying form of Professor Costello out of its way, which crumbled into large irregular chunks like dry, gray-blue clay. Dropping its dismembered limb, it used its remaining three arms to pry open the lab door, which moved aside in a spray of hot, steaming hydraulic fluid and electrical sparks. In the sudden scream of rushing wind, the creature was practically sucked into the corridor by the lesser atmospheric pressure in the now open passageway. The dense and cold Titan atmosphere roared its way into the passageway in a cloud of colored debris and condensed gases.

The thing retrieved its arm and was through the breached doorway in an instant.

●　　　●　　　●

Singleton yanked Arroyo around, almost flipping both of them over. "You fucking asshole!" he screamed as Captain Aamodt hopped up next to them. "Do you know what you just did?"

Lieutenant Sloan and General Newey's voices were yelling through everyone's helmet speakers. They were begging for information, the confusion of klaxons, sirens, voices, and static making their words nearly unintelligible.

"Major, Jamal's suit is seriously damaged, and his internal temperature's dropping fast," interrupted Aamodt. She could see Singleton's fury growing through his helmet faceplate.

Both men just stared at each other, with numerous voices sounding continuously in their ears.

"Major?" Aamodt yelled, trying to get Singleton's attention over the confusion. Through his helmet's faceplate, Singleton looked as if he wanted to kill Arroyo, and Arroyo looked as if he wanted him to try.

"Help her get Al-Yuzwaki inside," barked Singleton, looking tired and disgusted. "Lieutenant Sloan, we lost Nianta, and Al-Yuzwaki's down. Aamodt and Arroyo are bringing him in, alert Doc Tan. Do you copy?"

"Yeah, I copy," replied Sloan.

"What happened to the Major?" question Newey's voice.

"What do you mean, what happened?" Singleton found himself suddenly spinning out of control. "He's fucking dead! It threw him off the fucking mountain! What the hell kinda question is that?" Anger fueled the major's voice like a blast furnace. Realizing what was happening, his training kicked in, and he got himself under control again. "Sorry, sir. My apologies, I was out of line."

There was a long quiet pause, broken only by radio static, distant voices, and background sounds. After a moment, Sloan's voice came again. "We are registering numerous breaches in the structural integrity of the station, and a significant change of atmospheric pressure. Some key systems are offline."

Hesitantly General Newey Inquired. "Did you get it?"

Major Singleton did not reply, and Captain Arroyo did not move. The two officers just glared at one another for a moment, then Arroyo followed Captain Aamodt. He carried the empty recoilless rifle as if he wanted to drop it and forget it. With penned up fury, Singleton watched the captain move away.

"Did you copy, Major?" came Sloan again.

"Yes. The station took some explosive damage, and I am going to investigate." The major carefully ascended the ladder, and in the low gravity, hopped across to the blown out viewport. Using his suit lights, and with his weapon at the ready, he began looking for any signs of movement in the darkened and mangled remains of the room.

Entering the blackened wreckage that used to be a state-of-the-art biochemistry facility, Singleton's heart sunk as he discovered the body of Medical Technician Brauer. He knew he did not have to check to see if the young woman was deceased. The major followed a trail of crystallized blood and discovered the remains of Costello.

Part of Singleton wanted to look away from the ice-covered fragments on the floor, and the other part of him could do nothing but stare at the pieces. For a moment, the mess on the floor reminded him of the extrasolar entity when they had discovered it, back at Titan-Base Ksa. Staring at the fragments, the ghostly white, severed head of Professor Costello bothered him the most. The twisted look of pain and fear on the ice-covered face of the woman hurt him deeply. All of a sudden, it dawned on him. More people had died around him in the last three days, than in his entire professional career. That realization, at that moment, brought fear to him in waves of uncontrollable trembling.

After a minute, the major gathered himself and still shaking, moved on. He found the body of Professor Watkinski and noticed the fragments of broken glass and metal embedded in the dead man's face like blueberries in a muffin.

"Lieutenant, biochem lab three is *end-of-mission*. Watkinski, Costello, and Brauer were in the lab. I'm continuing my search."

There was no reply from Sloan. All but one of the background voices had gone silent. Only the voice of Lync could be heard, still babbling away in its usual monotone.

The major, switching off his weapon's laser-sighting beam, no longer felt afraid, he felt angry. "What the fuck are we going to do?" his voice was a barely audible whisper, as only cold hard gloom answered him.

# CHAPTER EIGHTEEN

General Newey, Colonel Rozsa, and Major Singleton sat around the Intelligent-conference table in the general's office. All three wore heavily insulated flightsuits, each color-coded for rank and position, and each sporting a variety of mission patches and insignias. The trio looked shell-shocked and haggard, and in need of a good days' sleep. In the last four days, they had seen more death and destruction than at any time in their lives. They had lost one complete base, eight friends, hundreds of co-workers, and the dreadful list just kept going. It was more than any of them had been prepared to handle.

Newey and Rozsa also had questions lingering in the back of their minds. They had questions about their monstrous intruder and how and if they could stop it. They had questions regarding their surviving comrades and about the long-term habitability of the station. There were more questions than answers. Even to a highly experienced officer like Newey, it seemed like months since they were all together, laughing and joking at the New Year's party. It took a moment for any of them to remember that it was only a little more than a week ago, that first names were in vogue. That five days ago, the most important matter to be dealt with was the failure of a science experiment, the planning of a party, and the outcome of a friendly game of Weiqi.

Singleton, with his down caste expression, offered, "Why don't we just abandon the base?" The exhausted major radiated distress all through the room.

The general cleared his throat weakly and pronounced in a tired voice, "As soon as Pulgar and Sloan get the communications array back up, we will be able to send a clear and secure message to the OSC." He flexed his still stiff and sore arm. "I think we can still save this situation."

Rozsa looked surprised but offered nothing in response.

Singleton just bobbed his head in disbelief. "And add to that another four hours or so before we get a reply. We could all be dead by the time we hear back from them."

Rozsa, her tone saying more than her words, added, "Besides, Marshall already gave you permission to evac if we feel the need."

"And tell them what?" Newey stared at Rozsa hard, "That we have an EBE running around down here, that half our people are dead. You know what they're liable to do." The deep disgust in his voice was mirrored by deep sorrow etched into his old face, and the faces around him. He knew, all too well, that as the commanding officer, he was ultimately responsible for everything that happened under his command.

"Worldfall," muttered Rozsa dropping her head into her chest. "Fuck."

The major sat up in his seat and quickly eyed Rozsa and the general, but said nothing.

Newey paid no attention to the woman's utterings. "Colonel, what's the condition of the station?"

Rozsa slumped back in her chair, "Arroyo; that oversized anal wart blew one mother of a hole in the engineering level, and another in biochem lab three."

"What's Arroyo's status?" inquired the general.

"As per your orders, Doc Stadts slipped him something, and he's out in his quarters," grumbled Singleton, his voice and expression, angry.

Rozsa looked over at Singleton. "Thanks to him, a good part of the science section is fucked. The explosion in engineering tore up a lot of very critical systems, even some emergency systems are offline."

"Repairs?" ventured Newey.

"All the bots are offline. Yoshida and Tounames are doing what they can to restore the vital systems. Central heating is operating at seventy percent. As long as we seal off non-critical sections, the rest of the base's temperature will hold at somewhere around seven degrees."

"Power?"

Rozsa shook her head and stared back at the general. "Main plant crashed; there is damage to some of the infrastructure. Backup power is holding; however, there is a power-drain someplace that is bleeding the system."

"Lync?" inquired the general, not knowing what else to ask.

"Spotty. LaRocque recommends we don't trust it for essential services. The blast in engineering exposed some of Lync's primary hardware to Titan's environment."

"That's why the bots are offline," interjected Singleton.

"He says there is extensive thermal damage." Rozsa's already gloomy expression instantly got more despondent as her voice dropped an octave, "The majority of the optronic relays for Lync are damaged, and the system is only operating at about forty-four percent efficiency. LaRocque said about half of the quantum logic blocks are fried beyond any hope of repair. Luckily, before its higher functions went down, Lync switched over most of the station's systems to emergency mode."

"Atmosphere?"

"It's holding for now," the colonel did not sound hopeful.

Newey glumly surveyed his officers. Neither of the two were looking back at him, and he felt like they were blaming him for their current situation. *Yes, mistakes were made. Rozsa shouldn't have brought that thing back to the station without consulting me first,* thought the general as he stared at the colonel. *Maybe I should have listened to Lori and McGilmer and did something to stop that thing when I had a chance. However, no great reward comes without some great risk and some great sacrifice.* "How's Jamal?"

Singleton looked up. "He's got severe cryo-burns over most of his lower body and to his lungs. NJ said with most of the key systems down, that gene treatment and cellular reactivation were out of the question. The autodoc is working on him, but it's recommending amputation of both legs and his genitals."

Newey exhaled and put his face into the palms of his hands for a moment before he collected himself. There was a long, painfully silent pause, then Newey asked, "How'd Tan take the news?"

There was another long pause. The look in Singleton's eyes could have answered the question. "After she stabilized Al-Yuzwaki, she went to her quarters. Reierstadt gave her something, and is staying with her."

There was another long moment of silence.

Rozsa unzipped a suit pocket and removed a small dataclip. "I thought you should see this. Sloan pulled this from the data recorders in the bio labs. They recorded what happened to Zuverink and the final moments of bio lab three." She slid the dataclip into a small slot in the tabletop and tapped out a set of commands on the holo-screen in front of her. The holo-screen expanded and flipped to the center of the conference table, so all could see.

The images on the holo-screens sped by for a second and finally stopped. It settled on an image of Sasha Zuverink sitting in a chair watching a vid. Motionless behind her was the lab worktable and its gray-white canopy, housing the extrasolar lifeform. From the time index glowing in the lower left corner of the ghostly image, Newey knew that these events were recorded approximately twenty minutes before he had arrived in the bio lab.

"Watch," Rozsa indicated a section of the image. The opaque canopy began to slowly open, as a mass of thick white fog began to settle to the floor surrounding the worktable. The scene instantly reminded all three officers of something from an ancient horror classic, something about an evil, undead thing rising from its funeral coffin, wanting blood. Indeed, the nightmarish thing began to sluggishly maneuver itself from the table. First, its movements were small and slow, as if its six limbs were painfully arthritic. However, within a minute it stealthily eased itself, spider-like across the lab floor and advanced toward the unsuspecting woman seated in the image.

"It moves like a skilled hunter," Singleton whispered to himself, almost subconsciously. His mind was fixated on the image of the strange entity like a chess player locked onto an opponent's queen.

"Why didn't Lync warn her like it did me and the com-center?" inquired Newey solemnly.

"She apparently deactivated the system's audio alert," replied the colonel, still watching the scene unfold.

The general slowly rocked his head in disapproval.

In the recording, the image of Zuverink appeared to be totally absorbed in the vid she was watching. It was apparent that she was unaware of their malevolent guest's ominous movements, just meters behind her. The thing scanned the lab quickly as if everything were a threat, then it moved quietly up behind the young woman. Newey wanted to shout a warning, as did Singleton, but they both knew that it was far too late to warn their friend.

Without warning, the expression on the young private-specialist's face changed. She looked to her right and behind her at the lab table. As she stood and turned toward the nightmare advancing on her, she froze. They appeared to stare at each other for what seemed like a full minute but was only a few seconds. The extrasolar lifeform made a series of sounds, but Zuverink, in a panicked motion, unholstered her Glock-Whelan and fired, emptying the weapon into the creature. Stumbling back two steps, the extrasolar was suddenly energized by the young private-specialist screams. It moved forward with incredible speed, its four arms reaching for Zuverink like some huge, demonic spider.

Zuverink's panicked screams halted instantly as the demonic entity snatched her up with such bone-crushing force and angry violence that it was painful even to watch. It reminded Newey of someone hitting a floppy doll with a cricket bat. Singleton thought the sick crack that, for an instant, replaced Zuverink's screams sounded like a piece of drywall snapping in half. Rozsa's stomach just flinched as the young woman instantly went limp and silent, the useless firearm falling to the floor.

Newey forced himself to watch in glum silence. He wished he had not stopped to talk to Reierstadt. Maybe he could have done something to save her, if only he had not stopped. The thought depressed him more, and he wanted another cigar and a lot of bourbon.

"She's still alive," mumbled Singleton, not wanting to watch, but not being able to turn away.

Zuverink whimpered weakly. She was conscious but limp.

The thing examined the private-specialist, manipulating her like a puppet, entirely oblivious to her distress. It reminded Singleton of the way wine connoisseurs held a glass to examine its color and clarity, or a jeweler examining a gem in the light. The creature issued an array of sounds that reminded Rozsa and Singleton of some familiar sounds, but played backward and at the wrong speed.

Zuverink let out a cry, and in response, the creature swung the young woman against the ceiling, ripping out the overhead panels, smashing several light fixtures. It flung the helpless Zuverink to the floor with such force that she rebounded at least a quarter of a meter. The AI must have sensed the change in light levels because the spectral patterns of the image changed to increase the picture's contrast.

"Turn it off, we've seen enough," Newey did not want to see anymore. Neither did Singleton.

Rozsa tapped the holo-screen, and the image fast-forwarded again. The strange entity ransacked the lab. It ripped open and went through drawers and cabinets like a thief pressed for time. It would stop to closely examine something, then proceed on with its search. Rozsa slowed the image. "This is what I want you to see."

The multi-armed, extrasolar-thing was paused over one of the lab's holo-screens. It was obviously examining the device. Its long fingers moved slowly over the holo-screen at first but soon grew to a speed equal to an expert. Bizarrely it stopped as if it had hit an invisible wall. It appeared to look the screen up and down for half a second, then moved off.

"I think it was trying to figure out our technology," announced Rozsa gently, still staring at the screen. "Like what it was doing in the greenhouse with the AI-interface terminals. However, keep watching."

The nightmarish thing was suddenly bent over Zuverink's body again. From the low groans of pain, the private-specialist was still alive. "What is it doing?" inquired Singleton, not wanting to know the answer to his own question. He was surprised, however, that she had survived the brutal encounter so far.

Zuverink let out a soft gurgling in the image, the sound of which made everyone's skin crawl. To Newey, it sounded like the last agony filled whimpers of a dying puppy caught in a coil of razor wire.

Singleton could taste his last meal and stomach acid in his mouth, as he fought back nausea.

Rozsa typed something into the holo-screen, and the image stopped. The colonel reached out and touched her index finger to a point between the image of Zuverink and the extrasolar lifeform. A transparent box appeared around the area on the screen, and she tapped it twice. The size of the box doubled to include the two figures. She then touched another icon below the image, and the picture zoomed into the box. Clearing, the unpleasant recording continued again.

The entity had apparently extended the length of one of its clawed fingertips and was using it as a cutting instrument, slowly opening up Zuverink's suit and chest with one razor-like cut. The screams that came out of the young woman's throat were like nothing human. Zuverink tried to move her broken body, but the creature held her still as it unzipped her flesh. The unfortunate woman began to choke as frothy red blood spilled from her quivering mouth. Mercifully, the young woman died after a few seconds, her eyes staring blindly at the thing that was methodically dissecting her.

Feeling as if he were going to be sick, Newey slumped forward. "In the name of all the divinities, why did we have to see that?" he looked at his holo-screen again as blood flowed out of the dead private-specialist's body. The extrasolar was covered in Zuverink's blood as it continued to work.

"It's studying her," Rozsa's face was steel hard and ice-cold. "It has never seen a human being, and its seeing how we are put together, how we work."

"I don't see how it could learn anything from that sick anatomy lesson?" Singleton avoided looking at the screen. After viewing this, he knew he was going to have nightmares. Observing the expressions on the faces of his colleagues, he knew all of them were going to have nightmares.

On the holo-screen, the extrasolar creature removed organ after blood-soaked organ, examining each and tossing it aside like so much uninteresting garbage. Unbelievably, and to the utter amazement of the three observers, Zuverink's blood and bodily fluids that had been covering the extrasolar form began to fade.

"I think it absorbed her blood through its skin," whispered Rozsa still watching the horrific scene as the last traces of dark red disappeared into the creature's skin.

After what seemed like an hour of unpleasant viewing to the three watching the recording, the four-armed demon finally got up and moved out of the frame of the image. It left behind a sloppy, blood-covered mess that only minutes before had been a human being, their friend, and coworker. The time index indicated that the whole examination took just over five minutes.

Rozsa zoomed out to the normal view of the lab. Their intruder appeared to continue its search of the lab, again. It ripped out more of the drop-ceiling and pulled itself up into the space, only to drop back down a second or two later. Finding the doorway after a few more seconds, it exited in a manner that indicated caution and stealth.

"There is nothing until you enter the room," Rozsa stopped the recording.

"So it's intelligent, but we knew that already." Newey was looking at the colonel, waiting for her to make her point.

"Yes, but it didn't attack Zuverink until she used her weapon. It tried to interface with Lync there, and once again later on in the greenhouse. The thing systematically searched the lab, and then it sat there and dissected her. It wanted to learn about us. It was trying to find out who we are and how we work." There was a silence as Rozsa waited for a question or comment. When none was coming, she continued, "This thing knows by now that we can't breathe Titan's atmosphere. If it wanted to kill us, it could just start knocking holes in the station."

Newey caught on to what Rozsa was getting at, "It's not out to kill us."

"If it doesn't want to kill us, then what the fuck does it want," Singleton looked to the general and the colonel for an answer.

"I don't know? Probably the same thing you'd want if you woke up in a strange place." Rozsa examined Newey's face.

"Those sounds it made were similar to the ones it made in Pulgar's quarters." Newey's shoulder was still aching. "It probably wants to find a way out of here, and back to its ship."

"That would be my guess," Rozsa removed the dataclip from the tabletop device. "And I think that is a bad idea. At least until we---"

"It's pissed off now, and whatever it's up to, I'm sure it's not in our best interest," interrupted Singleton.

"Is there any sign of it?" the general looked to Singleton, knowing the answer already.

"No," Singleton was looking more disheartened every minute, "but it's somewhere inside." Bizarre ideas, as to what their unknown guest was up to, were flashing through his mind.

"Professor Watkinski communicated that he thought that only extremes of temperatures and powerful electrical charges, would have an effect on this thing," explained a disgusted Rozsa, slowly surveying the other two at the table.

With a sarcastic tone, Singleton fired, "Maybe we could convince it to go fuck a power outlet?"

Somewhere in the back of the general's mind a light when on, "I got an idea," a grin breaking his exhausted, bearded face. "We've got lots of heavy-duty micro-cable and over a dozen of those portable nuclear generators."

"Those little cesium chloride bastards we use to power large equipment away from the station?" inquired Singleton, abruptly sitting up and paying attention.

"Yeah," Newey paused with his grin turning into a full-fledged smile.

Rozsa also smiled as she caught onto what the general was hinting at, "The best offense is a good defense."

"Exactly, we can set up several traps for it around the station. We can then lure it into one, and fry its ass for good." Major Singleton sat forward, but before he could speak, the general halted him, "Where is everyone?"

"Pulgar and Sloan are still working on communications. Professors McGilmer and Yee are taking care of Wai-Mun and Hiroshi," answered Rozsa, checking the memory of her PDI. "The trauma-specialist and the medtec are in the med-bay tending to Al-Yuzwaki. Reierstadt is with NJ in her quarters. Aamodt and Professor Eastman are holding down the com-center. LaRocque is in Lync's central-core trying to get some more systems back online. Yoshida and Tounames should still be in engineering, so LaRocque isn't really alone, and Arroyo should be down-and-out in his quarters."

"Okay, well I don't want to take Yoshida and Tounames off of station repairs," Newey looked questioningly at Rozsa, "and I want to keep Arroyo out of the fucking way. Do you think LaRocque, Pulgar, and Sloan can handle setting up a few electrical traps?"

The colonel nodded, "Yeah, if we don't get too fancy."

"Hopefully we can kill it or at least stun it with electricity, and restrain it somehow until help arrives." Newey looked at each of them in turn. "Now, if we do manage to capture it, what's our next move?"

Major Singleton was not looking at the general, but at Colonel Rozsa. "I say even if we kill it, we send a message to the OSC, take one of the hoppers up to the EET, and get the hell out of here."

"And if we do catch it, we drop it in one of the liquid helium tanks and see if that will freeze it," added Rozsa, "or at least slow it the fuck down. Then we go home."

"Not that simple." Newey, feeling another wave of exhaustion and depression coming on, rubbed his face briskly with both hands. "After all that has happened, we can't just go sailing off without permission. They'll tell the asteroid defense net to cancel our flight plan as sure as dogshit."

There was a moment of quiet anxiety, then Singleton continued, "I recommend that we send the civilians up to the EET while we trap this thing. After we capture it, we can bring them back down or we could---"

"I would rather have as many hands available as possible if we are going to try and trap this thing." The general stared thoughtfully at Singleton, "also, Yee and McGilmer may be able to devise another way of neutralizing our new friend."

"Yeah, like a Neanderthal trying to power-down a fusion reactor," snickered Singleton, his voice loaded with sarcasm, but the general and the colonel ignored him. They understood he had just lost a close friend in Major Nianta.

"We would also have to send Tech-Sergeant Al-Yuzwaki up with them, and one of us would have to fly," added Rozsa, looking the major coldly in the eye.

"Also, let's not forget another problem we have," Newey shifted uncomfortably in his seat. "We have to do something about Captain Arroyo."

# CHAPTER NINETEEN

Sergeants Yoshida and Tounames worked quickly and steadily in the shadows and dark areas created by the high-intensity emergency lights of the sub-engineering level. Their e-suits slowed their progress, but with the level exposed directly to Titan's poisonous atmosphere, they had no choice but to work around the restrictions of their suits to the best of their abilities. The damage to the guts of the station was beyond any hope of repair without the aid of the Marbs, which sat dormant at various locations across the rapidly cooling installation.

Both Yoshida and Tounames were surprised and dismayed by the unexpected appearance of Captain Arroyo. Colonel Rozsa had told them that Arroyo had been released from his duties. They were told he needed a few days' rest after the incident with the recoilless weapon. However, now less than a day after the incident, he was back.

Anxiously they watched the captain, disheartened at the apparent declining mental state of their colleague. He worked on the critical infrastructure, but Arroyo was unkempt and unshaved and was eerily silent. Yoshida and Tounames could see through his helmet visor that he was whispering feverishly to himself.

"We should get the fuck out of here," Tounames had his gloved hands in the innards of a large machine. "Assuming we manage to patch that whole upstairs, the science section is still fucked, and that thing is still running around."

"Chuck, hand me that point nine-eight, will yeah?"

requested Yoshida, pointing at the small tool and apparently ignoring Tounames' comments. "I'm almost done with this."

Tounames handed him the mechanical device without looking away from his own work, "Why don't we just go up to the EET or at the very least relocate to someplace like TBT?"

Yoshida did not reply. He knew the general would not abandon his command and order them up to their Emergency Evacuation Transport, which was sitting in orbit about Titan. He also knew that relocating to the abandoned Titan-Base Tui was an even poorer choice. Titan-Base Tui, like all the other Titan-bases, had been stripped of supplies, before being evacuated. There was probably nothing of use to them there. The Outer Systems Command did not leave valuable supplies just sitting around. Space exploration was very expensive, even in the thirtieth century.

"Hey, Capt'n you sure you are okay to be down here with us? You should be resting."

Captain Arroyo ignored Tounames and kept on working on the row of emergency de-icing units. The units were a mess, their metal casings were melted, Lync's control systems were obviously fried, and most of the operating circuits were coated in ice and carbonized black.

"Cap!"

"We are in trouble dumbass," Arroyo boomed, not looking at the two men. "You and Newey think I am just going to relax in my cabin?"

"Hey! I just wanted to know how the de-icers were coming along?" Tounames got defensive. "We'll have power for you in a few minutes."

Arroyo did not reply.

"Capt'n, you---"

Arroyo spun around to face Tounames, a lethal-looking hand-torch, its tip flaring a brilliant pale blue-pink, was pointed directly at Tounames. "Shut the fuck up and get back to work! I'll let you know when the damn things are working."

"Okay," Tounames was not going to press his luck. Looking through Arroyo's faceplate, the man's eyes did not look right to him. "Take it easy. I was just asking." He slowly rested his gloved hand on the Glock-Whelan next to him, in the event the situation turned ugly.

Yoshida, eyeing the captain, put his own gloved hand on

his sidearm as well.

Arroyo turned back to his work as if all of a sudden forgetting the other two men were present.

The two sergeants peered at one another. Tounames, with a wave of his hand, indicated that Yoshida should follow him. "Mitsu, lend me a hand upstairs, unpacking those plastocrete automolders." He started walking toward the exit, "We should have those things set-up and ready to go before the heaters come back online."

"Sure. The faster we can get that breach patched, the faster we can re-initialize the atmospheric controls, and get out of these suits." Yoshida glanced at Arroyo, who was still intent on his work. "We'll be right back, Capt'n."

Arroyo did not respond but remained focused on his task.

Wordlessly and carefully, the two men zigzagged their way through the ice-covered sub-engineering level. As they moved around the frozen and lifeless machinery, they kept nervously glancing back. They expected to spy Captain Arroyo or worse, their intruder, stalking them, but they saw nothing. Reaching the emergency ladder without any sign of impending danger, they ascended up to the main engineering level. Squinting back one last time, Yoshida slowly closed the hatch behind them.

In main engineering, Tounames could feel his nervous system throbbing with subdued fear, as he anxiously scanned the cold darkness. There was nothing, only an arctic stillness, and newly formed ice. The once brightly lit and busy engineering level that had been filled with numerous AI-controlled machines was now dark and lifeless. A large hole loomed at the bend in the room with vapors and wisps of super-chilled gases drifting like aimless ghosts through the opening. Irregular puddles of liquid ethane dotted the dark, debris-covered floor, like a cluster of kettle lakes.

Tounames swiftly held up three gloved fingers with one hand, as he changed the frequency of his e-suit intercom with the other.

Yoshida followed.

"Arroyo's out of it," whispered Tounames. He acted and felt as if the captain could still hear his short-range signals.

"I don't think he is even supposed to be down here," Yoshida whispered. "I could have sworn I heard the General order Doc Stadts to medicate him."

"Doesn't matter, I always thought he was wound a little too tight for this place, anyway."

Yoshida nodded in agreement, thinking about how Arroyo looked with that torch in his hand. "Do you want to jump him and take him to her?"

Arroyo was a big man, and Tounames was not sure if he and Yoshida could control him. Someone could get injured, and they had enough problems. "No. One of us should go get the Doc, and the other one watch him."

Yoshida looked back at the closed hatchway. "Look, you get Doc Stadts and I'll watch him." Yoshida really did not like the idea of being alone with Arroyo, even under normal conditions, and things had long since stopped being normal. "Just hurry the fuck back and tell her to bring a shot or something for this asshole, and try not to get killed before you get back here, please."

Tounames did not think that was very funny. He fired a cold eye at Yoshida, patted him on the shoulder and left, via the elevator. Yoshida swallowed some saliva that had been forming in his mouth, took a deep breath, and re-tuned his e-suit intercom. As Yoshida opened the hatch to the lower level, he saw Arroyo standing at the foot of the ladder. It appeared to him that he was adjusting his e-suit controls.

As another small Titanquake rumbled through the sub-engineering level, the two men stared at one another for a long moment, then Arroyo turned and walked off, muttering to himself.

Yoshida moved down the ladder, keeping an eye on Arroyo. The big man, illuminated by the bright emergency spotlights, moved back into the frozen disaster area that used to be the sub-engineering level.

●   ●   ●

After nearly an hour of consoling the grieving Doctor Tan, Doctor Reierstadt was relieved when the woman had finally drifted off to sleep. Between the physical and emotional stress and the sedative she had given the woman, Reierstadt knew her friend would be out for hours. Reierstadt fought to control her own thoughts, but she could not help feeling sympathy towards her colleague. The steadily flickering lights of Tan's quarters and the graveyard silence that issued forth from her interlink was only serving to demoralize and depress Reierstadt further.

The psychologist tried to work on her own report, but her own mental state was making it feel like a waste of time. However, with her PDI secured to her forearm, she began wandering around Tan's quarters, trying to force herself to struggle through her own growing depression. She hoped by the time Tan reawakened, they would all be off the station and headed home.

In her aimless wanderings around Tan's quarters, Reierstadt observed the half-dozen two-dimensional digital Image-blocks embedded in the smart-walls. They all were loaded with images of life on the station, before and after the evacuation. There were people and places that were important to Doctor Tan. Among the images were some of the recently deceased; Zuverink clowning around with Yoshida and others in the cafeteria; Lieutenant Fung, Private-Specialist Wong, and several others clad in e-suits working in some distant ice cave; a buddy shot of Singleton and Nianta at some station party. There were images of people she did not know and people who had been coworkers but had been evacuated. Most of the images were full of smiling faces and warm cheer.

Reierstadt spied a group image of Major Nianta, Captain Aamodt, and Professors Yee and Watkinski, all standing on the dark surface of one of Saturn's trivial little icy satellites. The faces of the four were just visible through the faceplates of their e-suits. She had seen the same image in Nianta's quarters, with the enormous face of Saturn looming in the background and the numerous irregular chunks of ice that were its rings taking up most of the sky. There were several recent images of Major Nianta, clowning around, hard at work, laughing in the cockpit of a skiff, swimming laps in the pool and smiling in the greenhouse.

The hydraulics of the main door to the quarters sounded as it opened suddenly, scaring the psychologist, who scrambled across the room and against the opposite smart-wall. It was Captain Aamodt carrying a Jones-Benelli coilgun, her index finger wrapped tightly around the trigger.

"Door close!" she barked as Reierstadt sighed with relief, the moisture in her breath forming a cloud of fog as it exited her mouth, "Did I---"

"Hell yeah," declared Reierstadt, moving back to the center of the room.

"Sorry, but the General ordered me to round up all the FA

staff and get them to the cafeteria." Aamodt's voice left no room for doubt that it was an order.

"Why?"

"Environment and power problems."

"I take it internal communications are still down?"

"Yeah, and the internal temperature is still dropping, so Doc can we get moving," Aamodt motioned toward the door with the barrel of the coilgun, "I still have to swing by the med-bay."

"What about her?" Reierstadt indicated the sleeping doctor in the next room.

"You can carry her," the captain moved so she could watch both the doorway and the majority of the room.

Reierstadt's face wrinkled, "How?"

"All right, I'll carry her, and you carry this." Aamodt held the weapon up, offering it to the psychologist, but still ready to bring it into action in an instant. "You do know how to use it?"

"Okay, I'll carry her, but---"

The main door opened again, and Aamodt wheeled around.

Tounames, still in his e-suit, minus the helmet, almost walked into the barrel of Aamodt's coilgun. "Hey!" his hands jetted high into the air, "It's just me!" The two women relaxed again, as Aamodt bought the weapon down.

"What's up?" inquired Aamodt, clicking her weapon's safety into place.

"I checked in with the com-center and asked about Doc Stadts," Tounames indicated the dark-haired psychologist. "The General told me where you were."

A wave of curiosity moved across Reierstadt's face, "What's going on?"

"It's Capt'n Arroyo."

"Fuck'em!" barked Aamodt with contempt. "Did you guys get the heat back up?"

"No, but---"

"The station's internal temperature is dropping, and the General wants all the FA personnel in the cafeteria until you guys get the environment back online," Aamodt's voice was tired, but still matter-of-fact. "I need to get to the med-bay to check on Lebowitz and Garcia. They are still with Al-Yuzwaki." She pointed to Tan, "You can carry her and see to it that they get to the cafeteria."

Tounames went into the bedroom and retrieved the unconscious form of Doctor Tan, "Is she okay?"

Reierstadt nodded, "I had to give her something."

The tech-sergeant understood. "I'll get her to the cafeteria, but you two need to go down to sub-engineering and do something about Capt'n Arroyo?"

Aamodt and Reierstadt traded a look, then the doctor pronounced, "He's asleep in his quarters."

"No, he's been working with us in sub-engineering for the last couple of hours and having full-length conversations with himself, and now he's getting violent," he adjusted Tan in his arms, cradling her like an infant. "Mitsu and I both think he needs to join her," he indicated the sleeping doctor.

"He was taking a milligram of Pantransytol before the incident," began Reierstadt, astonished. "And I gave him Deflexidizetine. The two of them together should have been enough to drop a camel."

Aamodt glanced at Reierstadt, each instantly knowing the other's thoughts. "We'll need e-suits down there," she added looking Tounames over, "Chuck, will you be okay?"

He smiled, "If I run into our friend, I'll drop sleeping beauty here and haul ass." He was obviously joking, and they knew it, and it relieved everyone's tension for a brief moment.

"Check in with Major Singleton in the cafeteria, tell him we are headed to engineering. Then check on Lebowitz and Garcia in the med-bay. If everything is okay with them, join us in sub-engineering."

He paused a moment as he surveyed Tan's comatose face.

"Let's go." Fingering the coilgun's safety yet again, Aamodt led the way out of Tan's quarters. Tounames ordered the door closed behind them as they moved quickly and silently up the corridor.

Aamodt and Reierstadt stopped in front of the elevator, Tounames slowed behind them. "You two take care."

"You just watch yourself," instructed Aamodt, the tension in her voice could be seen in the cold cloud of her breath, "and we'll take care."

"See yeah." Tounames carried Tan down the corridor as Aamodt and Reierstadt boarded the elevator. He threw the still unconscious doctor over his shoulders, checking the passageway for any signs of movement. The tech-sergeant walked, then jogged toward the cafeteria. The sleeping doctor slung over his shoulder like a sack of dirty laundry, never moved.

•   •   •

Captain Aamodt and Doctor Reierstadt entered the engineering level dressed in e-suits. Both women felt their adrenaline level rise as the eerie darkness of the dead engineering section closed in around them. The cold darkness made Aamodt tighten the grip on her Jones-Benelli. She was painfully aware that if their intruder were stalking them, her weapon would do little good, but it made her feel better anyway.

Just as Aamodt was about to make a comment, a shadow moved in the darkness. She whipped the barrel of her weapon up and her finger tensed on the trigger.

"Hold on," begged Yoshida, stepping out of the darkness and activating his e-suit lights.

The two women breathed a sigh of relief, "Smart, Sergeant, *real* smart." The shaken captain lowered the weapon.

"I thought you were *it*," added Yoshida, also relieved.

"I thought that of you?" Aamodt realized it might be time for her to activate the safety on her weapon, again. "Where's Arroyo?"

"The Capt'n still downstairs, I told him I had to check on Chuck," Yoshida frowned. "Where's he?"

"Busy. He'll be along shortly," replied Aamodt, nervously scanning the surrounding darkness with her suit lights.

Reierstadt held up a gloved hand. "You two stay up here while I go talk to the Captain, but stay close, just in case."

Without a word, Yoshida thumbed the safety on his Glock-Whelan, and loaded a projectile into the chamber, "As you said, just in case."

Reierstadt felt a little better knowing Aamodt and Yoshida were ready for trouble. Captain Arroyo was a physically powerful man and could do a lot of damage to her if he wished. Now she hoped, as she moved toward the hatchway, that their intruder would not show up to further complicate the situation. Things were going to be complicated enough she knew, for the only way to treat Arroyo was to get him out of the engineering level and out of his e-suit.

Climbing down the ladder to the sub-engineering, Reierstadt saw the tiny figure of Arroyo working on a giant machine across the vast expanse of the enormous chamber. The omnidirectional transceiver of her helmet speaker just made out the captain muttering to himself.

"Captain! I am glad to see you up and around, we could really use your assistance. Has Medtec Garcia given you your stim yet?" She felt it was a weak start, the second she voiced it. However, she knew she had to start him talking. "Newey's ordered everyone to be given stimulants to keep us working. Garcia was supposed to give the engineering team their injections."

The captain looked back and saw the psychologist descending the ladder. He immediately knew Reierstadt was not looking for Garcia. *The medtec would never come down to the sub-engineering level alone, especially in the dark with some alien-thing running around. They would have called us up to the med-bay.* Arroyo's face tensed behind his helmet faceplate as his thoughts raced. *They are up to something. They want me out of here. They blame me for damaging the station.*

"Hey, Captain, have you seen her? She was looking for you to give you a stim." Reierstadt rounded a buzzing machine and approached Arroyo slowly. Precipitously, her years of training began to scream at her. Something did not feel right, but she ignored the anxiety as it was growing in her gut. *It's just the darkness*, she thought as she felt her hands starting to sweat inside her gloves.

He did not respond to her. *I bet they blame me because the weapons didn't kill that thing. Yoshida and Tounames, those pricks can't do anything right. They probably fucked the weapons on purpose.* Arroyo flashback to when he first demonstrated the weapons to the general. Yoshida was leaning against the back wall staring at him with that look, that *pissy-ass* look. Tounames, that fuck was laughing at him, laughing! *They planned it! All along!*

"Capt'n, can you hear me?" Reierstadt was moving closer, whining her way towards him past towering machinery.

*They made sure the weapons wouldn't work on the thing. They blame me for Zuverink and the rest. It's just like Sisyphus all over again. Don't they know it wasn't my fault?* Arroyo moved to meet the advancing doctor. "You know Garcia wouldn't come down here," his voice was sharp with subdued anger.

"She was under orders to give you a shot." Reierstadt slowed her approach, reading his body language and not liking what it was telling her. "Are you all right? Mitsu said you were a little upset, and believe me you are not alone. We are all frightened and confused."

*I bet that little prickless wonder said I was upset. You think you are so damn smart, I'll show you.* Arroyo stopped next to a portable workbench. "I'm fine, but you're a liar." He stared at Reierstadt but allowed his gloved hand to slowly wander through the tools covering the bench. "Garcia isn't down here. She'd never come down here." His hand continued to fish through the hand-tools and instruments. He knew it had to be there.

Somehow, Doctor Reierstadt managed a nervous smile. "She had orders to give you, Mitsu, and Chuck a stim to keep you all going until we leave." Against her better judgment, she moved still closer to him. "Why don't you come with me upstairs? You can help me find Garcia. Something might have happened to her."

The glassy-eyed captain grinned. *You mean you want to strap me down in the med-bay, pump me full of drugs and let that fucking thing get me. You and the rest of these assholes will use me as bait while you all run for home. The general is probably going to place all the blame for the loss of the station on me.* "Sure you just want me to help you, Doc." He eased his gloved hand around the object for which he had been searching.

"Captain, all I want to do is to---"

"Blame me for destroying another station, just like Sisyphus." His index finger slipped around the trigger. "It wasn't my fault that the isooctane tanks ruptured and all those people burn to death. It wasn't my fault." The captain slowly wagged his head back and forth inside his helmet. "I didn't have any medical equipment, and no food or water." Arroyo brought the Jones-Benelli coilgun into view. "You didn't have to spend eleven days listening to people, your friends and coworkers begging you for water or to stop their pain. You didn't have to watch your own swollen, burnt blisters pop," he closed his eyes tightly for a long moment; images of a world on fire lit-up his mind. Burnt faces, charred bone, and blackened bodies streamed through his consciousness. Opening his eyes, he refocused on the doctor. "You didn't have to deal with the pain, the crying, the pleading, and the stench of infected pus and burnt flesh."

Reierstadt's mind was screaming in fear. She only saw the barrel of the coilgun and heard nothing of what Arroyo was saying. She wanted to turn and run but knew she would never make it. Instead, she reached out her hand, a forced smile on her face. "Captain, please let me help you."

The captain stepped back and chambered a projectile into the coilgun. "It was not my fault, just like Sasha and Wai-Mun and the Major. It wasn't my fault!"

Before Reierstadt could again speak or move, Arroyo unloaded one blast from the coilgun into her faceplate. The discharge took the top half of her helmet completely off in a multicolored spray of shattered helmet technology, escaping atmosphere and blood-soaked organic matter.

Doctor Reierstadt's mortally wounded body staggered back, as quickly freezing air and blood spurted from the missing section of her helmet. The partially decapitated body bounced off a silent machine and hit the floor, twitching. Blood pumped out of the missing section of the woman's helmet in a reddish-green slushy viscous mass.

Just as Reierstadt's body stopped quivering; Aamodt and Yoshida came through the upper porch hatchway. *"Chikushoo!"* shouted Yoshida excitedly as he pointed at Arroyo. Aamodt swung around her weapon and aimed, her targeting laser seeking out Arroyo's chest.

Arroyo darted behind several large machines, just as Aamodt fired two semi-automatic blasts. The captain's e-suit lights winked out, and he was gone.

For what seemed like an eternity, discharged projectiles, and fragments of projectiles, shattered pipes and machinery in the section of the sub-engineering level they were located. Arroyo, on the move, returned fire as if he were playing a VR-war game. Projectiles rebounded and ricocheted off pipes, machines, walls, floors, and ceiling, as Yoshida returned fire at the elusive captain. Most of the wayward projectiles found homes in piping or some other piece of unlucky equipment.

*"Chupa me, puto!"* screamed Arroyo, as the weapons fire stopped. "I told you it was an accident!" the Japotinian accent of his voice was barely audible over the helmet speakers. He sounded like he was on the other side of Titan.

Yoshida and Aamodt instantly switched off all the lights on their e-suits. They slowly eased down the ladder to the sub-engineering level, all the while listening to Arroyo as he murmured to himself. Reaching the foot of the ladder, the two split up and began their search-and-destroy mission to find the troubled engineer. Aamodt thought it felt like a combat scenario in one of the security forces VR-Weapon training sessions.

Yoshida knew his way around sub-engineering as well as Arroyo. He knew all the little places one could hide, all of the hidden, out-of-the-way spaces. The scary thing was Arroyo knew them too. He was the chief engineer, and this had been his place of business for years, not to mention his second home.

It was unnerving as the two stalked the one. The only sounds were the gentle humming and irregular rattling of several running machines, and the deep breathing of the three humans filtering through the helmet speakers. Even in the air-conditioned e-suits, Aamodt and Yoshida started to sweat like overweight, out-of-shape marathon runners. The tension was the all-consuming monster of the moment for all in the sub-engineering area, as eyes darted about, looking for movement. In the frigid environment, every shadow and every errant sound became a deadly threat.

Unexpectedly Aamodt caught sight of Arroyo, silhouetted by an emergency light. She quickly took aim, but just as she fired, he dove aside, and the shot blew a hole in a circuit box on the opposite wall. The box exploded with a crack of thunder into a bright white fireball, showering sparks and debris across the room. A variety of machines instantly stopped running.

There was a blaze of weaponsfire from all three in the sub-engineering level, as projectiles ricocheted around the area like a swarm of angry flying insects. A couple of wayward rounds blew holes in pipes, microcircuit boxes, and machinery. A few rounds slammed into delicate pieces of equipment, doing irreparable damage, but no one stopped firing. One by one, the bright, high-intensity emergency lights were blown out, but by the time Aamodt realized what was happening, it was too late.

The entire sub-engineering level was dark.

Not daring to activate his suit lights, Yoshida found a wall-mounted hand-light and illuminated the fleeing Arroyo. "Capt'n, up the ladder!" yelled Yoshida, as Arroyo scrambled through the open hatchway and vanished.

"Damn, come on!" Aamodt, turning on her e-suit lights, raced to the foot of the ladder with Yoshida in pursuit. "We can't let him get away!"

Reaching the ladder, both Aamodt and Yoshida reloaded their weapons before moving up the rungs of the ladder and through the hatch. Spying no one and no movement they both cursed, "The elevator!" Yoshida was half out of breath, as he switched on his suit lights.

Aamodt cautiously moved to the elevator and hit the button. It did not illuminate. "He must've cut the power." She hit it again, with still no response.

Yoshida, Glock-Whelan still in hand, jostled Aamodt and indicated a small hatchway. "Come on, the emergency ladder!"

"No," she stopped him, "that way." Aamodt indicated the dull orangey-red hole in the wall.

As the two dashed through the gaping opening in the wall, they came to an abrupt halt as they faced darkness. All the exterior lights on the station were out. All the viewports were dark. Only the emergency lights illuminated the exterior ladders and the airlock entryways.

It immediately dawned on Yoshida what had happened, "Oh fucking divinities! We must have blown the emergency relays. If we did, then the secondary buses for the whole fucking station are cooked!"

"You mean the power's out for the whole station?"

"Yeah, no doors, no lights, and worst of all, the rest of the environmental controls are out. That means no heat and no air." The fact that things had just gotten worse was written all over Yoshida's face, and he saw it mirrored in Aamodt's green eyes illuminated by her e-suit helmet lights.

"Get back in there and see what you can do," instructed Captain Aamodt, taking the hand-light from Yoshida. She quickly gave her suit a brief once over. "The life support system is the most important thing. That comes before anything else including the lights, understood?"

"Right, but you can't use the hand-light and the coilgun at the same time."

"Let me worry about that," without another word, she bounced off into the gloom, just as the wind began to pick up.

# CHAPTER TWENTY

When the lights went out in the cafeteria, and the main emergency lights failed to come on, a wave of panic began to wash over several in the room. Only three of the dull emergency lights illuminated the six cold and frightened people in the cafeteria. Nervous questions and panicked instructions echoed through the blackness. One of the dim emergency lights shown on the emergency equipment locker at the far end of the room. Another of the lights glowed over the disaster management control access panels at the front of the cafeteria, just under the huge hard-monitor.

Following Major Singleton's orders, Professor Eastman quickly moved to the emergency equipment locker and began handing out hand-lights, as the cold darkness began to close in around them. Professor McGilmer relaxed a little as Professor Eastman passed her a hand-light. Singleton, trying to hold a hand-light in one hand, desperately tried to undo the safety on the recoilless rifle with the other.

Professor Yee, opened his flightsuit, slapped an anti-nausea patch on to the side of his neck, and picked up the loaded Glock-Whelan from a tabletop and readied himself.

"You know how to use that?" asked Lieutenant Sloan, surveying Yee in the gloom.

"Played a few modified VR-games in my time," smirked Yee. "Besides, how hard is it to point a weapon at something and

276

pull the trigger?"

"Yeah," muttered Sloan, generating a loud mechanical noise that startled several in the room, as he chambered a projectile in his coilgun and moved to the doorway with Professor Yee behind him. "Why didn't we activate the DMC?" Lieutenant Sloan inquired aloud to no one in particular.

Professor Eastman just looked to Major Singleton in the near dark. For a moment, the major did not respond. He remembered what Colonel Rozsa had whispered several hours ago to herself in the general's office, *Worldfall*. Then he said, "If we activate the system, an automated disaster beacon starts to broadcast." He moved to join the lieutenant and Professor Yee at the entrance to the cafeteria. "Back home, they are already on edge because of what happened to T-One and TBK. I am quite sure they know we constructed weapons and that EBE is running around. If we start transmitting a disaster signal, they are libel to react harshly."

"I get that sir, but don't you think we should *react harshly* to this …this …*fuckama-thing*, or whatever you want to call it?" Sloan bounced the Jones-Benelli in his hands, glancing at the safety.

"I'd let the General make those types of decisions," he padded the younger officer on the shoulder, "don't you agree, Lieutenant?"

In the gloom, Sloan just nodded.

In the dark, the group sat quietly and motionless in the cold of the cafeteria, waiting. They all waited. They waited for the terror and horror of the unknown to strike at them from out of the frigid blackness. The only sound in the stillness was the gentle hum of the generator, powering the doorway trap. Several in the group checked their PDIs, only to have their hopes further crushed. The interlink system was still silent and useless. No text messages crawled across the tiny screens of their PDIs, no system updates beeped at them, only the local time flashed at them, as if mocking them. The lack of communication just added to the mounting fear, and the feeling of helplessness as Lieutenant Sloan and Professor Yee stood flanking Major Singleton. All three pointed their weapons at the open cafeteria doorway, and into the monstrous darkness beyond.

"So sir, what do you think happened? Do you think that thing's taken out engineering?" Sloan's voice was barely a whisper.

Ever since the station was damaged and Professor Watkinski and the others were lost, an ill feeling had been growing within him. A sense of dread was taking hold of the young officer, and the emotion was not unique to just him. All of them were beginning to believe that they were doomed. Sloan had considered telling Doctor Reierstadt about how he was feeling. He thought, maybe she would give him a pill or something to help get him through this. Then he thought if he had any chance of surviving this nightmare, he would need a clear head.

"That wouldn't explain the emergency lights." There was a long silence then Singleton added, "So how far are you into Darkness Falls?" He really did not care about the young man's VR-game but thought it might relieve some of the tension.

Sloan's face twisted in the dark, perplexed, "Sir?"

Barely visible in the near darkness of the room, the major's black face sported a faint hint of a grin. "I asked, how far along are you into the Darkness Falls chapter of the Rogue Colony Series?"

Sloan glanced over at Singleton in stunned bewilderment. "I haven't played in the last few days', sir. I've been kinda busy," the tone of his voice, stated it all. "Besides," added Sloan sarcastically, "I think this time, sir, I am playing the game for real."

"What the hell kinda question is that?" Yee's face was a cross between confusion and disgust, "especially at a time like this."

"Well, when the mining base is attacked, you get to meet the fog monsters," Singleton never took his eyes off the corridor in front of him. "They are the guard hounds of the *Remari*, the beings that are hijacking the mining trade that you have been tasked with protecting." He smiled to himself, "To survive the mining base attack, you have to---"

"Thank you, sir," Sloan abruptly interrupted the major, his face still half hidden in shadow. "I'm looking forward to finishing the game."

"You're an optimist?" Professor Yee's voice was cold.

Singleton nudged Sloan, "You'll get through the game and through this Lieutenant."

"I like a commanding officer who is optimistic," Sloan's tone stank of sarcastic pessimism, "that he actually thinks I'll want to finish a VR-game about aggressive EBEs, after this." The thick mist of Sloan's warm breath was making clouds in the beam of

Yee's hand-light.

"Did you check the rear exit?" inquired Singleton in a hushed voice. "Are the lights out there too?"

"Yes sir, looks like the emergency powers off for the whole level," Sloan quickly glanced back into the room, noting the glowing exit sign across the darkened expanse. "But the tripwires on the stairs are okay." He could see the towering blank holo-monitor at the front of the room, reflecting just a hint of the three working emergency lights.

It went quiet again. The ebony curtain in front of them ate up the minutes like some reticent cancer. There was a muffled groan in the darkness that sounded like it emanated from Doctor Tan, but no one was sure, and no one moved a light to investigate. There were a few brief whispers, but all else was still. Only the generator for the doorway trap softly droned on in the icy blackness.

A bright light mysteriously appeared at the distant end of the corridor, its source around the bend. From the slowly growing spot of light and its movements, the three men could tell the light source was moving closer, advancing up the corridor. The bouncing light was followed by a distant sound, and the tension level in the darkened cafeteria jumped to a new high, as Yee whispered, "Here we go."

Watching the light slowly advance, Singleton felt his heart rate increase and warm sweat starting to move down his cold face. Images of the bloody mess their violent intruder had left of Zuverink, Fung, and Wong flashed through his frightened mind. Singleton, like Sloan and Yee, hoped that if the light was a threat, that it was Captain Arroyo. All three knew their weapons could make short-work out of the crazed captain, but were next to useless against the thing that had invaded their home. Watching the moving light ahead of them in the corridor, and with Major Nianta's last panicked screams echoing in his ears, Major Singleton nervously readied the recoilless rifle. Taking a deep breath of chilled air, Singleton bellowed, "Who goes there?"

"It's me, Sergeant Tounames! I am with Medtecs Garcia and Lebowitz!" The tech-sergeant shouted from the corridor, his cautious voice booming in the stillness like a cannon. "Is that thing on?" his light played over the small metal plates mounted on the walls and floor in front of the cafeteria. The black metal plates were connected to the travel-case-sized cesium chloride generator by numerous black and red micro-cables.

"Hold on, Sergeant," replied Singleton as the crowd in the cafeteria nearly collapsed with relief.

Switching between the Jones-Benelli and a hand-light, Sloan moved into the corridor and deactivated the generator, "What happened to the lights?"

"No clue, sir?" barked Tounames as he led the two medtecs passed the electrical barrier. "The emergency backups are down; I'll need to get to engineering to find out what happened."

Sloan reactivated the generator as Tounames, Lebowitz, and Garcia moved into the cafeteria, hand-light beams and nervous questions greeting them. Buried in the sudden burst of noise from the cafeteria, Sloan thought he heard another sound. A faint metallic scraping echoing out of the darkness of the corridor, but there was nothing.

"I was on my way to the med-bay when the power went down," began Tounames, "Given the situation, I thought it would be best to get them back here."

"You did the right thing," Singleton surveyed the other two new arrivals. "How is Al-Yuzwaki?"

The note of sadness that swept across the shadowed faces of Medtecs Garcia and Lebowitz transmitted the answer without words.

"We did all we could for him. He was too weak, and the antibiotics didn't have enough time to stop the DHPN that was setting into his damaged organs." Lebowitz, catching Garcia's face in the darkness, frowned. She understood that only Garcia would know that DHPN was delta-hemolytic pseudomonas Necrosis, another nasty holdover from the bio-weaponry used during the Antarctican Resources War. "He died a few minutes before the Chuck arrived. He's still in the autodoc."

Professor McGilmer called out and tossed something at the two medtecs.

Lebowitz made a one-handed catch and looked at the bottle of *Okhotnichya*. "I think you could use it." Lebowitz gestured back to the professor, holding up the clear plastic bottle, then taking a deep swig from it. The very expensive Russian vodka, made on Mars and flavored with cheap port wine and genetically enhanced, cave-grown spices, hit the back of Lebowitz's throat like a fist. It felt good as it melted its way down to her stomach and sat there like a smoldering ember. Smiling, she passed the bottle to Garcia.

In the low light and cold fog, Tounames' dark, worn face looked ghoulish. "Sir, until we see what's going on I can't tell you anything. It could be the main power conduit from the reactor; it could be any one of ten thousand things."

Suddenly there was a tremendous moan, and the cafeteria vibrated like a giant's tuning fork. One of the illuminated signs over one of the exits winked out, as the sleeping Doctor Tan began to stir, but she still remained unconscious.

"That was a big one," whisper Tounames. "I better get going."

"Hold it," ordered Singleton. "Sloan, I'm going with Tounames, you're in charge here."

Sloan looked around at the shadowy faces in the room, then faced the major, "Yes sir." The three men moved back to the entrance to the cafeteria.

"If you don't hear from me or a superior officer in three hours," Singleton paused, looking the younger man up and down warmly and added, "Do what you think is best."

"Yes, sir," Sloan frowned, "Good luck."

As Sloan moved to deactivate the electrical trap, he paused. He thought he saw something black and silent move off deeper into the frigid darkness of the corridor, but it was nothing.

• • •

After a few minutes, both Newey and Rozsa realized that hammering on the com-center door was pointless. When the power failed, the door's hydraulics went offline, and the emergency release mechanism had not been re-installed during the repairs to the com-center. In spite of the obvious, both Newey and Rozsa tried everything they could think of to open the door. They rerouted circuits and even changed the fluid pressure in the hydraulic lines, but with no results. Even though the com-center had not been designed as a disaster safe zone, it had been engineered to keep its occupants alive and safe until rescue. It also appeared to the two officers, that it had been designed to prevent them from escaping as well.

Newey and Rozsa were trapped.

The two of them realized that the only option left to them to get the com-center door open was to blow it open. However, the only thing the two officers had, that was even remotely related to an explosive, was the fuel tanks from their ice-melters, and that was not an acceptable option. To explode one of the fuel tanks, in the confines of the com-center, was sheer suicide.

"What do you think happened?" inquired Rozsa, dropping herself into a seat. The emergency lights over the consoles flickered a little. *Must be a drain someplace,* she thought.

"No clue," Newey looked more tired and much older than he had ever appeared before. "Hopefully someone will come looking for us."

"Maybe they're all dead," Rozsa rubbed her face in her hands. "For all we know, most of the station is exposed to Titan."

The general ignored Rozsa's last statement and slammed an angry fist against the door, watching his own breath in the cold air. "The auto-disaster beacon didn't activate, so most of the station is still intact. If a large section of the station did go, at least we'll survive for a while. There are pressure suits in the emergency locker, along with rations, air, and water enough to last ten people a week." He turned around toward Rozsa, watching her reaction. There was none.

"From the way it feels in here now," Rozsa pointed at her own breath condensing in the frosty air, "I think the emergency heating is already offline."

"It's designed to keep us alive, no one said anything about comfortable."

"How long do you think the emergency batteries will last?"

"Well, there is a short someplace in the system that's draining power rather fast," began Newey, taking stock of the blank holo-screens and dead hard-monitors in the room. "The com-center has two hydrogen-helium power cells, so I'd say the power will probably last six, maybe eight months." He paused, grinned as if someone had just told him a dirty joke. "But little good that will do us, assuming everyone else is dead and we are trapped in here."

Colonel Rozsa hugged herself in her thick blue flightsuit, "Great, real great."

"Isn't it, though?" The general had a half-smoked cigar, a

stump really, in one of his suit pockets, but with an uncertain air circulation system, smoking was not the greatest idea. "Upside is, at least we won't die in the dark."

Rozsa leaned back in her chair, a smile curiously creeping onto her face. "You want to hear something funny?"

"Yeah, I could use a laugh right about now. What?" Newey scanned the control room. Maybe he'd missed an opportunity to better their situation. Not likely, he knew, but he also knew hope springs eternal.

"I just had a craving for peppermint-raisin ice cream," she looked at Newey, "Isn't that weird?" she smiled sheepishly.

He snorted a faint laugh. "No, it's not," his expression speedily changed again. "When I was laying in the autodoc, feeling that infrasonic beam fusing my shoulder and ankle back together, I thought about a lot of things. How the hell did we get ourselves into this situation? What could be going through that things mind, and what does it want?"

Colonel Rozsa refocused on the general, "And?" Memories of the argument in his office flashed through her mind.

"And it occurred to me that we missed something." Newey appeared to age ten years as he slumped into a sitting position in front of the doorway.

"What?"

"I think I figured out why this thing might have come out here." He stared at Rozsa. "I think in the middle of bio-forming Venus and Earth, it needed something that it determined it could get here, and something went wrong."

Rozsa shrugged, "What?"

"I think it needed something, probably water, and halted its bio-forming activities and located the purest, most uncontaminated source," the general gestured to Rozsa, who just nodded back. "We are terraforming Venus, and our biggest hurdle is---"

"Water," snorted Rozsa. "But we are taking it from the Jovian worlds and grabbing it from comets. Yeah, it's a long haul for water, but---"

"If you can cross tens of thousands of light years carrying the tools and technology to transform whole planets, a few billion kilometers to grab some ice is nothing." He rapped on the floor with his knuckles, "Less rocky material in the ice out here than at

Jupiter."

Rozsa sat forward in her seat, "So your scenario is these guys needed water to complete their bio-forming project and came out here and what?"

"I think something went wrong. I think they were trying to harvest one of Saturn's moons, something went wrong, the moon was destroyed, and their craft was damaged."

"And they crashed here?" Her reply came out as a cloud of warm breath, fogging the air in the cold room, and sounding aggressive.

"Or purposefully landed here, I am just speculating," he adjusted himself. "Suppose it was automated and that thing and its friends on the ship are the cargo?"

She waved him off. "An arc-ship? Like something out of some sci-fi vid?"

"Maybe," Newey just flashed a smirk, "or maybe just a group of builder-settlers. Like the ones that first settled Mars and Venus. They make it and then more show up."

Rozsa halfheartedly surveyed the cold, gloomy room. "So what do you think this thing is going to do now that it is awake?"

"What would be the first thing you'd do as a stranger in a strange land?"

The colonel sunk her face into her hands and rubbed for not quite a full minute, thinking. "Find out where I am, and where my friends are, and determine if there are any threats, and neutralize those threats."

Newey climbed back to his feet and began stretching his legs. "I think this creature is going to try and find its ship, and the only way it can do that is through us."

Rozsa snorted and added, "Unless it's got a built-in locator."

"Yeah, maybe," the expression on Newey's face rapidly grew hard and menacing. "It seems to have every other fucking advantage to help it survive." The general sat on the floor again and paused. He thought he heard something hit the other side of the door. It was nothing. "If it doesn't, it will have to trick us or force us to lead it back to its ship, and in order to do that, it will need to communicate with us."

"It had its chance," bitterly barked Rozsa.

"Bottom line, Colonel, we need to leave and recommend

Worldfall for Titan." Newey surveyed her in the dim light.

"We should disable every vehicle on the base first," Rozsa's voice was just above a whisper. "Just to make sure it doesn't get far."

"Better yet," Newey stared at Rozsa, "the station's self-destruct."

Rozsa chuckled, "Why the fuck not. There will be some much dogshit hitting the ground over this mess; no one is going to fault you. Hell, they might even give you a metal."

"Not after losing seven people."

There was silence again, and the two of them let the topic die.

After a few long minutes of numbing silence, the colonel began again, "Well, if we get out of here in one piece, I'm resigning my commission."

Newey scanned Rozsa a moment. He did not think that even a disaster like this would send her packing. "Resign? Resign and do what?"

"I've got some hard-currency putaway," the colonel continued, "and I was thinking of moving back to Earth, maybe to the NAC. I could buy one of those small resort islands off the southern coast of Georgia, in the New Gulf of Mexico."

"And do what? Run a hotel?" He could not imagine the colonel as just another citizen of the North American Commonwealth.

"No, an island ferry service. I was thinking about getting one of those prefabs, and a powerboat." Rozsa paused to examine the look of growing disbelief on the general's face. "You don't believe me. I could run a ferry service between the Americus seaport and the Orlando seadome. I could even run day trippers out to the Cape Canaveral Memorial or the ruins of Old Havana."

Newey grinned, "Shit. When I decide to retire, I am moving to Mars. I plan on buying a split-level living pod in the Southern Polar Region, and quietly spend the rest of my days, reading and writing, doing guest lecturing, and sleeping late." The two started laughing making large moist clouds in the dry cold air. Neither one took the other seriously, but both knew they were telling the truth.

There was a sound.

The laughing skidded to a halt. It sounded to the two

officers like someone trying to access the doors controls from the opposite side of the wall.

Rozsa popped out of her chair as Newey rose off the floor and hit the door. "Hey! Get us out of here!" Rozsa joined him.

Something dark exploded through the door with a sickening tearing sound. It began to wrench open the com-center door like a desperate rescue-worker trying to reach trapped children.

Newey and Rozsa stood transfixed in front of the quickly disappearing barrier. Trembling, Rozsa forced her eyes away from the entrance and surveyed their surroundings. She spied their ice-melters. "The melters," she spat backing away from the nightmare coming through the door.

"The backwash'll cook us in here." Backing away as well, Newey shoved Rozsa away from him, "Get over there and get down. I'll draw it in, and you take off and get the others out of here!"

"General!" was all Rozsa could get out as both Newey and the extrasolar entity entering the room cut her off.

"You have your orders, Colonel!" barked Newey, staring at the swiftly advancing thing. The four-armed, multi-eyed horror was suddenly looming over the station's senior officer like death itself.

Rozsa moved, but the creature was instantly five meters across the room, towering over the stunned colonel. Newey scrambled for his ice-melter in response, as one of the thing's arms hit Rozsa in the upper chest with such speed and power that it drove its clawed appendage deep into her body. The impact sent the stricken colonel cartwheeling backward through the air. She bounced off a console and landed on her knees, coughing and fighting for her breath. The dark thing dropped the fistful of blood-soaked flesh it had snatched from the colonel's body, as Newey reached the ice-melter.

Looking down, Rozsa was surprised at the raw, pink meaty hole in her chest that was quickly filling with dark blood. A second before, the hole had been her flightsuit and right breast. She tried to stand, but only staggered back and fell as the pain hit her, and the blood began to pour from her wound. She tried to scream, but only ejected sticky blood and bits of frothy red tissue.

Newey fired a stream of flame at their sinister assailant.

The creature danced forward, a riving mass of shrieks and

flame, but Newey continued to bathe it with fire. It raced blindly pass the wild-eyed general and bounced off a wall, and came charging back at the retreating Newey. It tripped over Rozsa's ice-melter and fell. Newey, full of terror-fueled insanity swept his melter down over the fallen creature, the backwash of flames engulfing Rozsa's ice-melter.

As the general, fighting the searing heat, worked his way towards the doorway, spreading fiery destruction with every step, he eyed Rozsa. The sad colonel, awash in reflected firelight, had agony on her blood-covered face as she reached out toward him.

•   •   •

LaRocque and Pulgar saw the glow and heard the unearthly scream and thunderous roar of the ice-melter coming from around the distant corner. Glancing at one another in the dim illumination from their hand-lights, they rushed forward towards the com-center, weapons at the ready. However, just as they rounded the corner leading to the com-center, an explosion thundered through the entire corridor.

A massive fireball of rainbow colors rolled and bubbled down the corridor, enveloped in a pressure wave that wrinkled the floor, walls, and ceiling as it moved towards them. The blinding ball of fiery hell lifted the two young officers off their feet and knocked the air from their lungs as it rolled past them, and dissipated up the corridor. They laid stunned and bewildered, covered in a cloud of debris and smoke.

LaRocque and Pulgar, choked by smoke and fine debris, got to their feet, both frantically checking each other on the way up. Nervously they stared up the corridor at the wall of flame and thick smoke that used to be the com-center. The whole room was in flames as black, toxic clouds of smoke billowed and rolled toward the two lieutenants along the hanging remains of the corridor ceiling. The only sound was the distorted and muffled crackling and popping of cooking carbo-plastic and frying electronics, the labored breathing of the two speechless officers, and the ringing in their ears.

"Divinities protect me," was all LaRocque could whisper as something began to move in the blast furnace, which moments ago, was the nerve center of the station. A flaming, four-armed figure, like some tortured spirit escaping the fires of hell, stumbled out of the roaring inferno as if it were intoxicated and lost.

With a sudden burst of sound, the damaged fire suppression system began pumping fire-fighting gas into the corridor, as the burning extrasolar spotted the two lieutenants and stopped. The thing just stood in the middle of the wrecked passageway and stared at LaRocque and Pulgar, as if it were not sure of what to do next. After a moment, LaRocque grabbed Pulgar by the arm and dashed back the way they had come.

The brilliant torch that was the extrasolar lifeform silently watched the two humans vanish around the corner. After another moment, it emitted an ear-piercing scream and lunged after the two fleeing humans, looking like some fearsome version of a flaming phoenix as it moved.

It was right behind them, pushing itself off walls, floors, and ceilings in its pursuit, moving fast. The two humans blindly ran through corridors and around corners until LaRocque remembered the traps that had been set for the creature. Pulgar swung her handlight around wildly looking for an escape, seeing screaming death closing on her at nightmarish speed. Her light fell upon a dormant maintenance-bot next to a half-opened doorway with the words: **SWIMMING POOL** engraved above it in big bold letters.

"In here!" shouted Pulgar, pulling LaRocque behind her into the dimly lit chamber.

"Go around to the other side!" LaRocque looked out of the doorway just as their pursuer skipped around the opposite corner. Part of the creature's body was still burning, casting shadows on the walls around it. It paused as if listening then began to move rapidly toward the swimming pool doorway.

As the extrasolar entity burst into the pool area, Lieutenant LaRocque fired two semi-automatic blasts from his coilgun. The rounds knocked the creature back against a wall. In the same beat, as it hit the wall, it bounced back to its feet like some bizarre, double-jointed gymnast and continued to advance toward the lieutenant as if nothing had just happened. At the sight of the creature's reaction to his weapon's fire, a cold wave of terror rolled down LaRocque's back, paralyzing him for a split-second.

One of the creature's hands just missed LaRocque's face as the lieutenant skipped backward deeper into the room. He darted and fell left, their nightmarish intruder charging after him.

LaRocque hit the tile floor, whirled around and fired at the same time as Pulgar. The explosive impacts from LaRocque's Jones-Benelli and Pulgar's Glock-Whelan knocked the creature off balance, and its momentum carried it forward. It tumbled into the huge ice-covered swimming pool.

The concussion from the arc-welder blast of blue-white electrical energy blinded LaRocque and Pulgar for half a minute. The deafening crack and subsequent deep electrical shriek reverberated around the tiled chamber several times as tens of thousands of amps of electrical current flowed through the water in the pool. Flashes, sparks, and arcs of electricity lit up the pool area in a ghostly blue light, as shrieks and howls echoed off the tiled walls.

For several horrifying seconds, the demonic entity riled and jerked violently in agony, its torment being frozen for a millisecond with each strobe-like flash of the artificial lightning storm. The arctic air in the room quickly filled with fog and the smell of chlorine, ozone, and burnt aluminum. As the unholy and unnatural wails and shrieks ended, and the echoes faded to a dead silence, the thing slowly sank to the bottom of the pool, twitching and convulsing. Only the gentle lapping of the waves against the sides of the pool could be heard in the sudden stillness.

Realizing she had been holding her breath, Pulgar took a gulp of ozone-filled air. "Is it dead?" she exhaled, trying to train her trembling hand-light on the spasm ravaged form at the bottom of the pool with one hand, and pointing the empty Glock-Whelan at it with the other.

The extrasolar twitched softly in the rhythmic motions of the water, as the generator emitted a series of beeps followed by a soft computerized voice.

"Are you fucking kidding me?" replied LaRocque, drowning out the generator's computer, staring transfixed at the motionless form in the water. "I'll give you ten to one it ain't," he glanced at the generator, still speaking and beeping for attention. "Let's get the fuck out of here."

As the two moved to leave the pool area, Pulgar noticed a message flashing across the generator's small screen. She was too deaf from the weapon's fire to hear what the machine had been saying, and was out of the room before she could read the message. However, she thought it said something about overloads and circuit breakers, but she could not be sure.

LaRocque and Pulgar headed back to the cafeteria at a dead run, both thinking similar thoughts. *That Singleton was now in command, and that he better get them out of there before more of them died.*

"What'll we do now?" inquired the out of breath Pulgar in a voice, weak and drained of strength. She thought of the general and Colonel Rozsa. "Should we check and see if they are both dead?"

"They're dead. Believe me." LaRocque looked around in the near darkness and for the first time felt the cold sinking in through his flightsuit. "It's really getting cold in here."

"No dogshit! The powers been off, remember?" Illuminated in the hand-light, Pulgar was dirty and looked small, terrified and worn out, "Back to the cafeteria?"

LaRocque nodded in the dark, grabbed Pulgar's hand and the two continued to run at breakneck speed to the cafeteria. As they moved along, they both could smell the sharp odor of ozone and burnt carbo-plastic. LaRocque led them to a door marked: **EMERGENCY ACCESS-WAY No. 3**. Moving the hatch out of the way, he and Pulgar began to climb the ladder as some of the emergency lights winked on in the cramped space of the access way. In the low illumination, they could see that frost was beginning to form on the walls, light fixtures, and rungs of the ladder. It was not a good sign.

When the two finally came out on the level of the cafeteria, they ran the entire way to the sanctuary. As they hurriedly advanced along the cold and gloomy corridors, both officers made very sure they did not stumble into any of the traps that had been set for their visitor.

Reaching the cafeteria, LaRocque and Pulgar noticed the lights were on, and most everyone was sitting around drinking steaming beverages and looking emotionally drained and generally ill.

"Where's Major Singleton?" inquired LaRocque, surveying the room as several of the others moved to join him and Pulgar.

"He and Tounames went down to engineering about an hour ago," Professor Yee handed LaRocque and Pulgar cups of steaming black coffee, and surveyed their faces. "The power literally just came back on not fifteen minutes ago."

LaRocque looked at Pulgar, then back at McGilmer,

thinking about how to tell them. "The General and Colonel Rozsa are dead," he had whispered it, but his voice was louder than he thought, for everyone in the cafeteria went silent with a look of surprise and disbelief.

Pulgar glanced unhappily at him. She thought *that was no way to tell them.*

"That's it, Major Singleton is in command. We can finally get the fuck out of here," injected Professor Yee, the hint of happiness in his voice was practically audible, as he looked to Sloan.

Professor Eastman, seated at the nearest table, stared blankly ahead for a long minute. Slowly, almost hypnotically she picked up the half-empty liter of *Okhotnichya* sitting on the table and took a long swig. She looked confused and lost, and probably for the first time, really looked scared.

"About time," added Sloan. "It was idiotic to have stayed here this long."

LaRocque looked over at Pulgar, warming her hands on her cup of coffee as he spoke to Lieutenant Sloan. "Look, I'm going to find Major Singleton. You get them ready to move."

"What about our friend?" Sloan quickly pointed toward the doorway.

"We gave it a hot bath in the pool, but I doubt if that'll stop it for long." LaRocque spotted the slowly waking Doctor Tan. Immediately Professor McGilmer and Medtec Garcia were next to her, Pulgar following to see if she could lend a hand.

"Well, you'd better hurry back." Sloan glanced over at Eastman and her bottle of flavored vodka, "These people are coming apart." He gestured at the group.

LaRocque's eyes scanned the room, "Who else did we lose?" He immediately became alert and worried again.

Sloan slowly motioned with his head in the negative, "Jamal didn't..." his voice trailed off.

LaRocque looked as if he was trying to wake up from a bad dream. "Fucking divinities," he whispered angrily looking over at Lebowitz. "If I'm not back in twenty minutes, get them all up to Hopper-Two and prepare it for launch." He took a gulp from his coffee, burning his mouth. "If nobody shows up in an hour, leave and link up with the EET. If you don't hear from anybody in another three hours, leave." He took another sip and glanced at

Pulgar, who was now talking with Doctor Tan.

"I don't want to be a ripped condom in this *fucking* plan of yours," informed Sloan, pointing to himself, "but I'm not a pilot, and I can't fly." He, like all the officers on the station, had been instructed in how to operate and pilot a hopper, but like most, he never really thought he would have to fly one in the real world.

"Neither can I, but you and Ariel can manage to get one divinity forsaken Grasshopper into orbit. How fucking hard is that? It has a fully functional AI!" LaRocque's voice went up several octaves and drew the attention of the others in the room. He, like most of the others, was too cold, too tired and too close to his breaking point to care anymore. "Ariel and I managed to ferry one from Tethys to Rhea a couple of months ago. You can manage to get one into fucking orbit!"

Sloan took a big step toward his friend. With his brown eyes wide with anger, he did not look so young and boyish anymore.

"Hey, Demitri!" yelled a muffled voice from the corridor, stopping Sloan before he could reply to LaRocque. "Turn this fucking thing off!" It was Major Singleton.

Sloan, LaRocque, and Yee vaulted to the doorway. Singleton and Aamodt, both in e-suits, were supporting a third suited figure. "Give us a hand," insisted Aamodt.

Sloan quickly deactivated the barrier and the five carried the person into the cafeteria. They laid the limp figure on a table and started opening the damaged e-suit. There were tears in the outer layers of the suit, and it was covered in brown and black dust, the small backpack and chest units were beaten and battered, and the faceplate was dirty and opaque. The internal helmet light-bar was out.

Professor McGilmer and Medtec Garcia moved to lend a hand with the undressing. All were glad to have something to take their minds off of the waiting. However, they were not happy it was another friend and coworker in need of assistance.

"I found'em on the ice, his suit's systems are fucked, and his suit batteries are low," Aamodt removed her helmet. "Vincent flipped out and killed Doc Stadts."

It was as if all the sound had been sucked out of the room. Garcia and the others paused a second and shot a hard look at Aamodt. They glanced at each other then proceeded to remove the e-suit, moving slowly. Everyone in the cafeteria instantly felt doomed, and that there was no escape.

Major Singleton removed his helmet as Professor Yee picked up his Glock-Whelan and, like an expert, thumbed the safety to the off position.

"Major," LaRocque's voice was little more than a whisper in the stillness of the room, "General Newey and Colonel Rozsa are both dead."

A grim look, followed by one of panic and confusion flashed across Singleton's tired face. He whispered something, but it was not audible.

When Garcia removed the helmet from the person on the table, they all stood stunned in disbelief and bewilderment. They all stared at the swollen, frostbitten face before them.

It was Major Nianta.

# CHAPTER TWENTY-ONE

Working frantically, Yoshida and Tounames struggled to bring life back to their dying home. They ripped open boxes of replacement parts and equipment and rigged up several makeshift networks of wires and cables. A bizarre spider's web of re-routed wires and cables grew across the sub-engineering level as they attempted to bolster their failing life support, and bring backlighting to the darkened installation. They knew it would take hours, if not days of work to restore the bare-minimum of essential systems. However, the two men were hoping that they would not be on Titan in a few hours, let alone for a few more days.

During their repair work and constant moving back and forth between the sub-engineering and main engineering levels, Yoshida explained to Tounames what had happened with Arroyo, and what the crazed captain had done to Doctor Reierstadt. Nevertheless, nothing could have prepared Tounames for what rested inside the remains of Doctor Reierstadt's e-suit helmet. As Tounames worked, he was not able to get the image of the remains on the ice-covered floor out of his head. Every time he had to walk past the doctor's body, he would avert his eyes, but the image was still there.

As the auxiliary engineering board showed several green and yellow lights, which had been red an hour ago, Tounames and Yoshida smiled at one another happily. Abruptly Yoshida's face turned hard and the forgotten matter popped back into his mind. "The Captain," he groaned coldly.

"Let's find him," suggested Tounames, feeling the rage well up in him. "Before he kills someone else," he armed his Glock-Whelan with a loud and angry motion.

Yoshida smirked and undid the safety of his weapon, "You know this isn't a VR-game, right? There is no reset on this dogshit."

His friend nodded.

"I never did like working with that asshole, anyway," Yoshida's helmet light illuminating his twisted smile. It made Yoshida's expression look genuinely sinister behind his faceplate.

"I knew you'd like it," replied Tounames, moving toward the hole at the other end of the L-shaped room. "Unless he uses one of the emergency power keys to open an airlock, the only way he is going to be able to get back into the station is through that hole."

After a pause to inspect the crude electrical trap they had set up around the hole in the wall, they checked their e-suits and stepped out onto the dark face of the icy mountain. The exterior lights of the station were still out, but the faint glow of the emergency lights gave the two men enough illumination to conduct their manhunt. Abruptly, both men extinguished their e-suit lights as if on cue.

The wind was blowing hard outside of the hole in the station wall. It carried bits of ice and dust into the gloomy, fog-shrouded night of Titan. Tounames and Yoshida looked around at the low hanging clouds that were racing by. They were backlit by the ghostly cold colors of the massive aurora high above them. It was a beautiful sight thought both men. However, it was too bad they could not enjoy it.

They gave each other the thumbs-up sign. "Keep an eye out for Major Singleton and Capt'n Aamodt," commanded Yoshida as the two men moved slowly and silently apart. Each man was ready to jump at the first flash of gunfire. "And don't forget, Arroyo is not the only threat out here."

Tounames could not look everywhere at once, but he tried nevertheless. As time passed with no sign of their prey or their extrasolar intruder, he began to lose focus. His concentration kept slipping, and his eyes kept wandering to the sky, as thoughts and memories of murdered coworkers drifted into his consciousness. He glanced up at the dancing light show in the sky, knowing that people back home would have paid hard currency to see such a beautiful natural sight.

•      •      •

In the two hours since starting the hunt, Yoshida's thoughts had not wandered. He had only one all-consuming thought, and that was to kill Arroyo as violently as possible. He was like a hungry animal on the prowl. Looking up and down, back and forth, he ignored the changing colors of the sky and the windblown debris. Unexpectedly, he spotted something on the top of the station. At first, he thought it was the changing sky playing tricks with his eyes, but then the shadow moved again. It was not a shadow; it was more like a shadow of a shadow.

He caught himself and did not call his companion over his helmet's transceiver. If it were Arroyo, he would know he had been spotted. Yoshida skipped ahead in the low gravity, movig along the edge of the darkened complex. He could feel his heart beginning to pound and the sweat beginning to flow down his face. He encountered another exterior ladder and scaled it as stealthily as possible.

Yoshida had only two thoughts as he ascended the ladder. One was; *if you're Captain Arroyo, you're going to get a big fucking surprise.* The other was, *and if you're our guest, I'll be the one getting the surprise.* As he approached the top of the station, he still had no clue if either thought was correct.

Reaching the top rung of the ice-encrusted ladder, he climbed up on to the roof and crouched low, scanning the area. Seeing nothing but the station's communications array, a stationary maintenance-bot, and a small sign indicating the direction to the landing pad, Yoshida advanced to the communications array. He checked the gloomy area again, noting the maintenance-bot, half encrusted in methane ice and looking like some bizarre snowman, then he moved next to it. Before he could crouch down, something knocked the weapon from his hand and sent him sailing across the roof like a child's toy.

"Why do you guys hate me?" Arroyo calmly asked as he turned on his e-suit lights and stood up from behind the maintenance-bot.

"Capt'n, we don't hate you," replied Yoshida in an

unsteady voice, his fear-gripped eyes trained on the massive weapon in the captain's hands. "We want to help you."

"Don't lie to me!" screamed Arroyo, swinging the barrel of the coilgun at Yoshida. "You assholes blame me for this mess." He started advancing toward the frightened tech-sergeant, "You guys sabotaged these weapons so they wouldn't stop that fucker, just to make me look bad."

Yoshida, on one knee, started edging backward as Arroyo closed the distance. "Capt'n you got it all wrong."

"But they worked well enough to take care of Reierstadt," the laugh Arroyo added scared the retreating Yoshida even more. "She thought she was so smart, I showed her how motherfucking smart she was."

The fear in Yoshida was starting to come to the surface, and it was turning to panic. He was trying to work his way back to the exterior ladder he had just climbed. "Capt'n let's just go back inside and talk this over," his voice was an uneasy balance between forced calm and blind terror. "We're not your enemy, that thing running around out here in the dark is." The tech-sergeant kept moving, circling back toward the ladder, the sound of his own blood thundered in his ears with every heartbeat.

Arroyo, snapping on the weapon's laser-sight, brought the Jones-Benelli coilgun up to level, taking careful aim at Yoshida's e-suit helmet faceplate.

The panic exploded in Yoshida, as he screamed, "*Urusai kono bakayaro!*" Turning to dive over the edge of the roof, his first step missed the lip and went right off the edge. His foot landed between the station and the top rung of the ladder. The momentum of his motion caught the frightened tech-sergeant by surprise, as the force of his forward motion swung him downward into the rungs of the ladder.

The crunching vibrations of his left ankle and knee, reached Yoshida's stunned mind long before he felt the blinding agony. As every twitch of his body sent lightning shooting up his left leg into his groin, the helpless tech-sergeant fought to control his pain and panic. He knew, from experience that his ankle was broken. The fire that burnt in the back of his leg told him that the ligaments behind his knee were torn, and the burning feeling was warm meniscus and blood pooling behind his destroyed joint.

"Mitsu!" cried Tounames, reaching the scene of the

encounter on the roof. He had heard the interplay between Yoshida and Arroyo over his helmet speakers and the distorted shriek of Yoshida's voice as he fell. He could still hear his partner's tortured cries of pain as he spotted Arroyo in the low light.

Arroyo, hearing Tounames' call over the omnidirectional helmet speakers spun around into a crouch, bracing himself. He fired blast after blast across the roof into the fog. Yoshida, screaming and half blind with pain did not hear the weapons fire. His whole mind was focused on freeing his destroyed ankle from between the ladder and the station, and stopping the pain.

Tounames dove to the right as Arroyo, stepping on Yoshida's broken leg, descended a few rungs on the ladder and used both the lip of the roof and Yoshida's body as cover. He continued to fire in Tounames' direction as Yoshida, flailing around like a scared and injured bird, continued to announce his agony in a series of unearthly screams.

The crippled tech-sergeant felt the jagged fragments of his shattered knee chew up the remains of his destroyed joint, as the force of Arroyo's movements folded his knee the rest of the way, in the wrong direction. Yoshida's brain decided that screaming was not helping anymore, it switched off, and Yoshida blacked out.

Tounames scrambled behind one of the communication dishes, then returned fire with his Glock-Whelan, "Mitsu!"

Arroyo answered for Yoshida with a blast from his Jones-Benelli Magnastar. The projectile hit just next to Tounames' helmet faceplate, and that was too close for the tech-sergeant. He jumped, rolled and bounced several times, then stopped and returned Arroyo's fire. One, two, three, and Tounames' weapon went silent, empty. He rolled again, popped up to his feet in the low gravity and skipped across the roof into the mist.

The crazed captain spotted Tounames' retreat and hurried to pursue. Stopping, he halfheartedly glanced back at the unconscious Yoshida, who was hanging by one leg twisted in the ladder. Arroyo blew Yoshida's foot completely off at the ankle, along with the top rung of the ladder. He grinned happily to himself as he headed after Tounames. Yoshida's body fell lifeless, and abnormally slow, down the side of the station.

Tounames scrambled down another ladder in the one-seventh gravity and landed on the surface of Lincoln Mons at a run, and automatically sensed Arroyo's pursuit. He looked left and right for cover, as he moved off into the darkness just as Arroyo reached the bottom of the ladder.

"You assholes wanted my job, that's why you were always backstabbing me!" He started off in Tounames' direction, "Thinking I didn't deserve to be here!" he paused, scanning the gloom, "I earned my place motherfucker! What about you?" There was a hint of unnatural humor in his voice, "Time for you to bend over and take a big hot one for the team!"

Tounames holstered his weapon and began climbing down the slippery face of the mountain. The fear in him was greater than any fear he had ever known. He could not move fast enough for himself. All that roared through his terror-ridden mind was *MOVE! MOVE! MOVE!* He slipped, he slid, but he kept moving downward, his body trembling uncontrollably. Jagged and sharp pieces of ice, as hard as carbon-steel, bit at his e-suit, but he did not see them or even care about the damage that could occur to his suit. He was in a nightmare panic, like a stampeding animal pursued by a furious predator.

"I see you," Arroyo's voice was eerily psychotic as a chunk of dark ice exploded into splinters centimeters from Tounames' gloved hand. It blew dark slush onto his faceplate. His mind cringed in blind fear, the sound of Arroyo's voice ringing in his ears.

Somehow, Tounames managed to move faster, his panic-stricken eyes trying to look in every direction at once. He was sweating, and his e-suit's air-conditioner was screaming, trying to lower his body temperature. He did not even hear his e-suit's AI announcing that he was experiencing a dangerously elevated heart rate, blood pressure, and body-core temperature. All he was aware of was the cool air and warm sweat on his body, and it only added to his fear. He now hoped that their monstrous intruder would appear and attack the pursuing captain.

Arroyo continued moving downward after the fleeing Tounames, his laughter nearly comical. He knew he had Tounames, he knew he could not climb much further. "Where are all those years of training?" he bellowed, "Remember what they taught yeah! Stop! Think! And remember panic kills!" Arroyo's mocking laughter echoed into Tounames' terror.

●　　●　　●

Confused and saddened, but relieved, Major Singleton listened to the report LaRocque and Pulgar made in regards to their encounter with the extrasolar being. When Doctor Tan had recovered from the shock of seeing Major Nianta again, she immediately snapped into doctor mode. Major Singleton approached his friend, trying not to get in the doctor's way. "Colin, we thought you were dead."

Nianta, holding onto Tan, answered in a slow, unsteady voice. "I hit a ledge on the shelf...I climbed back up...the mountain..." he leaned his head against Tan's chest and started to nod off.

"Colin?" The doctor pushed him back and held him up in a rigid sitting position, tapping his face. "Come on, stay awake. Stay awake, Major." She opened one of his eyes, as Trauma-Specialist Medtec First Class Lebowitz took his pulse and examined his frost-injuries. Tan checked the other eye and found both pupils were dilated, but with slightly different radii.

He opened his eyes again, "I'm tired, and I need some sleep."

"You are suffering from hypothermia," Tan looked to Lebowitz for agreement, "and you might have a concussion."

"I don't have a concussion," he lied. He knew his first aid well enough, "I'm just cold and tired from climbing," he started going out again. The major had used all his willpower and strength to claw back up to the station, and now he had nothing left.

"His pulse is a little rapid," Lebowitz announced as Garcia returned with some emergency medical supplies. The three women immediately donned surgical gloves.

"Alright let's get him out of this suit," ordered Tan dispassionately. "I want him on ten milligrams of Hyperinalizine and four milligrams of Eosinaphiline with a warm saline drip."

"I'll get some blankets," volunteered Garcia moving off again.

"Wait!" interrupted Professor Eastman. "Ten seconds after you open the emergency medical supplies the disaster beacon will trigger. There is no one in the com-center to override it."

"Professor, there isn't a com-center anymore," boomed Singleton, "and it doesn't matter at this point." He turned to Garcia, "Get what you need."

Garcia rushed away as Eastman stepped back and sat down at a nearby table, raddling a small bottle of flavored vodka that was there.

Tan and Lebowitz slowly stripped Major Nianta and began to examine every centimeter of his well-built black African body. His lower legs, hands, right forearm, head, and neck all showed signs of severe frostbite and minor frost-burn. The faint, putrid odor of warm pus was just noticeable, as the two medical professionals began to examine the purple and black blisters on his affected limbs.

"Major!" She shook him gently, "Show me you're okay and I'll let you sleep." Tan softly started feeling Nianta's head. The doctor's fingers gently probed through his short afro searching for signs of injuries, dislodging flakes of dandruff.

He nodded weakly.

Several minutes later, Medtec Garcia returned with a warm, battery-operated heating blanket and an I.V. cuff. She wrapped the blanket around the major and immediately began to place the I.V. cuff on the man. A few seconds later, she took a sample of his blood for analysis on a portable analyzer. "We've got a problem," whispered Garcia, trying not to draw attention.

Tan, Lebowitz, and Major Singleton all looked to Garcia, each expecting some more terrible news.

"A lot of the meds in the disaster kit are expired," the medtec whispered.

Singleton relaxed but quickly noticed the two medical professionals next to him did not.

"The blood-substitute? The pain meds?" questioned Tan, fighting to keep shock off her face.

Garcia subtly motioned with her head. "Six months to a year expired."

"So," blurted Singleton, not understanding.

Tan knew that with the evacuation of the majority of the base's personnel, dozens of routine things got postponed in lew of more critical and immediate tasks. Replacing the old and expired medical supplies in the disaster shelters was one of those tasks. "Modern synthetic blood-substitutes and most smart-drugs have very short shelf-lives. Most rely on short-lived isotopes like sodium twenty-two and sulfur thirty-five to make them viable. When the concentrations drop too low, they become ineffective." Instantly she began testing Nianta's mental and physical abilities. She fired off simple math questions at him while flashing fingers and open palms for him to touch. Moving her hands randomly, all the time she watched his eyes and noted his responses. At first, Nianta was sluggish like a punch-drunk boxer, but slowly he grew to the speed and accuracy to meet the worried doctor's flashing and moving hands. However, his nausea was so severe he thought he would puke in the concerned doctor's face.

"Okay, I want---"

"Already ahead of you," Lebowitz added quickly, as she and Medtec Garcia began spreading the bluish-green dermal regenerating gel over Major Nianta's cold and shivering body. They gave particular attention to the dark blisters, some of which had already begun to ooze bloody and watery pus. The scene gave Garcia a flashback of a training VR-simulation she had gone through in med-school, dealing with victims of the Red Death of Mars, a super pathogen closely related to the Marburg virus of Earth.

Singleton could not take waiting for the doctor to finish with Nianta, "That's enough," he stopped Tan. "Colin, both the General and Colonel Rozsa are dead, and our visitor is still on a rampage, plus Arroyo's gone *born-again* and is running around here someplace with a weapon."

"You handle it," Nianta started to lie back down on the table. Both Singleton and Tan stopped him.

"Oh no, I need you to fly us out of here," he pointed at the door, "and when we get in a hopper, you are technically in-charge." The fog of his cold breath washed over Nianta's face.

Everyone stared long and hard at Singleton for his insensitivity.

"We're all tired and hurt," added Aamodt, joining the small group, "and he is right."

Nianta looked at her, then around the room. They all were staring at him, wanting him to be in charge. "I'm in no shape to assume command," he could smell the combined stench of old sweat, stomach acid and unbrushed teeth coming to him from around the room, mixed with the foul odor of his own injuries.

"I don't mind assuming command, but I'm not a grade-one pilot," Singleton put his hand on Nianta's shoulder. "Yeah, under normal conditions I could get them up to the EET, no problem. But that storm is still raging, and with that cloud of blast ejecta in low orbit, we'd stand a better chance with a *real* pilot at the controls. And I, personally, am not going to carry your sorry ass out of here." There was a friendly edge to Singleton's voice as he scanned his comrade.

"Medically, his frost-injuries are not life-threatening, but it's going to be incredibly painful in a couple of hours as it starts to heal." Tan checked the results of his blood screening. "Right now, he needs some warm food and clothes, and rest. But he is going to need pain meds, soon."

Lebowitz, removing the stained surgical gloves, indicated her agreement, "But if he is going to move around, keep an eye on him for septicemia, especially with those blisters."

"We can bandage him," added Garcia, "I'll see if we have any clothes for him." She ripped off her gloves as she walked off.

"I don't like the idea of my patient walking around." Tan did not look happy.

Nianta flashed a grin at her, "I didn't think you would." He turned to Lebowitz, "Yara, give me something to keep me going."

Tan started to speak, thought better of it, and vocalized nothing. She had to sort out her emotions from her true medical responsibilities. This was an emergency, and certain things had to come first. She motioned for Lebowitz to get what the major asked for.

"The pain meds in the emergency kits, if they are six months to a year out-of-date, are going to be almost useless." Lebowitz looked at Tan and Singleton. "The only place that will have what we need is the med-bay."

There was a pause.

"Someone will have to go to the med-bay." Lebowitz's heart sank, and she immediately felt ill. "NJ, Miyo, and I are the only ones with access to the drug cabinets."

"Great," Singleton sounded dejected as he surveyed the messy cafeteria and the numb faces.

Lebowitz drew Garcia's attention from across the cafeteria, using sign language; she flashed a few words to her, then turned back to Major Singleton and Doctor Tan.

"Look, just fuck the med-bay and let's get the hell out of here, now!" shouted Eastman from the nearby table. She angrily knocked the empty bottle of flavored vodka to the floor, "Why are we fucking around, Major!"

"She's right," added Yee, perplexed. "Why don't we just carry him up to the hoppers and get the fuck out of here?"

"Because," Singleton turned to the disgusted professor, his tone sarcastic, "we still have people out there! Besides, he's the more qualified pilot." He was struggling to control his temper, "The atmosphere is a mess, and there is not only the remains of a solar storm raging, but a dogshit-load of low orbiting debris circling around up there. Do you really want me or her," he indicated Aamodt, "at the controls while flying through that?"

"Auto-nav it!" fired back Yee.

Singleton took a step toward the scientist, then checked himself. "You want to bet your life on that?"

Yee retreated in silence, shaking his head.

"I thought you said it wouldn't be that hard?" Sloan looked over at LaRocque with an expression of confusion on his young face.

"Positive re-enforcement, but the odds were still in your favor." LaRocque held up his mug of steaming coffee in a salute to Sloan, as Pulgar standing next to him softly quivered her head, disappointedly.

"In a way, he's right," Nianta stood up and instantly regretted it. Tan and Aamodt moved in quickly to catch him, nearly dislodging his intravenous arm cuff as they steadied him. "Look," he surveyed the room twice, "Where's Al-Yuzwaki and the rest?" He noticed he could see everyone's breath, including his own.

"Al-Yuzwaki is end-of-mission," Aamodt started counting off on her gloved fingers, "So are Doc Stadts, Professors Watkinski and Costello, Medtec Brauer, Colonel Rozsa, and the General."

Nianta reacted to the news as if someone had just jabbed him in the abdomen. He took Tan's hand and squeezed it as he leaned against the table. "Fucking dogshit," Nianta closed his eyes and pulled Doctor Tan closer to him for both physical and emotional support, "Give me the rest of it. What has happened since I've been gone?" He opened his eyes and focused on Singleton.

"The station is all but fucked. We have explosive damage to main engineering, the lab section, and according to LaRocque and Pulgar the com-center as well. Tounames and Yoshida managed to get some power back, but we are still bleeding to death, the Harlem system is still energized and grav is normal. We have electrified traps set up for our friend at key intersections and points of opportunity." Singleton glanced at Eastman, but she was no longer paying attention to the conversation. "Pulgar and LaRocque led it into one of the traps in the pool area, but odds are it isn't dead."

"What happened to the General and Rozsa?" asked Nianta, sorrow in his voice.

"They were in the com-center when there was an explosion," Singleton paused and exhaled loudly, images of his dead friend playing in his mind.

Nianta looked as if he had been kicked in the testicles, "Are you sure they were in there?" He whispered, still mournful.

"Yeah, LaRocque and Pulgar were on their way to the com-center when it happened. They said it came out of the flames after them." Singleton surveyed the room and focused on Eastman, as he searched his mind for anything else Nianta needed to know.

"And Tounames and Yoshida aren't back yet," quickly added Aamodt, looking around at the group.

"Yeah, and besides that, we now have Arroyo's crazy ass to worry about," concluded Singleton. "He killed Doc Stadts."

"What?" was all Nianta could say, trying not to be sick on himself. There was a moment of uneasy silence, then Nianta looked to Aamodt. "Do you think you can get down to engineering and find Yoshida and Tounames?"

"Probably, especially if I don't run into *It*," she held up her Jones-Benelli Magnastar, "But you want me to go by myself?"

"I'm going with you," volunteered Singleton.

"No," Nianta reached out and touched his friend's arm. "I am not a hundred percent, and we are low on OSC personnel." He scanned the slim, raven-haired captain. "Can you do this alone?"

"No problem," she grinned, obviously with false bravado.

Singleton, not happy about the idea of Aamodt going out into the darkened station alone, added, "Be careful and watch out for Arroyo." He knew, if anyone in their shrinking group could complete this task alone, it was her.

"If you see him," Nianta motioned at her coilgun. "Take his motherfucking head off."

"Trust me, not a problem," she exclaimed.

"Sloan, you take Lebowitz and Eastman to the med-bay," then Nianta turned to Lebowitz. "Get whatever you think we may need, bandages, painkillers, blood-substitute, anything and everything."

"I want a weapon," The professor stood up. She was not happy about being ordered to go, but she was not scared either.

Aamodt produced a Glock-Whelan from one of her e-suit pockets. She handed it to Eastman, handle first. "You ever play a first-person VR that used weapons?"

Eastman leered at the younger woman as if she had spat something rude. "When I was a teen, my mother almost got killed by a mentally-ill fucker, just after we got to Mars." The professor ejected the clip of stored projectiles from the weapon and visually inspected it. She then rammed it back into the Glock-Whelan, chambered a projectile, and toggled the safety. "She was nearly killed at the north pole of Mars because she didn't have a *real* weapon, and wouldn't have known how to use one if she did. She made sure I knew how to protect myself."

Professor Yee walked over to the group, "Lori you sure about this?"

She smiled, "I'm sure."

Garcia returned, handed Major Nianta a small, green and black capsule. "Sir, I am still looking for a flightsuit, but Professor McGilmer has a medical question." She gestured and walked off.

Tan flashed a smile and winked at Nianta as he swallowed the capsule. She and Lebowitz studied Nianta hard, but neither voiced anything as Aamodt and Sloan headed off with their weapons ready. Professor Eastman and Trauma-Specialist Lebowitz exchanged a knowing nod and moved off on the heels of Aamodt and Sloan.

Nianta closed his eyes tight. His head was spinning as the combined odors in the room made him gag. "NJ could you please get me some water." His hands and face were cold, but he could feel sweat on his forehead and back.

She nodded and moved off as Nianta waved Professor Yee over to join him and Major Singleton.

"Steve, you and Yee get everybody ready to move as soon as Aamodt and Sloan get back."

"Why did you send them for that dogshit in the med-bay?" inquired Singleton. "That stuff is on the EET, and there are emergency medical kits on the hopper."

"Suppose something else goes wrong, and we don't make the EET? We end up out on the ice or going to TBT?" Nianta was watching Tan across the room. "We are going to need all the supplies we can carry."

Doctor Tan returned with a large glass of water and a small crispy brown cake wrapped in a paper napkin. "I brought you a Chebureki, you need to eat something."

"Thanks." He took the glass and the fried meat pie with a grin; he was not hungry in the least. Sipping the cool water, he stared at the Titan-Lincoln mission logo etched in the glass and frowned.

Singleton, catching a subtle gesture from Tan, grinned and added, "Professor, come on, we've got some work to do." The major winked at Yee, casting a knowing glance at both Nianta and Tan. At first, Yee did not understand, but after a quick glance at the doctor, he got the message. The two men walked off, as a long and silent exchange began between Nianta and Tan.

They watched each other's breath in the cold air and ignored the gentle mutterings of the six other people remaining in the room. Nianta slowly took a bite out of his Chebureki, producing a cloud of moist steam. The pie was a combination of canine and feline meat, all seasoned with a plethora of herbs. "You know I am not hungry," he sat the glass of water and meat pie down and took Tan around the waist.

Tan did not say anything; she just checked his vital signs and his I.V. cuff. She also surveyed the major's nude body beneath the warm blanket and found that he was not aroused.

"So can I get some clothes?" he grinned. "Or do you just like seeing me naked?"

"Steady old boy," Tan cracked a grin. "First things, first," her voice quickly went back to being flat and emotionless, as she moved away from him. "You finish that and sit up for a few minutes, but don't move around. I'll be back shortly with some bandages and some clothes."

As the doctor turned away, Major Nianta had a sudden twinge of pain, as if someone stuck a fork in the back of his left eye. He took another sip of water, but let the steaming Chebureki sit on the table. Looking at Tan across the room, Nianta thought of the Cézanne portrait in his quarters.

# CHAPTER TWENTY-TWO

Tounames could not go any lower or any farther. There was a two-hundred-meter, nearly vertical drop below him and Arroyo was still coming after him. His fear mounted as he drew his firearm, and hastily ejected the empty clip, and slid in a new full magazine. Pulling back the slide, he chambered a projectile and waited. He aimed his weapon unsteadily up the glacial face of the mountain and waited. His breath was heavy, and his mind panic-stricken, as he readied himself.

A small moving light slowly appeared among the peaks and curves of ice and rock above Tounames' position. As he tensed on the trigger, the same phrase ran through his mind over and over again, like a broken playback. *One shot. One shot and I'll be---* The ice exploded in front of his faceplate, blowing sooty slush over it, blurring his vision. His Glock-Whelan slipped from his gloved hand and bounced down into the darkness below as the stunned tech-sergeant lost his balance and fell.

Tounames bounced and tumbled head over heels, even in the one-seventh gravity he was accelerating down the high angled slope. He could not get a hold of the slippery surface to stop his fall or even control his descent. It seemed to him like he had been falling for twenty minutes, but it had only been for a few seconds. As he collided with a boulder that spun him around and knocked the air from his lungs, he crashed onto an ice shelf. His left foot caught a fracture in the ice and the side of a rock, and his momentum twisted him hard. He gulped air as he grabbed his ankle. As it throbbed with pain, he hurriedly looked around for a means of escape.

Arroyo, with the Magnastar coilgun in one hand, stared down at Tounames. He grinned and started descending the steep slope in a controlled slide that no sane person would have attempted, even in Titan's one-seventh gravity. After sixty or seventy seconds of body surfing his way down the mountain, he finally landed on the shelf, just in front of his quarry.

The two stared at each other for a minute. Tounames feeling his heart sink in defeat, Arroyo smiling in victory. Then with a sharp nod of his head in triumph, the captain raised his weapon toward the tech-sergeant's helmeted face. The cold laser-targeting beam streamed through Tounames' dirty faceplate and fell on the bridge of his nose.

"Sorry, Chucky old man, but I can't afford anyone shit-talking me to the OSC."

As the trembling and whimpering Tounames squeezed his tear-laden eyes shut to block out the mind-numbing terror, he was barely conscious of his bowels letting go. He clenched his teeth tightly, bracing himself against the inevitable coilgun projectile that would splatter his head like an over-ripe melon. His mind screamed with fear. Fear of pain.

Fear of death.

Fear of the unknown.

"*Adios, Amigo,*" the captain squeezed the trigger.

Nothing happened.

At that moment, an observer of the scene would have been hard pressed to say who was more surprised, Arroyo or Tounames. Arroyo fumbled with the weapon, checking to see what the problem was. Tounames opened his eyes and stared in bewilderment at the fumbling officer for a moment, his mind not quite sure what had just taken place. It rapidly dawned on him what had just occurred.

With an animal like growl, Tounames launched himself at Arroyo, body-checking the larger man, sending him bouncing off the side of the mountain. The coilgun went cartwheeling into the frozen darkness, its green laser flashing its departure like some odd aircraft running light.

Tounames dove on Arroyo, trying to open the larger man's helmet seal, cursing him with every foul word that flashed through his mind. The tech-sergeant had suddenly become a wild animal fighting for its last chance at survival. There was no trace of humanity in the man's dark, twisted face as he snarled and struck at Arroyo. He was not just trying to kill Arroyo, but he *wanted* to kill Arroyo. Whatever was driving the tech-sergeant, it *needed* to kill Arroyo from deep down in it's being.

The two figures in e-suits struggled on the ice like two bizarre lovers on some dark, nightmarish beach, but love was nowhere to be found in the life and death struggle. In the violent wrestling match, Arroyo was by far the stronger, but Tounames was the faster. Grabbing and punching, kicking and screaming, the two men fought with such fury that the insides of their dirty faceplates clouded over. Huffing and puffing with the enormous effort, neither man heard nor cared that their e-suit's AIs were announcing warnings and voicing concerns about their suit systems.

Arroyo kicked Tounames against an outcrop of ice and then lunged at him. Tounames caught the bigger man with his good foot in the chest, slamming him hard onto the ice. Arroyo's helmet seal slipped, and he screamed, as bone shattering cold flooded into his e-suit.

The captain's face flash froze almost instantaneously. He could just smell the cold stench of hydrocarbons, like old syntha-oil and burnt carbo-plastic, before his nostrils and olfactory system froze. He tried to scream again, but there was no air as the soft pink tissues of his lungs transformed into hard gray blocks of ice. The crazed captain tried to reseal his helmet, but Tounames grabbed and held his arms. Spasms and waves of pain racked Arroyo's body as he lifted the smaller man, but it was too late, his arms slowly lowered. He would not move them again.

Tounames hurriedly removed Arroyo's helmet and threw it as hard, and as far as he could, then he sat there for a long moment, quiet. Exhausted, the victorious tech-sergeant began to giggle nervously. The giggling quickly became a fit of uncontrolled laughter. He looked at Arroyo's motionless body and his blue and gray crystallized face, and laughed harder still, tears rolling down his cheeks. Flopping back on the ice, he continued to roar with inappropriate laughter. He could not stop laughing as some primordial part of his brain celebrated. He was more than just *glad* to be alive, he was downright *elated*.

After a few minutes, Tounames tried, with little success, to wipe his faceplate clean. Then, feeling drained and centuries older, he began to make his way back up the mountainside. Using two screwdrivers, one from his tool belt and one from Arroyo's, he stabbed the ice face and pulled himself up.

The exhausted tech-sergeant began to pull himself up the mountain. His ribs and right elbow throbbed with pain, but he kept climbing. Every time he drove one of the screwdrivers into the ice, his ankle fired a lightning bolt of pain up his leg, but he kept going. He slipped and fell, but he continued to fight the pain and climb in the low gravity. His adrenaline surge was quickly wearing off, and fatigue was beginning to set in. However, he had managed to survive Arroyo, and he was determined to climb back to the station.

•   •   •

Sloan, his coilgun set on semi-automatic mode, moved along the dim, cold corridor slowly, ready to fire in any direction. He knew if they ran into Arroyo, that the weapon would come in handy. However, he also knew if they encountered the extrasolar creature, the ancient weapon would be next to useless. Nevertheless, like a campfire in a dark forest, it made him feel safer. Behind him crept Eastman, her mind was elsewhere, and her Glock-Whelan was held dangerously close to Sloan's back, as they moved up the corridor. Finally, bringing up the rear was an unsteady and very scared Trauma-Specialist Yara Lebowitz. She had the look of a trapped animal, and even in the cold air, she was sweating.

As they moved, Sloan knew that the temperature in the station was falling fast, for virtually everything they passed was coated with a thin layer of frost and ice. Even the few interior emergency lights that they encountered were encased in cold, crystallized water, which cut their illumination by almost half. Sloan could see their warm breath in the dull light, and the bursts of warm vapor in the cold air looked like the emissions from three primitive steam engines. Surprisingly he was not cold, but the gloom and dull yellow hue of the sparse light put him on edge.

In the beam from Eastman's hand-light, Sloan saw one of the emergency access-ways up ahead. "Come on," he motioned to the two women to follow him, as he examined the floor and walls, making sure he was not leading them into one of their makeshift traps.

They slowly climbed the access-way ladder to the level of the med-bay. For the first time, it occurred to the young lieutenant that the station sounded dead. Gone was the soft background hum of the united voices of the station's electronic systems. The place felt old and abandoned as they stealthily moved along the poorly illuminated corridors. Along the way, they encountered several room doors that had been knocked in or torn open, and half-frozen puddles of hydraulic fluid were everywhere. Room contents and debris littered the corridor. It reminded Eastman and Sloan of the aftermath of a riot, and to her surprise, the place had been looted. It is evident to the three that someone or something had been through the area, and was very angry.

They kept moving forward.

"Looks like someone's gone crazy," whispered Eastman.

Sloan just nodded, "Yeah, but was it our visitor or Captain Arroyo?" He continued forward. Sloan wanted to have the two women extinguish their hand-lights, but knew that Lebowitz would protest. He could tell that among them, she was the most frightened.

The three clung to the frosty walls like cautious mice, as they crept from one gloomy, ice-laden doorway to the next. Sloan did not know which was growing worse, the fear or the cold. He wanted to tell the two women to make less noise, but it was impossible to be any quieter and still breathe and move. His own breathing was like thunder to him, and their cautious, well-placed steps on the icy deck sounded like dog paws on a tile floor.

Just ahead, in the cold silence of the corridor, the illuminated: **MED-BAY** sign appeared. As they got closer, they could see that the door to the med-bay had been peeled open and pieces of medical equipment littered the corridor and the wrecked medical facility. Various colors and shapes of pills and broken glass covered the floor, and small pools of freezing liquid were everywhere.

"What the fuck?" whispered Eastman; her face was a mass of confusion.

Sloan could hear a faint sound emanating from the darkened med-bay, and his tension level jumped up fifty points. Alerted, the lieutenant signaled Eastman and Lebowitz to silently retreat back up the corridor. The three of them crouched against the corridor wall, and Eastman and Lebowitz instantly snapped off their hand-lights. The green beam of the coilgun's laser-sight was painfully bright in the cold darkness of the corridor.

Trembling, Sloan could feel the cold sweat on his hot forehead, and the drops of sweat tickling his armpits as they slipped down his sides. "I'll check it to make sure it's clear," he whispered, checking his weapon, his ears straining to catch the faintest hint of a sound.

It was nearly too dark for Sloan to see Eastman nod her nervous reply. "What do you think? Monster or Madman?" she was ready to flee at the first sign of danger.

"There's only one way to find out. Get ready to run. If dogshit goes bad, split up and head back to the cafeteria." The lieutenant took a deep breath and before he could lose his courage to the frosty gloom, ducked into the room.

For what seemed like an eternity, there was nothing, not a sound. Eastman felt the raw panic race up her spine as Lebowitz muttered something to her in a voice so low that she could not make it out. A minute later Sloan was back in the doorway, and even in the low, ghostly yellow light of the corridor, Eastman could tell something was wrong.

"Professor," Sloan's voice was weak and unsteady, "*Sie müssen das sehen.*" He gagged and sank to his knees, breathing heavy in the cold air of the doorway, generating clouds of frosty fog.

"What?" whispered Eastman, not understanding the lieutenant's Venusianized, neo-central European words.

"By all the love of the Divinities, you need to see this." The young man looked pale and sick. Even playing the illegal VR-games and working through the security forces VR combat scenarios, had not prepared him for the horrific scene in the med-bay.

Eastman and Lebowitz exchanged a concerned look and moved slowly past Sloan into the blackness of the med-bay. In the cold darkness, the med-bay smelled like an old moldy house with a backed-up toilet. Switching on their hand-lights, they scanned the room as Sloan moved in behind them.

In the beams of the two hand-lights, they could see that the med-bay had been ransacked. Drawers and cabinets were open, and equipment and instruments had been thrown aside. Puddles of liquid, pills, piles of dataclips, and containers of various sizes and shapes littered the floor. However, what immediately drew their attention was the bizarre apparatus rigged up to the remains of the autodoc, and the abomination within it.

Professor Eastman, seeing the assemblage in the former autodoc station, dropped her Glock-Whelan and slapped her hands over her mouth to silence her own scream. Her mind went numb with the sheer horror of the sight before her. Screaming uncontrollably, the planetary scientist urinated on herself.

Trauma-Specialist Yara Lebowitz did not speak. She could not speak for several seconds. All she could do was just stared wide-eyed at the nightmare before her as if expecting it to vanish at any moment. She had seen images of human pain and gore that had made her lose her last meal and not want another for days. She had seen images of human misery that gave her nightmares for months; however, what was before her left her speechless. All she could do is mutter in a perplexed whisper, "What the fuck is this?"

A cesium chloride battery that had been used for one of the electrified traps was now connected to the partly disassembled autodoc. Numerous fiber-optic lines, micro-cables, hoses, and pipes ran from the autodoc to a nightmarish amalgam of assorted machines and devices from all over the station. Several holo-screens slowly scrolled unintelligible colored symbols up and down their dark faces, as a transparent tank shone a dark red from deep in the autodoc. Floating within the tank and connected to the lid by countless wires were the severed heads of General Newey and Colonel Rozsa.

The burnt and blackened faces of the two officers bobbed in the slowly moving red fluid within the tank. Large patches of bare, charred bone were visible on both heads. Swollen and discolored brain tissue bulged through several cavities in both skulls. However, to the horror of all in the room, the bleached white eyes of both of the station's former senior officers were open and moving wildly, as if they were alive. General Newey's teeth, exposed by missing beard, cheek flesh and lips, gnashed at the single strand of gray tissue that held the remains of his blacken tongue to the inside of his mouth.

"Lori!" Sloan grabbed Eastman and turned her away from the horror in the autodoc, "Lori! Snap out of it! We need you!" With her mouth open in a muted scream, her eyes bulging with tears streaming down her face, she was clearly in terror-induced shock. He slapped her, but it did not do any good, "Lori!"

"This isn't Arroyo." Lebowitz began to examine the insanity before her, forgetting, for a moment, the cold and the horror.

Sloan turned to Lebowitz, his face a mixture of confusion and anger. "What the fuck are you saying?" He grabbed her arm, "You're saying that that thing did this?"

Lebowitz yanked her arm away. "It has to be," she could not take her eyes off of the stomach-turning construct before her. "Why would the Captain do this? How could he do this?"

Sloan angrily moved and retrieved Eastman's fallen hand-light and weapon. "How could it do this? Why would it do this?" Hurriedly, Sloan scanned the dark, cold room. His light instantly fell on a large naked human body lying face down on a table, covered in dark, frozen blood. The body, he recognized as Al-Yuzwaki's. His former co-worker's body had been filleted open like a freshly caught salmon. The man's spinal column and brain had been exposed with surgical precision. Turning at a sudden sound, he spied Eastman softly moaning and looking almost catatonic. She just stared at the modified autodoc and the ghoulish autopsy table beyond.

Yara Lebowitz slowly, but carefully continued to scrutinize the device. She examined the two floating heads and the holo-screens and ignored Sloan's repeated attempts to get an explanation from her. After a minute, she stepped back and whispered, "I think it is trying to access their memories."

"Dogshit!" bellowed Sloan shaking his head in disbelief.

"I think it is trying to keep their neuro-tissues alive, to record their bioengramatic memories," she played her light over the assemblage. "I think it's trying to translate them, see what's in their memories."

Sloan continued to rock his head. His mind was refusing to accept what the reality around him was presenting. "Yara! Find what you need?" He played the hand-light around the room again, then moaned, "We need to get out of here."

Still not taking her eyes off the horror in front of her, Lebowitz replied weakly, "Are you kidding," She stepped around an overturned cabinet, continuing to examine the device. "What are we going to do about this?"

"Destroy it," pronounced Sloan. The tension in his voice

was apparent as Lebowitz played her light on the ceiling and over the far walls. "Just get the dogshit we need, and let's move!"

Lebowitz nodded as she unpacked a medical satchel from under a table and attacked the remains of the medicine cabinet. She started stuffing bottles and boxes into the nylon sack as if she were on a time limit. In the dim light, she dropped to her knees and began searching the intact containers on the floor, putting the ones she wanted into her pack and discarding the others.

Sloan looked back and forth between Eastman and the strange autodoc device. He stood a nervous guard, wishing the trauma-specialist were a little bit quicker in her harvesting of the needed materials.

Professor Eastman slowly backed away from the autodoc and the ghoulish remains of the autopsy on the med-bay table. As she moved out of the small circle of light created by their hand-lights, and Sloan looked toward Lebowitz, the professor's life was taken with the softest of sounds, like the faint snapping of a cookie in two.

Lebowitz sighed in exhaustion as she zipped the pack. *Now we get the fuck out of here*, she thought, picking up her hand-light. Turning around and playing the light on Sloan, she screamed a cloud of steam into the cold air, dropping the pack.

Sloan dropped his hand-light and spun around with the Jones-Benelli Magnastar held high, the laser-sight zeroed in on his target. Behind him stood the towering dark form of their intruder with Professor Eastman wrapped in its four arms. Her head was oddly misshapen, and her eyes were no longer parallel with one another. Blood and gray matter leaked out of the motionless professor's mouth and nostrils, and oozed down her insulated flightsuit, forming cold, clear jelly as her body silently quivered.

For an instant, nothing moved in the med-bay. Sloan and Lebowitz stood frozen in horror and confusion, as time seemed suspended. The extrasolar entity held Eastman's broken body in its massive arms like some kind of morbid motherly embrace. The professor's dead eyes bulged around twisted features, fixed with the last seconds of terror. Only the sound of Eastman's blood and bodily fluids, eerily dripping onto the hard, cold floor could be heard.

Steam rose from the gory puddle of warm, dark blood on the cold floor as Lebowitz studied the thing's face, noting its teeth and the ridge of faceted eyes. Then everything happened at once. Sloan fired semi-automatic blast after blast into their attacker and the body of Eastman, knocking both of them back into a cabinet. Dark, fleshy chunks and bloody fragments of the professor's body painted the cabinet and wall behind it, as the Magnastar projectiles ripped her limp body apart on their way to their target.

Lebowitz exploded into a terrified scream, as the flash from the weapon momentarily blinded her. "RUN!" was all she could hear over the roar of the weapon and the inhuman wail of the extrasolar creature. The faint flash of light generated by every hypersonic projectile, superheated by air friction, illustrated the creature's movements like some bizarre strobe-light.

The Magnastar clicked empty. Their attacker laid against the wall, covered with the remains of Eastman. "Get out!" screamed Sloan, his voice breaking as he stared at the intruder and the barely recognizable remains covering it.

Lebowitz, with Sloan on her heels, bolted out of the med-bay door, the satchel of medical supplies forgotten. After a moment, like some unnatural tarantula covered in its victim's blood, the extrasolar sprung to its feet and followed the fleeing humans.

•　　•　　•

When Tounames finally reached the ridge where the darkened station rested, he was more exhausted than he had ever been in his life. Even in the low gravity, his leg felt like he had just spent the last eight hours bicycling the Appalachian Trail, none stop. Lying on his back for a long moment, fighting off the urge to close his eyes and sleep, he looked into the murky sky. A thick cauldron of dark oranges and blood reds rolled and boiled as the masses of clouds moved in to cover the warm pinks and blues of the aurora.

"Better get inside before it rains," he grumbled in a hoarse and broken voice. As he stood up, the frozen ground beneath him began to vibrate with the sound of rolling thunder, hurling him back to the ground. As the Titanquake rumbled past and died away, he again climbed back to his feet and began slowly hopping and skipping toward the installation.

The slow wind was blowing the dust and ice into swirls

and slow-motion tornados all around him. Large drops of sticky yellow liquid began to leisurely fall from the sky and slide along the ground in oily blobs and slick ribbons. The greasy, urine yellow rain quickly turned Tounames' already dirty faceplate into a blindfold. The tech-sergeant, practically at the end of his strength began to lose his footing and fall more and more. Even in the low gravity, every fall's impact ate at his waning energy.

After falling yet again, he laid on the ice glaring up through the nearly opaque faceplate. He spotted a pinpoint of light moving toward him out of the darkness. For a quick moment, he thought it was Arroyo coming to finish him off, but remembered their encounter. Then he thought it was their dark intruder, but reasoned it was unlikely. "Hey!" he screamed, "Mitsu! Help me!"

"Chuck?" answered a shadowy Captain Aamodt moving out of the fog swept gloom. "It's Tonja, I am here."

"Yeah!" Tounames replied as Aamodt moved down to him. "I got Arroyo." He tried to get up, and failed, "I took'em out."

"Are you injured?"

"My ankle's fucked." He clutched at his leg. Aamodt, still holding onto her weapon, lifted him to his feet. "I think Mitsu is on the roof." He swung an arm around Aamodt's shoulders.

"I found Yoshida," she informed him, "he didn't make it."

Aamodt could not see it, but Tounames had a look somewhere between disbelief, fear, pain, and exhaustion. His dark face was ashen and worn as he whispered. "Damn, damn, damn." The two sluggishly moved back toward the station, Aamodt still eyeing the gloom, looking for their one remaining adversary.

The captain and injured tech-sergeant entered the station through the damaged engineering section. They slowly made their way up an emergency access-way to the level where the cafeteria resided and headed for it at a pace somewhere between a walk and a hobbled-jog. The generator for the trap was still functioning, and lights and shadows were coming from the cafeteria.

Aamodt and Tounames opened their helmet faceplates in unison, releasing a cloud of warm air into the frigid, dry darkness of the corridor.

"Somebody, turn this thing off!" shouted Aamodt. A moment later, Major Singleton, Lieutenants Pulgar and LaRocque, and Professor Yee appeared outside the cafeteria doorway, all armed. "I got Tounames."

Singleton surveyed Aamodt half-carrying Tounames and switched off the current. Professor McGilmer rushed into the corridor to help Aamodt with the injured Tounames, as the group moved into the cafeteria. The major turned the generator back on, as Professor Yee and Lieutenant Pulgar repositioned the recoilless rifle, both while keeping a nervous eye on the corridor.

"Where's Yoshida?" was the first thing Nianta asked.

"Dead," Aamodt sat Tounames down in a chair without looking at anyone but the tech-sergeant.

Nianta dropped his head angrily, "Fuck!"

"Vincent killed him," Aamodt informed everyone in earshot as she sat her coilgun down. She removed her e-suit helmet and angrily tossed it onto a nearby table.

"Colin, I say we get the fuck out of here," the tone of Singleton's voice was practically a plea as he moved over to Nianta's side. "Sloan could be dead as well, and I recommend we don't wait around to join him."

Tounames, taking off his helmet, pitched it across the room. "I sure as dogshit, second that." The exhausted tech-sergeant immediately became aware of bad odors in the cold air. It was old coffee and stale sweat, mixed with that of alcohol and fear. Tounames saw the look in McGilmer's eyes and knew he looked like death warmed over because that was precisely how he felt.

"We don't know if Sloan is dead," Lebowitz stepped in, "We can't just leave him."

"Wanna fucking bet we can't leave'em?" coughed Tounames as McGilmer laid him down on a table and began opening his e-suit. "I am fucking done with this place!"

The room was dead quiet. Only the distant hum of the generator for the electrified trap could be heard, as the remaining Frontier Authority personnel; Tan, McGilmer, Yee, Garcia, and Lebowitz studied the surviving Outer Systems Command personnel; Nianta, Singleton, Aamodt, Pulgar, LaRocque, and Tounames. Everyone looked older and much fatigued. The faces of the men were unshaven, and not one of the survivors possessed neat hair or clean breath. E-suits and flightsuits alike were stained and dirty. Some of their suits were stained with the blood of friends or soiled with the oily grime of Titan.

Finally, Nianta looked up, "Steve, you and Aamodt get

them up to the hangar deck." He gestured at the others in the cafeteria. "Tounames, you and I have two things to---"

"Not on a broken ankle," interrupted Doctor Tan, as she and Garcia examined Tounames' foot through his still cold suit. His ankle was probably fractured, but broken was a good enough pronouncement. "And you still haven't answered my question," she continued removing Tounames' boot and glanced back at Singleton.

"Okay," Nianta started again. "Captain, you're with me. Steve, when you get to the hoppers, begin the launch sequence and wait forty minutes." Nianta glanced at Tan, who was watching in disbelief. "If the hangar door doesn't open by then, you and Professor Yee are going to have to get a generator hooked up to the hangar door motor circuits," he then paused a second. "Then set the main power core for self-destruct."

Everyone immediately crowded around the two majors, all looking equally stunned.

"Why?" Singleton voiced the same question that was on everyone's mind.

"Think about what Lebowitz told us. We both saw how fast it learnt to use an ice-melter. That thing is learning about us, studying our technology, and probably our biology. We don't know what happened at T-One, but if this thing gets back to its friends and its ship, who knows what it could do?" Nianta surveyed the group. "Its next stop could be Mars or even Earth." His statement made the room feel ten degrees colder, and no one said a word.

"I am all for stopping this fucker, but---"

Nianta cut Singleton off quick, short, and hard. "We can't take any chances! If we leave and this thing has free run of the place, who knows what it could learn!" The eyes of the two officers were locked. "And those secure servers are just sitting here. That thing could---"

"You don't have to convince me!" interrupted Singleton looking around in the dim light at the faces of the others calmly watching the exchange, their breaths forming clouds in the still chilling air. "But the main reactor is down, and so is Lync. Someone will have to enter the codes manually."

"I know the code," began Tounames, "but I don't think I can make it alone."

Still, there was silence.

"I'll go," Singleton glanced at Captain Aamodt. "Tonja will cover my ass. You have to pilot the hopper. I'll set the auto-destruct."

A wave of surprise swept across Aamodt's face, but she indicated nothing. Nianta wanted to disagree, but he could not fight the logic.

"Major," began Tounames, grimacing with pain as Garcia continued to work on his foot. "Mitsu and I got the power back up for the hangar bay."

"Nice, that'll save us some time," nodded Singleton.

"But what about Lieutenant Sloan?" pressed LaRocque, stepping into the conversation, "We can't just forget about him."

Nianta suddenly grimaced and leaned back on the table, drawing Doctor Tan's attention. He quickly made a visible effort to steady himself. "Look, we'll leave him a note. If he gets back here in time, great, if not, well we can't wait, and we are not going to look for him."

"After he and Lebowitz split up, he knew to head back here," added Singleton. Everyone knew that if Sloan were still alive, he would have been back a long time ago.

"Yeah, but that was almost two hours ago, and the thing followed him, not me." Lebowitz's tone was defensive and hard.

"The two of you split up so one of you could get back here unmolested, didn't you?"

Lebowitz did not reply, and LaRocque looked as if he wanted to, but did not.

"Okay, Captain, let's go." Singleton moved toward the exit.

Aamodt picked up her Jones-Benelli and automatically checked it. "Don't worry, Major, I'll watch his back," she grinned as she and Singleton led Nianta and Tan to the cafeteria entrance.

Lieutenant Pulgar and Professor Yee, who had been watching the corridor, handed Singleton the recoilless rifle and the small satchel of shells. Singleton switched off the trap's generator, and half heartily went into the darkness of the corridor. Captain Aamodt looked back at Major Nianta, gave him a smile and a wink, then vanished after Major Singleton.

Nianta's face was expressionless as he turned to Tan.

She was glaring back at him, negatively.

# CHAPTER TWENTY-THREE

Captain Aamodt, with her Jones-Benelli at the ready, fingered her e-suit lights. She walked slightly in front of and to the right of Major Singleton, who was carrying the recoilless rifle. She was not afraid, but she had known better days. The sight of Yoshida's frozen body with its missing foot and pale dead face haunted her thoughts. Images of all her dead friends and coworkers floated through her conscious mind like scenery on a long, unpleasant road trip. She knew it would be some time before she felt normal again.

Singleton fought to focus on his mission. His mind was torn between his duty and his fear. He was not afraid for himself, but for Aamodt. He knew she could take care of herself, but five million years of human social and biological evolution was hard to overcome, especially in the face of something as unfamiliar as the nightmare roaming the corridors. If they survived, he knew this incident could be, and probably would be *sanitized*. Those who did not cooperate with the cover-up would be shipped out to one of the government's *Special Personality Reconstruction facilities*. He did not want something like that to happen to Aamodt. In the last year or so, he had actually grown to care about her. He would have to make sure she understood the stakes.

After ten minutes of traveling through the cold, dark passages of the dying station, Aamodt slowed. "Hold it," she whispered, "There's one of those traps ahead."

The generator was smashed beyond any hope of repair.

The thin micro-wires of the trap were torn down and spread around the deck. Lying against the opposite wall, like some old discarded beverage container, was the small core of the generator's reactor. It's yellow and black casing horribly dented in the center of its radiological symbol.

"Looks like our friend's been through here," answered Singleton, quietly looking back the way they had just come. "Stay sharp."

"No shit," whispered Aamodt as they continued on, weapons at the ready. Descending an emergency access-way, which was coated in a fine layer of ice, the two officers proceeded on to the engineering level. Knowing that the engineering level was exposed to Titan's atmosphere, they sealed their e-suits and double-checked one another before entering the cold, dead section.

Moving past the darkened instrument panels and lifeless equipment; they headed for the red door embossed with pictograms and the black letters that read:

**DANGER!**
**MAIN FUSION POWER PLANT**
**EMERGENCY CONTROL CENTER.**
**AUTHORIZED PERSONNEL ONLY.**

A small illuminated key and scanner pad was mounted in the wall next to the door.

"It's got power?" Aamodt whispered.

"It's on a direct circuit."

"You do know the code?" Aamodt's voice was a mixture of sarcasm and disappointment. She was thinking that it would be their luck to come all this way and not have the access codes.

"Colin, Tounames, and I are the only ones left who do know the code," he punched out the seven-digit code and placed his gloved right palm on the scanner pad. The illuminated scanner activated and ran through a cycle under Singleton's hand. Even as it returned to it starting position, both Singleton and Aamodt knew they had a problem.

The tiny display on the scanner flashed: **UNABLE TO CONFIRM IDENTIFICATION. PLEASE ENTER EMERGENCY AUTHORIZATION CODE.**

"The gloves?" her voice was questioning, even though

Aamodt already knew the answer. The palm scanner could not read Singleton's hand through his e-suit glove.

The major quickly tapped in his emergency command override code and the seven-digit access code. A few seconds later, the door hummed to life and moved aside with a rush of pressure equalization.

As the door disappeared, Singleton, followed by Aamodt, entered rapidly. "Seal it," the major directed the captain with a wave of his hand as he sat down the recoilless weapon.

Aamodt hit the button on the control panel next to the door, and it slid closed. She surveyed the room with its extensive control laden central column, and numerous displays and holo-screens lining the walls. "What do you want me to do?"

"Watch the door," commanded Singleton as he studied the instrumentation that wrapped around the cylinder that dominated the room. He focused on a number of touch-driven consoles. One side of the cylinder was a white column with a hint of red at the bottom, and a digital counter at the top. There were thirty or so illuminated buttons and protected switches, and three holo-screens on the console across the white column just above waist level.

After a minute of no activity, Aamodt glanced at Singleton and asked, "You remember what you need to do?"

"I'm going to increase the D-T reaction rates and deactivate both the cooling systems and the helium venting pumps." Singleton started working the holo-screens, typing out commands furiously.

"Don't forget to activate the subroutines to disable Lync's emergency override for the WEP's venting systems." Aamodt pointed to the measurements graph of the waste energetic particles on one of the holo-screens but kept her coilgun trained on the doorway.

The major nodded but kept typing as Lync's voice responded. Singleton had to stop a few times to remember the codes for the subroutines that overrode the system's countermeasures. He was also that once the reactor began to operate outside of its normal parameters, Lync's automated subroutines would do whatever it could to bring the reactor back to standard operating conditions or simply shut it down. "I'm also deactivating the auto-shutdown subroutines for the magnetic confinement system."

Aamodt watched silently, checking the door and her wrist chronometer periodically, "How much longer?"

As if on cue, several different holo-screens around the small room came to life, and began to display graphs and scroll texts and numerical values. Singleton moved away from the console he had been working on, "It's done. We've got a runaway reactor." He picked up the recoilless rifle but kept his eyes on the column in front of him.

"I've never seen anyone intentionally start an uncontrolled reaction in a fusion system before," commented Aamodt, moving back to the door. "I hope I live to see it again."

"You and me both," the major opened the door and glanced back into the room. The hint of red at the bottom of the white column was starting to creep upward. "When that marker gets very near the top, the core reactions will begin exceeding the reactor's design capacity and will go critical." The two of them left the room and closed the door. "We've got about two and a half hours."

"Well, time to go," spat Aamodt moving away, only to be stopped by the major.

"Shoot the pad," Singleton instructed, "it won't keep it out of the room, but it will give it one less thing to peak its interest." Without questioning, Aamodt used her weapon on the illuminated keypad, destroying it. "Okay, let's take access-way number five, its closer. We can cut through storage unit seventeen to the hangar deck."

The two of them started up toward the emergency access-way and the hangar deck level. Aamodt moved toward the access-way in a combat shooting stance, her Jones-Benelli Magnastar held high, its laser-sight cutting through the darkness and playing over walls, doors, and motionless equipment. Singleton carried the recoilless rifle, his attention vigilant, and his fingers tight on the firing pad.

Climbing the ladder, Aamodt's e-suit light hit something up ahead on the next landing. It was half hidden behind an open hatchway door. Quickly she zeroed her weapon's laser-sight on the target, and just as quickly snapped off the beam. She closed her eyes and turned away from the gruesome sight. The blood-soaked body was pinned between the hatchway door and the wall behind it. Even though only a small bloody stump was above the shoulders, Aamodt knew immediately that the body was Sloan's.

"What is it?" Singleton was concerned that Aamodt had suddenly stopped ascending.

Aamodt took a deep breath, "It's Sloan." She moved up to the ice-covered landing.

"What?" Singleton slung the recoilless onto his back and moved up to examine the body pinned behind the heavy hatch. "The med-bay is on this level. It must have caught up with him after he and Lebowitz split up."

"You think?" Aamodt whispered her reply.

Eyeing the enraged captain, Singleton grabbed her shoulder with one hand. "Hey, calm down." He surveyed the surrounding scene, keeping his voice low. "It probably took his head back to the med-bay, with the others."

"What do we do? We just can't leave'em."

"There's nothing we can do for him." Singleton tried not to look at the headless form as he choked back a wave of nausea and grabbed the ladder for support. "Let's go."

They continued up through the cold dark shaft of the emergency access-way. Singleton made a comment that brought Aamodt to a sudden halt. "Damn!"

"What!"

"The data on the extrasolar," declared Singleton angrily, "The OSC will want it."

"To hell with that dogshit!" fired Aamodt. "Let's just get the fuck out of here! Every time we delay, somebody dies!"

"I'm not talking about the server data," Singleton's voice did not have the authority it had had only a few minutes ago. "Just the information we collected. Divinities know what the fuck this is and who knows what the fuck will happen next. It is learning about us, and we better learn about it. Newey had Eastman and Watkinski bring all the dataclips from TBK to his office."

"You're crazy! Look around!" Aamodt started up the ladder again but was stopped by the major.

"If the secure servers were not uploaded to the OSC or UESA, all of that data could be lost."

"You can take your data and stick it! No damn data is worth our lives!" Aamodt noticed the barrel of her weapon was in close proximity to the major's e-suit helmet faceplate. She had feelings for Singleton, he was an enjoyable romp in bed, and fun to be with, but at this point, she judged, he was insane to want to risk their lives for a bunch of dataclips. She stared at the barrel of her coilgun and thought that no one would doubt her if she said their invader had killed the major in some heroic battle. When the reactor blows, there would be no evidence to contradict her story.

The captain tensed her finger on the trigger of the coilgun.

"Will you listen to me?" Singleton paused, noticing the barrel of the coilgun only centimeters from his faceplate. "Now, you can get to the hangar door circuits. I'll go get the data." Singleton paused again, the sweat starting to form in his armpits and groin area. "Or vice versa, but we are not leaving that information. Our friends will have died for nothing if we don't at least try."

Aamodt bit her lower lip and stared at the major. "Alright dammit!" She had battled with the thought of killing him but finally decided against it. He was a good man and a decent *Fuck-buddy*. Besides, she had seen too much death in the last week. "Let's go get your dogshit data before our friend shows up."

"Good," grinned Singleton, "cause I didn't want to pull rank on you."

"Yeah, well I wanted to pull something on you." She was not smiling, "and I wasn't thinking of your---"

"Let's move," Singleton cut her off, flashing a grin. He knew what she meant.

They climbed back down the ladder to where Sloan's body was pinned. Aamodt quickly checked the body for ammunition for the coilgun.

A muffled klaxon started to wail, and several darkened, ice-encrusted lighting panels in the shaft began flashing red-warning lights. A calm, mindless Lync voice pronounced, "Danger! Danger! Reaction rate in the main power core has now increased beyond safety limits. The system is unable to initiate emergency procedures due to human intervention. An energetic disassembly of the main power core will occur in approximately one hour and fifty-nine minutes. Repeat. Danger! ..."

The major and the captain both stopped to exchange a long look and listen to the message as it repeated, Lync's North American Midwestern accent absent. Once the message concluded, they continued on. They let Sloan's mangled half-frozen corpse fall down the shaft, and watched as it banged against several rungs in the ladder, freeing caked ice as it fell. The body and the ice crashed at the bottom of the shaft with the sickening thud. Without a word, they climbed through the hatch and moved on.

They slowly jogged along the gloomy, half-lit corridors, the sound of the klaxon echoing in the darkness. Perspiration built on both their faces, more from nerves and fear than from physical exertion. Singleton knew from the amount of ice and frost in the station that the temperature of the installation must be down to around minus twenty degrees Celsius. The station's mindless AI made another announcement about the impending energetic disassembly, they had one hour and forty-five minutes.

They had to hurry.

Spying the general's office door, the two officers readied themselves. The door was nearly torn in two, but the interior itself looked more or less untouched. The embedded Image-blocks were dark, several workslates were spread over the floor, and a chair was overturned.

"Our friends been busy," Aamodt, in a security force's shooting stance, advanced into the room, the laser targeting light sweeping the cold, dark office space.

"Check those," ordered Singleton, dropping the recoilless rifle and falling into a chair with a groan. Emotions fought within him as he rummaged through the jumble of dataclips on the desk. He was ransacking through his commanding officer's desk. It was his job, and like so many things, it had to be done for the safety of all. He was tired. He was dead tired.

"Come on! They're down here!" Aamodt dropped to her knees and started collecting computer dataclips.

Singleton was next to her in an instant. He began removing his suit's chest unit and suit pack, then removed his helmet and opened up the front of his e-suit. He started to stuff dataclips into his e-suit, as the nightmarishly arctic-like air rushed into his open suit and chilled his sweating body. The ambient temperature had to be minus thirty or thirty-five Celsius.

"I hope this is worth it," Aamodt saw that the major was instantly freezing and was already shivering uncontrollably. "Fuck the OSC. If that fucker shows up…" Aamodt's voice trailed off as she shuffled the dataclips into a neat, small pile on the floor. As she started to unseal her e-suit, Singleton stopped her.

"I'll carry it," he eyed the stunned captain, his teeth chattering. "This situation could all go sideways on us."

"Fuck you." She started to pick up a hand full of dataclips, but Singleton stopped her again.

"I'm not joking, Captain!" His voice was strangely hard. "The OSC and the UESA may not look kindly on any unauthorized persons having seen this data."

"That's a lot of dogshit!" confused, Aamodt half-smiled as if he were joking.

The station's Lync-voice boomed over the room speakers, "Danger! Danger! The rate of reaction in main power core is now increasing beyond safety limits. The system is unable to initiate emergency procedures due to human intervention. An energetic disassembly of the main power core will occur in approximately one hour and thirty-five minutes." The message repeated again in the same unemotional voice.

Singleton put a gloved hand on her shoulder. "We don't have time for this, but I want you to know, you were initially just another---"

"Yes, I know," Aamodt smiled, "That is all you were to me---"

"But, Colin and NJ got me thinking, and now I think time has run out." Singleton took the dataclips out of her hand.

The mindless Lync voice repeated its warning, as Aamodt just stared at Singleton with a growing smile. "Yeah, okay," she picked up the recoilless rifle and slung it over her shoulder, "If we get out of this, I'm willing to see if we can make this work."

Zipping up his e-suit Singleton smiled back and added, "Divinities I want that."

Armed with the Magnastar coilgun, Aamodt eyed Singleton, gave him a sharp wink and a flash of a grin. Then she moved out into the corridor with the major on her heels. Aamodt's face was the very picture of concentration and determination, her mind focused on the main hangar deck control circuit closet and the motivations of the man behind her.

•　　•　　•

Nervously Major Nianta sat in the cockpit of the hopper.

Beside him sat Lieutenant LaRocque, both of them clad in e-suits, helmets off but at the ready. Nianta had performed all of the necessary pre-flight checks and had gone over the operation of the craft's controls with LaRocque twice. Now both men sat restlessly in the cramped cockpit, waiting. Nianta had trouble concentrating. He had a pounding headache that was growing by leaps and bounds, plus the annoying sensation of clotted blood far up in his nostrils. He knew he had a concussion, but he had a job to do, and he was going to do it.

In addition, like everyone else on the tiny hopper, he was not only worried about escaping the nightmare they all were caught-up in but worried about his three overdue comrades. He also feared for the woman he had grown to know and love over the past year. The major had no idea how all of this was going to play out when they were debriefed back at the OSC. Nianta's mind replayed the events of the last few days and knew this incident would leave lasting scars on all of them.

LaRocque's thoughts were a confused, nervous mess, centered on getting Pulgar, Sloan and himself away from this place before they became permanent residents. His thoughts rocketed back and forth between Pulgar and recently deceased friends and coworkers. Every time he closed his heavy, tired eyes, the memories and smiling faces of those who had recently died greeted him.

When the hopper's AI announced a core overload of the station's main fusion reactor, and the red emergency lights on the hangar deck began to flash, the two men almost panicked. It was only after they heard the soulless voice of Lync's bland countdown did they relax a bit.

They had time.

The two officers sat uneasily, both aware of what was happening around them. Both men could see the flashing red lights inside the hangar deck through the viewport of the hopper. They both could just make out the sound of the distant klaxon on the hangar deck. They both could hear Lync mark the time to energetic disassembly.

Time was running out.

"Major, let's go and open the hangar door," suggested LaRocque, his voice still showing signs of exhaustion. Even though the ship's air-conditioners were working, the inside of the craft was starting to smell like two-day-old sweat.

"Hold tight," Nianta had been watching the time as well. His headache eating away at his concentration, and now dizziness was starting to add to his discomfort. "We'll give them a few more minutes." He activated his intercom. "Yee, do you have an anti-nausea patch?"

A second later Yee's voice came back, "I still have the one I put on in the cafeteria."

Nianta frowned, "Do you have an extra?"

"No."

Immediately Tan's voice cut in, "Are you all right up there?" concern filled her voice.

"Yeah," he lied. "Just making sure we don't have any in-flight problems." He deactivated the intercom, cutting off her forming question.

"I can't take this waiting," LaRocque looking and feeling like ants were crawling over his body.

"Neither can I," The major glanced out the viewport. He thought the mindless Lync voice had just announced an hour and fifteen minutes until energetic disassembly, "but there's nothing much else we can do, but wait."

Minutes passed with a growing tension as the two men listened silently as the mindless Lync voice counted down the remaining time in five-minute intervals. After the one-hour mark was reached, they heard Lync's voice recommend the immediate evacuation of all station personnel, but still, there was no sign of Major Singleton or Captain Aamodt. The voice of the station's AI continued its ominous countdown as Nianta's dizziness got worse, and a background buzzing was growing in his ears.

By the time they reached the fifty-five-minute mark, both officers were fidgeting in their seats, both feeling the imaginary ants crawling up their backs and the sweat beginning to run down their faces. LaRocque had an uncomfortable feeling like he had to urinate, and there was no safe place to go.

Time was flying by with no word from Singleton or Aamodt. The hangar door remained closed, and Nianta could tell LaRocque was about to explode out of his seat. He knew what the younger man was thinking; *they should be preparing to go open the hangar door themselves. There was always the chance their guest could show up and spoil their escape.* Nianta realized his own right leg was bouncing and he put a gloved hand on it to calm his own nerves. The buzzing in his ears was growing louder, and he was uncomfortably warm.

"Sir, do you think this is the best course of action?" LaRocque's question caught Nianta off-guard.

"What?" between the noise in his head and the dizziness, he had not heard the lieutenant.

"Do you think you are doing what is best for your command?" the sweat and frown on LaRocque's face made him look mean. "I mean you are risking nine lives waiting to save two or three, assuming Demitri is still alive."

Nianta stared at LaRocque hard for a second. He wanted to be angry but felt too ill. "You and Sloan are old friends. Singleton and I are old friends. I don't know about you, but I am going to give them every possible second."

"Well, sir, the way I see it," began LaRocque, staring down the major. "Yeah, Demitri is my friend, more like a little brother, but if he were alive, he'd be back by now. And with all due respect, sir, if Major Singleton and Captain Aamodt were still alive, they would have been here by now."

There was a quiet moment, then Nianta replied, "We'll wait until I decide to leave. I am not leaving anyone behind if I can help it," The major turned his body in the seat to face LaRocque. "Do you have a problem with that?" He knew exactly what the junior officer was thinking because he and everyone else on the hopper were thinking it too. There was a long pause as the two men stared at each other, taking stock of one another.

"Yes, sir," LaRocque did not look angry anymore, but his tone had a hard edge to it. "I'd just like to know your plan, sir."

There was another long silence between the two men, as Nianta's dizziness continued to get worse by the second. The sound of jet engines roared in the major's ears along with the throbbing of his own heartbeat. LaRocque just sat nervously, shaking his head and looking out at the hangar deck as time passed ever so slowly.

Unexpectedly a deep shuddering moved through the cockpit, and the two men glanced nervously at one another, both knowing that that was the strongest tremor to hit the station since their nightmare had begun. There was no cognizant part of Lync left to announce the Titanquake, which added to the uneasiness of the situation.

It stayed quiet for several more minutes until Lync's mindless voice announced forty-five minutes until energetic disassembly. Then Professor Yee came up to the cockpit, looking worn and haggard, and like both Nianta and LaRocque, in need of a shave. "Any sign of them?"

"No," answered Nianta, purposely not shaking his head. Still, he nearly gagged with nausea.

"Shouldn't we be leaving?" Yee looked at Nianta and noticed the man's black face was ash gray and was sweating profusely. "You okay? You don't look too good?"

"Never mix tequila and scotch," the major grinned, attempting to be funny and failing. He looked to both Yee and LaRocque like he was riding a merry-go-round with a bad hangover.

"You know you really do look bad sir," LaRocque surveyed his superior. "Maybe---"

The hangar door started rising. The two atmospheres roared together in a storm of mixing gases, dark dust, and supercooled condensation. The men in the hopper cockpit were taken off guard by the sudden hurricane of mixing atmospheres that gently rocked the ship.

"Hold that thought! Overriding auto-launch sequence and bringing main AI online," yelled Nianta as he and LaRocque attacked the hopper's controls, "Inputting destination and alternate flight plan." He nervously watched the changing readouts on the holo screens and instruments set in the semicircular console before him. "Now, let's hope Steve and Tonja get back!"

"Yeah, but we can get the fuck out of here!" shouted Yee, as Doctors Tan and McGilmer, followed by Lieutenant Pulgar pushed up behind him.

Nianta, fighting back a wave of nausea, twisted around angrily. "Look, you and McGilmer get in the airlock and standby. The rest of you get back to your seats and strap in!"

Everyone moved out of the cockpit, but Doctor Tan hung back a moment longer than the others, studying the occupied major.

"Looks like at least one of them made it," added LaRocque, his eyes performing a waltz over his console, while his gloved hands did a coarse ballet over his holo-screens. "We've got green across the board; I think we can launch."

Nianta did not respond, as he gagged back a mouth full of stomach acid and black coffee.

The sound of the hopper's engines increased to fill the ship as everyone prepared for liftoff. Professor McGilmer and Professor Yee entered the tiny decontamination-airlock of the hopper. Bypassing the decon procedures, they opened the outer hatch and waited for a sign of Singleton and Aamodt.

Lync's voice sounded strange and muffled as it came over the hangar deck speakers, "Danger! Danger! Reaction rate in main power core now beyond safety limits. Unable to initiate emergency procedures, an energetic disassembly of the main power core will occur in forty minutes. Recommend immediate evacuation of all installation personnel. Repeat. Danger! Danger! ..." The message continued to repeat as liquefied gases began to run down the hangar deck walls and pool on the floor.

Suddenly the Kali-like extrasolar intruder was in the airlock doorway. For a short moment the nightmare, blacken and angry-looking, just stared into the hangar bay unmoving. Then slowly it began advancing toward the humming hopper, picking up speed as it approached. What was more stunning than the creature's sudden appearance was the fact that it was carrying one of the Magnastar coilguns in two of its four hands.

Yee and McGilmer started shouting to Nianta over their helmet transceivers, as the thing began to fire the weapon at the hopper.

"Get the fuck in here!" Nianta's voice boomed in terror.

"How the fuck did this thing know where to find us?" LaRocque's voice was a distorted shriek over their helmet transceivers.

A coilgun projectile just missed Yee as he and McGilmer brought their Glock-Whelans out and returned fire at their charred assailant. "Get us out of here!" screamed McGilmer, metallic, kinetic energy projectiles bouncing all around; one just barely missed the top of McGilmer's helmet, ricocheting off loudly. Ignoring it, she noticed that several projectiles from their Glock-Whelans had found their mark and staggered the creature backward, as other shells blew chunks out of the wall and doorframe behind it.

Just as Yee and McGilmer ceased firing and ducked back into the hopper's airlock, two suited figures appeared in the doorway of the hangar deck, just behind the extrasolar.

"It's Singleton and Aamodt!" shouted Yee as the hopper began moving forward toward the gloomy darkness on the other side of the open hangar door. "It's Singleton and Aamodt!" repeated Yee, "Hold on, Major! Hold on! It's Steve and Tonja!"

The hopper pitched to one side throwing Yee and McGilmer to the hangar deck floor. The craft settled down again, almost landing on top of the two fallen scientists. Both Yee and McGilmer quickly sprang back to their feet and moved toward the humming hopper. The extrasolar entity, towering like a dark, ugly mountain in the icy hangar bay, did not sense Singleton and Aamodt ducking to the floor behind it.

Nianta's voice was calling out over everyone's helmet speaker, trying to get information, but no one cared to respond. McGilmer and Yee fired again seeing, but not registering their comrades behind their target. They climbed the ladder and hopped into the airlock of the hopper. McGilmer and Yee both turned and fired again at their adversary, but McGilmer only had one shot left, and Yee had three.

Their advancing attacker did not go down.

"They won't make it!" McGilmer finally seeing her friends, started out of the ship again, but Yee stopped her. "We've got to help them!"

"What is going on, we can't see a fucking thing from up here! Someone talk to me, dammit!" thundered Nianta, his voice bathed in static with LaRocque's distorted voice just audible in the overlapping transmissions.

Captain Aamodt, remembering her weapon, aimed the coilgun at the creature's back, "I got this bitch!" she both fingered the safety and toggled the action switch to semi-automatic on her Jones-Benelli.

"You bet your sweet ass!" screamed Singleton bringing up the recoilless rifle. Just as he fired the weapon, Aamodt fired a three projectile burst from her coilgun. The blast of SIAP projectiles caught the creature squarely in the back of the head. It went over and down as if it had tripped while running at full speed, its weapon sailing across the dimly lit hangar bay. The missile from the recoilless rifle, sailed past the fallen creature, under the belly of the running hopper, and into the damaged skiff parked on the other side of the hangar.

The blinding white flash and the concussive wave flattened both Aamodt and Singleton. Aamodt stood up, and even in her e-suit, her ears were ringing, and her body felt like it had just been massaged by a landslide. She could see Major Singleton lying on the debris-covered deck, and from his movements and the tiny jets of erupting gas coming from his e-suit, she could tell he was in trouble.

Not surprisingly, the extrasolar creature was still intact, lying on the deck. There was no trace of half of the eyes on the left side of its head, just a confused chessboard of charred black flesh and oozing white holes. The entire back of its blackened head was dented and wrinkled like some bizarre, manhandled aluminum canister. White fluid poured out of the gaping holes in its cranium and down its neck.

Aamodt drunkenly moved to Singleton, coilgun still in hand. "Can you move?" she inquired, staring at the creature on the floor as it began to rise.

Singleton got to his feet, his e-suit's chest unit was damaged, and his e-suit's AI was rattling off a long list of problems. "My suit's fucked!" he cried, already feeling both the lack of oxygen and the sharp cold cutting at his body.

"Run! I'll cover you!" ordered Aamodt matter-of-factly, catching sight of Yee and McGilmer climbing back down the hopper's ladder. The ship appeared undamaged by the explosion of the skiff across the hangar, as Aamodt advanced on the slowly rising creature.

Singleton had no air left in his e-suit to argue, he just stumbled toward the hopper, trailing a thin cloud of cold oxygen like some human comet, the nitrogen of Titan's atmosphere forcing the oxygen in Singleton's e-suit out into the void of the hangar bay. With the last of his energy, he aimed himself at the two fading figures at the foot of the ladder. Yee caught him just as he fell against the hopper's ladder.

"Jeannet, help me get him up!" the two professors pulled the major up the ladder but kept their eyes on the captain and the angry unnatural being in front of her.

Aamodt quickly stepped up closer to the rising creature and fired another blast. The nightmare saw her approach and ducked. Aamodt fired again, but the extrasolar terror was too quick as it ducked around again. It swung up at Aamodt, knocking her head over heels. She cartwheeled in midair and hit the ground hard. The thing, without missing a beat, snatched up her useless weapon and smashed it down on her like a club, splintering the composite material of the coilgun. The captain screamed in her helmet, but the scream was cut short as a mass of blood and lung tissue exploded against the inside of her e-suit helmet faceplate.

Singleton heard Aamodt's final scream. He tried to call to her, but nothing but a whisper came out of his dry throat. He tried to break free of Yee and McGilmer, but he had no strength, as they dragged him up the ladder and into the hopper.

"They're in! They're in! Get us the fuck out of here!" shouted Professor McGilmer, half out of breath as she sealed the hatch.

The sound of the hopper's engines jumped several decibels, as it began to move toward the darkness of Titan, on the other side of the hangar deck doorway.

The horror that was their intruder caught sight of the hopper and with its remaining eyes, locked on to it as it dropped the coilgun and leaped. . .

Colliding with part of the wreckage of the destroyed skiff, the hopper bounced to the side, almost hitting with a wall of the hangar deck on its way out.

The tiny ship moved up and away from the station faster and faster, as the hopper's AI following its instructions, put on more and more power. A united moan rose in the hopper as both the human occupants and the structural supports of the small craft flexed under the induced gravity of acceleration.

At three and a half kilometers a second, the hopper broke Titan's cloud cover as if it were an angry bird being kicked out of its nest. A mere five minutes after leaving the station's hangar deck the small hopper arced in its course and entered a high orbit above the giant Saturnian satellite.

None of the occupants cared to take in the stunning view of Titan, its upper atmosphere awash in dancing lights and colors, courtesy of the distant sun and the Kronian magnetospheric plasma generated by Saturn's magnetic fields. Titan, in the last few days, had lost its appeal for the small group huddled in the hopper. Barely visible, like a thin layer of dust on a windowpane, were millions of small chunks of Titan, slowly orbiting just above the multicolored light show of the cloud deck. They had been blown there by the event at the T-One drill site.

The ten survivors of Titan-Base Ksa had barely stood the G-forces of their escape. They unstrapped their aching bodies from their seats and floated freely about the interior of the hopper. In the cockpit, Major Nianta turned to LaRocque, as bright blood drifted out of his nose. Before he could utter a sound, his eyes rolled back into his head, showing only white, and he began to convulse wildly.

LaRocque checked the atmospheric pressure and turned to Nianta, smiling. *"Merde!"* was all LaRocque could say, staring wild-eyed and surprised at the jerking and twitching man in the pilot seat, as his smile disappeared. "NJ, Yara, somebody get up here! The Major's in trouble!" he started unstrapping himself, trying to get to the violently ill pilot.

Trauma-Specialist Lebowitz popped into the cockpit, as LaRocque activated a cluster of AI auto control systems and helped the medtec wrestle the ill major out of the pilot seat.

Down in the main compartment area, the decontamination-airlock hatch opened with a loud hiss of pressure equalization. Yee and McGilmer pulled Singleton into the cabin and rapidly removed his helmet. Doctor Tan glided over to them as the gasping Singleton whispered one word, "Tonja."

"Doctor!" Lebowitz and LaRocque were already floating Major Nianta into the middle of the compartment.

"Colin?" Tan was instantly next to him. "Colin! Someone grab me a medkit!"

"Get him strapped down," ordered McGilmer, moving in to assist.

Blood was leaking from Nianta's nostrils and ears, the little oscillating dark red droplets floated away in several directions. The major's lower lip trembled as spasms spun his weightless body, and his eyes moved rapidly under closed lids. They floated him down to a seat and buckled him in, as McGilmer got out the medical kit. Lebowitz, using Singleton's discarded helmet, fished up floating blobs of Nianta's blood.

Major Singleton observed Nianta for a moment then took in the worried faces around him. He looked back at the empty cockpit. "LaRocque, back in the cockpit," ordered Singleton swimming through the air past the assembled group of survivors. "Status report?" He followed LaRocque back into the cockpit.

Tan angrily pulled herself down to Nianta, her tears moving away from her eyes with each movement of her head. "Come on Colin, don't do this! Colin!" the emotional doctor's voice was more of a sob than a series of words.

The major opened his eyes slowly. They were a soft pink and filled with tears that dripped out of the corner of his eyes and ran down his face, as he tried to focus on Tan. "Ning-Jing," he uttered hoarsely, his mouth straining to form the words, "did we make…" his words trailed off, and his eyes flickered back into his head again.

"Yeah, we made it, and you saved all of us," she looked back over her shoulder at Professor McGilmer, who was looking away. Both women recognized an acceleration induced cerebral hemorrhage when they saw it. "Where the fuck is that medkit?" Tan turned back to Nianta, knowing there was nothing she could do for him.

Nianta's eyes slowly stopped flickering, and his body appeared to relax.

McGilmer hugged Tan, as she hugged the lifeless form in front of them. Professor Yee joined them as Tan cried on McGilmer and the three slowly rotated in mid-air. For a long moment, the only sound in the small compartment was the hum of the engines and sobbing. No one moved, and no one spoke, until finally, Tounames whispered, "Dammit."

Pulgar turned and pushed off toward the cockpit leaving Tounames staring after her. McGilmer and Yee continued to watch Doctor Tan with sadness and pain in their eyes, as Pulgar floated silently up behind Singleton and LaRocque. "Major Nianta just…" she could not finish the sentence.

Singleton and LaRocque glanced at one another then turned disgustedly back to their controls.

"Did Demitri make---"

Singleton cut LaRocque off with a sharp shake of his head. His eyes were full of tears, as he added, "Tonja too."

The hopper's AI continued to mutter unemotionally to the cockpit crew, as Pulgar dropped her head and started to weep.

# CHAPTER TWENTY-FOUR

After two and a half orbits of Titan, the hopper found the emergency evacuation transport, sitting quietly in its parking orbit. The Saturn-Titan EET, formerly named the *Jejui-Gavana*, was a patchwork of floating metal and aging technology. At two hundred and fourteen meters in length, it was far larger than the hopper and had originally been designed as a transport and re-supply craft for the mining colonies. Its three and a half decks once ferried miners, equipment, and supplies to every part of the asteroid belt. Now the old ship, forty years past its intended service life, would no longer help tame wild asteroids and bring them into the service of humanity. Its scarred and overused structure only had one remaining task, to bring the personnel of Titan home in the event of an emergency.

The hopper's AI and that of the EET made an electronic handshake, checked each other's systems and agreed that the EET's AI should handle the approach and docking of the hopper. After some safety checks, the nine survivors of Titan-Base Lincoln, carrying Major Nianta's body, transferred to the transport and hurriedly changed out of their heavy flightsuits.

Tounames, LaRocque, and Pulgar inspected several critical systems in the old ship, as Singleton floated his way to the command bridge in the zero gravity. The EET's sensors had recorded several dozen micrometeorite strikes in the last few days, but none of them had done any real damage. They all knew that the EET's AI would have alerted them to any problems the second they docked, but procedures were procedures. The only problem the nine faced on the quiet cold ship was the lack of gravity, and the stale, metallic taste in the unrecycled air.

On the command bridge, Tech-Sergeant Tounames floated up behind Major Singleton and secured his good foot to the deck by the velcro sole of his footwear. "Everything's looking good," he announced.

The major stared blindly out of the viewport on the half circle of the command bridge. He slowly turned in the pilot's seat at the sound of the tech-sergeant's voice. "Great. Why don't you have Lebowitz or Garcia take care of your ankle?" the major halfheartedly scanned the array of consoles before him.

"No. Not yet. There are a bunch of things I have to check, first. I still have time before we hit the sleepers." Tounames moved into the copilot's seat and buckled himself in. The two sat and tried not to look at one another. Each man wanted to be alone with his thoughts, playing the recent memories in his mind like a holo-vid. Both men were physically exhausted and emotionally raped by their ordeal on Titan-Base Lincoln and the loss of so many friends and coworkers.

A bright flash in the dark tangerine clouds of Titan caught both men off guard. Slowly a glowing ignition pressure wave expanded across the gloomy, featureless face of the icy moon for several seconds, forming a perfect circle of continually fading colors. "Divinities," whispered Tounames, stunned by the beauty of the fading lemon yellow ring, "was that---"

"Yeah," the major cut off Tounames. An image of Captain Aamodt flashed through his mind, followed by a stream of memories. The transport's orbit was practically pacing the dying halo of death as it faded into nothingness. "Tonja and---"

"And all the others," Tounames finished Singleton's sentence. He fought to focus his mind on his job, pushing back thoughts of his dead friends. He tapped several icons on his console hard-monitor and flipped a row of protected switches on one of the overhead boards, "At least we got that fucker," muttered the tech-sergeant under his breath.

Singleton activated a tiny screen and watched a column of numbers and symbols file down the screen. "Our next pass back over the site isn't for another two hours and forty-seven minutes." He began frantically tapping hard-monitor icons in front of him.

Tounames was working his consoles and watching five small screens, "Maybe we can move one of the TiStars into a new orbit over the station?"

"Why? There won't be anything left to see," Singleton pointed at one of the small monitors, "Besides before we leave orbit, I want to park TiStar-Two over the T-One site. We'll have it monitor the site for the OSC."

Tounames nodded, still focused on his instruments. "I just thought that..." his voice trailed off. Somewhere in his injured mind, the tech-sergeant needed closure.

"Drop it. We have a lot to do before we leave orbit," proclaimed Singleton angrily, locking in the new instructions for the science scan platform. "LaRocque should have confirmed our AI's orbital departure vectors by now. I'll check with him, start running the secondary diagnostics on the NAG subsystems."

"You got it," Tounames voiced sadly, as Singleton started out of his seat. The tech-sergeant punched out a series of commands into his holo-screen, beginning his check of the navigational and guidance subsystems, as several of his hard-monitors switched to all new images. What appeared on four of the five screens was expected and of no real surprise. However, what appeared on his center screen was totally unexpected, and definitely unwelcomed.

It was the extrasolar entity.

The image on the monitor showed the blackened nightmare maneuvering its way across the surface of the transport. It went from one handhold to another with all the grace and skill of a well-trained zero gravity worker.

"No. No! No!" Tounames' voice quickly grew from an unbelieving whisper to a terror-stricken scream, as he felt himself trying to move away from the screen.

Singleton turned to look at Tounames and saw the image on the hard-monitor. "No fucking way! This can't be happening!" blurted the major, his mind starting to drift into shock. "What the fuck does it take to kill this sonuvabitch?" he exploded, slamming a fist against a wall. The action launched him into the back of Tounames' seat.

"What are we going to do?" panic was quickly creeping into Tounames' voice.

"How the hell am I supposed to know?" Singleton's eyes

were ablaze like a homicidal maniac.

"Because you're the one in charge!" shot Tounames, globs of errant saliva flying off into the cabin. "Think of something!"

The major just stared at the monitor screen, his mind racing to the point of physical pain. "Get everybody, except LaRocque and…" His voice petered out with sadness, confusion, and anger. Everyone his mind defaulted to was dead. "Garcia! Get everyone else up here. Tell LaRocque and Garcia to meet me at the storage lockers!" He glided away from the bridge, stopped himself, turned and barked, "Open all the outer doors to all the airlocks!"

"Are you crazy?" Tounames whirled his chair around to face the wild looking major, not even caring about hitting his broken ankle. "What the fuck for?"

"Do you want that thing tearing its way through the fucking hull?" Singleton launched himself like an arrow passed the two short rows of seats and toward the access tube at the rear of the compartment.

Tounames cursed under his breath, "I sure as Slovenian syphilis don't want it in *here*." He opened all the outer hatches and addressed the ship's intercom system. "Everyone, listen up and listen good! That fucker is back! It is outside on the hull! Probably hitched a ride up with us on the outside of the hopper! The Major wants LaRocque and Garcia to meet him at the main storage lockers," he paused for a second picturing the ship's layout in his mind, "on level three! Now everybody else is to haul ass up to the bridge! Move it, people!" He turned back to the center hard-monitor, not liking what he was seeing.

• • •

Terror and confusion raged through both Professor McGilmer and Trauma-Specialist Lebowitz, as they stood velcroed to the deck in front of one of the hibernation chambers on the second level of the ship. They looked up the elongated compartment lined with empty hibernation chambers, and at the small group loitering at the opposite end of the compartment. They both then turned to the small heavily insulated chamber next to them. Doctor Tan's partially nude body was strapped down and secured within the chamber, deep within a drug-induced artificial sleep. The EET's AI monitored the restrained form of the slumbering woman via the numerous lines connected to her.

"We got to leave her here." McGilmer snorted, as she surveyed the numerous monitors recording her unconscious friend's vital signs. "It's too late to bring her out of it," she noticed the doctor's body was down to the usual hibernation temperature of ten degrees Celsius, and that her levels of hibernation-specific proteins and tetra-Dadol-albumin complex were already at the maximum concentrations.

"But we can't---" Lebowitz was cut off by McGilmer, as both women unvelcroed themselves from the deck.

"No butts! Let's go!" McGilmer pushed Lebowitz toward the small group at the other end of the compartment with a little more force than was required in zero-g.

The memories of people recently deceased came back to the trauma-specialist in a wave of sorrow. "If it gets in here and finds her..." Lebowitz stopped herself and McGilmer just before reaching the cluster of people, as both women floated about like balloons, prisoners to the force of their own momentum.

The image of the severed heads in the transparent container, back in the station's med-bay flashed into Lebowitz's mind. "Don't stop! Keep moving!" she barked as she softly shoved herself along the corridor.

Yee, LaRocque, and Pulgar were hovering by the last of the thirty hibernation chambers on that deck. They stared into the darkened chamber that slowly flashed and beeped a level-one biohazard warning. The motionless person inside the darkened chamber did not need any life support systems or AI monitoring. Major Nianta's body did not require such things.

"How did that fucker get outside?" Professor McGilmer inquired, as she and Trauma-Specialist Lebowitz floated up to the group.

"The Tech-Sergeant said that it probably hitched a ride on the hopper," Yee was watching Pulgar and LaRocque. The two drifted silently, unblinking, afraid.

The corridor speaker came to life again, "Hey! Where the hell is everybody?" rang Tounames' voice, "Get up here, will yeah please!"

LaRocque and Pulgar embraced and held tight, the act causing them both to slowly rotate around a common axis. Lieutenant Pulgar's eyes were watering as the two kissed.

"Come on," whispered Yee under his breath. He was getting nervous, and the hint of Afrikaan in his voice was getting stronger. The professor was not really a religious man, but he was beginning to think that some deity had it out for them.

"I gotta go," LaRocque kissed her again on the lips and broke away from their embrace, launching himself toward the hatchway. "Make sure they get to the bridge," LaRocque floated to the access tube hatch, opened it and pulled himself down the ladder, and was gone.

"Let's move," ordered Pulgar, as she and the others followed LaRocque to the access tube, but instead of moving downward, they moved upward.

The four floated out onto the main level of the EET and went up to the bridge. No one was talking, but everyone was thinking the same thought, *who's going to be the next to die?* Pulgar closed her eyes and saw LaRocque lying next to Major Nianta in the hibernation chamber.

•   •   •

When LaRocque arrived at the main storage lockers, outside of the engine room, Major Singleton and Medtec Garcia were already working hard at some of the gear that they had taken from the locker. They had the equipment spread out over the deck, in a disorganized mess. Most of the materials came outfitted with magnetic fasteners or velcro pads to hold them in place, but stuff was still floating around the compartment. "Will you please explain to me, what the hell is going on?" It was difficult to tell whether LaRocque was more confused or angry.

"That thing's---"

The major was interrupted by Tounames' voice booming through his ear-mic, "Major! It has found airlock number two on level two!"

Singleton secured the metal tank he was working on against the floor, and tapped his ear-mic, "When it gets inside, seal the outer door, and open the inner one!" Even with his feet velcroed to the deck, he had to grab a handhold to keep from drifting into the bulkhead.

Tounames' reply was loud as it came through everyone's ear-mic, "You are fucking crazy! I'm not letting that motherfucker in here! You're out of your fucking mind!"

"Trust me! For the love of all of the divinities, trust me!" Singleton pounded the wall, holding on to the handrail. The sweat was beginning to form on his black face again and work its way into his fear-crazed eyes.

"Okay! But if you're wrong," Tounames' voice was a barely intelligible scrawl, "we've had it!"

Singleton was fighting to keep himself under control. "I'm not wrong! Look, close all the outer doors and open all the inner ones!" The major's shell-shocked brain wanted to drift off, to be someplace else that was mentally safe and secure. "Have the AI disengage all of the airlock door safeties."

"Okay, but what are you planning?"

"You'll see!" Singleton spun around to face the others, "Garcia, how's that suit coming?"

"You'd better check it. I've never done shit like this before." Garcia pushed herself off the floor and drifted away from the medieval-looking pressure suit, as Singleton moved to check her work.

"LaRocque, hook up those laser plate welders," the major pointed at the arrangement of composite tanks and the long rifle-like devices below LaRocque's hovering feet, as he gave the senior medtec's work a quick once-over. Finding Garcia's work satisfactory, Singleton began donning the metallic armor of the bulbous pressure suit with Garcia's help. It was stronger than a standard e-suit, designed for rough work in tuff environments. It lacked most of the amenities of a true e-suit but was durable, unattractive, inexpensive to mass-produce, and as uncomfortable as having a flaming case of hemorrhoids.

"What are you planning?" asked LaRocque, not taking his eyes off his work.

"You really don't want to know," the major did not sound like he was joking. "I know what I'm planning, and I'm scared shitless," he turned to meet Garcia's terrified stare, "and I'm the one who thought it up."

"Thank you for that." Garcia sighed sarcastically, "I'm already scared shitless, I don't need anymore to frighten me." She noticed for the first time since arriving on the EET that her hands were still trembling. Like every other survivor on the EET, she thought that her days of uncontrolled fear were over.

Tounames' voice came over their ear-mics, slow and calm, "Major, it's inside the lock. The outer door is closed, and the inner door is open. I hope you know what you're doing." The more or less calm tone of the tech-sergeant's voice sent a shiver through everyone in the corridor.

Singleton turned to Garcia and replied, "Be prepared to seal and over-pressurize any airlock I tell you to, as fast as you can." He motioned for her to assist him as he frantically checked his worksuit.

"*Over-pressurize?*" echoed Tounames questioning from the bridge.

"Yes, and shut off all the lights on level two, and turn on every warning light and siren on the ship!"

"Why?" asked Tounames.

"Hopefully, to confuse it and make it harder for it to see or hear us coming," bellowed Singleton, still working feverishly, "Now seal all of the access-tube hatchways on the ship. I want every deck and section isolated!"

"First intelligent thing you've said in twenty minutes." Tounames severed the link.

Singleton looked over at LaRocque and studied his work a second. "You've got the lines mixed up. It's red on the right, blue in the middle, and green on the left," Singleton moved to correct the connections, "just like the Mars planetary flag. Red for the planet Mars, green for the---" The sudden sounding of klaxons and sirens, and the flashing of both red and yellow warning lights interrupted the major.

The three looked around wildly for a second, feeling the adrenaline rush and fighting to control it. Coming back to the moment, Garcia sealed the heavy metal helmet onto Singleton's oversized protective worksuit, as LaRocque helped place the cumbersome welding unit onto the major's back. Slowly spinning in the middle of the corridor, the three looked as if they were performing some weird zero-g mating dance. A large number of objects were still drifting around the corridor, and it was hard to move without colliding with something. Tools, storage bags, bits of plastic, and tiny parts all sailed around, giving the area the appearance of being in the middle of some bizarre slow speed, low energy tornado.

Singleton activated his e-suit's AI, and his magnetized

boots. "Okay!" he began as his e-suit's communication systems came online, "Lieutenant, you and Garcia follow me onto level two. When we find our friend, we'll lure it into one of the airlocks. Tounames pressurizes the lock then we blow the hatch. The force of the decompression will blow the fucker all the way to Saturn!"

LaRocque and Garcia velcroed themselves down and put on their laser welder units and readied themselves. "That's why the pressure suit!" yelled LaRocque. The realization of the major's plan struck him and Garcia simultaneously.

It was a suicide plan.

"You're planning on being inside that lock with that thing," whispered Garcia, just audible above the scream of the sirens.

Singleton started moving toward the access tube. "Tounames, do you read me?" his voice sounded hollow inside his bulky e-suit.

A second later came the distant tech-sergeant's reply, "I still got you, Major."

"Unseal access tube One-B, between levels two and three," turning to Garcia he added, "Being inside the airlock is the only way to ensure that it goes in and stays in long enough for it to pressurize!"

Tounames acknowledged the major's request, just as he and his two companions reached the access tube hatchway. Singleton popped the hatch open with a hiss of pressure equalization and maneuvered himself into the narrow shaft.

"This ain't a good idea!" Garcia could not believe that this was happening as she moved in behind LaRocque.

The air inside the bulky suit tasted like aluminum, as Singleton added, "It's better than the one I had before I remembered the pressure suits."

"Even if you're still alive when the hatch blows, you're going to be shot halfway to Rhea with it!" LaRocque pulled himself up the ladder within the claustrophobic access tube. There was little space in the narrow passage for the three, plus their massive laser plate welder units strapped to their backs. The bottom of Singleton's boots was within centimeters of LaRocque's head, and the lieutenant kicked Garcia in the face twice as the group moved through the brightly lit tube.

"I thought that too, but then I remembered the emergency

tether lines in the airlocks!" Singleton stopped and opened the hatch leading out onto the second level, "If I can get to one---"

"What about the radiation levels outside from the solar flare?" interrupted LaRocque, slowly following the major out into the darkened corridor.

"Yeah, even with that e-suit you'll get a lethal dose of radiation inside of fifteen minutes," added Garcia, emerging into the corridor behind LaRocque. "And who knows what the neutron count is out there."

"Let's cross one bridge at a time, shall we," whispered Singleton straining to see in the near darkness of the empty corridor. The only illumination was the flashing of warning lights on the walls. The blaring of the klaxons, sirens, and alarms could almost be felt in the air.

"Major," came Tounames' voice over Singleton's helmet transceiver. "It's at the first junction, about fifteen meters up the corridor. I have both of you on the thermal imager."

"That's affirm." Singleton flashed a grin at the tech-sergeant's ingenuity. He knew that on the sensors for the ship's fire detection system, he and his two companions would appear hotter than the ambient air, and their target would appear colder due to its recent exposure to the extreme cold of space.

The terrified major felt dazed and confused by the flashing of the warning lights and the wailing of the sirens. His exhausted mind was tiptoeing back to thoughts of Captain Aamodt and the smell of green grass and flowers, but he snatched it back to the situation at hand by sheer force of will. "Let's do this."

LaRocque tapped the major once as the three slowly, and with exaggerated steps, moved up the dark passageway, the flashing lights playing tricks on both their eyes and their mind. The sweat from Singleton's face and forehead began to drift into his eyes. *Funny,* he thought, shaking his head in an attempt to redirect the trickle of saltwater, *after nearly a thousand years of space travel, the engineers have never come up with a practical way to wipe the sweat from a person's face, while they were e-suited up.* Singleton laughed aloud at the absurdity of the thought. However, his smile vanished as he saw the outline of their prey.

The extrasolar was tucked into a dark corner of the ceiling. The thing was hanging in the shadows, upside down like an enormous spider waiting to strike. It appeared oblivious to the screaming sirens and the strobing and flashing of the emergency lights. It was as if it knew they were coming and was waiting for them.

Suddenly the dark shadow exploded toward them with a speed and force that shocked all three humans.

Garcia and LaRocque both began to fire their welders at the advancing horror. The blue-green bolts of the welder laser light sliced into the gargoyle-like thing, and the bulkhead behind it. A bloom of multicolored plasma spalled off the creature in all directions as it shrieked and disappeared up the corridor and into more darkness.

"Hold your damn fire!" Singleton kicked off the floor and threw himself against one wall. Forgetting the darkness, he motioned for LaRocque and Garcia to do the same. Somehow, they saw his gesture and followed him. All three had to grab any available handhold to keep from rebounding off the corridor walls in the microgravity. "Be careful! You could burn through the hull or cut something vital!"

"Are we going after it?" LaRocque, like Singleton and Garcia, could not stop himself from drifting back and forth like a parade float, in the near dark of the corridor. There was something about darkness and free-fall that fostered terror in the human soul. A teenage memory flashed into LaRocque's mind. He was thirteen again, underwater for the first time, in the middle of the Atlantic Ocean with his Russian grandmother, and it was warm and black. Unnervingly he was pulled back to reality; it was still warm and black.

"Fuck this!" Singleton pushed off the wall and instantly moved forward. He flew through the air to the end of the corridor like a missile but stopped himself before he reached the bend. He did not take his eyes off the turn in the passage for a millisecond, forcing himself not to blink.

LaRocque and Garcia launched themselves after the major, and with velcroed boots and well-placed hands, just barely stopped themselves from flying out into the intersection.

"What now?" LaRocque readied his welder as his eyes fell on a missing handrail near a sealed hatch. The metal bar had been ripped from the wall. "Major," he pointed out the missing rail.

Singleton just nodded, "Cover me." He took a deep breath, whispered something, then hurled himself around the corner.

LaRocque was not ready as he drifted backward and raised his welder. Garcia looked more prepared to run than fight, as the two wafted about in the middle of the corridor like big holographic targets on a shooting range.

Singleton heard Tounames' warning, but it was too late.

Time seemed to slow down as the major, and the extrasolar studied each other. As the creature moved, it looked to Singleton much as it did the first time he had seen Lync's reconstruction of it. The damage that Aamodt's coilgun had done to the thing's head was almost healed. He could count the black, crystal-like eyes that were focused on him, and the number of teeth that were visible in the thing's mouth. He noted the ridges in the jagged end of the broken railing in its hand. Then the creature rammed the handrail into Singleton's midsection, as he fired the welder.

The major slammed into the opposite wall and bounced off hard. The laser beam from the welder caught the thing in the right thigh. A black mist expanded toward the four corners of the passageway, as a white fluid began to pour from the small hole in the nightmare's leg. The fluid formed a chain of connected blobby spheres as it drifted after the black mist.

LaRocque and Garcia, as a unit, turned the corner and shot the extrasolar in the face and upper body with their welders. The creature scrambled back and jetted down the passageway and through an open hatchway, trailing the chain of blobs of white fluid and black smoke. LaRocque and Garcia pursued it as Singleton kicked off a wall and swam through the air after them. The major's ribs felt broken, and each breath sent fire racing through his chest, but he kept moving.

"The airlock!" was the only thing that LaRocque could scream, as he grabbed the doorframe and directed himself into the corridor ceiling. Garcia was not as quick, as she and the extrasolar flew through the inner decontamination-airlock door and crashed into the outer door of the chamber.

As Singleton zoomed beneath lieutenant and into the lock, all LaRocque could do was to keep screaming, "Airlock-two-two!" into his ear-mic as the inner door slid shut, barely missing the bottom of the major's feet.

"Closed and pressurizing!" screamed Tounames, Pulgar's

panic-stricken voice could be heard in the background, but her words were unintelligible.

LaRocque was momentarily torn between telling them that Garcia was in the airlock and not saying a word about the senior medtec. It was his life and Pulgar's life, and the lives of the others, against the life of one person. He stared at the inner airlock door, his mouth open, but silent. All he could see was Pulgar's face, and all he could hear was the angry screams of the nightmare in the airlock with his friends. That thing had killed his best friend, Sloan.

He said nothing.

He did nothing.

Inside the airlock, Singleton and Garcia tortured the extrasolar with the laser fire from the welders and tried desperately not to hit each other. Garcia's boots were velcroed to the ceiling above the airlock's outer door, while Singleton's magnetic boots held him steady in front of the inner door. In the center of the tiny room, the screaming extrasolar-thing tried to reach a solid surface. The blue-green lasers cut deep troughs into the body of the dark thing, as atmosphere hissed into the room. The unstable creature, spinning and tumbling at several revolutions a second, tried to get at its tormentors. It batted at the laser light with its hands and feet, losing a digit in the process. The severed appendage tumbled away toward a wall, trailing blobs of white ooze.

As the trio continued to be a mass of barely controlled movement inside of the airlock, Singleton, using one hand, opened a small compartment in the wall, and removed an object that looked like a short-barreled flare-pistol with a grappling hook on the end. "Alain, secure the deck!" screamed Singleton into his helmet mic, his own words bringing him unbearable pain.

Without warning, Garcia began to thrash around, fighting for her breath, as she released her welder and clutched her throat and chest. The senior medtec had a stunned look of pain on her face as she gurgled a dry scream. Singleton glanced at a wall gauge, it read: **5.5 SEAs**. He realized that at five and a half standard earth atmospheres, Garcia was being crushed alive.

The spinning horror grabbed the struggling Garcia by the ankle and swung her like a fast meaty club into Major Singleton. The violent action stopped the creature's rapid rotations and sent it tumbling into the outer door frame. It bounced off with a swimming motion, moving back toward the two humans like a torpedo.

Singleton body blocked the out of control medtec. The blow bounced him off the inner door and blinded him with pain. However, not looking, Singleton with grappling hook launcher in hand bounced himself up and slammed a booted foot against the wall and launched himself at his oncoming attacker. The ill-aimed kick landed squarely on the emergency override control panel set in the wall.

An instant before Singleton and the extrasolar creature collided in the center of the small room; the explosive bolts blew the outer hatch into space. The inner airlock door slid open, and everything in the airlock roared into the soundless vacuum of space. Condensing gas and clouds of ice crystals all rushed into dark nothingness, following a trail to Titan.

The massive EET yawed sideways in its orbit as if it had been broadsided by a comet. The vessel's gyros went wild as its terrified passengers were thrown against bulkheads and stationary equipment.

# CHAPTER TWENTY-FIVE

The panic-crazed look on Garcia's face told the whole story as her sweat flash-froze on her skin. She was dying, and she knew it. She could feel her blood and body fluids beginning to freeze and expand in their restraining veins and capillaries, slowly ripping them to shreds. The senior medtec grabbed at nothingness as she fought for air that was not there. During her last fifteen seconds of life, Garcia's eyes went blurry as she saw her last chance to get home, tumble away into space. Just before her eyes froze over and ruptured in their sockets, Garcia saw the pale fuzzy ball that was Titan, one last time. It was set against a curtain of vibrant, out-of-focus stars, amidst a wall of blackness. Then the force of the exploding slush that erupted out of the medtec's eye sockets, nose, and mouth, sent the distorted remains spiraling off into space.

The extrasolar grabbed onto the doorframe of the airlock and swung around onto the outside of the ship, as Singleton sailed past it, following Garcia into the void.

Singleton fired the grappling hook just as he flew out of the doorway. The hook rammed into the airlock control panel on the other side of the lock. It held long enough to swing the major around, in a broad arc, back into the side of the ship. Singleton's ribs hurt so badly that he almost did not grab the exterior handhold, as he bounced away from the hull.

●　　●　　●

The outrushing atmosphere started the old ship slowly spinning and tumbling simultaneously. The erratic motion, coupled with the imparted Delta-V caused by the vented atmosphere, slowly began to make the vessel's orbit change.

LaRocque, pale and out of breath, had just reached the access tube hatch when the inner door opened. The sudden violent rush of escaping air and the sickening lurch of the ship came close to snatching him off the rungs of the ladder. He fought to shut the hatch behind him against the tornado of out-rushing atmosphere and the wail of the alarms. After a moment, the stunned lieutenant managed to seal the hatchway to the access tube behind him.

Once the hatch was closed, LaRocque floated there for a moment, hanging onto the ladder, trying to breathe and collect himself. As fresh air flooded into the access tube to replace the stolen atmosphere, the ship's AI was droning away about the decompression as the blaring of alarms continued. Bleeding from his lower lip and nose, LaRocque could just make out the moaning of stressed metal protesting the sudden and unexpected change in the ship's course. Cursing under his breath, LaRocque began to pull himself up toward the bridge.

On the command bridge, only two alarms were screaming. Tounames was watching the readouts on his HUD and nervously listening to the ship's AI make calm recommendations. In the background, he could hear the sickening sound of Professor Yee retching uncontrollably. The EET was falling toward Titan at two meters per second per second, and its rate of acceleration was increasing rapidly. Tounames barked several commands at the ship's AI through his ear-mic piece and tapped a series of icons on his control panels. He then crossed his fingers and waited.

The AI fired the appropriate maneuvering thrusters and the enormous craft's spin and tumble leveled off, to the joy of everyone on the ship. The AI had stopped the uncontrolled descend, but the maneuver sent every loose object and unrestrained person on the EET, flying hard into floors, walls, and seats.

LaRocque had to use several of the emergency overrides to open the access tube passage to the bridge level, but when he got there, he found Trauma-Specialist Lebowitz guarding the entrance with a large pipe wrench. LaRocque looked the frightened and bewildered medtec up and down as if she were floating there dressed in only a diaper, holding a baby's rattle. "You are fucking kidding me, right?" he pushed past the relieved woman. The sour smell of stomach acid and rancid food was thick in the air.

Pulgar and Lebowitz had been chasing floating amorphous blobs of Professor Yee's former stomach contents around when LaRocque popped through the access tube hatch. Pulgar immediately sailed to him and grabbed LaRocque so hard and sudden that it sent them both into a momentary spin. "We thought we lost you," she hugged him, then noticed the blood. "Are you all right?"

"Yes, but we lost Garcia and maybe the Major too," LaRocque quickly moved past her and Professor Yee, who was dry heaving into a biohazard bag. The lieutenant guided himself into the pilot seat and strapped in. "Try the exterior vid-units," barked LaRocque as Pulgar, McGilmer, Lebowitz, and Yee quickly moved in behind him and Tounames.

Tounames flipped through the different vid-channels until he got a useful image on his monitor screens. Major Singleton was standing on the hull of the EET firing the plate welder past the vid-camera.

LaRocque keyed up the channel for Singleton's e-suit com. "Major, this is LaRocque. Do you read me?"

"Yeah, our friend is between airlock two-two and the portside external cargo loading arm!" Singleton's voice had an undertone of pain, and his breathing was rapid. The crackling and popping of hot static broke his radio signal between each word, "I'm trying to laser it, but it can magnetize itself to the hull. I can't get a clear shot, and I don't want to risk damaging the hull." The end of his statement was a little distorted, but it was understandable. The computerized voice of Singleton's e-suit AI, on the other hand, was very audible. It was warning the major of the dangerous level of radiation in which he was now immersed.

"Even out in that radiation, that fucking thing just won't die," uttered LaRocque under his breath.

"It can absorb the radiation and use it as food!" shouted McGilmer, her ears ringing. "Radiation won't fry it!" The idea struck both Professors Yee and McGilmer at the same time, but it was McGilmer who spoke first, "Lieutenant." She pushed passed Pulgar and moved between the two men at the flight controls. "Fry it?" She had trouble stabilizing herself in position.

"The engines could do it," added Yee remembering

Watkinski's last report on the extrasolar creature. "They can generate the needed extremes in pressure and temperature."

LaRocque and Tounames both got the idea. "If the Major could lure it onto one of the ion-drive exhaust plates---"

"We'd fry its ass but good," LaRocque broke into a broad smile as he stared hard at his partner. "Major, we've got an idea…" began LaRocque, outlining their plan.

Listening to LaRocque, Trauma-Specialist Lebowitz whispered to Professor McGilmer, "What about the Major? If he lures it onto an engine exhaust plate, and it follows him, how does he get out?"

The doctor just forced a slight grin and hugged the young medtec for moral support. They both knew that the odds of him getting out of the way were slim to none. It was not what any of them wanted, least of all Singleton, but it was something they knew he would do to save the rest of them.

"…somehow you're going to have to fend it off long enough to get out of the way." LaRocque and the rest were watching the cockpit monitors and waiting for a reply.

"Right, okay." was all that came back to them. On the monitors, they could see Singleton starting to move toward the rear of the ship. He was taking quick steps for someone walking with magnetic boots in zero gravity, but for a man with hell's raging fury a hundred steps behind him, he was moving painfully slow.

The chase started abruptly as their demonic attacker, looking like an insane version of the ancient goddess Kali, moved against the fuzzy background disk of Titan with frightening speed. The white blobs of fluid that was leaking from numerous laser wounds were migrating back into the creature, the wounds healing practically before the major's eyes.

"Radiation is approaching lethal levels. Recommend evacuation of work area," Singleton's e-suit AI announced as he turned and fired the plate welder wildly, the shot missing.

"What's the radiation count?" inquired Professor McGilmer, moving closer to the small cockpit monitor.

Tounames tapped out a short series of commands on one of his hard-monitor and watched as one of his small screens changed to two columns of scrolling numbers, one red, and the other green. Two small fluctuating graphs also appeared beneath the scrolling columns, one red, and one green. "Internal ambient radiation is okay, outside is well within the red, even with a hardened e-suit he is still in trouble."

"We are still in the tail end of that level five CME," added Yee slowly shaking his head, "and Saturn's magnetic field isn't helping."

"We could rotate the ship; take the bottom of the hull out of the sun?" LaRocque glanced over at Tounames who was staring back at him with sunken, bloodshot eyes.

"Wouldn't help," spat Yee.

"And he'd be in darkness, and the exterior lights don't cover the entire ship." Tounames frowned, "Would you want that thing after you in the dark?" The memory of LaRocque's and Pulgar's previous encounter with the extrasolar, popped into Tounames' mind.

McGilmer leaned forward between the two men seated at the flight controls, "Major Singleton," she paused glaring at Tounames with exhausted, emotionally drained eyes. "Major, you'll need to get back inside as quickly as possible. You're getting critical---"

"I know, Professor, but it's way too late," Singleton cut off the concerned professor, his voice bathed in strong static. "Our friend is pissed, and I'd never make it to an airlock before it was on me!"

Tounames switched his cockpit monitor to another view. "Come on, Major! Move your ass!"

"Sound advice." Singleton's voice was barely audible over the incessant static. The rest of the bridge was as quiet as a morgue. Only a small caution light flashed and beeped to remind the cockpit crew that level two was still depressurized.

The six watched with nervous anticipation as Major Singleton, with the laser plate welder, slowly and steadily led their monstrous invader along the bottom side of the lengthy ship. Every few steps he would turn and fire the welder. Every few steps the creature would be just a little bit closer. Even the high-energy plate-welding laser appeared to be losing its effectiveness on the nightmare. Its wounds, when hit, appeared less severe and healed a lot faster than the previous injuries.

The extrasolar entity stopped for a moment as if it had a note of suspicion in its mind, but when its prey continued to retreat, unhindered by its lack of pursuit, it continued on. *It no longer needed a source of information. It had gotten most of what it required from the others, and now it was in space, and it had a ship. All it had to do was eliminate the troublesome occupants.*

The major climbed over and around various sensing equipment and other instruments mounted on the hull of the old craft. The creature, still following, was still closing the distance, moving faster. It had more agility than the exhausted major, and the distance kept shrinking.

As he leaped for a handhold, Singleton was violently yanked backward. The plate-welder was hooked on a small set of antennas near the rear of the spacecraft. The sudden stop sent a jolt of electric pain through his chest. He forced himself to take small breaths of air as the welder floated around him looking much like some strange tentacle.

"Oh dogshit," growled Singleton, glancing backward at his monstrous pursuer. It was still moving toward him like a big black hungry spider, and it was less than twenty meters away. The major started to pull himself toward the tangled welder but thought better of it. He began to madly strip the welder unit off his back with a low groan, more from fear than physical pain.

The extrasolar spotted the major's actions and quickened its approach. Tounames and LaRocque were screaming instructions at Singleton, confusing and frightening him even more. He could hear the shouts and cries of Pulgar, McGilmer, and Lebowitz in the background, all urging him to move faster. His side and chest throbbed and burned with fire as his faceplate began to fog. Without looking, he could instinctively feel that the creature was dangerously close.

He dumped the unit and launched himself towards a handhold, just a split-second ahead of the spidery creature pursuing him. Singleton swung himself into the engine assembly between the trio of triangular engine bells and pulled his suited bulk as far back into the complex array of pipes, cables, and large machinery as he could get himself.

Tounames switched through every vid-channel, but there were no vid-cameras on the engine assembly itself. "Major, I don't have a picture of your location. Watch yourself."

The six scrutinized the cockpit monitor in stunned and terrified silence, as the extrasolar entity carefully unhooked the tangled plate welder and with all the grace and skill of the best zero-g acrobat, swung the welder unit on to its lower right shoulder. The sweat from everyone on the bridge was starting to coalesce into tiny droplets in the air around them.

"Ambient radiation levels increasing," the major's e-suit's AI calmly informed him. "Lethal exposure in three minutes, recommend evacuation to a safe zone."

"Major! It's got the welder!" LaRocque's sweat was starting to drift from his forehead. "You handle maneuvering," commanded LaRocque, his hands dancing over several controls and consoles. "I'll handle instrumentation."

"Fuck me!" was all Singleton had to say.

Tounames' hands did a bizarre waltz on the controls. He flipped and threw covered switches to begin the main engine startup sequence.

"Main engine start is not permitted," began the craft's AI. "Personnel detected in close proximity of main reaction plates."

Without missing a beat, LaRocque fired, "Jejui, emergency command. Run nested script LaRocque EET One!" His Venusianized accent booming.

After a half second the AI announced, "Full access granted, full control granted, all primary systems report ready."

Tounames peered over at LaRocque as he announced without taking his eyes off his consoles, "An escape-hatch routine I installed several years ago, in case of emergencies. It basically lobotomizes the AI, temporarily."

"Nice," smirked Tounames.

LaRocque shook his head. "It only lasts for a few minutes. The AI macro-governing architecture will compensate and auto-correct for my ghost script."

"Too bad it doesn't work on our friend," spat Singleton from the console speaker. It was clear from the sound of his voice he was frightened, angry, hurt, and all but spent. His fear and anger, in spite of everything else, were the only things left pushing his aching and exhausted body onward. However now, he had no place to go and no place to hide.

The six on the bridge surveyed each other as their unwanted guest moved toward the engine assembly. The ship's primary AI suddenly announced, "Main ion drive systems online." On the console controls, three protected green buttons labeled: **MAIN ENGINE START** were flashing their readiness beneath transparent covers.

"You guys better strap in," Tounames flipped a switch, and a control stick and tiny keypad popped out from under the console. "We got to do this manually."

The soft-spoken AI announced, "Manual controls activated, DCS ranging activated, MDUs and SRP auto guidance to stand-by."

LaRocque looked nervously at Tounames. "Are you sure you can do this?" Deep down the lieutenant really did not want an answer to that question, but Tounames gave him one.

"No."

Yee, Pulgar, McGilmer, and Lebowitz retreated to the two lanes of seats behind the cockpit section of the bridge. They strapped themselves in with little concern for the momentum of flying seatbelt buckles or Yee's spasm of dry heaves.

"Major, talk to me," LaRocque and Tounames checked their seat buckles. Their eyes scanned all of the bridge controls, as Tounames directed LaRocque in the de-orbiting procedures. They punched buttons and flipped switches to ready the ship for main engine ignition.

"I'm in between the engine exhaust plates, but it's not coming in after...wait a minute." Singleton's voice went mute, but his rapid and heavy breathing could be faintly heard intermixed with loud, hard static. "Here comes the little motherfucker now. Get ready."

"Lethal radiation exposure in one minute, please evacuate to safe area," commanded Singleton's e-suit.

Tounames put his left hand on the control stick and opened the protective cover on the three buttons with his right. LaRocque frowned at his instruments and hurriedly typed in a series of commands on his console's keyboard, as the EET's AI noted a potential problem.

"Lethal radiation exposure in thirty seconds..." Singleton's e-suit's AI announced as it started an ominous countdown.

"I have a caution light on number two helium lines for the main MDUs. Re-routing number two lines supply to the alternates," added LaRocque, not looking away from his controls, hoping he was doing the right thing, and fighting not to hear Singleton's e-suit voice condemn his friend. "Main MDUs are still a go."

"Ten seconds to lethal radiation exposure. Nine, eight, seven..." the e-suit voice continued to count.

The extrasolar on the rim of the main engine exhaust plates slowly took aim at Major Singleton with the laser plate welder. It had him.

"Engage now!" exploded the terrified and static-laden voice of Major Singleton.

An alarm sounded as Singleton's e-suit announced, "Lethal radiation exposure..."

Tounames slammed his palm on the trio of flashing buttons. The three hyper-ion drive engines exhaust plates silently flared to life like a desert sunrise emerging from behind a cloud covered horizon. The entire vessel lurched forward with the deep mechanical lament of flexing metal and stressed composites. Everyone was pinned to the back of their seats, and Professor Yee was hit in the head by a piece of unsecured equipment as the ship accelerated.

# CHAPTER TWENTY-SIX

The gigantic blast of hyper-accelerated helium ions generated enormous heat and pressure on the extrasolar lifeform, and it exploded. It's remains were washed away by the intense stream of hypersonic particles from the engines. The seventy-nine thousand kilonewtons of thrust sent the millions of fiery embers, which had once been the source of so much terror and death for the members of Titan-Base Lincoln, rocketing into the endless reaches of deep space.

The engine thrust launched the EET forward into a constant acceleration around Titan. As it whipped around the large moon, it broke its orbit and began moving out away from the dull orange ball in the direction of distant Saturn.

"Let's ease her back," ordered Tounames, as he and LaRocque fighting the constantly changing acceleration induced g-forces, wrestled the massive vessel back under control. The ship's AI calmly commented, directed, and recommended actions to avoid disaster, which the two men followed to the absolute letter. "Cut power on all engines by one-third. Engage corrective retro-thrust, up two-thirds." The ship shuttered and vibrated, sending an eerie, specter-like moan throughout the virtually empty craft as if it were an old-time sailing ship run-aground.

"Retrothrust engaged," replied LaRocque, trying not to hit a wrong switch. "Power is up to two-thirds." Two rows of warning lights came on, as LaRocque and Tounames fought the controls.

"Warning! Excess structural torque detected in section C-eighteen through section A-four. Loss of enviro---"

"We lost environment in the main cargo bay, and have multiple electrical failures in attitude control Sixteen-L and Thirty-Two-R, and a structural integrity warning light on number one engine mount!" Tounames' voice boomed overtop the ship's AI.

"This old bitch ain't up to this," whispered LaRocque.

"Don't knock the old girl yet," replied Tounames, dealing with his instrument board. "She is still tight and wet, and got a run or two left in her yet."

"Jejui, priority command order, stop run of nested script LaRocque EET one." A number of screens and instrument readouts abruptly changed and the ship stopped vibrating and went quiet. The ship's AI started going through a systems checklist, as the force of acceleration released Tounames and LaRocque from the back of their seats.

"Okay, this is more like it." LaRocque broke a smile, his blue eyes sweeping his consoles. "AI has control. Cargo bay one has no leaks, fire suppression system is online and functioning, and AIC-nav beginning scans for nav-beacon lock."

"Engine number one is within seventy-nine percent of operational limits. I still have a serious suspicion we fucked up our de-orbit burn," concluded Tounames, still crazily working his controls. "Do you think we got it?"

"No clue." LaRocque stared out the main viewport at the not too distant Saturn. "Major, did we get it?"

There was no reply.

Tounames tapped a command into his board. "Main engines are offline. Okay, it's yours."

"Major Singleton, please respond," LaRocque called again, but only the static and the ancient noise of the dark, cold of deep space replied. The lieutenant, still downcast, zipped his index finger along a row of switches. "HC mode command unlocked, BBE command override off, auto mode engine override off, no beacon lock yet." He jabbed two buttons, "Activating sun sensors. Star trackers online," he searched his controls a second then flipped two overhead switches, "Proximity detectors checked, set and online." LaRocque looked over to Tounames, questioningly.

The tech-sergeant immediately stuck-up an index finger, "Wait one." Tounames continued to type instructions and commands into his hard-monitors for another half minute, before giving LaRocque a confirming nod.

Typing several quick commands into his own hard-monitor controls and hitting a short row of switches on the console, LaRocque added, "HC is offline, AIC main command is online, DCS ranging is still active, MDUs and SRP auto guidance switched to AIC. We have green across the board, and the AI has command," the tired lieutenant's voice echoing, and paraphrasing the Jejui-Gavana's AI's monotone pronouncements.

Tounames was startled as the control stick and keypad popped back under his console. He turned to LaRocque, a smirk on his face that quickly turned into an ear-to-ear smile. "I think we got the fucker this time."

LaRocque unbuckled and looked over at Tounames as he too unbuckled himself and started to drift out of his seat. "Run through the exterior vid-cameras, we've got to confirm that before we go celebrating," he caught himself. There was not a whole lot to celebrate.

"That had to get it," Tounames started activating the ship's exterior vid-cameras, "Thanks to the Major."

"It's about time you guys gave me some credit for something," Singleton's voice exploded over their ear-mics, drowned in static.

The shock of Singleton's unexpected voice would have killed anyone with a weak heart. It made Tounames jump and LaRocque's heart skip several beats. "Steve! You're alive!"

"That's very good, Chuck. Now that we know that I am alive, would you mind giving me an engine plate temp, so I don't burn through my suit getting out of here? I would like to get out of this bitch of a suit and into a good bottle of Scotch."

The stress rushed out of LaRocque and Tounames like the spring discharge of the river Beardmore of Antarctica. The two exhausted men began to laugh almost uncontrollably.

Professor Yee and the others floated up behind the two laughing men. "We don't have any good Scotch, but you've got it when we get home," added Tounames.

Everyone started smiling and giving one another cheerful pats on the back as they drifted behind LaRocque and Tounames. They were all happy and relieved, except for Professor McGilmer. She had not forgotten.

LaRocque relayed the current engine plate temperature to

Singleton, and Tounames gave him the okay to head for the closest airlock.

Singleton was way ahead of Tounames, as he climbed out from between the three hot, triangularly spaced engine exhaust plates. The physically and mentally depleted major made his way back to the nearest airlock in his slightly singed pressure suit. All the while, his suit's AI beeped a high radiation-warning signal.

•   •   •

Within an hour of getting back inside of the EET, Trauma-Specialist Medtec First Class Lebowitz had checked out Major Singleton and found that he had one broken and three very badly bruised ribs and a slight case of the Bends. None of that mattered, however; the major had received enough radiation during his struggle with the extrasolar lifeform to kill three men. He was already dead, but his body had not figured out that little fact just yet.

The exhausted major took the news well. He had a smile on his worn face that Lebowitz did not understand. As the major left the ship's medical-bay, the badly shaken trauma-specialist took several small pills and began making flavored drinks with grain alcohol.

The survivors of Titan-Base Lincoln attended to the minor damage to their massive escape craft. Major Singleton and Tech-Sergeant Tounames oversaw the minor repair work, then went up to the bridge and sat in the pilot and copilot seats. There the two men sipped a mixture of grain alcohol and mango-melon juice out of squeeze bottles labeled: *Distilled*.

Singleton would have preferred some of Aamodt's fifty-three-year-old Tennessee bourbon that she had been saving. However, it was gone. Just like she was gone, just like his best friend was gone. Singleton missed his lover, and he missed his friend. The major got teary-eyed at the thought of all his friends. He realized how much he loved all of them, but in different, but equally deep ways. Nianta was not just a friend and fellow officer he was a brother.

Tounames drank, silently remembering all the times he and Yoshida had traded stories over glasses of warm Brazilian saki. The man had been like a brother to him, and now he was gone. The tech-sergeant would not let himself cry as all the recent events came creeping back to him. It was as if some horrific memory that he had thought was just a childhood nightmare, but turned out to have been all too real. He, like everyone else who had survived, knew that the real nightmares would begin as soon as he entered deep sleep.

LaRocque entered the information from the dataclips that Major Singleton had retrieved from General Newey's office. It took nearly two hours to scan and record all of the data into the ship's AI-memory. After the exhausted LaRocque double-checked his work, he and Professor Yee had programmed in a beacon message for the Outer Systems Command. Pulgar ensured that the message was transmitted and coded for Commissioner Marshalls and Senator Robinson. Then the three of them headed to rejoin the rest of the survivors. On their way to check on Lebowitz and McGilmer, they met them on their way to the bridge. As they continued, Lebowitz dropped a surprise on them that was greeted with mixed emotions.

"Everything looks okay," informed LaRocque, he had dark circles under his eyes looking much like a burnt out drug abuser. "Lebowitz checked out Ning-Jing," he suddenly felt strange. "She's still sleeping like a baby." The frowning lieutenant looked back at Professor Yee as he moved next to him, his fresh anti-nausea patch visible on his neck. "Speaking of which, according to the bio-monitors, she is two days pregnant."

Singleton, just smiled, as he fought unsuccessfully to hold back tears. He surveyed the faces of Tounames, LaRocque, Pulgar, and Professors Yee and McGilmer. No one voiced a word for several minutes.

Pulgar finally spoke. "We all get monthly anti-pregnancy injections, how---"

"NJ is the senior medical officer," Singleton scoff, "She didn't take her own treatments. She wanted this." He started to tear up and laugh. Something of his friend was still alive. He only wished he and Aamodt could have had the chance.

There was silence on the bridge as LaRocque, and the others stared out the viewport at the distant disk of Saturn. LaRocque felt pain as he looked out into cold black space. Thoughts of Garcia dying in the airlock because he was too afraid to open it burnt his mind and his soul like a red-hot poker.

Looking at his friends next to him, he felt like a traitor.

Professor Yee was just about to speak when LaRocque cut him off, "I could have opened the inner hatch to let Garcia out of the airlock." LaRocque turned to face the three men and three women staring quietly at him. "But I was afraid of letting that thing back into the ship. I let her die."

Tounames saw the look of pain and deep sadness in LaRocque's eyes and added, "Hey, if you had, you probably would have been gone too." He paused and turned glumly to the viewport, "We all could have died. You did what you had to, just like I did when I killed Capt'n Arroyo."

Singleton said nothing.

It went quiet again for several long minutes as everyone on the bridge examined their own actions and reactions during the last few days. Only the gentle hum of the ship's systems seemed to mark time, as right and wrong, fear and guilt played across the minds of the people on the bridge.

"In the past, they use to call it survivor's guilt," Yee tried not to look at his companions, "why them and not me?" He sadly adjusted himself.

"You have anything to get off your chest?" Tounames, followed by the others stared at Yee.

"Everything," whispered the professor, lowering his head, "Nothing!"

Singleton stared back at Yee. He knew he and Yee should have protested Rozsa's decisions back on Titan-Base Ksa, but he knew nothing would have changed. "I would recommend that all of you," he indicated Tounames and LaRocque, "be careful how you write your reports. A lot of people died out here, and this whole mess is going to be a big loss for someone, and you survivors would make great scapegoats."

"You want us to cover up---" started Yee, before he was cut off.

"I want you to protect yourselves and your careers!" shot Singleton.

No one stated an opinion or voiced a word.

"Did you secure those dataclips?" Singleton grimaced. For the first time, he noticed dark blood pooling under all his fingernails. Strangely, thoughts of Aamodt filled his mind again. "If those secure servers never uploaded their data, those dataclips are going to be very important."

"Yes, those clips are secure, and the information is in the ship's AI-memory as well."

"Dataclips. That is all we have to show for the deaths of nineteen friends and over a hundred others?" Singleton smirked sarcastically. Deep down he knew it was worth it. They all did.

"Yeah, but they're possibly the most important dataclips in the history of humanity." Yee tried to sound optimistic, positioning himself down on the floor between Singleton and Tounames.

"Yeah, well that's what they use to say about the Torah, the Bible, the Koran, the Magna Carta, and the Constitution of the United Kingdom." LaRocque spat angrily.

"It's the Constitution of the United States," Singleton corrected LaRocque. After a few minutes, Singleton leaned back in his chair and looked at the constantly changing overhead lights of his console, but not seeing them. He did not say anything for a minute, and then he chuckled and rubbed his side, coughing a little blood. "Now I know how bacon feels." He tried to make light of the small mass of blood in his hand.

LaRocque, Tounames, and Yee all knew what twenty-five thousand plus millisieverts of gamma and neutron radiation was doing to Singleton's body. They knew he did not have much time left.

It was very silent for several minutes. Only the whisper of opening and closing relays and the hum of the ventilation unit broke the stillness. Everyone surveyed the faces of everyone else.

"Yeah, let's get it over with, so I can get into a chamber and forget some of this dogshit," shrugged the tech-sergeant as he moved out of his seat. He drifted behind McGilmer and Lebowitz as they led the way off the bridge.

"So people, let's get some sleep." Singleton unbuckled, got up and maneuvered himself away from the control section.

"I've got seven chambers ready and waiting," announced Lebowitz, turning to float back toward the exit.

"I know one thing," began Yee following Lebowitz. "Humanity is going to be able to leap to the stars with that. We will finally be able to see over the horizon."

"We can only hope," replied Singleton floating up behind the group. "But there is still the question of what happened at T-One."

"You need to get that ankle fixed?" indicated McGilmer, changing the topic and looking at Tounames with a concerned expression.

As the access hatch opened, Lebowitz followed by Yee, Pulgar, LaRocque, McGilmer, and Tounames floated off the bridge. Singleton took one last look around and then joined the others.

While Trauma-Specialist Lebowitz used the ship's autodoc to fix Tounames' ankle, LaRocque and Singleton did one last float through of the ship. LaRocque got back to the cryosleep area in time to ask Pulgar to marry him when they got home. She passionately kissed him and replied she would think about it after they lived together a few years and had a child or two. The both laughed.

After Tounames' ankle was repaired, he offered in his most solemn good-byes to Major Singleton. Then professor McGilmer and Trauma-Specialist Lebowitz safely lay to rest Tounames and Pulgar in their hibernation chambers. Tounames and Pulgar eased themselves to sleep with music pumped into their sleep chambers by the ship's AI.

LaRocque and Professor McGilmer followed them into the artificial dream state after their farewells to the major, knowing they would never see him again, alive. Singleton, being the senior officer, had to be the last to enter the sleep chambers. He and Lebowitz secured Professor Yee into his chamber to the sound of some traditional Gao-Hu music. Before Major Singleton closed the seal on Professor Yee's chamber, he added stone-faced, "There are a couple of things still bothering me. What caused that initial event? If that ship crashed here millions of years ago, why haven't their friends come looking for them? Also, if there were more like this one on that extrasolar craft, what is to stop the rest of them from waking up, and completing their mission?"

Yee shrugged, "We need to go back to T-One. We need to find out what the devil is doing in the dark." Singleton nodded and sealed the chamber with a smile.

Lebowitz preferred a modern ballad about lost love as she entered her cryosleep chamber. The trauma-specialist gave Singleton the name and dosage of a drug in the med-bay that could help him if he decided not to wait for the end to come.

He stood there a few minutes until Lebowitz and the

others were asleep, then he headed back to the command bridge. On the way to the bridge, he stopped to relieve himself. The dark blood and urine that vanished into the waste disposal system did not shock him as much as the fact that there was no pain. Looking at his ashen, black face in the mirror, he noticed several dark purplish blotches around his face and neck. He also noticed that his gums were bleeding and his teeth were loose. He simply grinned and continued on to the bridge.

He floated himself down into the pilot's seat and activated the ship's long-range transmitter. He tapped in a series of coordinates to re-align the vessel's long-range antenna, then punched in a security forces' encrypted prefix.

Singleton stared out the viewport at the stars and the bright little disk of the sun in the lower right-hand corner of the window. "Titan-Base Ksa and Titan-Base Lincoln installations have both been destroyed. The extrasolar vehicle may still remain at the T-One drill site. Information on extrasolar…" As Singleton continued with his report thoughts of General Newey, Major Nianta and Captain Aamodt flooded his tired mind in a tsunami of sharp images. He knew they would be coming back to Titan to recover the extrasolar craft. "…On board *the Jejui-Gavana*, are seven survivors, not counting myself. This is Major Steven Singleton, ending transmission to solarnet news headquarters, Danzig ecosphere, Luna." Singleton switched off the transmitter. He re-positioned the long-range antenna and erased the transmission log entries and AI-records of his work.

As the exhausted major drifted himself down to the cryosleep chambers, he fought back the urge to laugh aloud to himself. As he started to strip off his clothes, he stopped. *What was the point?* He thought, as he climbed into the hibernation chamber, hoping that history would remember him, his friends and his coworkers.

The major laughed aloud at the thought of climbing into the hibernation chamber, was like climbing into his own coffin, a cold box he was never going to leave. He glanced around the area once nervously, and then closed the transparent lid over himself.

He quickly checked the levels of hydrogen sulfide and nitrogen trioxide in the small sleep compartment. He then gave himself, first one injection of hydro-dobutamine and then a moment later, a second painful injection of tetra-Dadol-albumin complex. The major then placed the two used hypos back into their holders. He moved the two intravenous lines aside, knowing he did not need to be fed or hydrated when he was asleep. Tasting the faint metallic flavor of his own bleeding gums, he knew he did not have much time left.

The major typed out several commands on the small keyboard in the top of the chamber and scanned through the selections. Picking one, music started to filter into the chamber, and it surrounded him. It was an ancient song, written in the twentieth century, but the recording was still good. He had heard the mournful song at his grandfather's funeral and thought it appropriate. With a sigh, he finally closed his eyes and drifted off to sleep to the sounds of *Sitting on the Dock of the Bay* by someone named Otis Redding, and he dreamt. He knew these would be his last dreams, and he dreamt of old friends, lost loves and unanswered questions.

Singleton giggled to himself as he entered his final sleep. He was sitting on the dock of a vast bay, having a cold beer with his best friend and his woman, watching the sunset over the cool waters of the shimmering bay filled with sailboats. With a smile on his face, he started to whistle as he enjoyed the lazy summer evening.

# EPILOGUE

For months, news and rumors regarding the events on Titan flew around the inner solar system. Planetary congresses on Mercury, Venus, Earth, and Mars demanded answers and information from the United Earth-Space Administration, the Outer Systems Command, the United Security Forces, and especially from the administration of the United Governments of Earth. The fact that the discovery of extrasolar biological entities, and the recovery operations out at Saturn, had both been kept a secret only fueled the conspiracy theories. In addition, the fact that the survivors of Titan-base Lincoln had been sequestered at an undisclosed location did not help the situation either. There were calls for congressional investigations on all four terrestrial planets, votes of *no confidence* in the UGE senate, and cries of criminal penalties and impeachment for individual government leaders.

In the meantime, the News media could not supply information to the general public fast enough. Nearly every expert and university professor, in any of the fields related to astronomy, biology, chemistry, linguistics, and sociology were interviewed. Anyone who had ever worked out at Saturn was tracked down and interrogated. Dozens of outlaw religious cults sprang up and made themselves known in places as far-flung as the mines of Mercury and the icy satellite colonies of Jupiter. There were even several clashes between groups of believers, in direct violation of the Privacy of Religion act. Even though the melees were small and involved only a few individuals, fears that religious zealots could force a return of such meaningless violence, after four hundred

373

years of peace, prompted local governments to take action.

•     •     •

Commissioner Damien Marshall felt as physically and mentally exhausted as he appeared. In the ten months since the disaster out at Saturn, he had lost over ten kilograms and developed a recurring ulcer in his stomach. His doctor had informed him that the ulcer would keep returning as long as he was only consuming black coffee, cold food, and cheap bourbon, not to mention he needed to get some rest. He had not been able to get more than three hours of sleep a day since the second week in January. It seemed to him the only things he had done in the last few months were sit in meetings, testify before committees, and sidestep questions from the media. In the last week alone, he had been in meetings or had testified before committees in Cali, Orientale, Winnipeg, Amundsen, Jiayuguan, and lastly in the conference room in which he now stood.

Executive Conference Room Number Four had been modeled on archival images of the reception hall in the old Élysée Palace in Paris. That is before it was looted, gutted and burnt to the ground during the Second Dark Ages. There was lots of gold and silver trim in the blue-walled conference room. The long windows stretched from the polished granite floor to the stark white ceiling. A large spherical Intelligent-conference table was in the center of the room, encircled by twelve black, high-backed syntha-leather chairs. Seated at the enormous circular conference table were the General-Secretary of the United Earth-Space Administration, the Prime Minister of the United Governments of Earth, the Commandant-General of the United Security Forces, and the Senior UGE Senator from Mars, Anna Robinson, chair of the UESA oversight committee.

All of them looked unhappy.

Marshall turned to look again out the window, it was just becoming dusk, and the sky was engulfed in dark gray clouds. A heavy October rain was beating down on the attractively trimmed hedges and colorful bushes that lined the grounds of the United Earth-Space Administration complex. Looking south across the cityscape of Nairobi, he could just make out the large, curved glass structure of the historic McMillan Memorial Library, that lay at the center of the city. To his right, in the distance, lights were starting to come on in the housing units at the foot of Suswa, the twenty-three-hundred-meter high dormant volcano. In the gray, darkening sky, low flying aircraft were buzzing in and out of the Kenyatta transport center, on the other side of the city. "You know, that is one of the things I miss about Earth," lamented Marshall. "The rain, with its sound, its smell, and the feel of it as it hits your face."

"We got a report from Tran, during the last break," the commandant-general of the United Security Forces' voice was as tired as he looked. "The special unit arrived at Eunomia-Fifteen, late this morning, our time." The commandant-general of the United Security Forces was the youngest of the four seated at the table. He was square-jawed with features that hinted at a northern European ancestry, but with a dark skin tone that said black African. Only he wore a uniform, black with just a few insignias.

Marshall sighed; his brief moment of enjoyment gone, then he looked back toward the table. Anna Robinson instantly caught his eye. She was tall and slender, with shoulder-length hair that was a shade of cinnamon. For a senior UGE senator, she was also fairly young. "Good, I got an update, Yang is here. She just cleared security at the main gate."

"About fucking time," the general-secretary was a large, graying man of middle-eastern or Indian descent. He had been drumming his fingers hard against the tabletop for the last ten minutes. He wore an expression that would have killed a small child if one had been present.

"She shuttled up from Vishniac this morning." Anna Robinson did not look away from the workslate she was reading. "She knew what time our meeting began."

Almost as if on cue, the door to the executive conference room slid aside, and a middle-aged woman of mixed Asian and African descent entered. She, like all but the commandant of the Security Forces, wore the latest in professional office attire. "Sorry, I'm late. My DP linked me to tell me our house had some more damage from yet another quake. Deglaciation isostatic rebound is a bitch."

"Hope everything is all right?" Marshall was aware that Yang and her domestic partner lived in an area of Antarctica that had been experiencing large earthquakes for the last few months.

Smiling, the professor replied, "Not as bad as the last two quakes. It damaged a smart-wall in my son's room and took down one of our wind-turbines."

"It's good to see you again." Marshall walked over and shook Professor Yang's hand.

"So, have you read the plan yet?" Robinson was all business.

"Skimmed it. We are almost done with the data from both the T-One team and Vance's team at Ksa," smiled Yang, as she let go of Marshall's hand and moved to take a seat on the other side of the circular table. "I was truly shocked to hear about Lori Eastman and Ronald Newey," she frowned. "I know you and Lori had been friends for a long time." Marshall took a seat next to her.

Robinson's expression seemed to soften just a bit. "We were friends since we were thirteen years old. We grew up together on Mars."

"She was a good scientist. Her work will be missed."

There was an awkward moment of silence, then Marshall cleared his throat loudly. "So what have you learnt in the last week?"

"Yes, Professor?" The prime minister was seated between the general-secretary and the commandant-general. She was a graying brunette with ice-cold gray eyes and soft Slavic features. She too had a look as if she were going to knife someone.

"Well, madam prime minister, Professor Vance was correct in his assumption that these extrasolar biological entities were here on a bio-forming mission. All the data on the craft indicates that it was most likely designed to do that. However, we believe that they were wanderers and alone. That's why none of their kind came to finish their assignment."

The security force's commandant perked up. "You mean their species could be extinct?" His voice was baritone.

"No, sir. Based on the work of Professors Vance and Verdibello, and the analysis of the craft itself, we think they were refugees, probably more like exiles."

"Why do you say that?" The prime minister beat the general-secretary to the question by a millisecond.

"We think the craft was designed for a one-way trip and to complete one task."

"Do we know any more about their biochemistry or physiology?" inquired the security forces' commandant.

"Nothing more than what is in the last executive summary," replied Yang. "However, we discovered that Vance and his people coined a name for these extrasolars. They called them the Nephilim."

"Nephilim?" questioned the general-secretary, not recognizing the term.

"The AIs identified the word is from an ancient language, called Hebrew. There are three possible translations into the modern." Yang quickly accessed her workslate and created a secure datalink with the conference table. "But Vance and his people meant the old Americanized-English translation of this word." Holographic texts appeared over the table, each letter thirty centimeters tall, spelling out the origins and roots of the term.

"What is it?" inquired the general-secretary, his face hinting at disbelief.

Yang took in the faces at the table for a short moment, then answered, "Fallen Angel."

The prime minister smiled, "You know another name for a fallen angel is the Satan."

"Satan," chuckled the commandant-general. "The devil,"

"Yes, ma'am, I do," acknowledged Yang, ignoring the commandant-general.

The commandant-general of the security forces tapped out a few commands on the tabletop, and the large text disappeared, only to be replaced by a multispectral image of Titan. One spot was highlighted by a pulsating red dot. "The monitoring satellite network in orbit about Titan is still functioning and transmitting data. They indicate that a heat source with magnetic signatures has appeared at the location of T-One."

"We are sure there are others in the craft, like the creature that destroyed TBL, correct?" The general-secretary answered his own question.

"Yes, sir. Thirteen others."

A detailed schematic of the extrasolar spacecraft appeared next to the slowly revolving, multicolored image of Titan. "Your people still believe this craft is still viable, even after that first event?" The commandant-general was frowning.

"Yes, sir," Yang glanced over at Marshall. The man's right knee had started shaking beneath the table. "Given the level of technology involved, and the condition the craft was in, in spite of the fact that all the evidence indicates it formed Menvra crater and was subsequently buried for a quarter of a billion years, under twelve and a half kilometers of ice."

"All of us here read your weekly reports, and we have just re-read the reports from the survivors of TBL. We all agree these things are dangerous and damn near indestructible," spat Marshall.

The commandant-general coughed out a loud laugh. "Commissioner, our special operations team has been training for an assignment like this since before operation Quadriga went to pot. They'll have *real* weapons, not some dogshit thrown together by a mentally unstable engineer."

"Yes, but we are still operating in the dark here," injected Senator Robinson.

"Professor, we've spoken this morning at length," began the prime minister, glancing around the table, "and based on your recommendations, I will order the special operations team to Titan. Their orders will be to ascertain the status of the EBEs and their craft. If possible, they are to secure the technology and prepare the craft for transport to a secure facility on Mars." She looked to Senator Robinson, who gave an approving nod.

"Madam, Prime Minister, what if the other thirteen are awake when our personnel arrive?" questioned Marshall, his stomach was acting up again. "Based on the reports from Professor McGilmer, it could only take one of these things to---"

"Then we will invoke worldfall protocols," interrupted the general-secretary.

No one said a word for nearly a full minute, then the commandant-general of the United Security Forces said in a flat tone, "Don't worry commissioner, my people can handle this." He paused for a second as he surveyed the faces of the others at the table, then with a hesitated smile, he added, "This devil in the dark."